THE VISCOUNT'S KISS

Hannah's temper flared. "You had that boy spying on me? How dare you?"

"Looking out for you. And a good job he did so. I might have been too late."

She lifted her chin belligerently. "Well, I don't like it."

Theo rose and pulled her to her feet. He put a finger under her chin to force her to meet his gaze. "What don't you like?" he asked softly. "That I am here?" His lips brushed hers and she trembled, her lips automatically responding. He lifted his head momentarily. "No, that's not it, is it?"

Her arms crept up and around his neck. She leaned into him, responding to the next kiss with characteristic enthusiasm . . .

Books by Wilma Counts

WILLED TO WED

MY LADY GOVERNESS

THE WILLFUL MISS WINTHROP

THE WAGERED WIFE

THE TROUBLE WITH HARRIET

MISS RICHARDSON COMES OF AGE

RULES OF MARRIAGE

THE VISCOUNT'S BRIDE

Published by Zebra Books

THE VISCOUNT'S BRIDE

Wilma Counts

ZEBRA BOOKS
Kensington Publishing Corp.
http://www.kensingtonbooks.com

ZEBRA BOOKS are published by

Kensington Publishing Corp.
850 Third Avenue
New York, NY 10022

All Kensington titles, imprints and distributed lines are available at special quantity discounts for bulk purchases for sales promotion, premiums, fund-raising, and educational or institutional use.

Special book excerpts or customized printings can also be created to fit specific needs. For details, write or phone the office of the Kensington Special Sales Manager: Kensington Publishing Corp., 850 Third Avenue, New York, NY 10022. Attn. Special Sales Department. Phone: 1-800-221-2647.

Zebra and the Z logo Reg. U.S. Pat. & TM Off.

First Printing: July 2003
10 9 8 7 6 5 4 3 2 1

Printed in the United States of America

To Jane Jordan Browne, who made it all happen.

PROLOGUE

London, 1817

The butler ushered into the library the last of the four guests he had been instructed to expect.

"Welcome, Dickie." The host greeted the newcomer with the casualness of an old school chum—which he was. "We have been waiting for you." He poured a glass of port and handed it to his guest.

"Dickie" took the glass and the seat to which his host gestured. "I must admit to some trepidation about subjecting myself to this Tory bastion," he said jokingly and addressed one of the others particularly. "I am glad to see you here, Stubs. We Whigs have to stick together."

"Right." Stubs raised his glass to his fellow Whig and the others chuckled, for all five knew their alliance as longtime friends superseded any political labels.

Another—known as "Mer-man"—addressed their host. "So—now that we are *all* here—what is this about, Racer?"

The host responded with a gesture at the fifth man in the room. "It was Whitey's idea, really. I shall allow him to tell you."

The five had the easy familiarity—and trust—of men who had been together from youth on—who had played and wept and studied together, who had triumphed over bullies older than themselves, and endured headmasters who seemed to hate the youngsters in their charge. In some quarters they had been known as the "Fearless Five"; others had called them the

"Fearsome Five." Even today, some fifty years later, they were a formidable group. All were now peers of the realm with a great deal of prestige, riches, and power, both individually and collectively. In their little closed group, they delighted in using the schoolboy nicknames. Dickie bore the diminutive of his name, Richard; Stubs, who was now the tallest and slimmest, had once been short and pudgy; Whitey's shock of pale blond hair was now indeed white; Racer and Mer-man had been labeled for their athletic skills on the racecourse and in swimming.

Whitey cleared his throat, sipped his drink, then set it down and drummed his fingertips against each other. "You know very well that this is not the best of times for England."

"Finally!" Dickie said. "A Tory who admits that fact."

"Not that you Whigs have offered anything substantially better," Mer-man replied.

"Hear him out," Racer said impatiently.

"Whether one is in the government or in the opposition, it is often difficult to know what course to take."

They all nodded solemn agreement.

Whitey went on. "There are a number of Tories in our lot who cry vehemently for measures to maintain order and curb the excesses we see in events like that debacle at Spa Fields."

A few months before, a gathering of London working people had erupted into what some newspapers had labeled riots, in a place called Spa Fields.

"Many," Whitey continued, "are convinced that we are but a step away from revolution and anarchy in this country. Others say we must not take Draconian measures to restrict the rights of the people. We are, after all, civilized Englishmen, not quixotic, emotional Frenchmen."

"Hear! Hear!" Mer-man said quietly.

Dickie waved his hand dismissively. "Yes. We all know this. What, exactly, is your point?"

"Too often," Whitey answered, "we are merely the blind leading the blind. Parliament's pendulum swings too far this way or that simply because *we never have accurate information.*"

"And just why not?" Stubs asked aggressively. "Is the government not paying for spies in all those so-called 'Hampden Clubs'?"

Racer spoke up. "It is. But the information is unreliable. *And* it is too frequently filtered to us through the strainer of someone else's special interests."

"You're right," Dickie said glumly. "And our own people often seem to distrust us merely because we bear titles. People I've known all my life are guarded in their talk."

"As I see it," Whitey said, "what we require is that some—or one—of 'us' become close to 'them' so we may learn precisely the nature of the problems with which we deal—and what measures to take to alleviate the situation."

Stubs snorted. "You propose to place spies to spy upon the spies who spy upon the people?"

"Not exactly. Just someone to observe and report back to us."

"Dangerous," Mer-man said in his cryptic way. "People owning mills and mines have been killed for less. Remember the Luddites of a few years ago?"

Stubs spoke again. "'Twould be extremely difficult to find a member of the *ton* who could keep up such a disguise. His language alone would give him away. Think what could happen were he to be discovered!"

Dickie shook his head. "And it would have to be somcone who was virtually unknown to both the *ton* and the general populace. I certainly do not numbcr anyone like that among *my* acquaintances."

"I think I do," Racer said quietly.

One

Miss Hannah Elizabeth Whitmore was decidedly unenthusiastic about attending the Rollente ball.

The Duke and Duchess of Rollente were hosting the ball following an important civic event. Hannah knew she would enjoy the afternoon's ceremony of the dedication of a new bridge over the Thames. She admired the architecture and engineering skills that had gone into this new transportation marvel. She also heartily approved of having it named for the Battle of Waterloo. The name seemed a fitting honor for the men who had been lost in that costly victory. In part, Hannah wanted to attend the bridge dedication out of a sense of duty—attending would be a small way of expressing gratitude to those who had paid for victory with courage and blood.

An air of celebration always imbued such affairs. There would be a military band and grand speeches, as well as enterprising tradesmen to offer souvenirs, drinks, and food from various kiosks and carts. She anticipated an atmosphere like the country fairs she often attended at home. Hannah loved events that brought people of all walks of life together in a common purpose.

However, the Rollente ball was another matter entirely. The Duchess of Rollente was said to be a high stickler and very aware of her position as one of society's leading arbiters of who was who in the *ton*.

"Are you absolutely sure I must attend this ball?" Hannah asked yet again at breakfast one morning a good two weeks before the event.

Claudia, Baroness Folkeston, laughed. "Yes. For the tenth time—or is it the twentieth?—I am *quite* sure. You are turning into a true recluse, Hannah—and I will not have it! Besides, how else are you to meet an eligible gentleman? You cannot find a husband stuck away as you are in Derbyshire."

Hannah smiled in genuine amusement at her friend's stubbornness. "My dear Claudia. You never give up, do you? At six and twenty, I am quite beyond the stage of husband-hunting. Surely, you remember what a disaster my two seasons were. Two. Both failures."

Claudia's blond curls bounced as she shook her head. "You were not ready, that was all. And that aunt of yours managed to dress you like a veritable frump. Then, she kept harping at you so about the behavior expected of a vicar's daughter that you were afraid even to smile!"

"I was rather green and gauche, but it was not all Aunt Hermione's doing. She did her best and I was most grateful to her. I still am."

"Well, that feeling is all that is proper." Claudia reached for another muffin, then clearly thought better of it, and took another sip of coffee instead. "But that is all in the past—and you are still unwed. We simply must remedy that situation."

Hannah laughed at her persistence. "Has it not occurred to you that—contrary to what the gossips might make of it—I am quite satisfied with my life as it is?"

"Oh, Hannah—how could you be?" Claudia's usual optimistic gaiety gave way to earnest sincerity. "People are meant to go through life as couples—not as singles. Do you not want children?"

Moved by her friend's genuine concern, Hannah reached to touch Claudia's hand. "You must not worry about me. Try to understand that not everyone follows the same path through life. I am very happy for you and Folkeston. But this is not the journey Providence has planned for me."

"What about children? I know how much you love mine."

"I have the children of my school."

Claudia waved her hand dismissively. "Other people's children—and some of them mill children who may or may not benefit from your efforts on their behalf."

"They benefit," Hannah said firmly. "Any amount of education for them is better than none."

"Are you sure? Does it not concern you that you may make them discontented with their station in life?"

"That is certainly the view of many mill owners," Hannah said dryly. "But my students *should* be discontented. They *should* strive to better themselves."

Claudia sighed. "I did not mean to get you off on that again. Come now—what gown will you wear to the Rollente ball?"

"My lavender is suitable, I think."

"We have time to have new ones made up," Claudia suggested.

"Do you know how many books for my school I could purchase for what the mantua-maker charges for one gown?"

"Oh, for heaven's sake!" Claudia responded. "Let me buy you the gown."

"No. Absolutely not. I shall wear the lavender, and if it is not good enough . . ." Hannah knew she sounded inordinately stubborn.

"Oh, all right. I take that as your agreement that you *will* go."

Hannah nodded and changed the subject, glad to have Claudia distracted, however temporarily, from one of her favorite topics—Hannah's state of singleness.

Hannah loved Claudia dearly. They had been friends since their days at Miss Strempleton's School for Young Ladies. Now, Hannah customarily spent a month-long holiday each year with the Folkestons. Usually, the visit took place late in the summer at Folkeston Manor in the country, but this year, Claudia had insisted Hannah join them in town.

It had been a pleasant visit, despite Claudia's determined efforts to play matchmaker. Hannah had enjoyed seeing the sights of London again—one never tired of the city even if some of her citizens were less than fascinating. However, she hated the pretentiousness, the hypocrisy of much of the "social scene." Remembering all too well the tears and soul-wrenching pain she had suffered during her two seasons, she could not put aside her reservations about this ball. She admitted, if only to herself, that her reluctance to throw herself into such affairs came partly from cowardice. Perhaps there was a bit of hypocrisy on her part, for Miss Whitmore simply had not "taken" during her two seasons. Now, she was content to enjoy from the sidelines the musicales and an occasional rout. She had especially enjoyed trips to museums and the theater during this visit. But if this ball was so very important to Claudia, surely Hannah could exert herself to please her friend.

Theo Ruskin—Theocritus Euripides Ruskin—the Viscount Amesbury, and, until recently, a major in His Majesty's Army, strolled into the lounge of the very superior gentleman's club known as White's. He did so with as much aplomb as his slight limp and slightly outdated evening attire allowed him. *Nothing has changed in three years*, he thought. *The same deep leather chairs, the same hum of voices, the same odor of cigar smoke, and the same clink of glassware.*

Theo had fully expected to encounter two or three men with whom he was acquainted in this establishment. He had *not* expected to discover three of his dearest friends the moment he walked in. Trevor Jeffries, Samuel Jenkins, and David Moore were seated comfortably in a corner near a window. Judging by the level of liquid in a decanter near them, the three veterans of the wars with Napoleon had been there for some time. Trevor noticed the newcomer first.

"Theo! Are my eyes deceiving me? Is that really the intrepid major?" He waved Theo over.

Theo crossed the room, uncomfortably aware that Trevor's loud summons had brought every eye in the room to focus on his entrance.

"So!" Moore sounded a shade too hearty. "You've returned safe and sound."

"Safe, anyway," Theo said as he shook hands with each of them and awkwardly took a seat.

"Jenkins here told me you caught a French bullet at Quatre Bras," Trevor said. "So what kept you across the channel? Good God, man, Waterloo was nearly two years ago!"

"Wellington asked me to stay on with the Army of Occupation," Theo stated simply.

The three nodded and Theo knew they understood fully. None of them would have refused the duke's request either.

"Despite your injury?" Trevor asked.

"The wound healed quickly enough. I still have the limp—always will—but as you well know, we officers spend most of our time in the saddle. It was not a serious problem." A problem, yes, but not a serious one, he thought.

"I wager that will curb your forays onto the dance floor," Jenkins said sympathetically as he handed Theo a glass of port.

"Don't wager too much," Theo warned. "I still manage a passable waltz."

Trevor raised his glass. "Here's to your return."

"And to absent friends," Theo said.

"Hear! Hear!" the others responded and they all drank deeply.

"What are your plans?" Trevor asked.

"Plans? I have no plans," Theo said emphatically. "And believe me, that is just the way I want it."

Theo saw the three exchange puzzled, somewhat embarrassed looks.

Moore spoke with a longtime friend's teasing bravado. "Is this the conquering hero who came home from the Peninsula ready to take on the English world?"

"No. This is the would-be soldier who lost over a hundred men at Waterloo. That conquering hero nonsense is for schoolboys." Theo was aware that his voice was harsher than he intended. "Over a hundred good men," he added in a softer tone.

Jenkins raised a hand to signal a halt. "Hey! Moore and I

were there, too—remember? It was not your fault. The order came down—we all followed it."

"But we—I—should have countered it or . . . or something."

"Come on, Major. We all know what the chaos of a battle is like," Jenkins argued.

"Not to mention the consequences of disobeying orders," Moore said in a rueful tone that silenced them. Theo knew the others, too, remembered watching painfully as Moore was flogged in Spain for just such a dereliction—despite the fact that officers, even very junior officers, were rarely subjected to such punishment. They also remembered tending to his wounded back afterwards.

"Well, it is over now." Trevor refilled the glasses. "And I, for one, am very happy all three of *you* survived."

Trevor Jeffries had served in the Peninsula, but a growing horse breeding business and other family interests had kept him—reluctantly—out of Napoleon's final debacle two years ago.

"Theo, if you've no plans," the darkly handsome Moore said in a tone of clearly changing the subject, "you must join me in upholding the dignity and grandeur of the state of single men. Trevor, as you know, has long been a lost cause, and Jenkins here joined his ranks six months ago."

Theo looked at the redheaded, freckle-faced Jenkins, who was blushing. "You got yourself leg-shackled?"

"That I did," Jenkins said. "And I have to say 'tis a very happy state indeed."

"Actually," Moore offered in a tone of mocking mournfulness, "our friend here is as moonstruck as Trevor *still* is."

"Congratulations!" Theo said to Jenkins. Then he turned to Moore. "However, despite pressures to the contrary, I believe I'll wait to join their ranks."

Moore grinned widely. "Excellent!"

Theo gestured to a group of three younger men who stood near the fireplace at the other end of the room. "I may even join *that* lot." The three were dressed in the first stare of fashion with high shirt points, intricately tied cravats, and ostentatious waistcoats. They occasionally drew attention to themselves with a loud guffaw or a showy display of taking snuff.

Theo's group observed them silently for a moment, then Trevor said, "Uh . . . I don't see you joining that set quite yet . . ."

"Still," Jenkins said, "dashing hero like you. Heir to an earldom—every ambitious mama in the realm will have her eye on you."

Trevor set his glass down. "You should cut quite a swath through the field of beauties in the marriage mart."

Theo groaned. "Not you, too. My mother is already planning to parade a gaggle of females before me—and I've not yet been home a week!"

They commiserated insincerely with each other over the mysterious ways of women. As he joined their banter, Theo thought how grateful he was for these friends—and grateful, too, that, indeed, they had all four survived excruciating hardships. He also marveled at how quickly—despite prolonged absence from each other—they had fallen into the easy camaraderie that had marked their adventures as soldiers.

During a lull in their conversation, Theo and his companions became aware of a heated discussion in another section of the room. There were five men in the group: one appeared to be an octogenarian; two were in their mid-fifties; and two were younger—Theo judged mid-thirties or so.

One of the younger ones was saying, "Sidmouth is simply going too far. The man sees revolution writ large with the merest whisper of desire for change."

"And with good reason!" one of the middle-aged men said in an authoritative tone. "Just look what happened in France—that should show you what peasant demands can lead to. Chaos and regicide—is that what you would have here?"

"No, of course not," the first speaker insisted, "but we are likely to see chaos here, too, if the government continues to act in a repressive manner."

"In my day," the oldest member of the group said in a querulous voice, "we knew how to deal with revolutionaries."

"In your day," one of the younger men said flatly, "we lost the American colonies!"

The old man merely grunted in reply to this.

"What is *that* all about?" Theo asked of his own group.

"The old man is Lord Parkington," Jenkins said. "The others are Stremple, Marchand, and one of the younger ones is Wilkes. I think the other one is Ferguson."

Moore twisted in his seat to look. "Yes, it is."

"All three of the older fellows are members of Parliament," Trevor explained. "Parkington is one of those Toriest of Tories."

"So what is the fuss about?" Theo persisted.

Moore shrugged. "Who knows? Catholic emancipation, perhaps. Or, could be another bill against sedition and rioting."

"Welcome to a new kind of battlefield, Major," Jenkins said.

"Oh, no. I am having none of this," Theo said. "I intend to hunt and fish. Attend a few lectures, go to the theater. And dazzle the ladies at frivolous social affairs. No more battles for me."

Their little party broke up soon afterwards with Trevor and Jenkins going home to their wives and Moore off to an appointment with his current mistress. Theo drifted into the card room and played a few hands of whist before tossing down his cards and going home—more bored than he cared to admit, even to himself.

With luck, though, he might have drunk enough to keep the nightmares at bay.

Luck was not with him.

The dream had minor variations, but it was essentially the same, night after night.

He lay on a battlefield, pinned beneath his dead horse. What had been a rain-drenched field of waving grain was now a pool of mud and blood. Death and carnage were all around him.

He twisted his head in an effort to get a clearer view. In doing so, his gaze locked with the death stare of the youngest soldier in his regiment, a boy of thirteen years. Theo could not wrench his eyes from that astonished look.

"I'm sorry," he whispered.

He was cold and could not feel his legs. The horse's body was positioned so that breathing was difficult. He felt he was suffocating. Every breath brought pain. Then, suddenly, he felt a sense of release, of peacefulness, and he was floating high above the scene of death and devastation.

He did not want to look down. He struggled against doing so. He knew what he would see. He had seen it nearly every night for months now. Some power greater than himself forced him to look. It always forced him to look.

The dead lay sprawled where they had fallen. They stared vacantly at him—accusing him. Sergeant Cooper. Private Davies. Lieutenant Henderson. Miller. Edison. Morgan. Stevens. And many, many others. He could name them all. He did name them all. Over and over, he recounted their names.

Then there were voices.

"Why, Major?"

"You shoulda done somethin', sir."

"'Tis all your fault."

"You killed my friend."

"You—you—killed them all."

"No-o-o—!"

A warm hand was shaking his shoulder.

"My lord. Wake up! You are dreaming again."

His eyes flew open. Burton.

He raised himself on one elbow and wiped a hand across his face. He felt the dampness of cold sweat. "Thank you, Burton. I . . ."

"The same dream, sir?"

"The same." He sank back, suppressing a shudder. "Go back to bed, Burton. I'll be all right now."

"Are you sure? I don't mind sitting with you."

"It usually comes only once a night. I'm fine. Go back to your bed."

"As you wish, my lord."

Burton returned to his bed in the dressing room adjacent to Theo's bedchamber. Both he and the viscount were aware that it was unusual for the valet not to have a bed in the servants' quarters, but both agreed that there was no sense in waking the whole household with these events.

Theo had told the truth—the dream usually did come only once a night. But he was not "fine." He sometimes wondered if he would be ever again. He would sleep no more this night. He rose, lit the lamp near his bed, and picked up a magazine, *The London Review.* Surely something here would numb his brain.

Some writer calling himself "Gadfly" was carrying on about inequities in Parliamentary representation. *That ought to serve as a proper inducement to sleep*, Theo thought. However, he found himself caught up in the writer's argument that the nation's legislative body was far from representative of the people it was supposed to serve.

Interesting, he thought, *but nothing to do with me.*

In the next few days Theo prepared for the life he had described to his companions at White's. His years of army experience—over a decade—forced him to view his foray into society much as he would have viewed a military campaign. First, one reconnoitered the territory, observed the situation, and planned strategy. Only then could one take action.

His first step was to outfit himself in a new "uniform"—attire befitting the heir to a wealthy earl. He opted for less ostentatious garb than he had jokingly threatened, but there was no denying that he was now costumed for the part of his new station in life.

"You are looking quite handsome, my son," his mother

commented in the drawing room before dinner one evening. Theo was wearing a fine new jacket that had been delivered just that day.

"Why, thank you, Mother."

"Do you not agree, Edward?" The Countess of Glosson addressed her husband, who was busy at a sideboard preparing drinks.

The earl turned to hand each of them a glass of sherry. "Of course, my dear. After all, I married you to have beautiful children and you did not disappoint me."

"Really?" Her tone was mock surprise. "And all these years I have labored under the mistaken notion that you married me for my dowry."

"Well, there *was* that," the earl said. "Second sons are often forced to seek out rich heiresses. I was merely extremely lucky in the one I caught."

Theo sat sipping the sherry and only half-listening to his parents' banter. Everyone knew the Honorable Edward Ruskin, whose looks and status would have recommended him to an heiress of substantial means, had, instead, married a woman of good, but by no means rich, family. It had been a love match—and the love had not diminished with passing years.

The countess addressed her husband in a more serious tone. "So—tell us what went on at Westminster today, darling. What *is* Parliament up to now?"

"A great deal of talk—as usual," the earl replied. "The Irish—or perhaps it is the Chinese—have a curse. 'May you live in interesting times.' Let us merely say we live in *very* interesting times."

"Surely things cannot be that bad," his wife replied.

"They may be," he said grimly. "But come—we've more pleasant things to talk about and Morton is hovering at the door, trying to announce dinner—eh, Morton?"

"Yes, my lord," the butler said.

Theo was glad to see the large dining table was laid for a leisurely meal with three places at one end. The conversation centered first on family concerns—the countess had attended her daughter's latest lying-in and she oozed grandmotherly pride over the new addition. Then the talk turned to the earl's favorite topic—one shared by his wife and son—classical Greek literature.

"You have, of course, read that poem by Mr. Keats honoring the Chapman translations of Homer?" his mother asked Theo.

"Only recently," Theo admitted.

His father gave a derisive snort. "Hmphf! Misplaced accolades, if you ask me."

"Your father is a purist," the countess said. "He objects to what he calls Chapman's 'embellishments' of Homer, but I personally do not find them so very offensive."

Theo relished this discussion. Although his scholarship was inferior to his father's, Theo was well-schooled in the subject. With a name like Theocritus Euripides, he had felt he had little choice in that matter. He remembered complaining bitterly about his father's saddling him with a name certain to be the cause of schoolboy taunts.

"'Tis a wonderful name," his father insisted. "A great philosopher and one of the world's finest dramatists."

Later, his mother explained, "I think your father gave you that name to please me."

"To please you?" Theo had asked accusingly.

"Yes. I admired Theocritus, and when you were born I had just reread the plays of Euripides and loved them anew. Both men provide very positive views of women and the power of romantic love."

The child Theo had responded somewhat resentfully. "But he gave Francis a perfectly ordinary name—Francis Fitzwilliam."

"Francis is your father's heir," his mother had replied. "We were too young to give our imaginations free rein when he was born. We did what we wanted with you and your sister. I've always had a soft spot in my heart for Cassandra, the doomed princess of Troy."

The adult Theo had long ago accepted the name. Not since he was twelve had he resorted to fisticuffs over it. Indeed, he had been "Ruskin" and then "Major Ruskin" for a good many years—and "Theo" to his friends. In recent months, since his brother's death, he had, often as not, been simply addressed by his title, "Amesbury."

As the three of them left the dining room together, the countess linked her arm with her son's. "I am *so* glad to have you home at last!"

Theo chuckled and put his hand over hers. "Yes, Mother. You have managed to make that point daily now."

"Losing Francis was very hard on us—both of us." She glanced at her husband and then back to her son. "I hated your having to get that news in France—alone, with no family near."

"It was pretty shattering news, I must admit," Theo said, "but the routine of duties with the regiment helped."

"I suppose we all cope with such changes—such losses—in our own ways," she said. "Your father has virtually buried himself in Parliamentary matters. Cassandra, of course, is busy with her children."

"And you?" Theo asked gently.

"I have taken up music—again," she said brightly. "Francis always loved music so—and it makes me feel closer to him."

"She has been taking lessons on the harp," the earl put in. "And even with my poor ear for music, I can tell she has become very proficient."

"Good for you, Mother."

"It helped that I had had some experience with the harp previously."

"You must play for me," Theo said.

"I will. But not tonight."

They had taken seats in the drawing room again. Soon, Morton brought in a tea tray. As the countess busied herself pouring, Theo quietly savored this time with two of his favorite people.

"Now that you have a proper wardrobe," the countess said, having handed the men their cups and sipped at her own, "we must see to your being properly introduced—or reintroduced—to society."

"*Introduced* is the correct word," Theo said. "That brief period between Boney's original exile and his escape from Elba did not afford me much exposure to the *ton*."

"Good. Then you are not averse to taking your proper place in society," she said.

"Whatever that may be." Theo's tone was guarded. "We have discussed this before, Mother—and let me tell you again that I will *not* be offered up on the auction block of the marriage mart! I am simply not ready for that."

"But—in time you will be—and it will not hurt for you to survey what might be available in the way of a potential wife," she persisted.

Theo sighed. He knew his mother would not let go of an idea or "project" once she set her mind on it.

His father chuckled. "Give it up, son. You know you cannot win."

"All I am asking is that you *meet* some eligible ladies," his mother said defensively. "After all, you will marry some day, will you not?"

"*Some* day," Theo agreed. He then pointedly changed the subject and his mother seemed content to drop the matter, but Theo knew hers was only a strategic retreat.

Two

When his mother retired, Theo and his father remained in the drawing room, each occupying a comfortable wing-backed chair. The earl had a keen interest in his son's army experiences and asked probing questions.

After a pause the older man said in a regretful tone, "This country has not done well by her modern-day warriors."

Theo merely raised an inquiring brow.

"Comes from that natural English distrust of a large standing army," the earl continued. "As soon as we have no further use of them, we just turn them loose in the countryside to fend for themselves."

Theo nodded. "Where they swell the numbers of people out of work."

"Or they are forced to take low-paying jobs ordinarily done by women and children."

"I know," Theo said. "I visited some of my men at Chelsea Hospital the other day. The lack of jobs is a genuine concern for them—especially for those who sustained crippling injuries."

"Poor beggars," the earl murmured.

"Beggars, indeed. There is something inherently unfair about it."

"Yes. And that unfairness manifests itself in unrest—troubles in mines and manufactories—and in the mills."

"*Our* mill?" Theo asked, surprised.

"So far all the Glosson Mill has suffered is some grumbling from time to time. But others have endured smashed machinery and ruined products. Taggert keeps a strong hand on the tiller in the Glosson Mill."

"Is he not the same man Grandfather had as steward?"

"The very same. Knows his way around the running of the mill—which is more than one can say of the present earl." The "present earl" rose from his chair and went to a sideboard. "Leaves me free to pursue other interests."

"Such as the history of ancient Greece?"

"That—and Parliamentary concerns." The earl waved a decanter. "Join me?"

"Certainly."

They were both silent as the earl handed his son a glass, then sat down again. As they clutched their glasses to let the brandy warm in their hands, Theo spoke.

"So—you have taken up politics, have you?" He knew his father had always had a passing interest in public policy and that some of his parents' closest friends were important members of the established power structure.

"A seat in Lords came with the earldom. It was not something I ever expected, you know."

Theo did know. Five years ago the death of the present earl's brother had catapulted the Honorable Edward Ruskin to being Viscount Amesbury, heir to the Earl of Glosson. Early last year, within weeks of each other, the Viscount Amesbury had lost first his father to the wasting sickness, then his eldest son in a carriage accident. Thus had Theo's father succeeded to the earldom and Theo to the courtesy title Viscount Amesbury.

The official period of bereavement was long over, though Theo knew neither of his parents would ever quite get over the death of their firstborn son, the shining Francis Fitzwilliam. Indeed, Theo himself would never stop missing his brother.

The earl broke into his son's musings. "However, I find work with Parliament quite interesting."

Theo rose to refill his glass. He held the decanter out in an invitation to his father and noted the older man's glass was still sufficiently full. He ignored his father's slight frown of concern as Theo poured himself another, very generous portion. Anything to help keep the recurring nightmares at bay—but he need not burden his father with *that*.

"So you have joined the rest of the 'Fearsome Five' in Parliament," Theo commented. "What do you hope to achieve?"

"We always preferred *Fearless* Five. As to what we hope to achieve—perhaps just to be heard."

"Voices in the wilderness?"

"Perhaps. Some of us feel the government's fear of unrest—fear of revolution—may be unwarranted. But we do not *know*."

"I heard Lord Sidmouth had commissioned spies to inform on certain groups."

"The Home Secretary is, of course, doing what he thinks necessary. But frankly, the people with whom he chooses to work are somewhat questionable."

"Questionable?" Theo raised an eyebrow. "I confess I have not paid a great deal of attention to this issue." He shifted in his chair; a feeling of foreboding began to envelop him, but he did not want to be rude to his father.

"Sidmouth has pulled men out of Newgate Prison and sent them into the countryside to gather information," the earl explained.

"Prisoners? He is using criminals? I should not think them the most reliable sorts."

"Nor are they," his father said in a harsh tone. "The more scurrilous their reports, the better their rewards. Some of *them* have turned out to be instigators of the very unrest they report upon! No wonder the working people of England are so distrustful."

"Sounds a proper dilemma to me," Theo observed, trying not to appear overly interested.

If the earl noticed his son's apparent lack of interest, he chose to ignore it. "It is. The owners of the mills and manufactories—many of whom hold seats in Parliament—are agitating for harsher laws. Workers' groups —the few that can make themselves heard—insist the people are at the end of their rope."

"And you—?"

"I just do not know. We desperately need reliable information. *Reliable* information." The earl gave his son a meaningful look.

"And you think I can help somehow," Theo finally said reluctantly.

His father smiled. "You always were a clever lad."

"Father, I have no interest in politics. I do not want to become embroiled in the machinations of Sidmouth, Liverpool, Canning, and whoever else may be involved."

"I can understand that, son. God knows you have served the nation well already."

"But . . . ?" Theo prompted, perceiving that his father had much more to say.

"But *you* will be Earl of Glosson one day."

"Not any day soon, I hope."

The earl did not reply for some time. He sipped at his drink, then set the glass down. When he spoke, he seemed at first to take the conversation on a different path. Theo welcomed a change in subject, but he puzzled over the one his father chose.

"You know Francis was in Derbyshire when he was killed."

"Yes. You wrote that, but I am not sure I understood exactly *why* he was."

"He went there in my place." This admission carried a tone of something deeper than regret. "He was always more interested in managing the business side of things, you know. Even the estate in Wiltshire. I neither expected nor wanted to be the earl. Francis relished the idea."

"He always enjoyed organizing things—and bossing me and Cassie around." Theo was glad they could talk about Francis so casually.

The earl smiled weakly. "I was pleased when he took over the mill and the entire holding in Derbyshire. Your mother and I were content to shuttle between Ruskin Manor in Wiltshire and this house in town."

Theo tried to reassure his father. "Knowing Francis, I am sure he was satisfied with that arrangement."

"He was. But now . . ."

"I see . . ." Theo finally felt he understood where this was going. "You want me to take Francis's place in Derbyshire."

"Well, you *will* be the earl one day," his father repeated.

"Not any time soon, I hope," Theo repeated as well. "Father, I am a soldier by profession. You know I never expected to be anything else. Besides, you just told me this fellow Taggert handles things well."

"I *think* he does, but Francis said your grandfather had really let matters slide before he died. Your brother thought it best for a family member to take a closer interest."

"Francis *wanted* to do that. He knew what he was doing. I do not know anything about running an estate—or a mill. Tenant farmers, cottage weavers—what do I know of them?" Theo protested. "Granted, I am willing to learn— eventually."

His father's voice now carried a note of sadness. "I think the time is now, son." He let this sink in a moment, then added, "Not only for the family and our own people, but also for a larger interest."

"A larger interest?"

"We need someone we can trust to go among the workers and report on the degree of unrest among laborers in this country," his father said.

"We?"

"Certain members of Parliament. Most are Whigs, but some of us are Tories who do not entirely approve of measures proposed by the Liverpool government."

"The Fearless Five."

The earl nodded. "And others."

"Why me?"

"Well, you always seemed to get on well with the stable hands and farm workers. You have that wonderfully natural ability to mimic almost any dialect. I cannot think of anyone

I know who could do this job better than you could. What is more—I trust you. Implicitly."

Theo smiled. "Thank you for that vote of confidence."

"Will you do it?

"I will have to give it some thought. I never really liked being one of Wellington's 'correspondents'—spying on the enemy. I did it—but I did not like it."

"The working people of England are *not* the enemy," his father admonished, "though I daresay that is the view held by Sidmouth and his lot."

Theo was abashed. "I know, Father. I did not mean to suggest that that is *my* view, either. I had too much respect for the soldier in the trenches to believe now that his brother in the mills and mines would be an inferior sort."

His father nodded. "There *is* an element of danger, Theo. I would be remiss if I suggested otherwise. I would not present this to you if I knew of anyone I thought better qualified to do it."

Theo swallowed his impatience along with a strong swallow from his glass. "I said I will consider it. I have passed myself off as a Spanish peasant and a French soldier, but it might be easier to make a mistake as a common Englishman. *I* am not convinced I am the right man for the job."

"There is something else you should know, Theo." The earl seemed to weigh his next words carefully. "Your brother's death was not an accident."

"Wha-at?!" Theo felt all the air whoosh out of his lungs.

"It was made to *look* like an accident, but one of the axles of his curricle had been cut nearly through. Someone clearly knew of his love of driving as though the hounds of hell were in pursuit."

"Who did it?"

"We do not know. I have had Bow Street Runners working on it for months, but so far they have turned up nothing."

"Does Mother know?"

"No. It came to my attention a week after Francis died. Your mother was already prostrate with grief. I could not add to her pain. And now, I cannot think telling her would serve any useful purpose."

Theo nodded his agreement to this, still trying to digest such shocking news. "Were there no clues at all as to who might have been responsible?"

"A great deal of conjecture, but no concrete information. The most likely theory is that what happened to Francis was meant as a warning."

"A warning—of what?"

"Perhaps to terrorize mill owners—to make them more acquiescent to worker demands. Or, one of the runners thought it might be an isolated act of revolution. Or, possibly Francis had a personal enemy. The thing is, we just do not know."

"And you want me to find out."

"Among other things."

"My God . . ." Theo could not hide his despair.

His father stood. "Think it over, son. If you want to refuse, please know that neither I nor anyone else will hold it against you." He patted Theo's shoulder as he left the room.

Theo thought of little else during most of his waking hours in the next few days. A new dimension had been added to the familiar nightmare. Now, one of the accusing dead had the face of his brother. He struggled against the idea of taking on the task his father had outlined, but even as he chafed against it, he knew that, in the end, he could not refuse this mission, this calling. He owed it to his brother's memory to do what he could to ensure that Francis had not died in vain. He would, though, first find out all he could from the runners about his brother's death. Then, he would "test the waters" to see if he could indeed pass himself off as an English workingman.

Before that, however, he must deal with his mother's special "mission."

The countess had launched a concerted campaign to bring her son into society. Her first venture was a dinner party for some two dozen guests. Ostensibly, she intended merely to acquaint or reacquaint selected members of the *ton* with her long-absent son. However, she also clearly wished to introduce him to some eminently suitable young women.

While Theo appreciated his mother's efforts on his behalf, he rather thought he might be trusted to handle the issue of finding a wife without her assistance—preferably sometime in the distant future. The very distant future. Deterring his mother from any goal she set would be an uphill battle. The woman could be as tenacious as the proverbial dog with a bone.

Mid-morning the day after her dinner party, the countess summoned her son to her private sitting room. She reclined on a chaise longue and bade him take a chair nearby. Theo marveled again at what a handsome woman she still was—despite her having reached the half-century mark some years earlier, and despite the terrible loss of her eldest son only a year and a half ago. Her auburn hair was streaked with gray, but her blue eyes sparkled in as lively a manner as ever they had.

"Well?" she demanded in her blunt, no-nonsense manner. "What did you think?"

"What did I think of what?"

"*Whom*. What did you think of *whom*? Pray, do not, my child, play this silly game with *me*. What did you think of Lady Olivia Sanders? Or Miss Emily Wentworth? Or Miss Anne Bridges?"

"Tell me again which one was which."

"Theo!" She snatched up a pillow and tossed it at him. "Do behave."

Deftly, he caught the pillow and laid it aside. "Very well. They are all three prettily behaved *young* women."

"Not so *very* young. You told me you have an aversion to schoolroom misses. Miss Wentworth is nineteen—this is her second season. Miss Bridges may be twenty—I cannot recall of a certainty. And Lady Olivia is one-and-twenty. She was still in mourning last year, so missed the season. Her betrothed died from wounds he received at Waterloo."

"Yes, so she told me."

He knew his mother favored Lady Olivia, the statuesque, blond daughter of the Marquis of Wembley. In truth, Theo found her very attractive. Green eyes and dark lashes complimented her porcelain beauty. Unlike dark-haired Miss Bridges, who was noticeably shy, Lady Olivia was an easy conversationalist. Miss Wentworth was a brown-eyed sprite with red hair. Theo suspected the color had been toned down by a henna rinse—or whatever it was women used for that sort of thing. She might be twenty, as his mother said, but her giggle proclaimed her not long from the schoolroom he was anxious to avoid.

"Theo." His mother brought him out of these musings. "Tell me what you thought."

"They are all equally presentable, I believe."

"Well, yes—but surely you found one of them more 'presentable' than the others."

"Not at *this* stage of the game, my dear mama."

She turned his phrasing back on him. "'Tis not a game, my dear son. Each of these young ladies has a not inconsiderable degree of beauty, and each will have a suitable dowry—though I believe Lady Olivia has the edge there."

"I have no interest in a woman's dowry."

"Well, you should!" his mother said vehemently. "A prospective bride's dowry—and her bloodlines—these are important considerations in our circles."

Theo gave his mother a hard look. "I seriously doubt my father considered either of those factors when he chose *his* bride."

The countess had the grace to blush. "Oh, well . . ." She paused, then said, "Will you object to my inviting any of them again?"

"Of course not. 'Tis not my place to dictate your guest lists."

"That is not what I meant and you know it."

"Mother, the truth is, this is simply not a good time for this."

"Why not?"

"I . . . it just is not. I am not ready yet," he said lamely.

"Theo, you are one-and-thirty. When *will* you be ready?"

He was deliberately vague. "In time."

How could he tell his mother that he would not willingly consider taking a wife so long as his nightmares plagued him? It was bad enough that Burton knew of those dreams. And now, there was also this project for his father. He wondered how much his father had shared with his wife.

His mother gave him a curious look, but she sipped her morning chocolate, then said, "Well, at least you are not averse to society. There is no reason you cannot enjoy the rest of the season—what little there is of it."

Again, Theo recognized a strategic retreat when he saw one.

For the next several days, the Countess of Glosson insisted her son accompany her to this ball or that soiree, or excursions to the theater. Often his father, too, attended these affairs. The countess invariably said something to the effect of being escorted by the two handsomest men in the realm. And always, one, two, or all three of the countess's choices for her possible successor attended these affairs. Indeed, any of them might turn up as a member of the Glosson party.

Much to his mother's apparent frustration, Theo gave no indication of a preference for any of the three. He was equally polite and equally attentive to all of them. Privately, he admitted to a preference for Lady Olivia—but only because he suspected she might prove the most satisfactory bed partner. However, he knew if he indicated any preference, his mother would be making wedding lists.

He had committed himself to one last social affair before he would take up the challenge his father had laid upon him. The occasion was a ball given by the Duke and Duchess of Rollente. Earlier in the day, Theo had, along with his parents and Lady Olivia, attended the dedication of the newly opened Waterloo Bridge. Figuring prominently in the dedication ceremony had been the Duke of Wellington, who was also the guest of honor at the Rollente ball.

As the Glosson party made its way along the reception line at the ball, Theo heard the booming, rather nasal tones of his erstwhile commander.

"Ah! Major Ruskin." Wellington paused and cleared his throat. "Sorry. Viscount Amesbury. Hard to stop thinking of you as the capable soldier you were."

"Thank you, your grace."

"I understand you are not quite finished serving your country," Wellington said.

"It would seem so, your grace," Theo said before moving on.

The reception line was not the place to pursue this line of discussion, but Theo was surprised that Wellington seemed to know of his possible "service." God knew the man had always been three steps ahead of his subordinate officers, though. Theo shrugged off this distraction and set about the pleasurable and far-from-difficult task of charming Lady Olivia.

Sometime later, he stood with his parents on the sidelines of the ballroom, watching the dancers. He had danced only once—with Lady Olivia—and had proved that he did indeed perform a passable waltz. He was to take her in to supper later. That should provide sufficient fodder for the gossips to chew upon, he mused, as he caught the eye of the silvery blond beauty over her partner's shoulder. He smiled at her even as a young couple, along with another young woman, approached his parents.

"Ah, Folkeston." Theo's father extended his hand in greeting.

"Glosson." Baron Folkeston urged his wife and the other woman forward. "Lord and Lady Glosson, may I present my wife Claudia, Baroness Folkeston, and I think you know our friend, Miss Hannah Whitmore."

"Oh, yes. The vicar's daughter," the countess said with a meaningful glance at her husband.

"Of course," the Earl of Glosson said genially. "And may I present my son, Viscount Amesbury?"

Greetings were exchanged all around.

As Theo took Miss Whitmore's hand to bow over it perfunctorily, his glance caught hers only briefly, but he felt something pass between them. A disconcerted expression appeared in her eyes as she withdrew her gloved hand from his. His mother then engaged the woman in conversation—something about a village school—while Theo studied Miss Whitmore covertly.

She could be a beauty, he thought fleetingly—if she took the pains to be one. A more flattering gown and a modish hairstyle might have done her superb figure and those blue-gray eyes adequate justice. He only half-listened to what she and his mother were saying, then dismissed her as one of his mother's bluestocking acquaintances.

Lady Olivia appeared at his side, laid her hand possessively on his arm, and made a light comment about the exertions of the dance she had just completed. The Folkeston party was acknowledged and Theo then responded to Lady Olivia's request for some refreshment. When he returned, the Folkestons and their guest had gone. Theo shrugged off a twinge of regret. Later he noted the natural grace and elegance of Miss Whitmore's performance on the dance floor. He also noted that she went in to supper with the rather stodgy Walter Montgomery. Lady Olivia drew his attention back to herself.

That night, however, it was not Lady Olivia's laughing green eyes that flashed upon what Mr. Wordsworth called that "inward eye which is the bliss of solitude." It was Miss Whitmore's sober, assessing, blue-gray gaze.

Later yet, that bloody nightmare erased all trace of pleasant reflection.

As Hannah and the Folkestons settled into the baron's carriage for the return drive after the Rollente ball, Claudia turned to her friend.

"There. That was not bad, was it? I think you actually enjoyed yourself."

Hannah laughed. "As a matter of fact, I did. I had a wonderful conversation with Lady Hermiston and her niece, the Countess of Wyndham." She did not add that she now fervently wished she had opted for a new, more flattering gown. Perhaps the very attractive Lord Amesbury would have found her more worthy of his attention.

"And you danced four times!" Claudia exulted. "Though I could have wished for you to have gone to supper with someone other than Mr. Montgomery."

"Mr. Montgomery is quite an amiable gentleman," Hannah said defensively.

Claudia sniffed. "But hardly an eligible *parti*."

Hannah smiled in the darkness. She patted Claudia's hand. "Never mind. You can practice your matchmaking skills next year."

"What *am* I to do with her, Folkeston?" Claudia wailed rhetorically. "She ignores the fact that time marches on."

"Just love her as she is," the baron said matter-of-factly.

"Thank you, my lord," Hannah said.

Claudia ignored both of them. "I was sorry to see Amesbury so preoccupied with the Sanders chit. I had hoped you might like him, Hannah. I mean—after all, the Earl of Glosson *is* your father's patron and such a match *would* be perfectly acceptable . . ."

"The betting books are laying odds that Lady Olivia will bring him up to scratch sooner than later," the baron offered.

"I do wish gentlemen would not bet on people's personal lives so." Claudia was off on another topic as her husband idly defended the habits of gentlemen. Hannah was happy to have her friend momentarily distracted.

She was surprised at a niggling regret at the announcement of a possible match between the viscount and Lady Olivia. After all, what business was it of hers? She had started to dismiss him as one of those *ton* dandies, dressed as he was in the first stare of fashion. He seemed bored and distant—but all too eager to leap to do the Lady Olivia's bidding. The apparent respect with which the Duke of Wellington had greeted him was a bit of a puzzle, though. And even more puzzling to the usually self-possessed Hannah had been her own reaction when they were introduced. His grip was firm and she was unable to control a positively physical response to his touch and to a mesmerizing quality in his gaze.

She shrugged, assuring herself that she knew very well what men like that did with their time. Social soirees, balls, their clubs. Hunting parties in the late summer and autumn, then back to town for more social affairs— interspersed with occasional sporting events such as races and pugilistic matches. Hannah Whitmore had no time for people who led such idle, aimless lives.

Still—he *was* rather attractive. . . .

Three

A few days after the Rollente ball, Trevor Jeffries called at Glosson House and was shown into the library to await his host. When Theo strolled in, Jeffries gave a start.

"Good God! Is this the newest look among the dandies, then?" He looked Theo up, down, then up again, and shook his head in wonder.

Theo knew what Trevor saw—carelessly combed brown hair, a two-day growth of beard, rough clothing borrowed from a stable hand, and such boots as had brought the viscount's valet to the brink of tears.

"Hmm." Theo pretended to consider this idea. He smoothed his hands over his chest in a preening gesture. "Do you think Brummell would approve?"

"Be serious. Why is the man known as 'spit and polish Ruskin' looking like a dock worker?"

Theo looked down at his "finery" and answered Jeffries's question in an affected country accent. "Mayhap 'cuz that's what he be."

Trevor shook his head again. "What is this? What *is* going on?"

Theo explained in his own tone. "I am to become a common laborer for a time."

"A common laborer? Why? I know many people are feeling financially stressed in the aftermath of our fracas with Napoleon, but to have the heir to a rich earldom earning his own bread by the sweat of his brow—Well! that boggles the mind."

Theo dropped the mystery. "I have agreed to a mission of sorts. I am to test the pulse of the working classes."

"For whom?"

"Certain members of Parliament, mostly. My father suggested it. Should prove challenging."

"Oh, I see." Trevor's tone was ironic. "You did not get your fill of spying for Wellington."

"I will not be spying on an enemy," Theo said.

"No. On fellow Englishmen—and that is much worse." Trevor sounded indignant. "I've heard about Lord Sidmouth's commissioning spies to obtain information to use against agitators. Surely, you would not stoop to such a task."

"Of course not." Theo did not attempt to hide his irritation at the suggestion. He explained the situation to Trevor, including the information about his brother's death, knowing full well he would trust Trevor with his life. Indeed, had he not done so repeatedly in the past?

"Murdered?" Trevor asked. "Francis was murdered?"

"It seems so."

"Why? And—*who*?"

Theo explained what he had learned from the Bow Street Runners—which was little more than what his father had initially told him.

"What is it that you are expected to do?" Trevor asked.

"As I said—merely to take the pulse of the nation— though I hope to find out what really happened to Francis. I shall also, perhaps, try to help curb some of the more drastic measures being urged in certain quarters. You know as well as I do how some fear the specter of revolution in this country."

Trevor nodded. "Ridiculous, is it not? It has been nearly thirty years since the fall of the Bastille. If the French Revolution has not been exported to 'this sceptered isle' yet, it is highly unlikely that it will be."

"True. Nevertheless, there does seem to be a great deal of unrest abroad, and I mean to try to find out how serious it is."

"Why you? Good grief, Theo! Have you not done enough?"

"Primarily because I am not so well known. What with

serving in the Peninsula all those years, I have not been in England—except, of course, for those few months in '14 when everyone thought it was all over."

Trevor sat in silent thought for a moment. "This is risky business, you know. Some of those so-called 'Hampden Clubs' who advocate reform are pretty secretive. You have to be 'twisted in' with secret oaths and handshakes and what not. And if they think someone has betrayed them, they can be absolutely barbaric in seeking retribution."

"I am not out to betray anyone," Theo insisted.

"Some will view your just being you and in their midst as a kind of betrayal."

"*If* they find out about me, they *might*. But I doubt it will come to that."

"You cannot be sure, though," Jeffries insisted.

"Look, my friend. I was able to pass as a Parisian in Paris, a Breton in Brittany, and a native of Southern France in Toulouse. I was even a passable Spaniard in Vitoria. Surely I can pass as a Lancashire worker—in my own tongue yet."

"We all know of your prodigious facility with languages, but you take care. There will be no army at your back, you know."

"I shall be careful. In fact, I shall not undertake this assignment at all if I cannot pass myself off as an English workingman. I will know tonight."

"Tonight?"

"I am paying a visit to the Broken Anchor—a tavern down by the docks."

"Not alone!"

"Well, how else? I surely cannot take a fancy gentleman like you with me." Theo gestured at his friend's impeccable attire.

"I can manage to appear nearly as scruffy as you," Jeffries said. "I shall accompany you."

"No. I will not allow it." Theo's tone left no room for argument. "As you say, there *is* an element of risk. You have Caitlyn and your children to think of. Besides, it will be better for me to go alone, for if I cannot manage alone here in London, what will happen elsewhere?"

Jeffries continued to protest, but he finally conceded to Theo's reasoning.

That evening, Theo shrugged into the rest of his shabby attire, refusing the aid of the hovering Burton. At the last moment, in a habit left over from his army days, he tucked a knife into his right boot. He left Glosson House by the rear entrance and walked some distance to a heavily trafficked street. He hailed a hackney to take him to one of the more unsavory areas of the city. Observing his passenger's dress and hearing his destination, the driver made him show a coin before taking him up. Theo had him stop on the outskirts of the target area. He walked for quite some time, soaking up sounds and smells, and listening to the language. Night had fully enveloped the filthy streets before he felt he had a real sense of the place.

As he entered the chosen tavern, he observed that most of the men were drinking pints of ale. He ordered up a pint himself and sat at an empty table. He knew men such as these would not welcome a "pushy" stranger.

A buxom female with straggly yellow hair approached him. Her breasts overflowed her cheap dress. "You lookin' for some company, sweetie?" He noticed one of her front teeth was missing. As she bent toward him to give him an even better view of her cleavage, he caught a whiff of stale alcohol and body odor.

"Not tonight."

She shrugged and turned away. "Your loss."

He sipped his ale and pretended to mind his own business, but took in details of his surroundings. There were six others in the room besides the bored publican and the woman who had slunk back into what appeared to be her customary corner. One of the other patrons seemed to be a fishmonger, judging by the smell as Theo walked by him. Another, wearing a leather apron, was clearly a cobbler. The others all sported the nondescript garb of river men who worked the city's docks. Finally, one of these approached Theo's table.

"Ain't seen ye here afore," the man said.

"Ain't been here b'fore," Theo replied tersely.

The man waited and, when Theo did not elaborate, he asked, "Where ye from then?"

"Up north."

"Not a Scot, air ye?" the man asked doubtfully.

"Not *that* far north."

"Ye wouldn't be one o' them guv'ment spies, now would ye?" The man's tone was only half joking.

Theo snorted. "Not bloody likely."

"That's good. Cuz we don't take kindly to them folks. One of 'em turned up in the river jus' this week. Musta got drunk an' fell in." The man cackled mirthlessly.

"I tol' ye—I ain't no spy. Now you can join me with your pint—or leave me be."

"Can't hardly refuse a gent's invitation to drink, can I? Hey, Spence," he called to the publican.

Soon the other dock workers brought their drinks to join Theo and his newfound friend, whose name was Chester. Initially, the talk was of a general nature. The men recounted such tales as they had heard of the Prince Regent's marital problems—the Prince's estranged wife had recently returned to Italy. They also talked of the upcoming wedding of his daughter, Princess Charlotte.

"Don't see why royalty always marry furriners," one of them whined. The princess had recently chosen to marry Prince Leopold of Coburg, a German principality.

"Ye'd think an Englishman would be good 'nough for an English princess," another agreed.

"I say let 'er have it 'er way," the last one said.

Theo knew that Princess Charlotte, second in line to the throne, was generally well liked by the people. Her nuptials had been the cause of much speculation in higher circles as well. When she had made her choice, a considerable amount of money had changed hands among those on the betting books at gentlemen's clubs.

As the talk continued, Theo nursed his drink along, not

wanting to ingest too much of the strong brew in strange surroundings. He noticed that his companions had no such reticence. As they drank more, their conversation became more animated.

"Where ye workin'?" one of them asked him.

"I'm still lookin'," Theo replied. "Not much luck so far."

"These is 'ard times," another said. "Verra 'ard."

"If I don't get somethin' soon, I'll hafta go back home," Theo lamented.

"Ain't much anywhere these days," the eldest of the dock workers said. He was a grizzled fellow named Willis, who might have been in his forties.

"Workin' folks always get hit first and worst in hard times," the whiner said. "I hates ta go home fer the chil'ren cryin' they's hungry and my old woman a-naggin' at me."

"An' Willis's gel. Now that's a sad business," Chester said. When Theo directed a quizzical look at him, Chester went on. "She took to the streets this past week. An' her only fourteen, too." He shook his head dolefully.

Willis looked especially glum as Chester imparted this information.

"Them fellas as keeps cuttin' our wages now—ye don't see any o' *their* gels out on the streets." The speaker was a man who had given his name as Fred. He looked to be in his late twenties, and Theo gathered he was single but shared a "crib" with the whiner.

"Sure don't," the others agreed.

"I tell ye, if things get any worse, they's goin' ta be real troubles in this land." Chester spoke with the profundity of the inebriated.

"Hey, now. Curb that sorta talk," Willis warned with a glance at Theo, the stranger in their midst.

"I s'pose he's got the right of it," Theo said. Then he changed the subject by asking if they knew of any work available. No, they didn't. Times were hard, they repeated, but if he would hang out on a certain street, he might pick up a few pence for day work. Theo thanked them for the information and rose to leave.

As he did so, he became aware that the fishmonger had left. The cobbler ostentatiously ignored Theo and the others. Theo was instantly on the alert, especially when the cobbler slipped out the door just ahead of him. Ah, God. He did not want a confrontation. That was not his purpose this night. He stepped outside and stood listening for a moment. There were distant sounds—a shouted argument and someone singing off-key. It was dark in this area, the only light the faint glow from various windows along the street. The gas lighting in the richer areas of town had not made its way down here yet. The cobbler, who should have been on the street, was nowhere to be seen.

Theo stood on the stoop of the tavern, letting his eyes adjust to the darkness of the street, then he stepped away. Sensing a slight movement to his left, and catching the smell of fish, he lifted his right foot and retrieved the knife from his boot. He turned to his left just as the fishmonger raised a cudgel to strike at him. Theo slashed out with the knife and heard a howl of surprised pain. He brought the butt of his knife down on the man's head in a resounding blow. He heard a step behind him and to his right. He immediately turned to see the cobbler, who came from the side of the building. Seeing his companion felled and apparently observing both the weapon and the fighting stance of a man who knew his way around hand-to-hand combat, the fellow threw up his hands and said, "Steady there, I ain't meanin' ye no harm."

"Not now." Theo backed away cautiously, moving farther into the street. "Stay put!" he ordered and the would-be attacker did as he was told. The fishmonger began to moan incoherently where he lay on the ground.

"Take your friend and clear off," Theo said to the cobbler, who needed no further encouragement to do just that. The cobbler helped the other man to his wobbly feet. Theo heard them muttering about just needing extra coin as they beat a hasty retreat.

He made his way back to a busier street, where he hailed another hackney. He leaned back in the seat and breathed a sigh of relief. All in all, he was pleased with himself. He had, indeed, passed for one of the laboring class and he had lost none of his instincts or skills as a fighting man.

He thought of the soiree his mother had wanted him to attend this night. What a contrast to the evening he had had! He wondered idly if that vicar's daughter would have been there.

Two weeks after the Rollente ball, Hannah had returned to Derbyshire. Her brief meeting with the Viscount Amesbury was a distant, regrettable memory. She was once more caught up in the routine of her teaching and life in her father's vicarage, yet she often found her mind drifting to Lord Amesbury. What would it have been like to have danced with him? She frequently chastised herself for such idle thoughts, but they kept returning to plague her.

She tried to concentrate on the Crofton Parish Day School. That institution was now the center of Hannah's life, but she remembered well her family's reactions when she had first proposed the idea.

Three years ago, she and her parents had been sitting in the vicar's study, Hannah in a round chair, her mother perched apprehensively on a settee.

"You cannot be serious!" her mother had exclaimed. "Mill children, too?"

"Yes, Mama. The people of this parish need a school—a real school."

"Well . . . perhaps for the children of the village merchants and some of the farmers . . ." Her mother's voice trailed off.

"For *all* the children," Hannah insisted.

Her father spoke, apparently choosing his words with care. "I think that getting mill children and those of the cottage weavers to come to a school will be a most ambitious endeavor."

"Do you mean 'impossible'?" Hannah challenged.

"Perhaps," her father replied. "You must remember that cottagers and mill people rely on the income their children bring in."

"But if they could allow the children to have lessons even a few hours a day—or a few days of the week—" Hannah said hopefully. "I mean—consider little Georgina Foster. Her attendance is most irregular, but she has learned *so* much!"

"You can try it, daughter. You can try it." The Reverend Mr. Whitmore was clearly unconvinced. "But where do you intend to hold these classes?"

"The church? Just to start with," she said.

"Somehow I thought that would be your answer," he replied with a knowing grin.

"This is not a thing a proper young woman should do," her mother protested.

"Other women run 'dame' schools all over England," Hannah said.

"Older women. Widows and married women. *Not* proper young ladies," her mother responded.

"What could possibly be improper in a vicar's spinster *daughter*, instead of his wife, running a school?" Hannah asked.

"I am not sure, but there must be something." The vicar's wife directed a look of appeal to her husband. "Charles, darling, you cannot approve of this madness."

The Reverend Mr. Whitmore came from behind his desk to sit beside his wife. He placed a comforting arm around her shoulders.

"There, there, dear," he crooned. "Do not take on so. I seem to remember you proposed something of the sort yourself before our own children came into our lives."

"Yes, but I was a married woman. How will it look for a young maiden lady to do this?" she wailed into his chest.

"I *am* a maiden lady, Mama," Hannah said, "but at three-and-twenty, I am beyond being a *young* maiden. It will be all right. I am sure of it."

"Oh-h-h," her mother wailed anew. "You should be married already. That nice Mr. Robinson . . ."

"Was a penniless curate and a thundering bore," Hannah said. "Honestly, Mama—"

"You liked that handsome Mr. Smythe-Jones, did you not?" her mother asked hopefully.

"Initially," Hannah replied. "But he did not wear well." Horatio Smythe-Jones was the heir to a barony with property near Barnsley. The man was an Adonis whose mere presence would have impressed any woman. Hannah's interest had waned when she realized that his ardent courtship of her had begun only after he discovered that she would one day inherit from her godmother a small property that ran parallel to that which *he* would one day inherit. Besides, she could not abide a person whose favorite words were "I," "my," and "me."

"Well, Mr. Pettigrew, perhaps? He was studying to be a solicitor."

"Mr. Pettigrew's idea of the perfect wife is a woman whose most frequent utterance is 'yes, dear' and heaven forbid she should ever produce an idea of her own—let alone give it voice!"

"She has a point, my dear," the vicar said. "Our outspoken Hannah would have been miserable with such a man."

"You always did spoil her," his wife muttered. "Dorothea and Katherine are far more biddable."

"My sisters and I do not share the same interests," Hannah said. *And besides*, she thought, *they simply keep quiet and do what they please anyway; thus they* seem *more biddable than they are*.

When they were told of Hannah's proposal, neither of her sisters evinced the slightest interest in it. The four female members of the vicar's family had been lingering over breakfast one morning when Hannah brought up the subject of her school.

Dorothea, then nineteen and the recognized beauty of the

family, had been downright haughty. "I will not allow myself to be labeled a bluestocking." She gave an exaggerated shudder. "I wonder that you are willing to be so known."

"And you, Katherine?" Hannah asked the younger of her sisters. "Would you like to help in the school?"

Mrs. Whitmore answered. "She most certainly would *not!* I will not have another of my daughters associating with riffraff."

"Our neighbors," Hannah said stubbornly.

"In any event, I shall be going away to Miss Strempleton's school myself." Peacemaker Katherine thus carefully avoided responding to Hannah's question and simultaneously forestalled her mother's protest.

"It is one thing for *you* to do this, Hannah," Dorothea said spitefully. "After all, you have little interest in romance and marriage. Nor prospects, either."

"Dorothea!" her mother admonished.

"I am sorry, Mama, but 'tis only the truth. You cannot allow her to ruin our lives. I can only hope this mad scheme will not hurt my chances with Lord Randolph."

Squelching her inclination to retort to her sister's hurtful jabs, Hannah simply observed, "The man is besotted. I doubt anything would deter him."

"Yes, he is, is he not?" Dorothea patted her hair and lifted her chin, obviously pleased to have the conversation diverted to herself.

And besotted he had been. Dorothea and Randolph, third son of a marquis, were married the following year and Katherine had gone away to school.

Now, nearly three years after Hannah's outrageous proposal, Dorothea had borne Randolph a son and could not restrain herself from repeatedly boasting of this singular achievement to her older—still unmarried—sister. Katherine had returned from school a very pretty, very poised young woman who would start attending grown-up social affairs in the next season.

Having failed early on in finding an ally among the females

of her own family, Hannah found one in Jane Thomas, daughter of her father's friend, Nathan Thomas. Editor and publisher of *The Crofton Chronicle*, Thomas also ran a small print shop. Growing up together, Hannah and Jane had been inseparable, though their ways had parted for a while, as they were sent away to separate schools. As Hannah struggled to make her dream of a day school for the parish a reality, she welcomed Jane's offer of assistance. So it was that Jane Thomas, also a young maiden lady, became the second teacher in Hannah's school.

At first, Hannah and Jane had been content to work with only a few children of local merchants and better-off farmers. Soon it became a mark of distinction to have one's child enrolled in "Miss Whitmore's school," though it was officially known as the Crofton Parish Day School. By the end of the first year, the school had outgrown the limited facilities the church could offer, even though the body of students still included very few children of mill workers or cottage weavers.

The question, now that it had grown so, was *where* could the school go?

"You might approach Mayfield or Glosson," her father suggested. "Since they are not only the largest landowners in the area, but also owners of huge textile mills, it is just possible they may be able to provide space for a school."

"The Earl of Glosson is seldom in residence here," Hannah protested.

"True. The Earls of Glosson have always preferred town life. Thus, they have in my acquaintance with them been absentee landlords. Especially since his son died, the present earl—the seventh to hold the title—leaves most of the business of the earldom up to his steward."

"Mr. Taggert, you mean?"

"Yes."

"But he has another son, has he not?" As a child, Hannah had not known the seventh earl or his family except to see them in the village on rare occasions. Later, she had been too preoccupied with her school duties to be overly concerned.

"Perhaps the eighth earl, when he inherits, will take more interest in local affairs," Hannah said.

"I would not count on *that*," her father had replied two years ago. "I am told the man who will be the next earl prefers his Wiltshire property. Bookish sort of man. Amiable enough—I met him once. Meanwhile, Mr. Taggert is in control."

"Well . . ." Hannah said, "it seems to me that *someone* in that family is shirking his responsibility in leaving affairs here in the hands of Mr. Taggert."

"That may be. But Taggert is the one with whom you must deal."

Accompanied by her father, Hannah had called on Mr. Taggert in his office at the Glosson Mill. They entered the steward's office from an outside entrance that led them into an outer office where a young man acted as secretary to the steward. He announced them and showed them into a sumptuously appointed room with upholstered furniture and a fine Oriental carpet. Hannah thought the wall separating Taggert's office from the mill must be especially thick, as they could barely hear the whacks and thwacks of the dozens and dozens of looms in the five-story building.

Taggert greeted them with formal courtesy, due mostly, Hannah thought, to her father's position as the leading churchman in the community. The steward was a portly man of medium height with thinning hair. His beady, nearly black eyes peered around a rather bulbous nose and over fleshy cheeks. The odor of stale cigars permeated the room and Hannah noticed a half-filled ashtray on the desk. Taggert invited the vicar and his daughter to take seats before his huge, ornate desk and reseated himself behind it.

"What can I do for you?" he asked, steepling his fingers over a pile of papers on the desk. He directed the question to the Reverend Mr. Whitmore, virtually ignoring the clergyman's daughter.

"We have come on behalf of my daughter's school," Whitmore said. "I shall allow her to explain." Hannah caught her father's warning glance at her.

"School?" Taggert seemed disinterested and slightly annoyed.

"Yes." Hannah explained about the establishment and growth of the school, though she wondered how anyone living in this parish could fail to know of it already. She emphasized her desire to offer educational benefits to *all* the children of the parish, but they had outgrown the current location and perhaps the Earl of Glosson would be able to help them.

"All the children," Taggert repeated tonelessly.

"Yes," Hannah said firmly.

"Mill children and weavers' brats, too?"

"*All* children," she repeated, trying to ignore his negative tone.

"Preposterous!" Taggert sneered. "All the education these brats need they get right here in the mill. Why, I'd be a fool to deliberately aid in depleting my work force."

"The earl's work force?" Hannah asked innocently and saw a flash of anger in Taggert's eyes.

"Yes. Glosson Mill. Which *I* run."

"And the earl shares your view of educating workers' children?" Hannah probed.

"But of course." Taggert was smug as he toyed with his cravat. "As I said, I am in charge of the mill and the cottage weavers on Glosson property, as well."

Hannah shared a glance of despair with her father.

Taggert rose and said, "You'd best confine your little school business to the village kiddies. No sense stirring up the lower orders beyond their place."

"Still," Hannah said as she and her father also rose, "I would appreciate it if you would convey my request to the Earl of Glosson."

"Oh, I'll tell 'im, all right," Taggert said with a snide chuckle. "Good day, Miss Whitmore. Your servant, sir."

Outside, Hannah fumed. "That officious, odious, arrogant . . . toad! I doubt he will even communicate my message to the earl."

"Perhaps you will have a chance to do so yourself when next the earl visits here," her father consoled.

"Whenever that is likely to be," she muttered, not yet ready to let go of her anger.

"There is still Baron Mayfield. He may prove more amenable in the search for a location for the school."

"I hope so," she said.

It was a hope doomed to disappointment.

Baron Mayfield received them more cordially in the formal drawing room of his elegant house. He was a young man and reasonably good-looking, with very black hair and brown eyes. He was dressed in a fashionable coat of blue superfine, buff-colored pantaloons, and highly polished shoes. His neckcloth was tied in an intricate manner that Hannah thought must be "all the crack," as the young dandies would put it. He seemed to fancy himself something of a ladies' man and flirted mildly with Hannah, holding her gloved hand just a shade longer than necessary.

He listened politely and smiled indulgently, but in the end, he proved to be no more helpful than Mr. Taggert had been.

"A pretty young lady like you should have more to concern her than teaching ignoramuses to read and cypher. Perhaps you will allow me to take you driving one day?" This last was addressed half to Hannah and half to her father, who had accompanied her again.

"Perhaps . . ." she said vaguely, not wanting to close the door completely. Nevertheless, she doubted there would be any help from that quarter.

A week later her father met her in the foyer as she returned to the vicarage from teaching her afternoon classes.

"Come into my study when you have put off your things," he said. "There is someone here you must meet."

She quickly divested herself of her bonnet and cloak and smoothed her hair, tucking in errant strands. As she entered the study, a dignified, middle-aged man with a shock of white hair rose to greet her.

"This is Mr. Andrew Bellenham, my dear, from near Doncaster. My daughter, Miss Whitmore, sir."

When Hannah and the gentleman had exchanged greetings, she seated herself. As the men resumed their seats, she mulled over the visitor's name. "Bellenham. Bellenham. I feel I should know that name, sir."

"Indeed you should, daughter," her father said. "Mr. Bellenham owns the building that once housed the Bell and Hammer carriage works."

"Ah, yes." She still did not fully comprehend the man's presence in her father's study.

"He has offered the use of that building for your school," the vicar said.

"He has—" Hannah echoed. "Oh! Sir! How very, very wonderful!"

Bellenham flushed at her enthusiasm. "Well, now, I'm not so sure you'll feel that way when you inspect the place closely. 'Tis really rather a big barn of a building, and it has been sitting empty for these five years and more since we moved the carriage-making business over to Doncaster. I'm in no position to put anything into the building, and I'm of no mind to sell it, but if you want the use of it, perhaps we can work something out."

Hannah felt tears threaten. "Oh, sir. You have provided the answer to my prayers. To *many* prayers. But how . . . ?"

"I received a letter from your father explaining something of your dilemma here."

"I merely requested that he call upon us if he were in this area," her father said.

"I shall be glad to see some good use made of the building," Mr. Bellenham said. "I hated seeing it deteriorate. Already vandals have broken all the windows."

There was more discussion of a similar nature and the details were ironed out; then Mr. Bellenham took his leave. When he had gone, Hannah hugged her father tightly.

"Oh, Papa. You did it! You found a place for my school. And it is *so* perfect—right between the Mayfield and Glosson mills—they will *have* to allow the children to attend!"

"Now. Now." He patted her back. "Do not get your hopes up too high. Mill people can be stubborn—and I refer to owners and workers alike."

On first inspecting the building two years ago, Hannah had been dismayed at the enormity of the task of turning that neglected monstrosity into a school. Three months later, though, the Crofton Parish Day School was a reality in its new location. At first, it was largely parents of existing students who donated time and goods to renovating the building. From his Sunday pulpit and during parish visits, Vicar Whitmore encouraged further participation. Soon "*the* school" became "*our* school"—a project for the whole parish and a source of community pride.

However, Hannah and Jane were well aware that the pride was not universal within the parish. There were those who disparaged the establishment of a school as totally unnecessary, even wrong in that it might lead to the dissemination of radical ideas. Support came from an unexpected quarter, though. Her father's ecclesiastical adversaries—the dissenting sects such as Methodists—enthusiastically endorsed the school.

Francis, Lord Amesbury, eldest son of the eighth Earl of Glosson, had come to Derbyshire for a period of a few months just after the new school was established. Hannah had not met him, though her father had called upon him and found him an amiable gentleman. Then had come that terrible carriage accident. After that, the earl himself paid a visit, but he came alone and stayed only a short time. It was said that the family, reeling from the death of the eldest son, had then focused their attention across the channel with the remaining son who served in the Army of Occupation. Until the new Viscount Amesbury counted himself ready to assume control of things in Derbyshire, the earl declared, they would remain in the apparently capable hands of Mr. Taggert.

"In other words," Hannah groused to her father, "the earl is unwilling to take an interest in matters here so long as he reaps the rewards from his enterprises."

"Perhaps," her father ventured.

Hannah put this matter from her mind as she and Jane surveyed the miracle that had been wrought by people working together. Partitions had been established, and crude tables and benches of varying sizes made their appearance in the old Bell and Hammer building. An army of workers, devoting their time after long hours at paying jobs, replaced the windows, repaired a leaking roof, and installed ceramic stoves in each room. Finally, they whitewashed the walls.

A festive air spread among the people as "our school" neared completion and the parish declared a half holiday one Saturday to celebrate. Hannah and Jane kept pinching themselves to be sure it was all real.

The dream was realized—almost.

The building was there. Supplies were meager, but sufficient—thanks in part to the Countess of Glosson, who had answered an appeal for that much support at least. However, three years since Hannah had first promoted the idea, the students were still largely the children of merchants and farmers. Very few children from the textile mills or weavers' cottages attended.

As Hannah returned from her visit with the Folkestons in London, she was more determined than ever to change that situation.

Four

Theo arrived in Derbyshire in mid-July. Determined to *be* the person he claimed to be, he had walked most of the distance from London, though he had cadged occasional rides from farmers and carters hauling goods to market. Within a week of his arrival in Crofton, he had obtained a job at one of the machines in the Mayfield Spinning Mill. Necessarily shunning the elegant house of the Earl of Glosson, he also found a place to stay in an establishment for single men run by a woman named Peg Thornton. Peg's husband and six of her seven children—all but the eldest daughter, Doreen, a girl of sixteen—also worked in the Mill. Peg and Doreen took care of their boarders in a house rented from the mill owner, Baron Mayfield.

Doreen appeared to be a comely armful. She had ash-blond hair and clear blue eyes that managed both innocence and seduction—simultaneously—a look Theo had seen often enough among camp followers on the Peninsula. Early on, she seemed to view Theo as a likely partner for her kind of fun, though he politely avoided her as much as possible.

As she served a meal, she would "innocently" brush a breast against his shoulder. If he chanced to meet her in the hallway, she managed to brush her body against his or touch him. He found her machinations more amusing than exciting and dismissed her as a child trying to pretend to grown-up allurements.

In his years of army campaigns, Theo had been accustomed to the meanest of living conditions: meager rations at times, and long hours of arduous, boring marching. Nevertheless, he found it difficult to adjust to standing at his machine for twelve hours a day with only a few minutes off in mid-morning for breakfast and a half-hour for lunch. He also found it repugnant to have to ask permission for such a simple matter as a call of nature.

The work itself was a monotonous matter of performing the same motions over and over, with the pace determined by the machines—and woe betide the human unable to keep up. An "overlooker" paced about the room with a long whip which he was not loath to swing upon the back of any he determined to be a sluggard—man, woman, or child.

The mill was a building of five stories. Each floor consisted of a vast, barn-like room housing dozens of machines lined up facing the same direction. During the day, light filtered in from windows too dirty to allow one to see the sky or weather. The windows were kept closed, so the air, moist from the steam used to run the machines, was always a stale combination of dry cotton, harsh dyes, and unwashed bodies. The air was so laden with cotton lint that mere breathing proved an unpleasant experience. When it grew dark, lanterns using tallow candles added their noisome odor. The monotonous clunks of the machines were broken by occasional screeches of metal crying out for oil—and the frequent crack of the overlooker's whip.

There was little sound of the human voice. No songs such as one might have heard at sea or in a field. Talking among the workers was forbidden. Theo learned the hard way the penalties for being late to work by a mere five minutes—and for talking with the man at the next machine. At the end of the week his pay had been docked for these infractions.

Despite his being in generally good physical shape before embarking on this mission, and despite his improving upon that state by walking to Derbyshire, Theo found his first few days to be exhausting. His ankles swelled from long hours on his feet and the leg injured at Waterloo ached abominably. He often returned to his lodging too tired to taste much of the unchanging supper of boiled cabbage and boiled potatoes laced with bacon grease. He would fall into the bed he shared with another worker, too tired to worry about the possibility of the dream's disturbing him—or others in the room. Morning arrived all too soon.

One evening as he trudged up the walkway to the boardinghouse, he decided he was simply too tired to face that unvarying evening meal. He would go directly to bed and hope his body would be more cooperative on the morrow. As he opened the door to the room he shared with five other mill workers, he found Doreen Thornton bending over the bed he shared with Tim Hessler, smoothing out the single blanket. In doing so, she displayed a good deal of plump, young cleavage.

"Leave it," he said in a tired voice, and began to shrug out of his jacket.

"I couldn't do that, now could I?" She cocked her head flirtatiously, then hurried around the bed. "Here. Let me help you with that."

She stood close and put her hands out to help him remove the jacket. He quickly stepped away and pulled the jacket back in place.

"That won't be necessary," he said.

"Oh, don't be such a prude." She pursed her lips in a pout. "I'm just being friendly, after all. We could be real good friends, you and me."

Theo stood with his hands on his hips and gave her a hard look. "Miss Thornton. I am honored by what you seem to be suggesting, but it won't do. It won't do at all."

"Why not?" she challenged brazenly.

"Well, for one thing, you shouldn't even be here in this room alone with me. If your ma knew, she'd take a whip to both of us."

"Just who do ye think suggested ye might like some company?"

Theo was taken aback by this information, but somehow

knew Doreen spoke truthfully. "Still, it ain't proper," he insisted.

She turned toward the still-open door, but instead of leaving the room, she closed the door and stepped closer to him. She put her arms around his neck and pressed her body to his.

"Ye want me, Leo. Ye know ye do," she whispered, using the name Theo had given when he arrived.

Theo was truly concerned now—not on his own account, but on hers. What if one of the other men—or her mother—walked in? He reached up to loose her hands from around his neck and thrust her away from him.

"Miss Thornton, please—"

"Doreen. You can call me Doreen," she said in a tone she must have imagined to be seductive.

"Miss Thornton," he said firmly as he reached to open the door. "You must see reason—"

"What'sa matter? Ain't I good enough fer ye?"

"You're a lovely young woman," Theo said, thinking to save some of her pride. "But you are half my age—and to be brutally honest—I am simply too tired for what you have in mind. Now, if you will excuse me—" He held the door and gestured for her to leave.

She shrugged. "Oh, well. Another time, maybe."

As he closed the door, Theo heard Peg call from down the hall. "Doreen?"

"You're too late, Ma."

Theo took off his jacket and lay on the bed fully clothed. He briefly congratulated himself on that narrow escape, but soon enough exhaustion took over.

Gradually, his body adjusted to the abuse. As he had done with the dock workers in London, Theo—who had presented himself as "Leo Reston"—did not push himself on his companions. He was not unfriendly, but neither did he invite quick intimacy. In time, they readily accepted him and began to invite him to join them "for a pint" at a local tavern, The Silver Shield, whose shield, if it had ever existed, was long gone.

Some of the men were veterans, but Theo did not announce his own veteran status, nor did he take part in discussions that involved sharing war experiences. He did have a close call when one man talked of an officer known as "Spit-and-Polish Ruskin."

"Made sure all the buttons was polished, he did," the man said, making wet circles on the table with his tankard.

"Yours or his?" a companion asked.

"Both. He were a real stickler."

"Pretty boy officers," another sneered. "Out there playin' soldier and like as not gettin' men killed."

Theo kept his head down and his mouth shut as the first speaker responded. "Major Ruskin weren't just a pretty boy. I weren't in his regiment. Been better off if I had a been. Took care o' his men, he did. And he weren't afeared o' wadin' inta the middle o' things. Leastways, that's what I heard."

"Ah, well . . ." the second speaker dismissed the subject and Theo was glad when they went on to another.

He listened carefully to these discussions, listening especially for signs of serious unrest among the people as a whole. He did find a great deal of worry and discontent. Men complained about the long hours and short wages and how hard it was to make ends meet, even with their wives and children working, too. The conversations varied, but the same topics came up repeatedly.

"Trouble is," a man of forty or forty-five named Henshaw said one evening, "we can't do nothin' about it."

A group, including Theo, sat around a large table in The Silver Shield. Others stood around the table, having just heard a rather well-dressed man named Henry Franklin read to them from a recent London newspaper.

"Oh, I wouldn't say that," a younger man replied. His name was Jack something or other, Theo remembered. "We just need to get together."

"That's union talk," an older, grizzled fellow warned. "I ain't lookin' for the law to come down on *my* head."

Several others nodded and murmured agreement.

"Well, I say ol' General Ludd had the right of it," Jack challenged.

"Breaking up machinery don't make jobs—it jus' puts more folk out o' work," the older man explained in the patient tone of age reasoning with youth.

"Besides," Henshaw agreed, "the Luddites didn't achieve much with their smashing machinery. I heard they was more army here in the Midlands in '10 and '11 than they was with Wellington—Wellesley, then—in the Peninsula."

"That's right. An' we coulda used them soldiers in Spain." The speaker this time was Farley, who, Theo knew, had been a sergeant in the Peninsular campaign.

Jack was not willing to let the conversation veer into soldiers' reminiscences. He set his tankard down with a bang. "I still say we need to get together and present our case *together*—united."

"And I still say that there's union talk and unions is illegal," the old man said. "Ain't that right, Mr. Franklin?"

"Yes, it is," Franklin said. "The acts forbidding such 'combinations' are still in effect."

Theo studied the man, Franklin, covertly. He was a local solicitor, much respected by the workingmen of Crofton. Theo had been told that Franklin had actually trained at Lincoln's Inn—one of the Inns of Court in London—but had returned to Crofton to offer his services to his neighbors. Once or twice a week, he would frequent this tavern, bringing with him newspapers that he would read aloud to the others, who were, of course, mostly illiterate. This was a common practice in country towns and villages. As a young man down from Oxford, Theo had himself been pressed into being a "reader" once in his native village in Wiltshire.

"O' course," the old man was saying, "them acts was meant to limit owners as much as workers, wasn't they?"

The lawyer raised a brow in apparent surprise. "Why, yes, they were."

The old man cackled. "Hah! Fooled ye, didn't I, Harry? Jus' cause a man can't read don't mean he can't 'member things."

Franklin gave the man a sheepish grin. "You are right again, Mr. Gordon. I shall not underestimate the powers of your memory in the future."

"Well, that law seems to work only one way, don't it?" young Jack sneered. "How else do you explain the fact that wages are the same in most mills? Folks in the Glosson mill get the same as we do—both low! You can't tell *me* Mayfield and Glosson don't get together on that!"

"Right," several others murmured.

Apparently emboldened by their agreement, Jack went on. "We got to take hold of our own lives—like the Americans did—an' the French."

"Whoa, boy!" Henshaw warned. "You don't wanta be talkin' like that. Never know *who* might be listenin'."

"Revolution," someone said softly.

"Well, maybe it'll take a revolution," Jack muttered in a less vehement tone.

Theo rarely took an active part in such discussions, preferring to listen. What he learned was neither new nor surprising. He *was* surprised when Henshaw later invited him to a meeting of the Crofton Corresponding Society.

"Corresponding Society?" Theo asked, pretending ignorance. He knew very well such groups existed in any number of towns and in London, where they had started. They often agitated for democratic reform and citizens' rights, and for this reason alone they might have incurred the government's suspicions. It was not against the law for like-minded people to meet to discuss political issues, but some leaders in government distrusted *any* organized group not directly under their supervision. Henshaw's description of the Crofton group fit what Theo already knew.

"The Society ain't preachin' revolution—though young Jack would have us doin' exactly that," Henshaw added.

"I see . . ." Theo said tentatively.

"Anyways, you might find it int'restin'."

Theo agreed to attend the next meeting.

Before he could do so, however, he found himself an interested bystander in what he later thought of as a confrontation of classes.

Having just finished work for the day, he was looking forward to a quiet evening of study, for he had picked up a copy of William Cobbett's *Political Register*, a publication that often attacked government policy. *At least Cobbett is never dull*, Theo thought.

It was still early when he and his fellow workers left the Mayfield Mill. The days were getting shorter, and there was a nip in the evening air, but there was a good deal of daylight left. Two women, in better clothing than those around them, stood in the middle of the thoroughfare encircled by women and children of the mill. On the outer edges of the group a number of men hovered, several of them husbands of female workers. Theo was mildly surprised that he recognized one of the women in the center. It took him but an instant to summon up the name—Miss Hannah Whitmore.

He deliberately stood so that he was obscured from her view. He thought it only a slight possibility that she would connect a rough, unkempt mill worker with a gentleman in a London ballroom, but he was taking no chances. Still—what *was* going on? What was a vicar's daughter doing associating with mill workers? She wore a plain gray gown, high-necked and long-sleeved, but it failed to hide an enticing figure beneath—and did very little indeed to dim the sparkling intelligence of her eyes.

"Do you not want a better life for your children?" Miss Whitmore asked.

"O' course we do," one of the mill women, who clasped a child's grubby hand in her own, replied in a hurt tone.

"Then—please—allow them to come to school. Education can be their key to a better life."

"I—we—can't!" the woman said. "They's too many mouths to feed. We needs their wages."

"Could they not come for just a little while?" the vicar's daughter pleaded. "Or even just one child in a family?"

"Well . . ." The woman, who seemed to be the leader, looked around her, and Theo sensed hesitation and a glimmering of hope among all of them.

Just then a handsome carriage drawn by a team of four matched blacks approached. Theo noted an ostentatious crest on the door. When the carriage stopped, a man emerged before his footman could jump down from the back to open the door and set the step. The passenger was a relatively young man—Theo gave him no more than ten years beyond his own age. The newcomer had black hair and brows. He was of an unprepossessing height, but the crowd immediately parted for him.

"Mayfield," someone near Theo muttered.

"Just *what* is going on here?" Mayfield's demand was issued in a loud, authoritative voice that, along with the short whip in one hand, immediately had a cowing effect on most of the onlookers.

But not on Miss Whitmore.

She gestured to her companion. "Miss Thomas and I have come to discuss our school with these children and their parents."

"Miss Whitmore." His voice was condescending—as though he spoke to a lackwit. "I thought I made my position perfectly clear to you some time ago."

"Oh, you did, my lord. Indeed you did. However, I am no longer asking your assistance. I am—we are—merely offering the services of our school to *all* the children of the community."

"My workers have no need of your services, madam."

"Oh, I don't know," one of the men near Theo murmured. "I wouldn't mind the 'services' of one as looked like that."

Theo gave the man a hard stare and the fellow turned red, then moved away.

Miss Whitmore was standing her ground. "That is a decision for the parents to make."

"Not if they wish to keep their jobs." Mayfield glared at the assembled workers, then turned back to Miss Whitmore. "Now I suggest you two *ladies* take yourselves off. You've no business here in the first place."

Miss Whitmore raised her voice to be heard by the others. "Lord Mayfield, it may have escaped your notice, but the people assembled here are on a *public* road. I believe freeborn Englishmen and women have a right to be here."

Mayfield advanced toward her, towering over her and fairly sputtering. "*Miss* Whitmore, I'll thank you to make no more trouble."

When Mayfield moved in her direction, waving the whip, Theo pushed through the men on the fringes, ready to grab the weapon if necessary. Only later did he think that such action would mean the premature demise of his mission.

Before Theo was required to act, another voice was heard. The lawyer, Franklin, had shouldered his tall, lanky frame through the group.

"Miss Whitmore? Miss Thomas? May I be of assistance?" He might have been passing cakes in a polite drawing room.

"Get them out of here," Mayfield growled.

"Well, certainly—if they wish me to do so," Franklin said calmly, offering his arms to the two ladies.

"No! We have a perfect right to be here." Miss Whitmore sounded decidedly angry and there were two spots of color on her cheeks.

"Fine! You stay then," Mayfield shouted. He swung around to the crowd and waved his whip in the air. "But anyone who works for me had best be gone—now! Anyone still here five minutes from now will be turned off. Is that clear?"

Theo could tell that the workers resented his tone, but they dispersed quickly—if reluctantly. One of the last to go, Theo lingered to be sure there would be no further altercation between Miss Whitmore and Baron Mayfield.

"That was meanly done, my lord," Miss Whitmore challenged.

"But effective," Mayfield replied smugly.

"Ladies." Franklin tried to usher the two women away.

"Know this, Baron Mayfield," Miss Whitmore said calmly. "I am not finished."

"Oh, I think you are. Here, at least." His smugness had risen a notch.

Seeing that no harm was likely to come to the two women now, Theo quickly caught up with his fellow workers.

That night Cobbett's fiery words kept losing out to the image of a fiery schoolmistress, gray eyes flashing, standing up to one of the most powerful men in her community. Theo knew of few women—few men, either!—who would have stood up to someone like Mayfield. Obviously, Miss Hannah Whitmore was a woman not easily intimidated.

"I hear there was quite a commotion near the Mayfield Mill yesterday," the vicar said over supper the next day.

By now, Hannah had had time to let her temper cool, but she felt herself color up at her father's gentle teasing. She glanced from his smiling face to her mother's unsmiling countenance and Katherine's look of eager curiosity.

"I heard about it as well," her mother said. "Mrs. Grimes could hardly contain herself in telling me."

"I am sorry if she taxed you with that, Mama," Hannah said contritely.

"What *were* you doing alone in the midst of all that riffraff?" her mother asked. "That might have been very dangerous."

Hannah could not help the defensiveness that crept into her voice. "I was not alone, Mama. Jane was with me and it was still very light out. We certainly had every right to be out in public."

"Right and wisdom do not always go hand in hand," her mother replied. "It could have been dangerous—even disastrous."

"Really, Mama, there was no danger at all. I get on quite well with the workers and their families. So does Jane."

"She does, you know," the vicar assured his wife. "So does Miss Thomas. Comes from their being willing to help—like with that siege of chicken pox last year. No, dear, our Hannah was in little danger on a public street in broad daylight. I am sorry I brought up the topic if it distresses you."

"Were you not frightened when Baron Mayfield ordered you away?" Katherine asked.

"Oh, my. I see Mrs. Grimes had a great deal to say," Hannah said dryly. "Frightened? Not exactly. I admit to a bit of apprehension, though."

She smiled at Katherine to make light of this admission. She then changed the subject to one she knew would appeal to both her mother and her sister. Katherine's attendance at adult social affairs, though still rather limited, was a focal point in the lives of the other two women at the vicar's table.

She did not tell her family that her apprehension the previous day had dissipated when one of the workers had emerged from the crowd to stand behind and to the side of Baron Mayfield. She *should* have been frightened of such an apparent show of force for the mill owner, but somehow she had felt—incongruously, to be sure—that the man's intent was to protect *her*. Ridiculous! she told herself later, but the idea would not go away.

There was something about that man that intrigued her. She almost felt she should recognize him, but how could she? She knew many of the *women* who worked at the mill—and some of their husbands, but this man was not of that group. He was taller than many of the others. He had worn a cap pulled low on his head and the familiar rough trousers of the working class. His shirt, opened at the top, revealed a strong neck arising from powerful shoulders.

When he walked away, she had noted a slight limp. Perhaps he had been a soldier. . . .

Oh, what romantic nonsense, she told herself. *Perhaps the man was staggering drunk and fell down some stairs*!

However, she could not quite dismiss him entirely from her mind.

Five

The Reverend Mr. Whitmore was far more prosperous than most of his counterparts. Both he and his wife came from well established families. Crofton's vicar might have been a squire or gentleman farmer, but he had heeded the call of the church. The Whitmore household now consisted of the vicar, his wife, two of their three daughters, an indoor staff of three, and an outdoor man who served as gardener, groom, and handyman. One of the maids was Elsie, a rather plain, broad-faced, apple-cheeked young woman whose age fell between Hannah's twenty-six and Katherine's eighteen. Elsie Britton was the daughter of a tenant farmer for Lord Glosson and came to the vicarage only during the day. She was generally cheerful and optimistic, with a ready smile and a host of amusing anecdotes about her brothers and sisters—of whom she had ten.

"An' all survived! Mum says most women lose at least one to some malady—an' usually more 'n' one."

"True," Hannah said. "'Tis sad that so many children do not live beyond infancy."

As the eldest of the Britton brood, Elsie had a ready store of tales to tell. One morning a few days after the confrontation with Baron Mayfield, Hannah found the normally bubbly Elsie to be absent-minded and unusually quiet. Hannah sat doing some mending in her favorite spot in her room—the windowseat, which provided good light for fine work.

"Is something wrong, Elsie?"

"Oh, no, miss."

"You seem distracted and you just put the clean laundry in the hamper for soiled linens," Hannah said.

"Oh, no! Did I?" The maid rushed to the basket for soiled things and lifted the lid. "I did. I'm that sorry, Miss Hannah. I did not mean to do it."

"I had not intended to beat you too severely for such a simple error, Elsie. I'll save the beating for something huge—like washing my handkerchiefs with the red tablecloth."

This bit of nonsense elicited only a wisp of a smile from the maid, who retrieved the clean laundry and put it away properly.

"All right." Hannah put aside her sewing. "Here. Sit down." She pointed to a chair, which the troubled maid took with a resigned expression. "Now—out with it," Hannah ordered. "Perhaps I can help."

"Oh, miss. 'Tis not my place to burden you with my troubles."

"Elsie, we have known each other for too many years for such nonsense. Is someone in your family ill? You know you have only to ask to attend them if you are needed at home."

"No, 'tis nothing like that. I wish it was."

"Well, what then? Oh, Elsie. You're not . . . You haven't . . ." Hannah found it hard to say what she was thinking.

Elsie blushed a brilliant pink. "Oh, no, miss. I'm a good girl, I am."

Hannah breathed a sigh of relief.

"It's me brother Bennie—I mean Benjamin—he insists on the grown-up name even though he has only fourteen years."

"What about him? Is he in some kind of trouble?" Hannah was alarmed, for she knew Benjamin well. He had been one of her pupils early on, but he had recently left school to take a job in the Glosson Mill.

"I'm . . . I'm not sure," Elsie said. "He's taken up with a rough lot of older boys. At first they seemed harmless enough, but now they . . . they go out late at night an' they practice marching with sticks and pikes and they talk about getting guns."

"How do you know all this?" Hannah asked.

"I followed him last night when he sneaked outta the house."

"Elsie! You should not be out alone at night!"

"I know. But I had to find out, you see. And I figured I could yell if something happened and Bennie— Benjamin— would have to help me. But nothin' happened."

"You were lucky," Hannah said, trying to ignore the silent voice telling her she sounded like her mother. "Who are these other young men?"

"Da says they're a bunch of malcontents and he warned Benjamin to stay away from them."

"But Benjamin has not done so and you are worried about him," Hannah said matter-of-factly.

"Yes, miss." Elsie sighed heavily. "They are going to some meeting tomorrow night. Benjamin is feelin' real important because Jack Slater asked him along."

"You mean the Crofton Corresponding Society?"

"Yes. That's the one. I jus' don't think Benjamin has any business bein' there."

"You may be right," Hannah said. "However, it is not exactly a secret meeting. There will be a large number of people there."

"Women, too?" Elsie asked curiously.

"I do not think females are forbidden. Perhaps I can find out what this is about and put your mind at rest."

"Oh, would you, miss? I'd be ever so grateful."

"Well, you will have to accompany me. I can hardly attend such a gathering without an escort or a maid," Hannah declared.

"'Course I'll go," Elsie agreed.

As she thought about it later in the day, Hannah welcomed the idea of going to the meeting. After all, the people attending would be discussing matters she considered important—such as Parliament's suspension of habeas corpus in February. More than six months later, the lawmakers still had not reinstated such an important protection of people's rights.

As a result, local magistrates could now hold people indefinitely on the flimsiest of excuses without producing solid evidence or credible witnesses against them. This was a matter dear to Hannah's heart, for George Kinney, the father of one of her students, had been accused of poaching and, though no witness or evidence had been produced, he had been incarcerated now for two months. So far, Henry Franklin had been unable to secure his release. Meanwhile, Kinney's wife and children suffered in dire straits.

The Crofton Corresponding Society met in the larger of the two rooms of the Crofton Parish School. Hannah felt allowing the community use of the school was one small way of repaying people for making the school a reality. When she and Elsie arrived at the meeting the next night, they immediately encountered two attendees they knew—Henry Franklin and Elsie's brother Benjamin. The boy had red hair, brown eyes, a profusion of freckles across his nose and cheeks, and a trace of fuzz on his chin.

"What are *you* doin' here?" Benjamin challenged his sister. "I don't need no nursemaid."

"I got as much right to be here as you," Elsie said.

"Well, you just see you stay out of *my* business."

Hannah thought Benjamin sounded exactly like the sulky schoolboy he was trying not to be. He stalked off to sit with his friends.

Franklin steered Hannah and Elsie to seats in the front and sat with them, thus lending his countenance to their being there, though, in fact, a smattering of other women attended as well.

"I was not aware that you planned to be here tonight," he said to Hannah.

"I decided only yesterday," she replied.

"Why?" There was no challenge to his question, just curiosity.

"For two reasons, actually. Maybe three. I wanted to hear what was being said—and since many of these people are parents of mill children, I thought after the meeting I might continue what Baron Mayfield interrupted the other day."

He grinned at her. "You don't give up easily, do you?"

"Not easily."

"That was two reasons," he prompted.

"I also came because Elsie here is worried about her brother."

"Young Benjamin. I know him. He's a bit of a hothead."

"He is merely young," Hannah replied. "Young people are by nature zealots—they see the world in absolutes. Black or white—no grays."

"Thou speakest like an aged granny," he teased, "but your own enthusiasm is well known, my friend."

"And yours is not?" she asked archly.

"I suppose we are both a couple of revolutionaries at heart."

"Reformers. I prefer the term *reformer*."

"As you wish," he said as the officers took their places in the front of the room to begin the meeting.

Theo, accompanied by Henshaw, arrived late and had to stand in the back of the crowded room. He leaned one shoulder against the wall as various speakers sought support for this or that favorite cause.

"Universal suffrage."

"Make Parliament representative."

"Better living conditions."

"Higher wages."

"Steam engines and power looms take away jobs."

"Restrict child labor."

"Restrict Irish immigration—they take our jobs for lower pay."

Finally, the chairman recognized a well-dressed man who introduced himself formally as Squire Richardson, the local magistrate. He droned on for several minutes about how he agreed essentially with many of the ideas being voiced here tonight. "However," he cautioned, "I would urge a 'wait and see' approach. Given time, I am sure many of these problems will simply resolve themselves without undue government interference."

A woman in the front raised her hand.

"The chair recognizes Miss Whitmore."

Theo's attention had drifted while the squire spoke, but it now riveted on Miss Whitmore. *Good God! What was* she *doing here*?

"I would remind Squire Richardson," she said in a calm but carrying voice, "that the people have been waiting for a very long time—and they have yet to see much progress on any of the issues laid out here tonight. I would urge that immediate action be taken."

Theo surprised himself by standing straight and holding up his hand. He had not intended to draw attention by taking an active role in the meeting.

"The chair recognizes the gentleman in the back."

"Leo Reston, Mr. Chairman." Theo remembered to maintain a country accent. "I'm just awonderin' what the gentle lady up there in the front means by 'immediate action'—is there some partic'lar proposal?"

The chairman looked toward Miss Whitmore.

"Why, I . . . uh . . ." she stammered.

"Smash the looms!" a voice called out, interrupting her.

"Burn the mill!"

"Get Kinney out of gaol!"

"We'll show 'em!"

Henshaw looked worried. "This is gettin' out of hand," he mumbled to Theo.

Several people who had been sitting now stood to add their voices to the general din. The chairman pounded his gavel and called "Order! Order!" to no avail. There were about fifty people in the room—not enough to turn into a real mob—but Theo knew fifty people on the rampage could do a good deal of ill.

A tall man in front stood. "Gentlemen! Gentlemen!" he called in a booming voice. "Oh. And ladies, too," he added, getting a laugh, but also focusing the crowd's attention and thus calming them. It was the lawyer, Franklin.

He had been sitting next to Miss Whitmore, and Theo remembered that Franklin had shown up to offer her his assistance at the incident outside Mayfield's Mill. So—were the two sweethearts? The question popped into his mind, but he dismissed it as merely idle curiosity. He ignored any inkling of regret or envy at the thought.

Turning his attention back to the situation at hand, he was glad to observe that the lawyer's words were having a calming effect. There would be no acts of violence perpetrated this night. Theo and Henshaw slipped away.

Hannah was shocked at what had happened at the meeting. She had been furious at the squire's complacent call for accepting the status quo. Then the abrupt and vehement response to that call of "Smash the looms!" had taken her by surprise and shaken her to the core.

Although she and Elsie had walked to the meeting—it was not even two miles—she readily accepted for both of them Franklin's offer to see them home in his carriage.

"I didn't know. I just did *not* know," she kept repeating.

"Know what?" Franklin asked. "Why, I myself have heard you go on at length about most of the issues presented at tonight's meeting."

"Yes, but I expected them to be *discussed*—rationally. I had no idea that feelings run so deep and that violence is so near the surface. I should have remained quiet."

"Or—maybe that Reston fellow should not have asked his question," Franklin said. "It was not your fault."

"Thank goodness you were there, Henry. There is simply no telling what would have happened had you not been."

"Someone else would have spoken up, I'm sure," he said.

"Perhaps . . . In any event, let us hope cooler heads prevail in future." She sat in silent thought for a moment and her mind focused on the man who had asked her that off-putting question. "Henry—do you know that man Reston?"

"No. Not really. I have seen him at the tavern now and then.

He's new. He does not say much, but I have an idea there's more than meets the eye there."

"I have the same feeling," Hannah said. "He was among the bystanders when Mayfield went into his tirade the other day."

"Was he now? I seem to remember him with Henshaw—and Henshaw works at the Mayfield Mill." There was silence for a moment, then he turned to speak to Elsie. "So. Miss Britton. Your brother is associating with a rather rough lot, is he?"

"Yes, sir. We are that worried about him. Dad's afraid Benjamin will end up transported like Uncle Stephen was in that Luddite business several years ago."

"Stephen Britton's sentence should be up by now," Franklin said.

"'Twas up a year ago," Elsie said. "But he stayed on in New South Wales. Dad thinks the family will never see him again." There was a forlorn note in Elsie's voice and she sighed. "An' now Benjamin."

Hannah patted the maid's hand. "Try not to worry. Benjamin is a good boy. He will not allow himself to get carried away."

"But he wants so much to be part of that Jack Slater's lot, you see," Elsie said.

The subject was dropped and none of them said much before their good-byes at the vicarage, where Elsie would spend the night on a trundle bed in Hannah's room.

Hannah found it difficult to fall asleep. She tried not to thrash around too much so as not to waken Elsie, but she replayed the evening over and over in her mind. These were her neighbors—many of them were friends—but obviously their level of frustration had reached a higher pitch than she had realized.

She supposed that, if she were wise, she would leave matters in the hands of the men who had more power and authority to deal with such issues than women had. But when had wisdom ruled Hannah Whitmore in such things? Bow out and give free rein to the likes of Squire Richardson? Not likely. Her mother's comment came to mind—"Right and wisdom do not always go hand in hand."

Well, so be it.

She drifted off to sleep finally with the image of the man Leo Reston before her. She could not remember finding any other local man so . . . well . . . innately disturbing. It was as though she *anticipated* more with him—or from him. She gave herself a mental shake. Her obsession with this man was getting more and more ridiculous! He wore the same attire as many of the others at the meeting. His hair was longer than, say, her father's or Henry Franklin's. His speech was that of a country dweller. He certainly blended in with other workers.

Yet there was something about him. . . .

Hannah would have been surprised to learn that *she* was the cause of sleeplessness on the part of the man she knew as Leo Reston. Theo, too, mentally replayed the meeting. It had brought some order in his mind to major issues troubling the people in general. Then he considered specific persons. The vicar's daughter might have got in over her head. Trying to bring students into her school was one thing. Meddling in workers' issues was quite another.

He had to admire her courage, though. Theo Ruskin had seen many displays of bravery in his day, but this was a different sort of courage. Of course, sometimes there was a very narrow line between courage and foolhardiness. In the opinion of the heir to the Earl of Glosson, the presence of the vicar's daughter at a workers' grievance meeting was simply foolhardy. It was no place for a lady. No place at all.

When he finally slept, the dream came again.

He moaned in pain at the horse lying on his legs. The eyes of the young soldier again accused.

He woke with a sharp elbow in his ribs. "Be quiet, Reston. You'll wake the dead with that moaning and groaning."

In the predawn light coming through the window, Theo blinked at the man lying next to him. "Thanks, Tim. Sorry."

"Go back to sleep!" another voice in the room muttered.

Later that morning, as they walked to work, Tim Hessler mentioned the dream.

"Sounded like you was on a battlefield," Tim said. "I never knew you was a soldier."

"Learn somethin' new every day, don't ye?" Theo asked flippantly.

"Yeh. Ye do," Tim replied thoughtfully and let the matter drop.

Three weeks later, the cat was truly out of the bag.

Six

Theo had settled into the routine of his life as a worker in the spinning mill. It was a hard life, but it had its moments, especially those shared in the camaraderie of men—and women, too—engaged in achieving a common goal. He was grateful that he was getting this insider's view of the realities of the life lived by a large segment of England's population. He had grown fond of many of the people with whom he worked. Nevertheless, he was profoundly glad that, for him, this was a temporary way of life. He privately vowed that, in the future, he would do whatever was in his power to improve matters for those who came within his realm of responsibility.

For a while, Doreen still cast calf eyes at him during the evening meal, but Theo had ensured there would be no repeat of the earlier incident. About a week ago a new boarder had arrived, a young man in his mid-twenties named Ian Cochran, and the fickle Doreen seemed to have transferred her affections and her less-than-subtle flirtations to young Cochran.

"Better watch out, Reston. Cochran will be winning the day with your lady fair," Tim Hessler teased.

"Well, so be it." Theo made a show of mock regret. "May the better man win."

Theo had even grown used to the ribald jokes and suggestive comments from women on the way to and from work and during the all-too-brief lunch breaks. At first he had been shocked at such language from females in England, but they were not so very different from their sisters who had followed the drum in the Peninsula, were they?

"Our Leo here ain't much fun anymore," said a middle-aged crone with few teeth left. "'Member how he used to blush so pretty?"

"Ah, Flora, findin' out you was already took jus' fair left me bereft with sadness."

This brought a girlish giggle from Flora and smiles and snickers from those around her.

"He gotch ya, Flora."

A man slapped him on the shoulder. "You're all right, Reston."

Among the dozens and dozens of people who worked in the Mayfield Spinning Mill were a couple in their mid-twenties named Molly and Tobias Tettle. Molly worked on the third floor along with Theo; her husband was assigned to the fifth floor. Theo had seen them out strolling on a Sunday afternoon with their three children and an older woman. Molly had proudly introduced her husband and children and her mother, who lived with them and cared for the children while the parents worked. Theo thought the Tettles a nice family—the sort his Wiltshire grandmother would have referred to as "salt of the earth" folks.

Even though she had borne three children and obviously led a hard life, Molly Tettle was a comely woman with blond hair, a clear complexion, and—so far, at least—all her front teeth. With a ready smile and a kind word for nearly everyone, she was unfailingly cheerful and optimistic. Her mere presence made the workplace less unpleasant.

Nor had Molly's attractiveness escaped the notice of the overlooker on the third floor, a brute of a man named Logan. Early on, Theo had thought the man far too free with his whip on women and children. Logan seemed to be more wary of using it on men. He was also prone to covertly touching the women indiscreetly. Theo had seen him caress one woman's breast and pat another's behind.

Theo was sure Molly tried to avoid the man as much as

possible, but Logan began to hover near her. The closer he got, the more nervous she appeared. After several days, Theo noticed less cheerful ebullience and more worry on her part. He overheard Tobias ask if she were feeling well.

At one end of the large, barn-like rooms housing the spinning machines on each floor, there were small offices for the overlookers. A large window allowed each overlooker a view of the sea of machines and workers in his charge. A curtain could be drawn across the window for privacy. The curtain on the third floor was drawn for about an hour most afternoons.

"He's got ta have his nap, don't ye know?" a woman said softly.

"At least he ain't out here with that blasted whip then," another said just as quietly.

"Amen to that!" yet another said. "I really hate it when he uses it on the children."

One morning several days after the meeting of the Corresponding Society, Logan seemed especially agitated. He had been even freer with his whip than usual. Then he stopped at Molly Tettle's machine.

"Come into my office," he ordered.

"But . . . but . . . my machine," she stammered.

"It'll keep," he said.

She followed the overlooker, but Theo could see that she did so with an air of dread and resignation. Logan closed the door and drew the curtains.

"Looks like Logan'll be busy a few minutes," some man said with a leer.

"She's been askin' for it," a woman said. "Flirtin' all the time with all the men."

"Aw, yer jus' jealous," another woman said. "Ol' Logan lost interest in *you* soon enough."

But Theo noticed that most of the women wore solemn, rather pinched expressions, and he sensed a feeling of pent-up, helpless anger about them.

Mother of God! he thought. *Surely this cannot be happening.*

But it was.

He had to do something.

But what?

Hesitating only a moment, he deliberately wrenched at one of the spindles on his machine, which then ground to a screeching halt. He went to the office door and lifted his hand to knock. He heard Molly's voice.

"Please, Mr. Logan. No. I can't do this."

"You can—if you wants ta keep yer job—*and* if'n ye want yer man ta keep his." Theo's stomach turned and his temper flared at the note of smug triumph in the man's voice.

"*Please* don't make me do it," Molly sobbed.

Theo pounded on the door.

"What—?" After a moment, Logan jerked open the door. "What the hell do *you* want? Don't you know that drawn curtain means 'private'?"

"Yes, sir." Theo forced himself to sound humble. "Somethin's wrong with my machine an' I can't fix it."

"Incompetent fool," Logan muttered, but Theo knew Logan feared for his own job if production were seriously impaired. "If there's any damage," Logan threatened, "it'll come out of your wages! Come on, then." He glanced at Molly, who was repositioning her bodice. "You get on back ta work."

Molly sidled past the two men, but she flashed Theo a grateful look.

Out on the floor the other workers continued silently at their own machines. Some cast admiring looks at Theo; some nodded their heads in approval; and a few shook their heads as though in wonder at his foolishness.

"My God!" Logan said, inspecting Theo's machine. "There's some serious damage here. What the hell happened?"

"I don't know, sir," Theo lied. "I jus' heard a poppin' sound and then lots of screechin' an' it jus' quit."

"Looks deliberate to me," Logan accused. "An' like I said, it'll come out of *your* wages." When Theo did not reply, Logan went on. "Well, goin' to take a while to repair this. Take over Baxter's machine. 'Bout time he was replaced anyway—that ol' coot can't keep up."

Baxter was a frail old man whose fear of losing his job was well known.

"But I need this job," Baxter whimpered. "Me an' my woman . . ."

"Can go to the workhouse, for all I care," Logan said, never turning his attention from the machine to the man.

Baxter gave Theo a look of utter despair. Theo knew his own eyes must mirror that despair as he glanced from Baxter to Molly Tettle and back. He had not counted on his rescue of Molly ending in consigning this old man and his wife to a life of dependence and near starvation.

Lord! Had he not learned by now that every action, every decision might have unforeseen consequences?

Well, he could do nothing for those who haunted his dreams, but here was a situation about which he *could* do something. The question was—how? How could he do so without revealing himself? He was a stranger in this area. He had no idea whom he could and could not trust. This much, however, was an absolute certainty—Mr. Baxter would not suffer for some action of a man named "Leo Reston."

That evening he wrote a note to the Glosson steward, Taggert, and enclosed it in another to the butler, Knowlton. Knowlton's note instructed him to give the enclosed note to Taggert without telling the steward where it had come from. Both notes were then encased in yet another sheet of paper, which carried only the butler's name. Both the inner notes carried the seal of the Earl of Glosson.

The earl had given his son his own signet ring as an emergency precaution as Theo set out on his journey. "It might come in handy," the earl had said. Then he had added, "Knowlton, the butler, is totally reliable. He was a young footman when I was a child. His wife is the housekeeper and most of the rest of the staff were new when I last visited Glosson Hall."

Having written the notes, Theo was faced with the problem of how to deliver them. He could not just walk up to the front door—or even the back one—of the Hall. The solution presented itself later that same evening in the form of a young footman from Glosson Hall who appeared at the Silver Shield in his Glosson livery. Theo drew the young man aside.

"Be ye workin' at the Hall?"

"That I am. Name's James." The young man offered his hand, which Theo took.

"Leo Reston. An' ye know a man named Knowlton, do ye, James?"

"Yes. He's the butler."

"Seems this Knowlton was some family connection to me da," Theo said. "He—me da, that is—asked me to deliver a letter. An' I wonder if you might save me the trip to the Hall?"

He drew the missive from an inner pocket in his coat, hoping no one else in the tavern saw him do so. Theo smiled inwardly at the demotion in status for his father—or promotion for the man Knowlton—but it was the least Glosson could put up with for involving his son in this situation in the first place.

The young footman eyed Theo with more interest now. "Why, of course. Be glad to. Might earn me a few points with the old man."

Theo gave him a sympathetic smile. "Fella can always use an edge, eh?"

James put the papers inside his own coat. "You got the right of it."

"I think it's important," Theo said, pointing to the man's chest and hoping to ensure actual delivery, "so maybe it'll earn you even more points." He then offered to buy the footman a drink as payment, which the young man readily accepted.

James was an open, friendly sort who responded readily to the questions of his newfound friend. Theo learned that James was a local boy whose father was a cottage weaver for the Glosson concerns. James's older brother would be taking over for their father eventually.

"There wasn't a place for me with the weaving, but my da, he made sure I had some learning. Sent me to Sunday school, then to Miss Whitmore's school, he did. She helped me get the job at the Hall."

"Did she now?" Theo asked, to keep the conversation flowing.

"She did. She's helped others to jobs, too. Nice lady." James laughed self-consciously. "Daresay all the boys in the school was in love with her at one time or another."

"Friendly like, were she?"

"Friendly enough. But she can be real demanding, too. Makes you learn more than you think possible."

Theo stored away these bits of information about the intriguing Miss Whitmore and shifted the conversation. "Is it true there's none of the family in residence at the Hall?"

"Only old Miss Stimson. She were sister to the former countess. The family has always took care of her. She keeps pretty much to herself—rarely leaves the grounds." Theo remembered meeting this great-aunt a time or two and was glad to hear there was little danger of her accidentally identifying him in the village. "We had the earl's heir here for a bit a year or so ago, but he died in a carriage accident."

"Is that so?" Theo urged.

"Real nice he were, too. At least to the staff at the Hall. I heard he ruffled some feathers elsewhere."

"Oh?"

"Some sort of trouble at the mill, but then it was all hushed up when he died."

"Carriage accident, eh?" Theo said. "Some of the nobs ain't such good drivers after all, are they?"

"Oh, Lord Amesbury were a good whip. Reg'lar out-and-outer. I don't know what happened, though one of the grooms told me there was something wrong with an axle. Amesbury liked to drive real fast, he did."

"I see." Theo hoped James would say more about Francis, but the young man finished his drink and took his leave.

Two days later, Molly and Tobias caught up with Theo as they all trudged to work.

"Did you hear about Mr. Baxter?" Molly asked.

"No," Theo replied honestly.

"He's not going on the dole after all."

"Is that so?" Theo pretended surprise.

"Seems that steward from Glosson hired him as an assistant gardener at the Hall."

"You don't say."

"He gets the same pay as he did here, too!" Molly seemed unselfishly pleased for Baxter. Then she turned thoughtful. "Strange how things turn out, ain't it? I never heard much good about that Mr. Taggert before."

Theo wondered what she had heard that was bad, but he dared not seem overly inquisitive.

A few days later it no longer mattered.

Theo had gone to The Silver Shield one evening, largely at the invitations of Henshaw and Hessler.

"Some new chaps hired on over at the Glosson Mill," Henshaw said. "Farley says he knew one of 'em in the army and he's an all right sort of fellow. They'll be at the Shield tonight."

Theo tried to beg off but when Tim Hessler joined in Henshaw's urging, Theo gave in. After all, he was here to mingle with the workers, was he not? Lord knew he had learned a great deal more at the Shield than he had at Mayfield's mill!

Theo and his friends were seated at a table and well into their first pints when Farley and the newcomers entered. Henshaw waved them over. Later, Theo remembered thinking how lucky these men had been in their ready welcome—so unlike the tentativeness bordering on suspicion that Theo had encountered at first.

One of the new men, slightly behind the chunky Farley, was halfway across the room when he stopped dead in his tracks.

"Major! Major Ruskin!" A pleased smile split the man's face as he fairly jumped to offer his hand to Theo. "God! I never thought to see *you* again, sir. I heard you'd got hit bad at Quatre Bras." He used the soldiers' term for the worst of the Waterloo battles. "I am *that* glad to see you, sir."

Henshaw, Hessler, Farley, and half the men in the room stared in wonder—then suspicion—at Theo, who sat in stunned silence for a moment.

"Leo?" Tim Hessler said in a wondering tone.

Theo finally stood and clasped the hand of the former sergeant who had repeatedly saved the life and reputation of a very green, newly commissioned lieutenant in the Peninsula. "Sergeant Yardley. Good to see you made it home."

Shock and animosity on the faces around him apparently registered on Yardley's consciousness. "What—? Is something wrong?"

"I don't know about 'wrong,' but they's somethin' mighty curious goin' on here," Henshaw said. "Care to explain, Reston? Or is it Ruskin?" It was more a threat than a question and carried a hint of betrayed friendship.

"Leo?" Tim questioned again.

Theo looked at the faces around him. These were men he had worked with, lived with closer than he had lived with anyone since the Peninsula, men who had shared their dreams and confidences. Their expressions were closed, their eyes hard. He knew that in a less public place, he would be in serious danger—and that he was none too safe here and now. After all, some of those secrets involved matters that were hanging offenses. Fear and potential danger to themselves could inspire them to turn on him in an instant.

Theo slowly sat back down and gestured for the others to be seated as well. He motioned to the barmaid to bring pints all around.

"God! Major, I didn't intend— I mean—well . . ." Yardley's voice trailed off in confusion but he regarded Theo with warmth while the others were rapidly shutting him out with suspicion.

"We're waitin', Reston. Ruskin. Whatever," Henshaw prodded, his tone almost menacing.

"Ruskin. That's Glosson's family name, ain't it?" someone asked.

"Yeh . . ." This voice held even more suspicion.

"Bloody gentry. Pretendin' to be somethin' they ain't. Playin' stupid games!" Theo recognized this voice coming from another table. It belonged to Ian Cochran, who shared quarters with Theo and the others.

The barmaid brought the pints and quietly set them down without her usual joking and flirtatious smiles. She soberly pocketed Theo's money.

"It is, indeed, Ruskin," Theo said quietly, no longer feigning the country accent.

"You been sneakin' around here all this time . . ." Henshaw angrily accused, but his tone held hurt, too.

"Why?" Tim asked. "We trusted you."

"And I hope you will continue to do so," Theo said. "I promise you—no malice was intended. I merely wanted to find out what *really* goes on with working people. I did not want people telling me what they thought I wanted to hear. Nor did I want to hear a lot of prejudiced complaining. I wanted a true picture."

"So you lied to get to the truth? Seems mighty strange to me," Henshaw said.

"Yeh," Farley agreed.

"Why?" Tim asked again with nothing more than curiosity in his tone. "Why would gentry do such?"

Theo was quiet for a moment. Finally, he said, "How else to know—truly know? Henshaw, would you have invited Viscount Amesbury to attend the meeting of the Corresponding Society with you? Would you?"

"Hell, no!"

"Just so," Theo said. "But I learned much at that meeting—and meeting with you here—just working with all of you."

"Spyin' on us, you mean," Farley said. "So's you can report us to the magistrate like them poor fellas in Pentrich."

"I promise you that *I* have reported nothing to the magistrate," Theo assured them.

"But—but he's *your* man," Henshaw said.

"What do you mean, 'my man'?"

"He acts on behalf of the Earl of Glosson," Henshaw explained.

Yardley came to Theo's defense. "The major ain't the earl."

"Same thing. He's the heir now," Farley said.

Theo sensed their belligerence, and even understood it. He tried to think what he could salvage from this debacle. He had already decided to be as forthright as he could.

"Looks to me like we got us a guv'ment spy in our midst," a sneering voice called from the next table. Again, Theo recognized young Cochran's voice.

"Not exactly," Theo said quietly to the men at his own table, but he spoke distinctly so his voice would carry. "However, there *are* members of Parliament, including my father, who are keenly interested in the lives of working people—and who really care about making things better."

"That's what they *say*." It was Cochran again. "But remember—actions are stronger than words. Theirs or ours," he added ominously.

"Yeh. Yeh."

Theo looked into the faces around him, where he discerned only suspicion and anger.

"I am sorry," he said. "I am sorry for having deceived you. But I am even more sorry that you cannot see your way to trusting me."

With that, he rose to take his leave. As he did so, he laid a hand on the shoulder of the former sergeant.

"Don't worry, Yardley. It was bound to come out. I would like to have had more time as 'Leo Reston' . . . but so be it . . ."

As he walked stiffly to the door, he felt every eye in the room drilling into his back. As soon as the door closed, he heard the muffled voices—angry and threatening. He wondered if any would follow or try to ambush him. His only weapon was the knife in his boot. Several of those men in The Shield were ex-soldiers like himself. He would not stand a chance if they came at him en masse. His back tensed for a blow all the way to the boardinghouse.

* * *

More devastated than he had let on by what had happened, Theo gathered up his meager belongings. It was late when he made his way to Glosson Hall. He braced himself for another confrontation. His only communication with the Hall had been that note to the butler, and even then he had not indicated he was even in the area. He had been a child of perhaps ten years the last time he had stayed here. He had seen his grandparents on rare occasions, but almost always in London.

A footman responded to his knock.

"Yes?" The servant barred the door and eyed askance the workingman's garb of the man before him.

"I should like to speak with Mr. Knowlton, if you please," Theo said. *And even if you don't please*, he thought sourly.

"Sorry. Knowlton has already retired," the footman said and would have closed the door had Theo not quickly placed his foot in the way.

"Then rouse him—now!" The evening's events had taken their toll on Theo's patience.

Something in Theo's tone must have given the young man pause, but his voice was haughty as he asked, "Whom shall I say is calling?"

"Viscount Amesbury." Theo's tone was equally haughty.

"Viscount—? One moment, please." He opened the door for Theo to step into the foyer and then scurried away.

Soon he reappeared with an aged retainer who had wrapped a woolen robe about a frail body—and still managed to look dignified.

"Sir?" the aged man asked, apparently unwilling to take chances on the identity of this visitor.

"I am Viscount Amesbury. I want a bath and a comfortable bed. Now—if you please."

The old retainer looked at Theo for a long moment. "Yes, my lord. You do have the *look* of young Master Theo—but I hope you will not take it amiss if I require that you produce some means of identification?"

Theo grinned. He was going to like Knowlton. "Will this convince you?" He produced his father's signet ring.

The man considered it carefully. "Yes, indeed. It will do very well. Welcome home, my lord."

Theo breathed a sigh of relief.

Seven

The gossip mill in Crofton worked just as regularly— and just as productively—as the spinning and weaving mills. At least, this was usually the case. However, two days after the incident in the Silver Shield, Hannah had not yet heard the gossip. She and Jane had spent those days in Manchester consulting with certain educators who were said to be obtaining excellent results. The two teachers from Crofton Parish School had returned home exhausted the second evening, but also full of enthusiasm about trying new ideas.

First, though, Hannah had promised Henry Franklin she would join him and two other men—a cottage weaver named Cranston and a mill worker named Melton, both of whom were Glosson employees—as they met with the Glosson steward, Mr. Taggert. One of the things they were to discuss was the attendance of mill children at the school. Hannah, running late, had sent a hasty note to Franklin that she would meet him at Taggert's office. She arrived just as the three men were being ushered into the inner office.

"There's something you should know—" Franklin started, but he was interrupted by a greeting from the Glosson steward.

Mr. Taggert viewed the latecomer with an insincere smile. "Ah, Miss Whitmore. Come to pitch your school idea again, have you?"

"Among other things," she replied with an equally insincere smile. Well, at least they were starting off politely.

Taggert greeted the two weavers brusquely and the better educated Franklin with more civility. He told his secretary to bring two extra chairs and then sent him off on an errand. Seats were arranged around Mr. Taggert's huge, ornate desk. Hannah was seated with her back to the door, directly across from Mr. Taggert. Franklin sat to one side, the two Glosson workers on the other side at an angle.

"Now, what is this all about?" Taggert asked, apparently attempting to sound genial.

Cranston, the cottage weaver, spoke up first. "We been gettin' inferior wool. There ain't no way a weaver can make quality goods with it."

"You get what's available," Taggert said.

"Stuff in the mill seems better," Cranston replied hesitantly.

"Then maybe you should come and work in the mill," Taggert said and made a note on a piece of paper.

Hannah suspected the note would indicate even more inferior goods to a weaver named Cranston.

"Mr. Taggert," she said, "is this perhaps a way of pressuring the cottage weavers to give up their independence and become mill workers?" She knew the cottagers prided themselves on the quality of their handwoven work over that mass-produced in the mill.

"Now why would you suggest something like that?" Taggert sounded offended.

"Because it has been done repeatedly elsewhere," Hannah said.

Taggert gave her another of his vacuous smiles. "Perhaps, Miss Whitmore, this meeting would progress more efficiently if you confined your comments to your school business." Before the fuming Hannah could reply, he turned to the other worker. "What is it you are complaining about, Melton?"

Hannah could see the challenging tone of the question disconcerted Melton.

"W-workers' hours," Melton said.

"What about them?" Taggert maintained that same challenging manner.

"Th-they's too long."

"Too long?" Taggert scoffed. "The workday is twelve

hours. That is standard everywhere. In this day and age, I doubt you will be able to find a job with less hours—though you are welcome to try."

Franklin spoke up now. "I think Mr. Melton's point is not necessarily a twelve-hour day, but that the day often exceeds that and, in fact, many work fourteen and fifteen hours on a shift."

Melton nodded. "That's it. An' with nothing extra in wages."

"Well, production demands have to be met, after all." The steward spoke as he might to children. "If the workers cannot maintain production on twelve hours, they must simply put in a little extra time."

"But we been producing more an' more," Melton said.

"Not according to my books." Taggert slapped his hand down on a stack of ledgers on his desk. "But as I say, you are welcome to try elsewhere."

The steward made another note and Hannah thought Melton would find himself working even longer hours.

Again, Franklin spoke up. "Mr. Taggert, this has been an issue for some time. A number of mill workers have kept records of hours worked—*and* what was produced. I wonder if you would be willing to compare your records with theirs?"

Taggert's face turned red. "What—? Absolutely not! Who's been keeping records? False ones, I'm sure." He slapped his hand on his ledgers again. "These are the only records that matter!"

Hannah saw defeat written on the faces of the men and it both saddened and infuriated her. She thought to change the tenor of the discussion by changing the subject.

"Mr. Taggert, I wonder if you have communicated with the Earl of Glosson about allowing the mill children a few hours of schooling each week?"

"I have. It's as I told you before—mill children have no need of your school, Miss Whitmore."

"The children have no need of education and they and their parents can stand at those infernal machines for hours while an absentee owner takes little or no interest in the plight of these families." Hannah's voice had risen slightly in bitter vehemence. "Meanwhile, elevated members of the *ton* blithely go about their own meaningless lives doing little of value for the lives of people for whom they are responsible. I tell you, it is deplorable. Simply deplorable. They and their families are but parasites feeding off the labor of others!"

Her tirade finished, Hannah finally noticed a smug grin on Mr. Taggert's face—not at all the reaction she might have expected. Cranston and Melton wore shocked expressions and were frantically gesturing to her.

Franklin touched her arm. "Enough, Hannah."

She turned to him. "What? You agree with me, Henry. You know you do."

Before Henry could respond, there was the sound of someone applauding behind her. "Bravo! Miss Whitmore."

She whirled on her chair to see the very elegant Viscount Amesbury leaning casually against the door frame.

"That was quite a performance, Miss Whitmore." There was neither admiration nor amusement in his eyes. "You must repeat it for my father one day." His gaze swept beyond her, dismissing her. "Taggert, I trust I am not too early for our meeting?"

"Not at all, my lord. We have finished here." Taggert rose to usher Hannah and her companions from the room.

She had never felt so humiliated in her life! Would she *never* learn to hold her tongue? There was an awkward silence as she and the others prepared to leave. Then she stood before the viscount and held his gaze with her own. It flashed through her mind that she had been just as spellbound by him in that London ballroom. But there was something else, too. . . .

"My lord," she said, "I apologize."

"For the sentiment—or my having heard it?" he asked.

So. He was not going to do the gentlemanly thing and let it pass. "To some degree, both," she replied. "I will not deny my view that many people suffer for the luxuries a few enjoy. However, I would you had not heard me carrying on so. I would have chosen to be less . . . less adversarial had I known . . ."

He cocked his head to one side, still holding her gaze with an expression she could not read.

"I see." As he stepped farther into the room, she barely noticed a slight limp. "You shape your views for whatever audience you happen to have. Is that not rather hypocritical?"

She felt her face flush with anger. "You . . . you are deliberately twisting my words, my—" She clamped her mouth shut abruptly, for suddenly, she saw him—really saw him! The limp. That square jaw. This was the man on the pavement as she accosted Mayfield, the man at the Corresponding Society meeting!

Viscount Amesbury. Clean. Stylish haircut. Stylish clothing. No undergrowth of beard, not a speck of dust or grease about him, and not a syllable of country accent. Every inch a viscount, but still the very same man! What was the name he had given? Leo. That was it. Leo Reston. Just what kind of game was he playing? What kind of trouble would he make for the likes of Cranston and Melton?

She had to get away from here. Get Henry and Cranston and Melton away. She had to tell them—warn them. She turned to Franklin. "I . . . I think we should go now."

"Yes," he agreed.

"One moment, Franklin," the viscount said. "I should like to call upon you tomorrow afternoon, if I may?" That it sounded more a polite request than an imperious order surprised Hannah.

"Of course, my lord." Franklin handed the viscount his calling card. "Here is my direction."

As they awaited their carriages, Hannah asked of Henry, "Did you know the viscount and that man Leo Reston are one and the same?"

"Yes."

"And you did not tell *me*?"

"I started to do so, but Taggert interrupted. I thought you might not have heard."

"I have rarely been so profoundly embarrassed."

"How could you know he would arrive just then?" Henry's tone was all sympathy.

"If I had, I certainly would have curbed my babbling tongue."

"We tried to warn ye, miss," Cranston said.

"Yes, I saw that—too late. I was so caught up in myself, I did not see it before." She twisted her reticule in her hands. "I just hope his ever-so-noble lordship and that toady, Taggert, do not hold my outburst against *you*."

"The viscount does not strike me as being that kind of man," Henry Franklin said.

"Hah!" Hannah snapped. "He is the type to go sneaking around pretending to be something he is not!"

"Hmm," Henry said. "I wonder why he wants to visit me?"

Hannah gave what she hoped was a ladylike snort. "Perhaps he is already involved in a particularly nasty bit of litigation and needs a local solicitor."

"I doubt a man with access to the finest legal minds in the country needs *my* expertise," the lawyer said.

"*Yours* is a very fine legal mind!" she insisted. "But—mark my words—there is something very peculiar going on with the viscount."

"Don't be so hard on the man," Henry said, handing her into the gig she had driven to the meeting. He and the two weavers turned toward his vehicle standing in front of hers.

"And don't *you* be so trusting of him," she called out to their backs.

Henry waved a hand in response.

Theo had not intended to eavesdrop on Taggert's meeting, but he had arrived early, the secretary was nowhere to be seen, and the door *was* ajar.

"How much of that did you hear, my lord?" Taggert asked.

Wondering at a note of apprehension he perceived in the steward's tone, Theo chose to be guarded in his reply. "Enough to know Miss Whitmore has a rather low opinion of ranking members of society."

"Meddlesome woman. She's one of those bluestocking do-gooders," the steward said.

"She seems to be well respected by working people," Theo replied.

"Oh, yes. She has *them* fairly eating out of her hand. See her as their champion, they do."

"Well, I suppose they need *someone* to take up the banner for their cause," Theo said.

Privately he thought her cause might be better served if she controlled what appeared to be an unbridled tendency to leap to conclusions. Nonetheless, her comments had stung—all the more because there was a grain of truth to them. He was annoyed, but he shoved his reaction to her to the back of his mind—expecially his reaction to her person. This was no time to be disracted by a woman's flashing eyes or the way emotion colored her cheeks.

The steward clearly did not agree with Theo, but he just as clearly did not wish to pursue a disagreement with his employer. "Maybe . . ." he said slowly, "but Miss Whitmore is too enthusiastic by half. The woman's a troublemaker!"

"In what way?"

"Always carrying on about that infernal school of hers."

"I gather she has approached you before." Theo deliberately kept his tone neutral.

"Several times." Taggert managed to sound much put-upon. "I've told her there's no reason to stir up trouble by sending mill brats to any damned school—just give 'em ideas above their station."

"And my father and grandfather agreed with that view?"

Taggert's tone became expansive, ingratiating. "Well, actually, I saw no reason to trouble them with every little issue that came up." The steward went to his desk, opened a drawer, and removed a large ring of keys. "You wanted to tour the mill, my lord?"

"Yes. And see the accounts—all of them, not just the mill's. Perhaps you will instruct your secretary to have the books ready for me when we return."

"But of course, my lord." Taggert was positively obsequious in his manner. He spoke privately with the secretary for a few moments, then accompanied Theo to the mill.

The mill seemed to run efficiently enough, but Theo did not like what he saw in the faces of the workers. Their expressions ranged from sullen resignation to numb vacantness. They were people who obviously saw little to enjoy in life.

He took his time in this, his first inspection of the mill. Accompanied by a groom the previous day, he had ridden out to visit the tenant farmers and cottage weavers. It had been an exhausting day, but he had managed to visit over thirty families—and had drunk more cider in one day than in all his life before! As he had done with the farmers and cottage weavers, he asked penetrating questions of the workers in the mill.

He found the actual working conditions not unlike those he had experienced in Mayfield's spinning mill. There was a stale smell of wool. The interior of the vast weaving rooms was dim and lint filled the hot, damp, still air. Silence reigned at the machines. Theo surmised that this atmosphere was not unlike that endured by other workers all over England, though there might be slight variations depending on the product being extracted or manufactured. That it might be common in no way inured him to its unpleasantness.

The workers did not welcome him with open arms. They did regard him with intense curiosity, for, after all, this man wielded great power over their lives. Theo knew that among the things uppermost in their minds were the tales of his having posed as a worker like themselves. He also knew that the consensus was not in yet on whether his lordship was a dilettante amusing himself by playing a role—or something more sinister, one who sought reasons and means to suppress them even more. Some few—like the former sergeant, Yardley—

might think him an all right fellow, but Theo knew very well the majority were adopting a wait-and-see attitude.

There was one citizen of the district who was *not* adopting a wait-and-see approach. The morning after the debacle at the Silver Shield, Baron Mayfield called at Glosson Hall. Mayfield arrived early; Theo had only just arisen. On his arrival at his ancestral home, Theo had been pleasantly surprised to find that his father had sent Burton to the Hall—along with Theo's belongings.

"Show the baron into the drawing room and provide him coffee as he waits," Theo told a footman as Burton struggled to get the neckcloth tied just so. "Enough, Burt. This one will have to do."

"Yes, my lord."

Theo entered the drawing room to find his guest pacing the floor, his face set in a stern expression.

"Good morning." Theo extended his hand and for just a moment he thought Mayfield might refuse the gesture, but the baron clasped Theo's hand very briefly.

"Morning."

"Will you have a seat?" Theo asked politely.

"No, thank you." The baron's manner was brusque. "My business is brief. I want to know precisely what you were about in that little charade you were playing in my mill. Did you think to steal some secrets of production? Find some way to undermine my business?"

"Whyever would you think that? You deal in cotton. My people produce woolens."

"Spinning is spinning and weaving is weaving. *Why* were you spying on me?"

Theo went to the tray a servant had brought in earlier. "Coffee?" he asked.

"No, thank you. I *will* thank you to answer my question."

"Please. Be seated and I shall try to explain."

With reluctance written all over him, the baron finally took the proffered chair. "Well?"

Theo weighed how much of the truth he should reveal.

"I was attempting to measure the temper of the working classes."

"Why?"

"Because someone I respect asked me to do so and because it seemed a reasonable thing to do."

"Why did you come into *my* mill? Why not your own?"

Theo answered the belligerent question calmly. "I am interested in the latest technology and I think your mill is far more up-to-date than ours. There's been no new machinery here since my grandfather installed power looms in the early nineties."

"So you *were* spying on me!"

"No. Just trying to learn."

"You could have done that in your own mill."

"Not as a common worker. The Glosson Mill was not hiring when I arrived in Crofton and I did want to be an ordinary worker."

Mayfield gave a contemptuous snort. "That simply does not make sense. A peer pretending to be a peasant! And I resent the underhanded way this was done. You might have come to me as an honorable man and told me what was going on."

"I *might* have," Theo agreed, "but would you have seen a common laborer named Leo Reston?"

Mayfield waved his hand in a gesture of dismissal. "That is beside the point."

"No. That *is* the point. I was to try to find out how common laborers think and feel. Unfortunately, the mission was aborted before it fairly began."

"Mission!" The baron sneered. "Seems to me you are behaving exactly like one of those radicals—the likes of Cobbett and Hunt. It would not surprise me to find you in league with them—them and that interfering teacher, the Whitmore woman."

Theo had had enough. He rose. "I could hardly be in league with Mr. Cobbett. The man has fled to America."

Mayfield took the hint and rose himself. "He still publishes his trash here, though."

"That may be. But I give you my word as a gentleman that I am not 'in league' with anyone."

"Well . . ." Some of the bluster was gone from Baron Mayfield. "Nevertheless, in future, I require that you stay away from my mill and my workers."

"I can only promise that I will not trespass on your property." Theo bowed slightly and saw his less-than-welcome guest to the door.

Theo found the premises of the lawyer Franklin without difficulty. On the first floor of a building that housed a mercantile store on the ground floor, the lawyer had two rooms as an office on the front, with living quarters in the back. Theo entered the first room of the office and announced himself to a young man with his nose in a law book.

"I am Amesbury. Here to see Mr. Franklin."

The young man jerked to attention. "Yes, my lord. He is expecting you." He ushered Theo into the inner office. "Lord Amesbury, sir."

"Thank you, Larkin." Franklin came from behind his desk to offer Theo his hand, then gestured to a set of matching chairs with a table between them. "What can I do for you, my lord? I assume this is not merely a social call."

"No, it is not. I confess to having eavesdropped on much of your conference yesterday with Mr. Taggert."

"And—?"

"I found the entire discussion . . . shall we say . . . interesting?"

"I cannot believe the workers' complaints of long hours and inferior materials came as much of a surprise—not considering how you have spent the last few weeks."

"I did not say 'surprising'—I said 'interesting.' Perhaps *puzzling* would be more accurate."

"I see . . ." The lawyer's tone indicated that he did not see at all. "Uh . . . may I ask just what it was that you found so intriguing, my lord?"

Theo gave the man a direct look. "For one thing, I find it unusual for you to be speaking on behalf of working people. They do not usually put their trust in a man like you."

"A man like me?"

"Educated. Apparently gentry. I am wondering what interest you have in becoming involved in such matters."

The lawyer raised a questioning brow. "This curiosity from a man who lately passed himself off as a working man? Tell me, my lord, do you find my involvement offensive?"

"No . . . though perhaps I should amend that to say I have not so far found it to be so."

"Very well." Franklin waited.

"You seem to have gained a position of trust among the employees in both Mayfield's works and ours."

"Yes, I believe I do hold such a position," Franklin said, quietly matter-of-fact. "But then, I grew up in Crofton, you see."

Theo decided to lay his cards on the table. "I, on the other hand, seem to be in a state of limbo with them."

"Neither fish nor flesh, eh?"

"Something like that."

"Is that so surprising—given your rather sudden change in status with them?"

"No, I suppose not," Theo said. "But I would have their trust."

"Men of Derbyshire do not give their trust easily," the lawyer warned. "It is earned over time, and I am sorely afraid that you are off to a bad start."

"That is, in part, why I am here. I think you can help me gain their trust. Or *re*gain it, in some instances."

Franklin shifted about in his chair. "Why? Why do you care whether people trust you? The law gives you the power to do as you will—short of murder and mayhem."

Again, Theo decided straightforward honesty would be the best approach. "True. But great power always entails equally great responsibility. In the few weeks I was a common laborer and in a few days of close inspection of Glosson properties, I would surmise those who have wielded power here in the past have much to answer for."

"That is a refreshing view, my lord. Would you care to elaborate?"

"I have not by any means completed my investigation, but it would appear the Hall and its concerns—including the people who are dependents—have suffered a great deal of neglect."

Franklin sat forward and clasped his hands between his knees. "As you probably know, your grandfather was quite ill for the last ten years of his life. I was away at school much of that time, but I was told he did not want his family to know just how sick he was. The last five years were particularly difficult for him because he had lost his eldest son."

"My Uncle Matthew. Grandfather doted on him."

"After that the old earl—who had always spent much of his time in town—rarely returned to Derbyshire. He just left things up to Taggert."

"Taggert pretty much had a free rein," Theo conceded.

"We thought when your father inherited . . ." The lawyer's voice trailed off.

Theo shifted in his chair. "My father is a scholar—and something of a politician. A caring one, mind you, but he prefers to avoid the business end of *anything*. That is why he turned matters over to my brother—and now to me."

"Your brother certainly meant well," Franklin said. "He asked all the right questions—and people took to him right off—but then there was that accident . . ."

A long pause ensued during which both men were silent. Theo unconsciously rubbed his once-injured leg. "You mentioned the existence of a set of records kept by workers at Glosson Mill."

"I did," Franklin admitted.

"I should like to see them—if they really exist."

"They exist."

"May I see them?" Theo wondered at the man's terseness.

"Why? Why do you wish to see them? I must tell you that

if your intent is to punish the men who kept them, they are unlikely to be available." Franklin seemed adamant on this point.

"I assure you that is *not* my intent."

Franklin merely waited for him to go on.

"What I *intend*—once I have a clear picture—is to effect some changes. Changes that I think will not come amiss to people dependent on the Earl of Glosson. However, I would rather not make changes until I have a complete picture."

Franklin shifted back in his chair again. "And you think—"

Theo interrupted. "I think you can save me a great deal of time and effort by allowing me to do what you yourself suggested—compare those records."

"I see . . ."

"So—I am asking you—will you or will you not supply me those records for study?"

The lawyer sat in deep thought for some moments. Finally, he said, "My lord, I would myself be inclined to take you at your word and turn over those documents to you now. The truth is, though, I do not have them. I will contact those who do and see if they will cooperate."

"Will you advise them to do so?"

Again, the lawyer was thoughtful. "Yes. I rather think I will."

"Thank you." Theo rose and offered his hand. "I will await word from you." He started to leave the room, then turned back. "Uh, Mr. Franklin? I would ask that you tell no one of this conversation unless you find it absolutely necessary to do so."

"Understood, my lord."

Eight

After the fiasco in Mr. Taggert's office, Hannah spent a great deal of time berating herself for her runaway tongue. She flinched inwardly as she recalled the enigmatic expression in Lord Amesbury's eyes. Her inclination—which propriety quickly quelled—had been to run to him and say, "Oh, but I didn't mean it." Only she had. The tone and manner had been far too strident, but the substance of her criticism was valid. She knew it was!

Still, she wondered if she had, in a matter of a few minutes and with a few ill-chosen words, undermined much of her own work of the last three years. When she voiced these thoughts to her fellow teacher as the two walked home after school one afternoon, Jane tried to comfort her.

"You must stop beating yourself so, Hannah. It was an honest mistake. Mr. Franklin told me about that meeting."

"Once Lord Amesbury tells his father what I said, there will be no hope of changing their minds about education for mill children."

"You cannot know that for sure," Jane said.

"Oh, Jane. You should have seen the look he gave me!"

"Lord Amesbury, you mean? Was he so very angry?"

"I . . . I am not certain *what* emotion he felt. He . . . he just looked at me in a most puzzling way and then ignored me." Hannah had been as much chagrined by his seeming to dismiss her as by his subsequent accusation of hypocrisy.

"Ignored *you*?" Jane's tone was disbelieving. "You are a hard woman to ignore, my friend."

"Well, he did, believe me."

Both were silent a moment. Then Jane said thoughtfully, "You know, I wonder if the earl—or his son—has ever really heard of our offer to teach mill children?"

"Mr. Taggert said he conveyed the message. And certainly the earl knows of our school—why, his wife mentioned it to me in London. And she has helped us with supplies."

"But do you know for a fact that the earl knows of our—your—proposal?"

"You think Mr. Taggert lied," Hannah stated rather than asked.

"I think it entirely *possible* that he did so," Jane said slowly. "Mr. Taggert seems to be a man who wouldn't scruple about the means to achieve his ends."

"I agree with you on that point," Hannah said. "I thought perhaps I was merely being too judgmental."

"Harry—Mr. Franklin—feels as I do," Jane said.

"*Harry*, eh?" Hannah teased. "Not even *Henry*, but *Harry*. Well done, my dear Jane."

Jane's blush reached to the roots of her golden blond hair. "I . . . uh . . . it was a slip of the tongue. Mr. Franklin and I are merely friends—just as you and he are."

"Oh, no. Not just as he and I are. He does not look at *me* the way he looks at *you*. Nor do I blush profusely and start stammering when he turns his attention to me—as someone I could name does."

Jane appeared abashed. "Surely I am neither that transparent nor that silly."

"Only to someone who knows you both as I do," Hannah gently assured her.

"You must not tease him about me, Hannah. Promise me you will not. He has no idea how I feel. I would be so embarrassed . . . Promise."

Hannah laughed. "I doubt Henry recognizes his own feelings—yet. Comes of the three of us having grown up together. Very well. I promise."

Jane heaved a small sigh of relief and returned to the

original subject. "So? What do you think we should do about persuading the earl that mill children need to be educated?"

"Rumor has it that the earl and countess will be arriving soon for an extended stay—perhaps I—we—can approach *her*."

"Good idea. She obviously approves of the school."

"In theory, at least," Hannah said with a chuckle. "However, the final word on mill children attending rests with her husband—and, perhaps, her son."

"Oh, dear."

"'Oh, dear' indeed. For I have just offended the son in a monumental way."

Jane murmured comforting words until they parted. Hannah schooled her mood to be more cheerful when she arrived at the vicarage. Her father had officiated at two funerals this week. One of the deceased had been a particular friend of the vicar. He certainly did not need his eldest daughter adding to the general gloom. She let herself in the front door and was surpised to hear laughter coming from the drawing room. Her sister's tinkling, ladylike merriment blended with her father's guffaw of genuine amusement.

"Oh, la, my lord. That is too funny for words," Katherine was saying as Hannah entered the room.

She was dumfounded to find Viscount Amesbury sitting in the family drawing room.

"Ah, here she is," her father said.

He and the viscount rose as Hannah joined them, nervous in the presence of this particular guest. She noted that here, in this setting, the viscount seemed even taller. He *was* taller than her father. He was also disturbingly attractive in soft doeskin breeches, a russet-colored waistcoat, and dark gray jacket. His shirt points were modest, barely reaching his jaw, and his neckcloth correct, but casual.

Mrs. Whitmore poured a glass of lemonade. "His lordship was just telling us of a caper in his schooldays at Eton."

"I see," Hannah replied.

He nodded respectfully in her direction. "Good afternoon, Miss Whitmore."

Hannah took the proffered glass and seated herself next to her mother on the settee.

"G-good afternoon, my lord." She glanced at him, but quickly lowered her gaze. She was embarrassed at having to confront him with no warning. Had he come to make her uncomfortable? Retribution for her outburst in Mr. Taggert's office? Her discomfort—her irritation—increased upon seeing that the viscount seemed perfectly at ease here.

An awkward pause ensued, which Hannah's mother sought to fill with a comment about the weather. Then, with much flashing of her lashes, Katherine asked their visitor a question about London sights to which he responded politely. There followed a few minutes of social chitchat, but Hannah took little part in the conversation, her mind in turmoil all the while.

Then he turned his attention directly to her. "I wonder if I might persuade you, Miss Whitmore, to take a turn in the garden for which I am told your mother is so justly famous?"

Hannah raised her brows in surprise and shot her father an inquiring glance. The vicar gave her a reassuring smile and a slight nod. She had told him about her caustic exchange with the viscount.

"As you wish, my lord." She tried to appear calm, dignified—just as though there were no insects flitting about in her innards.

Her apprehension grew, for Lord Amesbury said nothing as she led him out to the garden where they would be fully visible from the drawing room window. Finally, having looked around him appreciatively, he said, "Mrs. Knowlton was right. This is a spectacular garden."

Hannah stopped and faced him. "Yes. It is. But I somehow doubt you suggested this walk merely to admire Mama's shrubbery."

He gave her an assessing look, apparently weighing his response. "No. It was not."

"If you mean to take me to task over my imprudent remarks the other day, I might point out that I have already apologized." The challenging tone she had used earlier was still with her.

"My, my," he said mockingly. "You are a prickly little thing, aren't you?"

"Now I am prickly as well as hypocritical. Have you any additional negative observations to make of my person, sirrah?"

She saw a look of annoyance flash across his vivid blue eyes. The truth of his comment had raised her hackles. She *was* being "prickly"—and she knew her own defensiveness was at fault.

As he regarded her in silence, she lifted her chin and refused to hold his gaze.

"Miss Whitmore, we seem to have got off to a rather bad start. The truth of the matter is that I probably owe *you* an apology for the other day."

"Because . . . ?"

"I could have made my presence known earlier, but I chose not to."

She gasped. "You were spying even then—just as you have been for the several weeks you have been in Crofton?"

She noticed his jaw twitch in annoyance—or anger. His eyes took on a flat, stony quality, but his voice was calm. Cold, but calm. "I have *not*, madam, been 'spying.'"

"Well, what would you call it then, my lord?" She made her tone deliberately sweet.

"I came here as I did to gather information—"

"Is that not what spies do? You must know—from your 'gathering information'—that people in this area do not take to spies very well—especially after that so-called event in Pentrich." She referred to an uprising that had taken place in the town of Pentrich in June. A march of workers and unemployed that was intended to involve hundreds, perhaps thousands, as it swept from one town to another, had ended with arrests in Pentrich. Dozens of men had been arrested, charged with treason, and now awaited trial.

"I did not come here this afternoon to wrangle with you

about matters of which I have no direct knowledge—or responsibility."

"So? Why *did* you come?"

"To discuss your school."

For a moment she was nonplused. "M-my school? Wh-what about it?"

His eyes changed and a softening about his mouth revealed deep smile lines. He seemed amused at having caught her off guard. How was it that she was always so . . . well . . . sort of "off balance" around this infernal man?

"Suppose we sit over there?"

He pointed to a stone bench under a great elm tree. It was Hannah's favorite spot in the garden. She hoped he was not going to change that. She perched primly on one end of the bench, her hands folded in her lap, and waited for him to continue. As he seated himself, she was uncomfortably aware of his physical presence. She tried not to regard the way his breeches fit smoothly over strong, athletic thighs. Or her own heightened senses at his nearness.

He cleared his throat. "Among the things I overheard that day was your questioning Taggert regarding schooling for mill children."

"Mr. Taggert said mill children have no need of schooling." She could not prevent the tinge of bitterness in her voice.

"That *is* his view. He told me a little of your proposal or request, but I should like to hear from you what you have in mind."

"Are you telling me the earl has no knowledge of Crofton Parish Day School?"

"So far as I know, he does not not. He did not mention it to me—and he was quite thorough in preparing me for my journey here. However, I do know my mother has an interest in local infant schools."

"The Countess of Glosson has been very supportive." Hannah wanted to believe him. After all, what reason would he have to lie about such a matter? Yet Mr. Taggert had assured her . . . She considered this silently.

"Well?" He cut into her musings.

"Well, what?"

He rolled his eyes slightly. "Are you or are you not going to tell me about this school business?"

"You—you are quite certain you know nothing about it?"

"No. I mean, yes. I am quite certain. That is, madam, why I am here. To obtain the information straight from the horse's mouth, so to speak."

Hannah's posture stiffened momentarily, then she giggled. "What a marvelously gallant way of putting it."

He ran a hand through his hair and smiled ruefully. "Oh, Lord. You are right and I only meant . . . well, it's an army saying, you see. Our orders came from the Horse Guards, as you know. My apologies, Miss Whitmore."

Hannnah smiled. Somehow having caught the elegant viscount in a minor *faux pas* made her feel more at ease. "What would you like to know about the school?"

"Everything. Especially whatever it is I am supposed to know already."

So, she told him. With an occasional interruption as he asked a question, she explained the establishment of the school, her taking on an assistant in Jane Thomas, the struggle to find a suitable location when the numbers of students increased, and, finally, of her fervent desire to enroll children of mill workers and cottage weavers.

"Though, as a matter of fact," she finished, "we do have a few cottagers' children."

"But none from the mills?"

"Only one. A young girl named Patsy Tettle. Her parents work in the Mayfield Mill."

"I know them," Amesbury said. "Molly—Mrs. Tettle—worked at a machine near mine."

She groped for something to fill the ensuing silence. "Nice people."

"Yes," he agreed absently, then seemed lost in thought. Hannah wished he felt comfortable enough to share those thoughts with her.

"Lord Amesbury?"

He started at her prodding.

She hardly dared hope as she asked, "Will you consider the idea of education for mill children—or," here her voice became harder, "do you share the views held by Mr. Taggert and Lord Mayfield that education is wasted on the 'lower orders'?"

He turned the full scope of those deep blue eyes on her. She felt something shiver—not at all unpleasantly—deep within her.

"No," he said. "I do not share such a view."

"Then you will allow mill workers' children to come to school?"

"I did not say that."

She jumped up from the bench. "Oh. So you, too, think such children unworthy of benefits others may take for granted." Her tone was challenging, accusatory.

He rose and faced her squarely. "Do *not*, madam, presume to know what I think!" His eyes had gone all stony again, his voice cold. "I will consider your proposal and discuss it with my father and others who may be concerned. More assurance than that, I cannot give you now."

She felt her shoulders slump in defeat. "I think I can predict the outcome."

"Then you know far more than I," he replied. "But thank you for clarifying the issue for me. Now, if you will excuse me, I must be off."

She accompanied him back to the house, where he bade her parents and sister good-bye, retrieved his hat and gloves, and then he was gone.

When the door was firmly closed, her father asked gently, "How did your interview with him go?"

"I do not know," Hannah said, still frustrated at the way the conversation had ended. "That man is so . . . so—"

"Handsome," Katherine interposed dreamily, "and utterly charming."

"*Arrogant*, I was about to say," Hannah said sharply.

"How odd that you should find him so," her mother said. "We found his conversation quite amiable."

"Luckily—or unluckily—we cannot all always have the same opinions of things—or people," Hannah replied.

Theo left the vicarage vastly irritated at the clergyman's pretty eldest daughter. Just what on God's green earth did she expect of him? That he could just wave a magic wand and make things go her way? He had no idea if the workers at Glosson Mill even *wanted* their children to attend school. Would they willingly give up the pitifully small wages the children brought in? *Could* they do so? What would be the impact upon the mill's production—could the earldom afford such a magnanimous gesture? How would a change in Glosson concerns affect other workers in the area?

He admired Miss Whitmore's dedication and determination, though. Moreover, he had enjoyed watching the play of emotions on her face—and the way her eyes changed from blue to gray and back as she recounted the establishment of the school and her dreams for its future. He had also noted how a soft breeze loosened tendrils of her brown hair and how the late sun managed to pick out red highlights in it. He chafed at her assumption that he would object to her plan because of some misguided sense of superiority toward people of the so-called "lower orders." What did *she* know of his views—republican or otherwise?

He decided to work off some of his irritation by riding through the village before going home to the Hall. His boyhood memory had been of a thriving, but rather sleepy, country village. However, in the last twenty years, expansion of both Glosson and Mayfield Mills had brought in a huge influx of people. It was no longer really a village. More of a town, Theo thought, though not on the scale—yet—of a Manchester or Leeds. But those were actually *cities*, not mere towns. He hoped Crofton could maintain some of its country atmosphere.

As he trotted his horse through certain areas, however, his nose told him something would have to be done soon about a proper sewer system. He supposed it would be up to him—and, perhaps, Mayfield—to initiate a change. The practice of throwing refuse into the unpaved streets and letting erratic rains wash it down into the river was smelly, unsightly, and surely unhealthy. He was especially dismayed at seeing children playing in such an environment. He recalled his own childhood—romping on green lawns, climbing trees in an orchard, fishing in a clear stream—and tagging after the inimitable Francis.

What *had* happened here to Francis? Where should he start in finding out? Francis's groom was still employed in Glosson stables. He might know something. There was also the footman's comment about some fracas at the mill.

Meanwhile, Theo still had those infernal ledgers to peruse. He hated working with columns of numbers. In the army he had usually managed to assign such a task to a subordinate. He had not yet received word from Franklin regarding the "other" ledgers, but there was no reason to delay looking through those that Taggert had given him.

Theo had settled very quickly into life at Glosson Hall. He renewed his acquaintance with his great-aunt Stimson and found her a delightful dining companion. She was nearly eighty years old, but her wit was sharp and she was well read. He knew his parents would enjoy her company when they arrived.

Returning from his interview with Miss Whitmore, Theo had a light supper with his Aunt Stimson, during which he told her of the encounter. He did not, however, mention Miss Whitmore's intriguing eyes or the tantalizing trace of lilac that made him want to lean closer, if only to determine that it *was* lilac.

"The vicar's eldest daughter has done much good in the parish," the elderly lady said. "Far more than her mother, as a matter of fact. Or those sisters. The mother is rather shy, I think, and the middle girl was simply more concerned with herself than anything or anyone else. Of course, the youngest one is only just coming into her own."

"You approve of Miss Whitmore, then?"

"What is there not to approve? Except perhaps that she does not toe the line in what society generally expects of a lady of the gentry. However, *I* am the last person who should throw stones at that glass house!"

Theo chuckled. He lifted his wineglass in a salute to his dining companion. "Miss Whitmore does seem to be an original."

"I quite agree. I hope you have not crossed swords with her over this school of hers."

"Now why would you think that?" he asked, feigning a wounded tone.

"I may be something of a recluse, but that does not mean I am deaf and blind, dear boy. Besides, Hannah has been in the habit of visiting me and she has not been here since you took up residence."

"Hmm." Theo did not know how to respond to this. He did not relish the idea that the intrepid Miss Whitmore might be wary of him.

The meal over, Theo reluctantly retreated to the library and the ledgers.

He had written his father of the turn that events had taken in Derbyshire. He also assured his father that he intended to stay on at the Hall "to see this business through as much as possible." His parents' joint reply was to have him instruct the staff to ready the Hall for an extended house party. The earl and his countess planned to be in residence several weeks—perhaps through Christmas and until the opening of Parliament early in the new year.

Theo groaned inwardly. Much as he loved his parents, he knew exactly what motivated his mother in hosting a house party of some duration. Her first words on arrival—and the appearance of Lady Olivia as one of her traveling companions—left no doubt on that score.

"If Mohammed will not come to the mountain, the mountain will come to him," she said.

Later she informed her son that Miss Bridges and Miss Wentworth would arrive soon, along with as many as twenty other guests.

"Including," she said brightly, "your friends Mr. Moore, Mr. Jenkins, and Mr. Jeffries—and, of course, the wives of Mr. Jenkins and Mr. Jeffries."

"Of course," Theo murmured in defeat. He recognized that bit of information for what it was. Strategy. She was not only surrounding him with eminently eligible young ladies, but she also was putting these happily married young men—his own friends—directly in his path in hopes that they might inspire admiration or envy. The first item on her new battle plan was a grand ball to be held in late September to celebrate the harvest. She would, of course, invite a number of local families to attend as well.

After his mother and Lady Olivia had retired that first night, Theo and his father removed to the library, where they sat savoring brandy and cigars.

"I am sorry, Father. I wish I had had more time as a mill worker. I knew there was a possibility of my being discovered. I just did not think it would come quite so soon."

"Not something we could foresee or forestall," the earl said. "So—what *did* you learn? Whitehall is up in arms about that Pentrich affair, you know."

"I do know. And it amounts to a tempest in a teapot," Theo said. "The leader is supposedly a simple man named Brandeth. His talk was full of bread, rum, and 'a hundred guineas' for those who marched with him—not a word about suffrage or parliamentary reform."

The earl blew a perfect smoke ring, then sipped at his brandy. "A workers' revolt then, but hardly a revolution."

Theo gave a rueful chuckle. "Hardly. Seems Brandeth's idea of a 'provisional government' was one that handed out provisions!"

"Do you hold with the view that this fracas was largely the work of a government spy?"

"Yes, I do," Theo said. "The talk in the tavern here centered on that, anyway. Someone called 'Oliver the Spy,' who traveled around trying to stir things up. He did not find many takers until he got to Brandeth."

"That name was bandied about in Westminster, too. Too bad. Heads are bound to roll on this one." The earl sat in silent contemplation, then changed topics. "Were you able to find out anything about Francis's death?"

"Not much more than what you told me earlier. There was something about a dispute of some sort, but I've not been able to explore that yet. In general, though, Francis seems to have been well liked for the short time he was here."

"Francis was always well liked."

"Apparently not by everyone."

Nine

The vicar, accompanied by his wife and two of his daughters, paid a courtesy call upon the newly arrived earl and his countess. It meant rearranging her schedule of lessons, but Hannah welcomed the visit as an opportunity to enlist the countess's aid even further. She scarcely admitted to herself that she also looked forward to seeing Lord Amesbury again.

As they were ushered into the drawing room, Hannah was surprised at the number of people gathered there, despite having learned earlier of the arrival of yet more guests at Glosson Hall. Her gaze was immediately drawn to the viscount, who made a point of joining his parents to welcome the vicar's party. Hannah knew, however briefly, most of the London guests, but introductions were made to acquaint the rest of her family with Miss Bridges, Miss Wentworth, and Mr. Moore. There were also both of Miss Bridges's parents and Miss Wentworth's mother, as well as a Captain Phillips of the Royal Navy. A tall, blond man in his mid-thirties and tanned by years at sea, Captain Phillips seemed somewhat at a loss in this on-shore environment.

Miss Stimson made a point of sitting next to Hannah. "With the war over, Phillips is home on half-pay. He is Margaret's cousin." Hannah knew that *Margaret* was the countess's given name. "Comes in handy for filling out numbers at table, don't you know?"

"Now, Miss Stimson," Hannah admonished softly, "a man who has risen to captain must have more to his character than that."

"Oh, he is probably brave enough, but the man cannot speak of anything but ships and water routes."

Hannah laughed and set herself to observing others in the room. She was amused to see Katherine—who was engaged in conversation with Miss Bridges and Mr. Moore—trying to hide her eager wonder at being in such elegant company. Perhaps Miss Strempleton's training in proper decorum will have taken with *one* of the Whitmore girls, Hannah thought.

The elegant Lady Olivia and the rather flashy Miss Emily Wentworth seemed to be engaged in a subtle—ever-so-ladylike—struggle for the attentions of Viscount Amesbury. At one point, the viscount looked over to Hannah's part of the room. She saw a rueful little smile play about his lips as their gazes connected. Well, at least he was not unfriendly to the vicar's "prickly" daughter.

"My money's on Lady Olivia," Miss Stimson whispered. "More class. I doubt poor Theo could stand that giggle for long."

"Miss Stimson!" Hannah's admonishment was punctuated by a burst of giggles from Miss Wentworth at something the viscount had said. I doubt it was *that* amusing, Hannah thought sourly. Then it struck her that she was jealous. Jealous of his attentions to these other women? *Where* had that preposterous notion come from?

Soon—too soon for Hannah's purposes—it was time for the vicar's family to leave. As they extended their farewells, the countess pulled Hannah slightly aside.

"Miss Whitmore, I am sorry we did not have more time to talk. I should like to visit your school, if I may."

"Of course, my lady. Miss Thomas and I will be most pleased to welcome you."

"My son tells me I might find it quite interesting."

"I hope you will, my lady."

Now what did that mean? Hannah asked herself. Still, the school had obviously been a topic of conversation between the viscount and his mother. Surely that was a good sign, was it not?

* * *

With the steady arrival of an army of houseguests, Theo found less and less time to pursue the mystery surrounding his brother's death. Moreover, the trial in Pentrich of the would-be revolutionaries was having an impact throughout the working classes of northern England. People were reluctant to talk. Theo noted increased alienation between the classes. The subject came up one evening after the ladies had left the gentlemen to their port and cigars in the dining room.

"I have a feeling this Pentrich thing will not turn out well," the earl said.

"Serve them right if the whole lot were hanged," Mr. Bridges muttered.

"Doubtless some will be," the earl responded grimly.

"And others will be transported," Mr. Moore observed.

"Much as I should like to be back at sea," Captain Phillips said, "I would not welcome the duty of transporting prisoners to New South Wales."

"Just another cargo, I should think," Mr. Bridges said in a vastly superior manner.

"No, sir," argued the captain. "'Tis little better than a slave ship. Mind you, I never served on a slaver, but I docked next to one being unloaded in Charleston once. The stench was overwhelming."

"Blacks. What could you expect?" Bridges sneered, readily accepting the wine decanter as it made its rounds again.

"I daresay their color was irrelevant," Theo put in. He found Bridges's comments mean-spirited and distasteful. "Had you ever been on a ship bearing English troops to war, sir, you might have experienced much the same."

"Right," Moore echoed.

"Luckily, I shall never be forced into such a repugnant situation." Bridges managed to make his non-participation in the recent war a matter of superiority.

"Yes, luckily." Moore exchanged an ironic look with Theo.

The conversation drifted to sporting matters. The earl offered his guests opportunity for shooting, though he was told the pheasant were rather scarce this year. Plans for entertaining the gentlemen also included a "mill" to be held in a neighboring town between two well-known pugilists. Theo's attention drifted.

Theo knew Bridges and his wife had been invited only to lend their presence to their eminently marriageable daughter, but he found the man's attitude offensive. On a purely intellectual level, Theo wondered why so many people thought to elevate themselves by pushing others down. What was it in humans, as opposed to other species, that made distinctions in dress and speech, skin color, and other physical attributes cause for valuing or devaluing another?

On the other hand, perhaps it was nature's way after all. He remembered seeing a flock of chickens peck the frailest, weakest one to death. It was not uncommon for animals in the wild to turn on the ones least able to fend for themselves. But thinking, reasoning man was supposed to be different. Did his religions not proclaim him so? Perhaps it boiled down to mere jealousy born of feelings of inferiority. Somehow that explanation seemed too simple, too easy. Surely the problems that gave rise to events like the Pentrich revolt were more complicated than that.

His father's voice jolted him out of his abstract speculations. "Gentlemen, 'tis time to rejoin the ladies."

Entertaining the Hall's guests took up much of Theo's time. Sporting events for the gentlemen were balanced by shopping and sightseeing expeditions for the ladies, who, of course, required the escort of gentlemen for such outings. Theo did not truly mind these demands on his time, for was this not precisely the life he had aspired to only a few months ago?

At least this was what he told himself during the day. Night brought a different outlook. The nightmares continued, though they came erratically now. Sometimes he would sleep deeply through the entire night. On other nights, they woke him two or three times. There was no Tim Hessler to shove an elbow in his ribs, but Burton resumed the duty of keeping his master from waking the whole household.

Sometimes his brother appeared among the battlefield dead; sometimes Francis appeared as an onlooker, beckoning Theo closer to hear—what? A plea? A story? A warning? Theo never knew, for he always awoke at that point with his brother's name on his lips and in his throat. He knew it was foolish, but he could not shake the feeling that Francis was trying to tell him something.

He had spoken with the groom who had accompanied Francis to Derbyshire. Hallem showed him the axle that had caused the accident.

"I kept this here axle, my lord. I jus' hope someday we catch the scoundrel what done this."

Theo examined the offending shaft of wood and metal. Clearly it had been tampered with and would have caused a serious accident even without the extreme speed that Francis so loved.

"I hope so, too," he said. "Have you any idea—any idea at all—who might have done this? Did you notice anything out of the ordinary?"

The two were standing in the doorway of the stable, a two-storied building with sleeping quarters for grooms and coachmen above. A light rain was falling and the clean smell of horse and hay of the indoor air contrasted with the fresh-washed scent of the outdoors.

"No, my lord. But afterwards . . . ye know how things come back to ye *after* somethin' happens?"

Theo nodded encouragingly.

"Well, afterwards, me an' Elmer, we remembered how the horses seemed 'specially restless early that morning—I mean, real early when it was jus' gettin' light out."

"I assume you checked on it."

"We did, my lord, but we didn't see nothin' and the dogs hadn't made no fuss, either."

"So an intruder managed to silence the dogs somehow," Theo said, thinking aloud.

Hallem nodded. "My guess is they tossed 'em a chunk of meat."

"You are probably right. A practiced thief has a few tricks in his bag."

"I'd say this fella knew his way around machinery—at least, around carriages."

"Oh?" Theo raised an inquisitive brow.

"The man knew exactly where that shaft would be weakest and he managed to hide it so's it wouldn't be seen in a quick once-over look. Master Francis—I mean, his lordship—he always looked things over purty good afore he climbed into the driver's seat. He drove fast, but not foolish." The groom, who had been around to teach the young Francis his driving skills, ended on a note of pride.

"Thank you, Hallem."

The groom's conjecture that the axle had been tampered with by someone with specialized skill gave Theo something to chew upon. The next step would be finding out more about that dispute in the mill. Theo had casually asked Taggert about it in the presence of Dawson, Taggert's secretary, but both men denied knowledge of any such incident. Mill workers professed equal ignorance. Theo decided it was time to enlist some aid.

He sent the young footman James—dressed in something other than his fine Glosson livery—to seek out Tim Hossler and the former sergeant, Yardley. Theo, himself attired in the clothing he had worn as a workman, waited for them in the stable behind The Silver Shield.

"You left the tavern separately?" he asked as they arrived nearly together.

"Yes, Major—uh, my lord. Just as the lad said," Yardley answered.

"I need your help," Theo said bluntly.

The two spoke at once.

"What kind of help?" Tim asked.

"Anything. Just ask, Major," Yardley responded.

"I am trying to learn why my brother died—and who might be responsible."

"So them rumors about it was no accident—they was *true*?" Tim asked.

"Yes," Theo said and Yardley sucked in his breath. Theo explained about the broken axle.

"So what do you want of us?" Yardley asked.

"Mostly just to keep your eyes and ears open—since I no longer have the freedom to move among workers as I once did."

"I'm real sorry about that," Yardley said.

"Never mind," Theo said. "It was, as I said, bound to happen. Now we just have to deal with it."

Tim, who had been quiet, now asked suspiciously, "You ain't askin' me to spy on other workers, are you?"

Theo gave an exasperated snort. "I wish to bloody hell folks would stop using the word *spy* in connection with me all the time! No. I am not asking you to 'spy.' I am trying to find out who killed my brother—and why."

"Sorry. I had to ask," Tim said. "Besides, I work for Mayfield—how can I help?"

Theo thought for a moment, wondering how much to tell them. He trusted Yardley implicitly—the man had saved Theo's life, limb, and sanity repeatedly. Instinct told him Tim would be just as trustworthy. So he explained the Bow Street Runners' theories about his brother's death.

"Whoever was behind it, the person or persons who actually did the deed probably worked in this area. If it was a personal grudge of some sort, the guilty person may be a Glosson worker. If a dead Francis was meant as a warning to mill owners in general, it could be anyone. But *someone* in Crofton knows who—and why. Now, will you help me?"

"Yes," Tim said simply.

"O' course," Yardley said. "I owe ye—that saber would have got me for sure at Vitoria."

"If you and I are to discuss who 'owes' whom, Yardley, I

will end the greater debtor, as I am sure you know. But I thank you. My thanks to both of you." He shook hands with them, then added, "You are *not* to put yourselves in harm's way over this. *If* you come across anything useful, let me know and I'll take it from there."

They agreed and left separately. Theo waited several minutes, then he, too, left the stable and hurried home.

The next day he accompanied his mother and Lady Olivia on a visit to the Crofton Parish Day School.

Pride would not allow Hannah to make special preparations for the countess's visit.

"Although we *can* dismiss early that day, Lady Glosson should see us just as we are—warts and all," Hannah insisted over Jane's hesitant protests.

"Nevertheless, I shall have some tea and biscuits to be served in the office," Jane said.

"That will be fine," Hannah agreed, for she and Jane, along with volunteers who came to help from time to time, often shared similar refreshments in the office.

The countess arrived in mid-afternoon, accompanied by her son and Lady Olivia Sanders, who was dressed in a very fashionable walking dress and a perky straw bonnet. Hannah was immediately glad that she *had* made enough of an occasion of the visit to don her most flattering "teacher" attire that morning, a soft blue-gray kerseymere with white lace at the neck and wrists. The color of the gown matched her eyes perfectly.

So, Hannah thought on seeing Lady Olivia descend from the carriage, *Miss Stimson was right. It appears the countess is training her successor*. But she could not think why she herself should find this idea so objectionable. It quite simply was not her place to judge personal choices made by the earl's family. Telling herself this, however, did not make her welcome Lady Olivia's presence, though she greeted the countess's protégée with all due civility.

The countess insisted on visiting both classrooms, Jane's group of younger students and Hannah's older ones. Lady Olivia and Lord Amesbury seemed to hold back, allowing the countess to set the pace and tone. Lady Glosson took her time, stopping occasionally to ask a particular child a question. She listened with apparent pleasure as a child of six years read aloud, complimenting her with a "Well done, my dear!"

When she came to the room for older students, she found them studying Shakespeare's *Henry V*. Once again, the countess posed interested questions to the students. Hannah was surprised at how relaxed and natural Lady Glosson was with young people. Even more surprising was the countess's intimate knowledge of the play. She soon had the youngsters involved in a lively discussion of the character of one of England's great warrior kings.

"My son knows this play quite well," the countess announced. "Amesbury, did you not memorize whole portions of it once?"

"That I did," he affirmed. "It was punishment for a bout of fisticuffs with another lad, as I remember. However, I was later glad I had done so."

"Oh, I'm sure," a disbelieving voice called out.

Hannah recognized the familiar sarcasm of Billy Daniels. She shot him a baleful glare and saw him slink down in his seat.

"Why were you glad?" asked Lucy Williams, who could always be depended upon to ask the right question or provide the right answer.

"Army life offers a great deal of boredom between small moments of action," the viscount explained. "I would often recite things to myself as we were marching or when I was on guard or something. It helped to pass the time."

"Oh, yeh?" This time Billy's skepticism was quite open. "Can you recite any now?"

"I think so. Hmm. Let me see . . . *Henry V*, eh?" Lord Amesbury then launched into Henry's inspiring speech in the center of the play, in which the young king urges English troops to extraordinary bravery against the French. "'Once more into the breach, dear friends, once more . . .'"

When he had finished, there was a moment of utter silence; then the whole class applauded with the countess, Lady Olivia, and Hannah joining in. Viscount Amesbury looked embarrassed, as though he had been caught out at something inappropriate.

"Sorry, Miss Whitmore. Mother. I . . . uh . . . did not mean to monopolize . . ."

"Oh, no, my lord," Hannah assured him. "I thank you very much. Perhaps my boys will more willingly do their memory work now." Her smile included both the viscount and the now-less-skeptical Billy.

This effectively ended the lessons and Hannah dismissed the students, who were ecstatic to be released early. She invited the guests into the office, where Jane had already laid out a table with tea and biscuits.

Lady Olivia had said little during the entire visit. Unlike the countess and her viscount son, the younger woman seemed to hold herself aloof from the children. Hannah, seated next to the beauty, thought Lady Olivia might be bored by the whole excursion.

"Have you an interest in schools, my lady?" Hannah asked by way of making conversation.

"My interests lie elsewhere, I fear," Lady Olivia replied. She gave a tinkling little laugh. "I was never what one might term a diligent student."

"We all have our separate interests and talents," Hannah said politely as an inner voice warned her not to expect much support if this one became the future mistress of Glosson Hall.

"My dear Miss Whitmore," the countess said. "I must say I am most favorably impressed with what you have achieved here."

"Thank you, my lady."

"Now tell me," the countess went on in what Hannah now

recognized as characteristic bluntness, "just how you wish to expand the school."

Hannah glanced nervously at the viscount, but found his expression to be neither encouraging nor discouraging. Once again she explained to a member of the Ruskin family the direction she fervently wished the school to go.

"You mean to add a number of mill children? But *where*?" the countess asked. "The two classrooms you have would not accommodate very many additional pupils."

"That is true, my lady. However, had we more students, there *is* room. You may have noticed that we are using less than half the space afforded by this building. I am sure," Hannah said, warming to her subject, "the same parents and parishioners who helped us achieve this would do so again. All we need are the children."

"And furniture, and books, and supplies, and . . ." The viscount's practical voice trailed off.

Hannah bit her lip, annoyed at his dampening tone. She gazed at him directly. "We are accustomed to sharing and making do. And," she added boldly, "we hope the mill owners will see some advantage to having a better-educated workforce and thus lend their support."

"Why do I not find that surprising?" His grin took the sting out of his words.

"I will certainly bring your proposal to my husband's attention," the countess promised.

"However," the viscount cautioned, "there are a number of factors that must be considered. We cannot give any assurances at this time, you understand."

"Yes, my lord," Hannah said rather tonelessly. This dratted man was going to do little—or nothing.

"We must be going," the countess announced, placing her teacup on the table as she rose.

Lady Olivia gave what Hannah took to be a sigh of relief and followed suit. They took their leave, offering Jane and Hannah farewell handshakes. Once again, Hannah felt a flush of warmth pervade her body as Lord Amesbury clasped her hand.

"Don't give up hope yet," he murmured for her ears alone.

She looked at him in surprise. There was no consistency in this man. None at all.

When the three visitors had left, Jane began clearing the tea things.

"I think that went well," she said.

"The *countess* seemed positive," Hannah replied. "I am not sure about her son."

"He will come around. You shall see."

"I hope so. I do hope so."

Ten

Theo sat in the carriage with his back to the horses, facing his mother and Lady Olivia, his thoughts still on the unique Miss Hannah Whitmore. The woman baffled him. On the one hand, he found it most unusual for a woman to have the organizational skills and ability to follow through on a plan such as she had shown—and he was not sure he approved of such in a female. On the other hand, he found her very tempting—her eyes had alternately shone with sincerity and amusement and kindness; her hair caught and held sunlight; and she walked with both determination and a natural grace.

"What did you think, Mother?"

"Miss Whitmore has achieved far more than I would have thought possible," the countess replied.

Theo merely nodded.

The countess turned to the woman seated next to her. "Olivia, dear, you were inordinately quiet during our visit. Did you not admire what we saw?"

Lady Olivia cast a quick glance at Theo, then lowered her lashes. "I . . . I cannot judge what a school should or should not be. I suppose there is much to admire in this one . . ."

"But . . . ?" the countess prodded.

"But I cannot admire a woman who steps outside accepted roles for our sex."

"And what roles might those be?"

Theo recognized the dangerously soft tone his mother used, though he doubted the younger woman did. What he did not recognize—indeed, what came as a shock to him—was his impulse to defend Miss Whitmore. After all, Lady Olivia had merely given voice to his own opinion of a woman who chose to speak for workers, who thought nothing of verbally assaulting a gentleman in the midst of a public thoroughfare, and who went far beyond the simple feminine task of teaching children. He listened carefully to Lady Olivia's response.

"I believe a woman's place is at home—she should comfort and support her husband. She should manage the servants well and . . ."—she blushed prettily—"and she should provide her husband an heir. She should be a reflection of her husband's good judgment in choosing her."

"I see . . ." the countess said. "You see no reason for this paragon to be a person in her own right?"

"Why, no." The younger woman sounded surprised. "She should have no need to do so."

"You will make some lucky man the perfect wife." The countess patted Lady Olivia's hand as she gave her son an oblique look. Lady Olivia looked pleased and Theo knew she had missed the irony in his mother's tone.

The perfect wife. Well, perhaps she would be, Theo thought. As his mother had pointed out in her none-too-subtle way, he *was* one-and-thirty. He supposed he should marry and have children before he reached his dotage. So what if the marriage had not the excitement and warm affection he saw with Jenkins and Jeffries—and his own parents. Even Cassie had married for love. Theo doubted the likelihood of love's becoming a factor in *his* life. Lust, perhaps, but not love. He knew of plenty of successful unions without that upsetting distraction. Lady Olivia seemed as likely a candidate as any to become Viscountess Amesbury and—eventually—Countess of Glosson. When his thoughts drifted to the marriage bed, though, it was not silvery blond strands he envisioned spread over a pillow. No. It was a stream of brown hair with reddish highlights. He shook his head, refusing to allow that wholly unsuitable image to go any further.

* * *

Hannah dressed for the Glosson ball with almost as much reluctance as she had for the Rollente ball some months earlier. The vicar's family, along with adult members of all local gentry families, had been invited to join the earl and countess and their London guests. Katherine was beside herself in anticipation of her first grown-up ball, and Hannah was determined to say or do nothing to dampen her sister's pleasure.

Several days had elapsed since the countess's visit to the school, during which the earl and his family had been significantly silent on the issue of mill children attending school. Granted, they had a house full of guests to entertain, but surely they could have made a simple yes or no decision by now. Hannah vowed that she would display neither anxiety nor annoyance this evening.

The receiving line consisted of only the earl and his family, including his daughter Cassandra and her husband, who had arrived two days earlier. Hannah passed from one to the other, her smile firmly in place. Again, she experienced that physical rush as the viscount took her gloved hand in his own, but she had steeled herself in anticipation of such. They exchanged only the briefest of pleasantries, then she joined other guests.

Her attention was immediately drawn to Lady Olivia, who was holding court, as it were, with several gentlemen clustered around her. She wore a silk gown of pale green with a long, sheer shawl of emerald green draped around her arms. She wore an emerald bracelet over her long, white gloves and emeralds adorned her neck and ears.

Having learned her lesson in London, Hannah had procured a new gown for this ball, but upon seeing the elegant Lady Olivia, she felt decidedly dowdy. Hannah's gown was a cream-colored Indian gauze that flowed freely when she moved. There were soft blue flowers embroidered in a twining design on the skirt. Her only jewelry was a gold locket.

She covertly watched Lady Olivia, though she found it difficult to know why. Certainly there were many attractive people—women *and* men—who might have commanded her attention. Perhaps it was envy. The woman was inordinately lovely. No wonder there were rumors of a match between her and Lord Amesbury.

When the dancing began, Lord Amesbury partnered Lady Olivia in the first set and Hannah, sitting on the sidelines, noticed that he managed quite well despite his slight limp. They were a very attractive couple, his dark evening attire complementing her lovely gown. Hannah averted her gaze. Then her attention was drawn by another of the dancers—Lord Mayfield.

Obviously, the Ruskin family had a very short memory if they had sent *him* an invitation. Everyone knew of the confrontation between Lord Mayfield and Lord Amesbury, for the baron had made no secret of the meeting.

Apparently noting the focus of Hannah's attention, Miss Stimson said behind her fan, "I think Glosson is trying to smooth the baron's ruffled feathers."

"Is that so?"

"Edward says social gatherings are one thing and political matters quite something else."

"The earl has a point," Hannah said, and vowed anew not to introduce the subject of workers or school to a single soul at this gathering.

However, she could not help taking a keen interest in watching how the baron and the viscount dealt with each other. The two men seemed coolly polite when they met, disappointing any guests who anticipated a heated exchange. She had to admit the baron looked quite splendid in evening attire. *Handsome is as handsome does,* she silently reminded herself—and in her view the baron was only moderately good-looking.

Hannah was surprised to see Mayfield join the cluster of men around Lady Olivia. Sitting close enough to hear much of the bantering conversation, Hannah was intrigued by the way the lady managed to manipulate her various admirers with flirtatious smiles and cleverly feminine use of her fan. Hannah stared openly until Miss Stimson distracted her.

"She thinks to make Amesbury jealous by flirting with Mayfield. It will not work, though."

"What makes you think so?" Hannah asked, deploring the gossip even as she engaged in it. "Surely Lady Olivia knows the two men have been at odds with each other."

"She knows. Probably one of those females who feels that adds spice, though. Maybe she thinks Theo is the type to rise to such obvious bait."

"Are not all men rather territorial about women for whom they care?"

"Some more than others, I would say. In truth, though, I would conjecture that Theo's heart is far from engaged."

This observation made *Hannah's* heart do a little jig. "I was under the impression they would make a match of it."

"Well, they may yet. Certainly the lady and her papa have that in mind, but, take my word for it, it will not be a love match."

At this point Hannah decided she had indulged herself in gossip quite enough and she changed the topic. She did notice, though, that so long as Mayfield hovered near Lady Olivia, Lord Amesbury occupied himself elsewhere.

Well aware of Lady Olivia's machinations, Theo could summon only indifference to them. If he considered the matter impersonally, Lady Olivia and Baron Mayfield would appear to be a good match. Her silvery beauty complemented his dark good looks, and vice versa. Probably more important to the financially embarrassed Mayfield, Theo thought, was the fact that Lady Olivia would go to her marriage bed with a *very* substantial dowry. Her father had made that abundantly clear, though Theo had not yet seriously considered approaching him for his daughter's hand.

The Marquis of Wembley, along with his wife, had arrived at Glosson Hall only two days ago and had immediately established their consequence among the other guests. The pretentious Mr. Bridges had come in for a set-down that Theo thought justly deserved, but he also knew it was demeaning of the marquis to give it.

His lordship's superior attitude toward David Moore set Theo's teeth to grinding. Moore's grandfather had been in trade, but the family fortune would rank with those of the top half of the *ton*, and Moore men had always managed to marry quite well. David might be a mere "mister" in the *ton's* pecking order, but the man was loyal, brave, and ever willing to serve his country—or his friends. People like Wembley, Theo thought, owed their superior places in life to people like Moore.

Theo looked around to find Moore engaged in conversation with Miss Bridges. Theo had seen the two dancing together earlier. He grinned. Those two had often had their heads together in the last week or so. Moore looked up to catch Theo's grin. A moment later, when Miss Bridges took to the dance floor with another, Moore strolled over to where Theo stood.

"And just what is it that you find so amusing, my lord?" Moore asked.

"You. And do stop 'my lording' me, David."

"What about me?" Moore was defensive.

"Well . . ." Theo spoke slowly, teasingly, "it occurs to me that if you are not careful, you will be as firmly locked into the parson's mousetrap as you accuse Jenkins and Jeffries of being."

"Oh, come now," Moore blustered. "A bit of dalliance—is that not expected at country house parties?"

"One 'dallies' with married women—or demireps—not with the likes of Miss Bridges."

"Oh, I say, Theo. Have I encroached on your domain? I . . . uh . . . I thought you and Lady Olivia . . ." Moore's voice trailed off in embarrassment.

Theo gestured impatiently. "No. Of course not. I have no ties on any of the ladies here—despite my mother's wish to see the succession neatly arranged."

"Then you will not mind if Anne and I . . ."

Theo raised a brow at his friend's inadvertent use of the lady's given name. "You *are* smitten, aren't you?" He laughed. "And you were the one issuing dire warnings to *me* a few weeks back!"

Moore turned red and admitted sheepishly, "I suppose I am. I don't know—it . . . well, it just *happened*, you see."

Theo clapped him on the shoulder. "If that is the way it is, snatch her up, my friend."

"Thanks, Theo, but I think her father is set on reeling in a viscount and future earl."

"He is doomed to disappointment then. Miss Bridges and I have never been anything but politely friendly. The field is all yours as far as I am concerned." Theo grinned and added, "Though I shall not envy you such a father-in-law."

"About like Wembley, eh?"

"Wembley would have apoplexy if he heard you say such."

They both laughed at this and they were joined by Jenkins and Jeffries, whose wives had gone off to the ladies' withdrawing room together. Theo listened as the three of them talked horses and carriages. Then his attention was arrested by the sight of Miss Whitmore on the dance floor, partnered by Henry Franklin.

He had seen Franklin dancing earlier with someone else, but he had not then noted who the lawyer's partner was. He certainly noted now, however. The vicar's daughter shone to advantage in a pearl-colored gown that flowed enticingly with her every movement. She seemed perfectly at ease with her partner, laughing and talking animatedly. Theo felt a distinct twist of envy grab at him.

There were enough potential dance partners at this ball that Theo felt no obligation as a member of the hosting family to present himself to each and every female guest. However, he deliberately presented himself to Miss Whitmore.

"If you have not yet promised it, may I have the next dance, Miss Whitmore?"

She seemed confused and a little breathless. "Why . . . why, of course, my lord."

He wondered at a look of surprise and apprehension that crossed her face when the orchestra played the first bars of music. It was a waltz. Theo opened his arms and she stepped forward to place one hand decorously on his shoulder and the other in his. He put his other hand at her waist and suddenly there was the music and this woman in his arms. He was conscious of nothing else. Truth to tell, he was barely conscious of the music as the two of them seemed to flow with it.

Theo could not recall ever reacting so to a mere dance. Be honest! he told himself. It was not the dance, but the dance partner. He looked down to find her gazing at him in wonder and he knew she experienced the same sensations. A fleeting look of panic in those blue-gray depths told him she was also as surprised and—yes—afraid as he was.

They danced in silence for what seemed a long while. He hesitated to break the spell, but was it not expected that one would converse with one's partner?

"You dance very well, Miss Whitmore."

Her eyes sparkled with amusement. "I shall convey your compliment to my father."

"Your father?"

"He taught me—and my sisters—to dance. We had no dancing master."

"Our vicar is a man of many talents, I see."

They danced in silence for a few more moments, then he leaned close to whisper, "It is your turn now." Her hair smelled of sunshine and lilacs.

"My turn? My turn for what?"

"To come up with an inane topic of conversation. That is what dancers do, you know—they talk of inane matters they no longer remember when the music stops."

"'Tis a hard and fast rule, is it?" she asked, ultra serious.

"Oh, yes," he answered, matching her tone. "Passed from fathers to sons and mothers to daughters since we staggered out of those infernal caves."

Laughing at this bit of foolishness, she allowed her gaze to lock with his again. It was a hearty laugh, albeit feminine, genuine and free. He grinned down at her. Then their merriment changed to something far more profound. He covered his own confusion by swinging her into a series of graceful circles. As the music ended, she was out of breath.

Disconcerted by a subtle something that had taken place, he returned her to where she had been sitting between her mother and his Aunt Stimson. He thanked her and retreated as quickly as he politely could.

Hannah took her seat in a great state of inward agitation. What was it that made her react to this man as she had reacted to no other—ever? After all, she was not some schoolroom miss enthralled by the idea of an attractive Prince Charming. Prince Charming, indeed! Heretofore, the man had been a great deal *less* than charming. She must hang onto that thought and forget about being carried away by the music, the faint scent of spice and herbs, the feel of his arms.

His arms. She had walked into them in an almost mesmerized state. Once there, she had felt—incongruously—that it was utterly *right* to be there. Now—was that not positively ridiculous? Such a man was not cut out for a vicar's spinster schoolteacher daughter.

Her mother brought a welcome halt to this line of thinking. "Hannah, you looked absolutely radiant during that waltz."

"Why, thank you, Mama."

"It just goes to show what a handsome, amiable partner can do for one."

"I suppose you are right, Mama." Hannah did not want to discuss that dance with her mother. She did not want to discuss it with anyone. She wanted to hug the memory to herself—at least until she figured it out.

For the remainder of the evening, she tried to put the interlude with Lord Amesbury out of her mind. She danced her share of dances, though not as many as the London ladies. She took great delight in seeing Katherine's enjoyment. Her pretty younger sister would surely be a "diamond of the first water" when she went to London for the season early next year.

Hannah went in to supper with Captain Phillips. She happily discovered that there were, indeed, topics besides ships and sea lanes that interested him. They were seated with Mr. Moore and Miss Bridges and, to her dismay, with the viscount and Lady Olivia.

"*Hannah* is your given name, is it not, Miss Whitmore?" Captain Phillips asked as he set plates of food for both of them on the table and took his seat next to her.

"Yes, it is."

"It is a very pretty name. Biblical, is it not? Meaning 'grace or favor.'"

Hannah looked at him in surprise. "Yes. I do not remember anyone else ever mentioning that on learning my name before. You are a well read man, Captain."

He chuckled. "There is not much room on board a ship for a vast library, but we always have a Bible."

"It seems a most appropriate name—for a vicar's daughter." Lady Olivia's tone suggested she meant "for a *mere* vicar's daughter."

"Is there some unwritten rule that clergymen must give their children biblical names?" Miss Bridges asked innocently.

Hannah laughed. "If there is, I doubt my parents knew of it. My father wanted to call me Helen. He had just been immersing himself in the Trojan War, you see. My mother wanted to name her new babe Anna for *her* mother. They compromised on *Hannah*."

"And a happy solution it was," Captain Phillips said.

"I wonder what name Princess Charlotte and Prince Leopold will choose for their child," Miss Bridges asked, then blushed at the delicacy of such a topic.

All England knew the princess was due to be confined very soon. And all England had high hopes of an heir to a throne that had too long been beset by madness, dissipation, and scandal.

"If the child is a girl, I doubt she will be named for her grandmother as the princess herself was," Lady Olivia said with a snide little laugh.

"The current Princess of Wales has not proved to be a paragon of propriety," Hannah said, "but one cannot help feeling sorry for her all the same."

"A boy might well be another *George*," Mr. Moore said. "That would certainly please the Prince Regent."

"Swell his sense of his own consequence even more, you mean," Captain Phillips said.

"Perhaps a boy will be called 'Leopold' for *his* father," Viscount Amesbury suggested.

Lady Olivia giggled. "Can you not just hear it now—'King Leopold'? Or perhaps 'King Leo'? For an *English* king? Oh, too, too much."

The others smiled politely with her and the conversation turned to other matters. The evening eventually ended for Hannah on a happy note as she listened to Katherine's raptures over every detail of her first ball.

Ten days later, the entire nation was plunged into grief as Princess Charlotte died after giving birth to a stillborn son.

Eleven

As all England floundered in a sea of grief and uncertainty about the future, the midlands suffered a double blow. The trial of the Pentrich revolutionaries ended as many had predicted: with transportations and hangings. Of the forty-five or so arrested, only a handful escaped punishment. The leader, Brandeth, and two of his cohorts were hanged. The rest were tranported with sentences of fourteen years, rather than the customary seven.

As winter progressed, unrest among workers—already seething with anger over the severity of those sentences—became even more pronounced. When wages of many were cut yet again, there were rumors of a revival of General Ludd and the violence of some years previous. Owners of mines, mills, and other manufactories became increasingly fearful. As a result they and their stewards and overlookers became increasingly oppressive—with full approval of agents of the local and national governments.

"It is as though a charge has been set and we are merely waiting for the fuse to be lit," the Earl of Glosson said to his son. The earl and his wife were traveling to London the next day for the upcoming opening of Parliament. Once again, father and son were enjoying a late *tête à tête* in the library after the countess retired.

"Parliament has the power to defuse the situation," Theo pointed out, "but do you think they will use it?"

"No. As a legislative group we will sit around and wring our hands and make proclamations." The earl sighed heavily.

"I hate to agree with the likes of writers like Cobbett and that Gadfly—whoever *he* is—but they have the right of it."

"It does rather seem that the government runs around putting bandages on the injured limbs of the body politic as an insidious cancer eats away from within."

The earl shifted in his chair. "That's one way of putting it. Until there is real reform of Parliament, things are likely to stay the same. And reform is a long, long way off."

"Careful, Father. You'll be accused of being a Whig," Theo teased. Then he became serious. "Like so many in Lords, you yourself control several seats in The Commons. Will you give up that control?"

"Personally? Gladly—when there is a system in place to ensure real representation."

"And in the meantime?"

"In the meantime, it is my duty to see that responsible, honorable men occupy those seats."

"Unfortunately, Father, yours is still very much the minority view among those wielding power. There is a vast army out there—an army of working people—waiting more and more impatiently for changes."

"And no one seems to know just how to deal with the changes that have already just erupted around us. Factory workers are not the same as farm laborers. Those infernal machines have changed the whole character of England!"

Theo grinned at his father. "Ah, there's the good Tory talking again!"

The earl merely grunted and turned the discussion to problems closer to home. "Still no word about what happened to Francis?"

"A great deal of conjecture and idle gossip from outsiders, but nothing of real value from people who might have had the most contact with him."

"Our own mill workers, you mean?"

"And cottage weavers. He was visiting cottage weavers that day, you remember."

"Somebody *must* know something," the older man groused. "Good grief! Next month will make it *two years*!"

"I know."

"Tell me again what your man Yardley had to say."

Theo rose and stood in front of the fireplace, allowing the warmth to soak into his backside. "He said people are afraid. There *is* something out there in the way of information, but to quote the dauntless sergeant, 'People is terrified to come forward.'"

"If I ever find out who is responsible, he—or they—will have cause to be terrified," the earl vowed.

"Seems there was an altercation of some sort between Francis and one of the overlookers, a man named O'Reilly."

"Over what?"

"I don't know. It was apparently an argument that took place in the overlooker's office on the third floor. People on that floor could see but not hear anything."

"Did you confront the fellow—or Taggert—about it?"

Theo nodded. "That fellow and another Irishman named Duggan left about two months after the accident. I asked Taggert. He said he knew nothing about it and that those two were simply homesick for Ireland."

"They left about the time the Bow Street Runners would have started asking questions. I'll have Bow Street check on their whereabouts now." The earl rubbed his hand over his chin. "If only we knew what they quarreled about . . ."

"Something of value may turn up yet. I will continue to work on it."

The earl drained the last of the brandy from his glass. "I'm for bed," he announced, rising from his chair. "Your mother wants an early start tomorrow. So, I leave it in your hands, son. All of it. Do whatever you judge to be right."

"Thank you, Father."

"You are now *thanking* me for unloading nearly the entire earldom on you? Now, that is a turnabout."

Theo returned his father's grin. "No, sir. I thank you for your confidence in me."

"Hmphf. Well, good night."

"Good night, Father."

When his father had gone, Theo refilled his own brandy glass and lighted a lamp on the desk. He pulled out those bothersome ledgers again, along with the most recent additions to them. His gut feeling told him that these columns of numbers contained some of the answers he sought. But where? Everything seemed perfectly in order. Production was steady and profits were as good as might be expected in these hard economic times.

He recalled a recent discussion with Henry Franklin. Theo had gone to the lawyer's office to ask about those "other" ledgers again.

Greetings over, Theo asked, "Am I ever to see those books, Franklin? It has been over three months now. They do exist, do they not?"

"They exist," Franklin said. "It is just that people are apprehensive—more than ever after those hangings in Pentrich."

"I have no intention of killing the messenger should he be bearing bad news."

Franklin smiled briefly at this weak joke. "I doubt it is you who is feared. Your steward, rather."

"Taggert? Why?"

"He has had a great deal of power for quite a long while and, frankly, he is rather heavy-handed in wielding it."

"For instance?" Theo did not particularly like Taggert personally, but the man was an employee, not a friend. As long as he did his job . . .

Franklin gave Theo a direct look. "I am not one to bear tales, but it is well known that workers are dismissed or fined or punished severely for matters that would require mild reprimands were there not so many unemployed wandering the highways looking for work. Any work."

"And hours?" Theo asked. "I recall that was a complaint earlier."

"So far as I know, there has been no change in hours." Franklin's tone was faintly accusing.

Theo had thought there would be some reduction in hours, since he had himself instructed Taggert to look into the matter and make changes where possible. Now, as he sat in Franklin's office, he remembered exactly how vague had been Taggert's report that the issue of hours worked had been "taken care of."

Theo was embarrassed. He knew he had mishandled things. As an army officer, he would not have failed to follow through on orders he gave, but he had done just that here as a civilian. True—he had been distracted by that extended house party in the autumn. He had spent a good deal of his time then in the pleasurable business of halfheartedly courting Lady Olivia—well, keeping up his end of a continuing flirtation, at any rate. There had been drives and sightseeing expeditions, and even—to Theo's surprise—a dinner invitation from Lord Mayfield that had been extended to the Glosson household and their London guests.

Following the visit to Miss Whitmore's school, Theo had been slightly confused and vastly amused at seeing his mother's enthusiasm wane in her championing of Lady Olivia. One day when their guests all seemed occupied in their own pursuits, the countess persuaded her son to walk in the garden with her. In her usual manner she went directly to what was on her mind, but to Theo's surprise, her tone was rather subdued.

"So, my son, are you or are you not actively courting Lady Olivia?"

"I admit only to exploring the possibility. Why do you ask?"

"Oh, no reason. Just put it down to a mother's curiosity."

Theo chuckled. "Now, that won't wash, and you know it. What is on your mind?"

"Just that if your interests truly lie in that direction, you had best exert yourself a bit more. Or have you failed to notice that Mayfield seems intent on fixing *his* interest with her?"

"Well, if she is receptive to his attentions—" Theo shrugged.

"If you are so indifferent to Lady Olivia, perhaps you would find Miss Wentworth more to your liking," his mother suggested.

"I thought you were set on Lady Olivia as your eventual successor." Theo stalled for time. He really did not want to discuss his own ambivalence toward the green-eyed beauty.

"Lady Olivia is a lovely young woman." His mother was beginning to sound exasperated.

"Yes. She is." Theo refused to commit himself.

"She would surely be an *agreeable* wife."

"You make her sound like some sort of toady."

"Oh, I do not *mean* to do so. I should just like to see you settled, dear."

"In time, Mother. In due time."

Privately, Theo was neutral about the idea that Mayfield, too, might be pursuing Lady Olivia. Theo knew very well that if he wanted it—*he* had the inside track. The trouble lay in deciding if he wanted it.

Eventually, the house party came to an end and the guests departed. The Christmas season, with its attendant festivities and obligations, followed. Theo's sister and her young family stayed through the holidays and Theo often found himself in the nursery with her children. But there was also the ongoing investigation into his brother's death.

None of these were matters that *should* have so distracted him from the tasks at hand. Yet that is precisely what had occurred—and Theo Ruskin, Lord Amesbury, was the man who had allowed it to happen.

He shifted uncomfortably in his chair, but met the lawyer's gaze directly. "Get me those books. If they prove the allegations made earlier, I can promise there will be some changes made. But I cannot—and will not—act without solid reason for doing so."

Two days later, Franklin appeared unexpectedly at the mill.

"I had a hard time running you to ground, my lord," the solicitor said, slightly out of breath and apparently unaware of the humor of his statement, as he had just climbed all five flights of stairs at the Glosson Mill.

Theo rose from the floor, where he had been helping to repair a broken loom.

"There. That ought to do it. If it breaks down again, let me know. Let *me* know," he repeated with a pointed look at the fifth-floor overlooker. He noted the interested, even amazed, looks of the workers gathered around.

"Thank 'e, my lord." The worker who manned this loom pulled at his forelock.

"'Twas rather like mending an artillery cart," Theo said with a deprecatory shrug, then acknowledged his visitor. "Good afternoon, Franklin."

Theo wiped his hands on a cloth a woman handed him and shrugged back into the jacket he had removed earlier. He knew that, with dust and stains on his clothing and muck on his hands, he presented a poor picture.

"I have something I need . . to . . . uh, discuss with you," Franklin said, choosing his words guardedly.

"All right. I am finished here, I think. Back to work," he added in a slightly louder tone for their audience. "Do you want to talk here? We could use the overlooker's office."

"I think not," Franklin replied.

Theo gave him a quick look and the lawyer nodded ever so slightly.

"Well, then," Theo said, "I am for a cup of coffee or tea. Will you join me?"

They descended the stairs, exchanging comments about the weather, comparing this year with the previous one, and speaking of other mundane matters until they were clear of the building.

"We'll go up to the Hall," Theo suggested. "I fear we will have to use your carriage, though, as mine is to return for me in—" he consulted his pocket timepiece—"about an hour."

Once they were ensconced in Franklin's hired carriage, the

lawyer reached under the seat to retrieve a small packet, under which he handed to Theo.

"The books, I take it," Theo said.

"The books."

"At last," Theo breathed. Then he said in a stronger voice, "Thank you, Mr. Franklin." Both knew his gratitude was for more than just the books.

As the carriage pulled up in front of the Hall, Franklin said with what Theo took to be genuine regret, "I will have to pass on the coffee, my lord. I have an appointment that cannot be missed. I just wanted to deliver these directly into your hands and as discreetly as possible."

"Of course," Theo said, offering his hand. "My friends call me *Theo*—or *Amesbury*, Mr. Franklin. I should like you to do the same."

Franklin took his hand warmly, hesitating only slightly as he responded, "Amesbury. To *my* friends, I am *Henry*—or *Harry*."

Moments later, Theo entered the Hall highly agitated, eager to peruse these ledgers. He laughed at the idea of his being eager to deal with unending columns of numbers. But first, a bath.

He spent the remainder of the afternoon and evening comparing the two sets of books. The set Franklin had given him was obviously not kept by anyone experienced in keeping accounts. Nevertheless, there was a ring of truth in that amateur quality. It was readily apparent that there were vast discrepancies. The accounts Taggert had given him showed steady production and a good, if modest, profit. The books Franklin had supplied showed a far greater production—which *should* have translated into a more substantial margin of profit.

The next day, Theo confronted Taggert. Careful to protect his source of information, Theo went directly to the steward's plush office. He carried only the ledgers Taggert had given him.

"Given the hours workers have apparently put in, I wonder that production seems to be so low," Theo said in a deliberately amiable tone.

"Workers are simply lazy, my lord. It is hard to get good help these days."

"I see." Theo looked at the expensive furnishing around him, knowing full well where some of the unreported profit had gone.

Taggert apparently sensed Theo's skepticism. There was a moment of silence, then the steward said, "I am told that the lawyer Franklin visited you yesterday, my lord. I do hope you are not . . . uh . . . influenced by his misconceptions of what happens at this mill."

"His misconceptions?" Theo kept his voice neutral.

"He hears things from only one source and thinks that is the truth. He's given us a lot of grievance, let me tell you."

"Really?" Theo hoped he sounded merely curious. "Can you give me an example?"

"He was here some months ago complaining we worked folks too hard. But we were shorthanded until this past summer," Taggert asserted.

"Strange. That was not noted here." Theo tapped what he thought of as the Taggert ledgers.

"An oversight. I'll get Dawson right on it, my lord. My secretary is actually the one who keeps our books in order. The mistake will be rectified immediately, Lord Amesbury."

"See to it," Theo said, as though he believed what he had just been told. As he left, he thought he heard a great sigh of relief behind him.

His next step was to arrange another clandestine meeting with the trusted Yardley. The former sergeant came to the rear entrance of Glosson Hall and was shown into the library.

Theo invited him to the seats he and his father had occupied so often and explained the situation he had uncovered.

"Somehow, I ain't surprised," Yardley said.

"Why?" Theo asked.

"Well, the overlooker on my floor, see, he's a secretive son of a bitch. And meaner than a snake about producing more an' more ells of stuff. I mean—'tis a very personal matter to him."

"Does he mistreat the people under him?"

Yardley shrugged. "Some. Mostly the ones that will take it, that won't—or can't—stand up for themselves at all."

"That would not be you," Theo said.

"No. He mighta tried, but 'tis well known that I served with you in Spain and Belgium. I doubt he'll bother with me as long as you stay in the area." Yardley gave his former commander an inquiring look. "I somehow doubt you had me come here tonight to talk about that rotter, though."

"You're right. I should like you to talk with workers on other floors and see if they have the same stories you do."

"They do," Yardley interrupted.

"It appears to me that Taggert and Dawson have a sweet thing going here." Theo explained what he knew and what he conjectured to be the result—Taggert and others skimming off profits from the mill at the expense of both the workers and the Ruskin family. "As I see it," he continued, "this could not happen without the cooperation—and complicity—of the supervisors on each floor. I need to know just how many and who is involved."

"The overlookers, certainly."

"Yes."

"I expect you're right about that," Yardley said. "They're a hard lot, that's sure. It's a shame. Most of the people are workin' real hard."

"I know." Theo paused. "And—Yardley? Be careful. Be very careful."

The other man simply gave Theo another inquiring look.

"I strongly suspect my brother stumbled onto this mess—and it led to his death."

Yardley nodded solemnly. "I'll take care. Won't be no untimely accidents happening to *me*."

Yardley was right. When it came, the accident was not to him. But it *was* an accident—more or less.

* * *

The winter months always weighed heavily for Hannah. So many of her pupils were ill-fed, ill-clad, and ill-housed. Try as they might, she and Jane simply could not provide for all who needed help. Many times she took leftovers from the vicarage table to feed hungry students. She tried not to allow the children to see the tears that sprang to her eyes when she ushered a thin, shivering little body nearer the stove for warmth.

She was grateful to neighbors and merchants who were willing to help and she tried not to be *too* much of a pest to them. Among the most helpful in seeing to the physical needs of the children had been the Countess of Glosson, who had made it her business to see that several bolts of material from Glosson Mill were made available for winter cloaks for parish children.

"I must tell you, though," Lady Glosson confided with an amused, triumphant chuckle, "that Mr. Taggert was not best pleased. I had to remind him just who it was who owned this mill!"

Hannah would have loved to have seen that exchange, but she merely smiled and thanked the countess.

An appeal to Lady Mayfield—the baron's mother, who resided with her son—had met with less success. The Mayfields donated only a bit of stock from their vast inventory. Privately, Hannah thought they did *that* much only to avert adverse gossip after the Glosson household had done so much.

In mid-November, the vicar's family was invited to another social event sponsored by a leading family in the area. This time it was the Mayfields who were hosting a dinner party at which the London guests still at Glosson Hall would be entertained.

"Are you quite certain thc invitation included *me*?" Hannah asked her father when he announced to his wife and daughters one evening that he had received it. Mrs. Whitmore and Katherine had been quietly gossiping over their embroidery as Hannah sat reading several poems she planned to teach on the morrow.

"Yes, my dear. Your name is here, plain as day," he answered. "And why should it not be?"

"Lord Mayfield has been decidedly cool to any request regarding the school. I think he has a rather acute dislike of me in particular."

"That may be, but he could hardly invite the rest of us and exclude you," her father said.

"Besides," her mother added, looking up from her embroidery, "the invitation quite properly came from the hostess, Lady Mayfield, not her son."

"You may be sure this is *his* party," Hannah said. "You know how reclusive Lady Mayfield usually is."

"She is that," Mrs. Whitmore agreed.

"Were I a more refined sort," Hannah mused aloud, "I suppose I might decline this invitation as far as it pertains to *me*—but it might be fun to tweak Mayfield's whiskers, so to speak."

"Hannah!" her mother admonished in a shocked squeak. "You must promise you will do nothing untoward. Promise!"

"Yes, Mama. I promise to be on my best behavior." She shared an amused glance with her father. "Perhaps my presence alone will be enough to discomfort him, however slightly. And that is a man who could use a bit of discomfort, I think."

Her mother laid aside her embroidery to give her eldest daughter a stern look. "I do hope you will remember that you should set an example for Katherine and the other young ladies of the parish."

"Mama!" Katherine protested. "I should like to think *my* behavior is such that I need not model it after another's."

"Yes, dear. Your behavior is always all that is proper," her mother comforted.

Hannah rolled her eyes, but neither her mother nor her sister caught this expression.

More amused than apprehensive about the prospect of dining in style at Mayfield Manor, Hannah actually looked forward to the event. She always found that such doings provided endless opportunities for that most intriguing of pastimes—watching others perform in this comedy of the human condition.

She dismissed from her mind any importance attached to the fact that all the persons from Glosson Hall would have been invited, too—including a certain viscount. Nevertheless, she dressed carefully in an apricot silk that she knew to be particularly flattering to her coloring.

As Lady Mayfield sorted out her dinner guests prior to their removing to the dining room, Hannah was amazed and inordinately pleased to find that *she* was to be partnered by Lord Amesbury. She had noted earlier the baron's rather effusive greeting to Lady Olivia and then his discreet flirting with her. At the table, the Marchioness of Wembley was properly accorded the place at the host's right, but instead of the Countess of Glosson, it was Lady Olivia—looking especially elegant in the palest of pinks—who occupied the place to his left. At the other end of the very long table, the baron's mother was flanked by the Marquis of Wembley and the Earl of Glosson. Hannah and the viscount were seated halfway down the table.

"Well, not exactly below the salt," the viscount murmured for her ears alone. His eyes twinkled in amusement.

Hannah smiled at him, caught in the intimacy of the moment. Then she noted that she and the viscount were placed on the same side of the table as Lady Olivia, making it impossible for that lady and the viscount to make eye contact. The Countess of Glosson was on the opposite side from them and *she* was able to make eye contact with her son. Hannah saw her distinctly, but discreetly, wink at him. Hannah searched her mind for something to say that was witty and sophisticated, but her mind was blank.

"Have your students finished *Henry V*?" he asked politely, taking his assigned seat at her right.

"Oh, yes. Some time ago." She gave him an arch look. "I am surprised you remembered that."

"Why? You think me such a dunce as not to recall something as simple as the title of a play?"

She thought his tone was only half teasing.

"No. That is not what I meant at all. And, really, my lord, it is most unseemly of you to suggest that I did."

He gave an exaggerated sigh of wounded vanity and said quietly with an air of addressing an unseen arbiter, "Ah, now the teacher is chastising me for improper behavior. How *will* my dignity bear such a blow?"

"Lord Amesbury!" she admonished.

He grinned and said in a perfectly normal voice, "Henry V happens to be one of my favorite characters in literature, though I think I prefer him as Prince Hal in *Henry IV* more than in the battle-ridden play you were doing."

"But his father so overshadows him in the earlier play," Hannah protested.

They then engaged in a lively discussion of the merits of the two plays, though proper etiquette forced them both to devote equal time to diners on either side of them. Hannah found herself impatient with propriety and eager to make this or that point.

She was also acutely aware of the man seated on her right, as his shoulder occasionally brushed hers and a now-familiar warmth coursed through her. There was simply no denying that this was one very attractive man!

Caught up in their conversation, Hannah scarcely noticed what she ate, and she was mildly surprised when Lady Mayfield signaled that the ladies should withdraw. Hannah conjectured—correctly—that the baron would not allow the gentlemen to dawdle for long over their port. Not while the beautiful Lady Olivia sat in the drawing room.

When the gentlemen did rejoin the ladies, it was not the baron who dominated that lady's attention, but the viscount. At the lady's subtle invitation he took the place next to her. Hannah recognized the twinge she felt at this for what it was—jealousy. She tried to tell herself she simply wanted to continue an interesting discussion.

On the way home, her mother noted, "You and Lord Amesbury seemed to be getting on well this evening, Hannah."

"Yes. He was surprisingly amiable."

"Why do you find that so surprising?" Katherine asked. "I have ever found him an amiable gentleman."

Hannah succeeded in remaining amiable herself on this topic. "Yes, I suppose he would seem so to you. Let us just say my encounters with him have not been the same as yours." She then changed the subject by drawing Katherine's attention to the gown Miss Bridges had worn.

Hannah could not have said why, but she was not yet ready to discuss Viscount Amesbury with her family. She wanted to hold every nuance of the evening to herself for a while.

Twelve

On Saturdays, the Crofton School dismissed early. As Hannah left one Saturday afternoon in early March, she noticed a small child huddled on the steps, her face crushed against one of the balusters. The child was sobbing.

When Hannah approached her and touched her shoulder, the little girl turned her tear-stained face up to Hannah's. Hannah recognized her as Patsy Tettle, one of Jane's students in the younger class.

"Patsy? What is it, darling? What is wrong?"

Patsy put her hand over her face and lowered her head, sobbing even harder. She mumbled incoherently through her sobs.

Hannah put down the bag of books and papers she had been carrying and knelt on the step below the girl. She pulled gently at Patsy's cold hands.

"Come, sweetie," she crooned. "It helps to share your problems. Perhaps I can help."

"No-o-o," Patsy wailed, "no one . . . can . . . help." She took great gulps of air between words. "It . . . it's . . . my mama."

Alarmed, Hannah asked, "Is she ill?"

"S-she's goin' to die, Miss Whitmore. My mama's goin' to die."

"Are you sure? Sick people often get well, you know."

"Th-there was blood. I seen it. Lots of blood. Gramma didn't want me to see, but I did. My mama's gonna die." She ended on another high-pitched wail.

Hannah moved to sit on the step beside the little girl and pulled the small body close to her own.

"We don't know that, Patsy. Only God can know for sure."

"But . . . but there was blood." Patsy's sobs had diminished to whimpers now. "An' I'm scared, Miss Whitmore. Real scared."

Hannah hugged her tighter. "Of course you are. I would be, too."

"Truly?" This bizarre idea seemed to divert the child for a moment.

Hannah smiled down at her. "Yes, truly. Now—would you like me to walk you home? It looks to rain soon."

"Oh, yes, please."

"Just give me a moment." Hannah dashed back into the building to ask Jane to inform the vicar of her whereabouts and to have him send a carriage for her later. She returned to the front steps, picked up her bag in one hand, and took the worried Patsy's small, cold hand in the other.

A quarter of an hour later, they arrived at the Tettles' flat, which was a basement apartment, half below the street level. There were steps down to the door, and once inside, Hannah noticed only two small windows high on the wall. Rough planks laid directly on the damp earth beneath made an uneven floor. The apartment consisted of a large front room that obviously served as a kitchen, dining room, sitting room, and even a bedroom for some members of the family. There was a much smaller room in the rear from which an older woman with iron-gray hair emerged on hearing Hannah and Patsy come in.

"Patsy? Oh. I beg your pardon." The woman peered at Hannah. "You're the teacher, ain't you?"

"One of them," Hannah said. "I've just walked Patsy home. She was quite upset about her mother."

"Poor dear," the grandmother said, opening her arms to enfold Patsy.

"Is Mama all right?" Patsy asked. "Can I see her?"

"She's resting right now," the grandmother said, but Hannah

noticed she evaded Patsy's question. The old woman knelt down beside the child. "You be a big girl now, won't you? I want you to run up to Mrs. Thompson's and help her take care of your little brothers. Can you do that?"

Patsy nodded. "Aw'right."

When the child had gone, the old woman turned to Hannah. "I thank you, Miss— Miss—"

"Whitmore," Hannah supplied. "Is there anything I can do? Patsy feared her mother was dying."

The old woman sat down heavily on a chair and leaned her head on her fist, obviously fighting tears. "She is. My daughter won't make it through the night."

"Are you sure? Perhaps the doctor—"

"He's already been here. He only told me what I already knew."

"Patsy's father . . . ?" Hannah left the question dangling.

"He's gone. Soon as he heard the news, he spent some time in there with Molly and then lit out of here—a terrible look on his face. Terrible."

"Do you know where he went?"

"No. But there's murder on his mind. I just know it."

Hannah pulled a chair around the table and sat next to the woman. "Tell me, Mrs.—"

"Hacket. Molly—Patsy's mama—is my daughter."

"Let me help, if I can, please."

Mrs. Hacket heaved a heavy sigh. "Not much anyone can do now. 'Tis in God's hands—an' He don't seem likely to do anything."

"What happened? Did she just suddenly fall ill—or what?" Hannah asked.

"Don't suppose it matters much now—Molly ain't goin' to be here to pay for her sins in this life," Mrs. Hacket said wearily.

"P-pay for her sins?" Hannah was apprehensive. Was the woman some sort of religious zealot?

"Molly went to see the Widow Stanton day before yesterday."

"Oh, no." Hannah knew the Widow Stanton had a small

cottage a few miles out of Crofton. She dealt in roots and herbs and offered home remedies for everything from warts to liver complaints. She was also known to help young women who found themselves in "an interesting condition."

"But . . . but *why*?" Hannah asked. "Mrs. Tettle has a husband."

"Tobias Tettle was not the father," Mrs. Hacket said flatly.

"Not— not—" Hannah stuttered. "Surely that cannot be true. I have seen the Tettles together. I cannot imagine—"

"'Tis true, all the same. Molly told me all yesterday when she started bleeding again. I told her not to tell Tobias, but I think he wrung it out of her."

"But . . . *why*?" Hannah was appalled at the very idea of what Molly Tettle must have been through.

Mrs. Hacket stifled a sob. "She told me she just couldn't bear to have a babe not fathered by Tobias—and certainly not by the likes of that beast, Mike Logan."

"She knew for sure the babe was Logan's?" Hannah asked.

"Yes. She said she and Tobias had not . . . well . . . you know—" Mrs. Hacket paused, clearly embarrassed. "Anyway, they wasn't together—you know?—when it would have happened—though I expect I shouldn't talk about such with a young unmarried lady like yourself."

"Never mind, Mrs. Hacket. I am not such a young one. I do know where babies come from," Hannah assured her. "But I do not understand. Surely Mrs. Tettle and Mr. Logan were not—"

"No!" Molly's mother said vehemently. "He forced her."

"Oh, my God!" Hannah said in a horrified whisper. "He . . . he . . . *raped* her?"

"Same as done so," the old woman said. "He told her that her and Tobias would both lose their jobs—be thrown out on the street! They been savin' to have the baby's foot operated on. He was born with a club foot, you know."

"I am so sorry," Hannah murmured. "So terribly sorry." She sat for a moment trying to absorb the scope of the other woman's pain. Then she asked gently, "Do you have any idea where Tobias has gone?"

"I ain't real sure. But I think he probably went after that . . . that vermin, Logan."

"Oh, dear."

There was a groan from the other room, and almost simultaneously a knock at the door. Mrs. Hacket was too distraught to deal with both demands on her attention.

"You see to Molly. I'll see to the door," Hannah said, knowing it was probably the vicar's man coming to fetch her. As it was. She called a quick good-bye to Mrs. Hacket, promising to return soon.

All the way home, Hannah wracked her brain for something *she* might do to stop Tobias Tettle from bringing even more disaster upon his young family. The truth was, she had no idea of where to start. Perhaps her father . . . Then it struck her. No. Had Lord Amesbury not said he once worked with the Tettles? Surely he knew this Logan person, too. She quickly instructed the driver to go to Glosson Hall.

Knowlton was obviously surprised to find *her* at the Hall's entrance at this untimely hour.

"Miss Whitmore!"

"I must speak with Lord Amesbury," she said.

"He and Miss Stimson have only just sat down to supper," Knowlton said.

"This is an emergency, Knowlton. Please ask him to see me now."

"Yes, miss."

Theo looked up as the dining room door opened.

"What is it, Knowlton?"

"Miss Whitmore is here, my lord. She . . . says it is urgent that she speak with you."

"Show her to the library. Please excuse me, Aunt." He laid aside his napkin and rose.

He found the vicar's daughter pacing in the library.

"Good evening, Miss Whitmore."

"My lord. I am sorry to disturb you at supper, but this would not wait."

"Please. Have a seat and tell me how I may help."

"I'm not sure *how*—or even *if* you can, but I had to try," she said, taking the chair indicated.

He sat across from her in a matching chair and calmly crossed his legs. "Well, until you enlighten me, we will neither of us know, will we?"

"Oh, I *am* sorry. It is just . . . well, you once said you were acquainted with the Tettles, did you not?"

He felt a premonition slither through him. "Molly and Tobias. Yes, of course. Has something happened to either of them?"

"Something terrible. Too, too awful." She sounded very distraught.

Theo went to a sideboard, where he was happy to find a pitcher of water along with the usual assortment of liquors. He poured a glass and handed it to her.

"Thank you." She drank deeply.

"Now—suppose you start from the beginning."

When she had finished, Theo sat in stunned silence. He should have foreseen something like this. He put his elbow on the arm of the chair and covered his brow with one hand.

"I should have known," he said in an agonized whisper. *Hell! I* did *know and just let it slip from my mind. I knew about Logan—what kind of man he is*. "Poor Molly," he said aloud.

Miss Whitmore seemed to have regained her equanimity even as he was losing his. "I think Molly is beyond our help, my lord. But perhaps we are not too late to prevent Mr. Tettle's doing even more damage to himself and his family."

"Right." Suddenly, he was once again the "officer in charge." "I shall find Tobias. Perhaps you would go back to the Tettles' place and wait for him—for us? I shall see you home afterwards."

"I will need to stop by the vicarage first."

They set an hour by which he should turn up at the Tettles'. Later, Theo wondered why he had asked her to involve herself further. It did not immediately occur to him that *he* wanted her help in this crisis, that *he* gained comfort from her very presence.

Theo had no idea where to start looking for Tettle, but he did know where he might find Logan. The man was a despicable cur, but he should be warned about the rage of the man whose wife he had wronged. The Wild Boar was a tavern that prided itself on serving a certain "wilder" element of the district.

As Theo entered the establishment, a hush fell over the room. Wearing a dirty apron over a huge belly and brushing a hand at his greasy hair, the proprietor hurried forward.

"May I help you, my lord?"

"I am looking for Michael Logan," Theo said without preamble. He saw several men exchange wary looks.

The publican made a show of looking around. "He don't appear to be here."

"It is vitally important that I find him," Theo said. He raised his voice for the benefit of their avid audience. "It is in his interest that I find him."

"Uh . . . he was here a while ago," someone offered.

"Went out back, I think," someone else said.

Theo assumed "out back" meant answering a call of nature. "How long ago?"

"A long time," the man answered in dawning surprise.

"Show me the way," Theo ordered the publican, who quickly grabbed a lantern.

Several of the customers followed the two out the back way. There was no sign of Logan—and, to Theo's relief, no sign of Tobias Tettle.

His relief was short-lived.

"Over here," someone yelled, clearly alarmed.

The lantern revealed the man's grisly find. Some distance from the tavern, curled into a fetal position, lay the body of a man—Michael Logan. Nearby was a piece of wood that might once have been part of a fence railing.

"Oh, God. I am too late," Theo said.

He saw that Logan had been beaten far beyond mere punishment. This was the result of insatiable rage. Theo conjectured that some of the blows to the head and torso had been delivered long after Logan had been rendered insensitive to any more injury.

"Sweet Jesus," murmured one of the men, turning Logan over. "Somebody did a right proper job on 'im."

"Who coulda done such a thing?" another man asked.

"Lotsa folks mighta *wanted* to," yet another answered. "Logan was a mean one, he were."

"Yeh, but to do *this* . . ." the publican said in awe.

"Well, I know someone as would of had *reason* lately," still another said importantly.

They all paused and the publican shifted the lantern to illuminate the speaker's face.

"And who would that be?" one of the others demanded.

"Tobias Tettle, that's who. Logan was messin' with Tettle's woman."

One man whistled.

Another murmured, "You don't say so."

A sick feeling invaded Theo's gut. He could not help thinking he might have prevented this—somehow. Not that he cared about Logan so much. It was Tobias and Molly and their pain that shattered him.

"Notify the sheriff and the magistrate," Theo ordered the publican. "There will have to be an investigation."

Theo entered the Tettles' flat some time later to find Miss Whitmore sitting at a table with an older woman she introduced as Mrs. Hacket, Molly's mother. Theo acknowledged that he had met Mrs. Hacket in happier times when she walked out on a Sunday with the Tettles. Miss Whitmore's maid sat with them, looking somewhat stunned. The three were drinking tea from cracked pottery mugs. It occurred to him that Miss Whitmore had probably supplied the tea in the poor household. Mrs. Hacket had her arm around a young girl of eight or nine, and Miss Whitmore had a small boy of perhaps five years in her lap; a toddler lay asleep on a couch. He recognized the Tettle children.

"Is he here?" Theo asked.

Miss Whitmore rose, handed the boy to her maid, and stepped nearer him. He caught a scent of lilac that offset the smell of earth from the floor and of tea in the room.

"Yes, he is," she said softly. "He came in here looking disheveled, but calm and determined. He did not speak a word to us. I doubt he even saw us. Just went directly to his wife's bedside. He has not left it."

"Is she . . . ?"

"She died about half an hour ago."

"Oh, God," he murmured. He felt an urge to draw the woman before him into his arms and bury his own guilty pain in that mass of lilac-scented hair. But no gentleman could do such a thing.

Miss Whitmore touched his arm and spoke even more softly. "My lord? I think you should know there are . . . blood spatters on his clothing."

"I am not surprised," Theo said. He drew her farther away from the others and in a tone barely louder than a whisper, explained what he had found at The Wild Boar.

She drew in a long, shuddering breath. "I feared as much."

"As did I." He ran a hand through his hair. "I should have prevented it—all of it."

"You blame yourself?" she asked in surprise. "Somehow I missed hearing your name as the perpetrator of these heinous deeds."

He smiled fleetingly at her tone. "What is to be done here? The sheriff and the constable will undoubtedly be here soon."

The words were no sooner out of his mouth than there was a pounding on the door. Theo opened it to find the two law officers. The sheriff was obviously surprised.

"Wha—uh, good evening, Lord Amesbury. Didn't expect to find you here," the sheriff said.

"Sheriff. For the sake of these children, let us handle this matter discreetly," Theo said in a voice that was more an order than a request. "If you will just wait outside, I will bring you your prisoner."

"'Tis highly unusual . . ." the sheriff blustered, "but . . . all right." He backed out the door, taking the second man with him.

Theo entered the dark inner room, which was lit only by a single candle. The smell of burning tallow permeated the room, along with the stale, decayed smell of illness and death. Tobias Tettle knelt beside his wife's inert body, still holding her hand. He seemed to sense Theo's presence. He turned up a smudged, tear-stained face. He had not shaved in some days and he looked at least twenty years older than when Theo had last seen him.

"My Molly's gone," he said simply. "She's gone."

Theo laid a hand on his shoulder. "I know."

"But I made that bastard pay for what he done. Oh! Sorry, Molly. I know you don't like rough language." He patted the dead hand. "I got 'im, sweetheart. He won't never do this again."

Theo squeezed Tettle's shoulder. "Come now, Tobias. It's time to leave Molly be. You must come with me."

"Come—ah." Comprehension flickered in Tettle's eyes. "I . . . I suppose the sheriff is here, eh?"

"Yes. He is waiting outside. You may bid your family good-bye if you wish."

"Good-bye, my darling." Tettle leaned over to his wife's still cheek and then reluctantly released her hand.

In the outer room the little girl ran to her father and threw her thin arms around his waist. "Papa!" Her brother quickly joined them.

Tettle knelt and gathered them to him. There were fresh tears in his eyes as he kissed the top of each fair head.

"Patsy?" He looked intently at his daughter. "You take care of Toby and Jem for Mama and me now—you hear?"

"Yes, Papa."

"I must go away for a while. But you remember—always—that I love you. I love all of you *so* much." It was an anguished cry.

Theo, himself near tears, saw that all three women in the room were crying softly.

Tettle went to the couch and kissed the sleeping baby, kissed each of the older ones again, then straightened and faced Theo.

"I'm ready."

Hannah wiped at her tears as Lord Amesbury ushered Mr. Tettle out to the men waiting beyond the door. In a matter of minutes, the viscount returned. He regarded the three children solemnly. Hannah could see *dilemma* written all over his face.

"Mrs. Hacket and I have discussed the situation, my lord. Elsie and I will take the children to the vicarage for a day or two. There is a neighbor who will help Mrs. Hacket take care of matters here."

"Very well," he said with what she thought might be relief, but also admiration, and that thought pleased her inordinately. Then she wondered curiously if he had assumed she would fall to pieces in a crisis.

Mrs. Hacket gathered some meager belongings for the children and stuffed them into a cloth bag. Within minutes, it seemed, they were ready. To Hannah's surprise, Lord Amesbury picked up the sleeping toddler, handed him to Elsie, and himself picked up the other boy and settled him on one arm. He took the bag in his other hand.

"Ready?" he asked Hannah, who had hold of Patsy's hand.

Patsy twisted her hand from Hannah's and ran to her grandmother. "Gramma? Do I gotta go? Can't I stay with you?"

Mrs. Hacket hugged her. "No, honey. You go with Miss Whitmore now and I'll see you tomorrow."

"Promise?"

"I promise." The older woman looked to Hannah for confirmation. Hannah nodded.

Three adults and three children made for rather close quarters in the carriage. The children, emotionally and physically exhausted, fell asleep almost instantly. Hannah, sitting next to

Viscount Amesbury, was intensely conscious of him every time the carriage hit a bump and jostled them together. There was a prolonged, uncomfortable silence.

"I . . . I wish to thank you, my lord," she said quietly.

"There is really no need to do so," he said. "In fact, I thank you for making this easier than it might have been—both for me and the Tettle family."

"What is to happen to them now? I mean, the children and Mrs. Hacket."

"I do not know. Something will turn up, surely."

"It would be a shame were they to be separated," she said.

"It would," he agreed, but said no more until they arrived at the vicarage. He exchanged a few words with her parents, then bade them all good night and he was gone.

It crossed her mind that most men of his social status would just wash their hands of the Tettle family, but she somehow doubted that he would.

Thirteen

Within a few days, members of the Tettle household had been resettled, at least temporarily. Tobias Tettle was, of course, to be held in Crofton's gaol until the next meeting of the assize court—whenever the traveling judge put Crofton's issues on his docket. After conferring with Mrs. Hacket, the vicar had soon resolved the problem of the grandmother and the children. He caught Hannah as she and Patsy returned from school on the Monday following the incident. Hannah sent Patsy up to change into play clothes and followed her father into his small library.

"Turns out our Mrs. Hacket was married and widowed twice. Her first husband was Barclay," the vicar said.

"As in—" Hannah prompted.

"As in John Barclay. Liam Barclay, one of Glosson's tenant farmers, is her oldest child by the first marriage. Mrs. Tettle was her youngest—by the second."

"And Barclay is willing to take them in?" Hannah was surprised and pleased that it was working out so smoothly.

"He is," her father affirmed. "He and his wife lost their only child in that fever two summers back. His wife has never been very well. Seems he tried to persuade his mother to live with them before, but she felt her place was with her daughter."

"He will take the children, too?"

"Seemed glad of the idea of having young ones around again. He says it might be a bit crowded until he can see his way to adding another room to his cottage, but they will make do. After all, they are family, he said." The vicar was obviously pleased with the arrangement.

"What about Patsy's attending school?" Hannah asked.

"Barclay accepted the idea. Said it would be good to have someone in the family who could read and write."

"Well, then," Hannah said, "it does appear that 'all's well that ends well.'"

"Strange how disaster in one corner of God's universe opens up opportunity or provision in another," the vicar said.

"And wonderful." Hannah smiled. She knew already the topic of her father's next sermon.

In the days following, Hannah saw nothing of Viscount Amesbury. She heard talk of him, of course. There was no escaping hearing about him. "The viscount this" and "the viscount that" seemed a favorite topic of gossip wherever she happened to be. His polished appearance, his fine figure on a horse, his gracious manners, his ease of conversation—all recommended themselves to shopkeepers, to Hannah's students, and to callers at the vicarage. Most of the talk seemed approving—he was what one would expect of a member of his class.

Just what one would expect, Hannah thought grimly.

So far he had taken not one step to answer the very legitimate complaints of the workers in his mill. So far as she knew, he had simply walked away from the Tettle family without a backward look. Honesty forced her to admit that he had indeed been there during the worst of the immediate crisis—and that the principals in the affair were Mayfield's employees, not Glosson's. But had the viscount not claimed some acquaintance with the Tettles?

Perhaps he was simply too preoccupied with other matters. The gossip also informed her that Mr. Moore had returned to the Hall. She wondered if the two elegant young men were too busily engaged in sporting events to trouble themselves with anything of a serious nature, then mentally chastised herself for such an uncharitable thought. She had also heard that Lady Olivia Sanders and Miss Anne Bridges were visiting a Sanders relative in Manchester, which was only an hour or so away.

The problem was, she thought, she found the *man* intensely disturbing, but the mill owner, the high-ranking member of society, was an enigma. He *seemed* concerned and caring, but so far in the weeks and months he had been in Crofton, there had been few changes for Glosson's working people. On the other hand, there were four new children enrolled in the Crofton Parish Day School. The parents of three of them worked in the Glosson Mill and the other was the son of a Glosson cottage weaver. They were older children, ranging from ten to thirteen years; two were from the same family. She wondered if Lord Amesbury had had anything to do with their enrollment, but, in fact, all four had simply appeared one morning requesting admission. Hannah welcomed them warmly.

"It's a start," she said to Jane later.

"But you have no idea why they suddenly appeared now—when the school year has only a few weeks left?"

Hannah shrugged. "I have no idea. But I am *not* looking the proverbial gift horse in the mouth."

"I would venture to say that Lord Amesbury had something to do with it," Jane mused aloud.

"He may not have voiced strong objection, but I don't know that he encouraged such a step. Frankly, I doubt he cares one way or the other."

"You are rather harsh in your judgment," Jane said mildly, but she dropped the subject.

Throughout the winter and early spring, Hannah had attended, albeit sporadically, meetings of the Crofton Corresponding Society. She mostly went to such gatherings with Henry Franklin, though occasionally she was accompanied by her maid and the two of them welcomed the reluctant escort of Elsie's younger brother, Benjamin. Some in the parish undoubtedly considered Miss Whitmore's attendance at these meetings rather peculiar—even scandalous, if truth be known—but the workers accepted her. Even young Benjamin seemed to do so, though he chafed at having his sister involved in his "business." Still, he seemed to take manly pride in providing escort for the two women. Elsie had quietly thanked Hannah for helping to curb Benjamin's enthusiasm for the more outlandish suggestions of the group led by Jack Slater.

Thus, Hannah attended a meeting with Elsie and Benjamin one evening while Tobias Tettle yet languished in gaol—along with the accused poacher, George Kinney. In Hannah's mind, these two were both victims of injustice; she thought of them whenever the Society's heated debates turned to the suspension of habeas corpus and the helplessness of common people in opposing measures taken by "them." *They* and *them* needed no explanation—the Society meant both the London government as a collective oppressor and any members of the upper classes, who, of course, made up the government.

Occasionally, there would be an out-of-town speaker to help maintain worker enthusiasm—someone from a connected Society in a larger town, even London. On this night no such speaker was planned, but Hannah sensed a high degree of tension in the room when she arrived.

The chairman rapped for order and started through the usual schedule of business. Hannah breathed a little easier. Then a man rose in the middle of the room.

"Mister Chairman," he said decisively, "I move we suspend the usual order of business to listen to Jason Osborn's account of what happened to his little girl today in the Glosson Mill."

"Hear! Hear!" several others agreed.

"I shall take that as a second to his motion." The chairman's tone was ironic. "All in favor?"

Soon a somewhat nervous and obviously distraught man in the nondescript garb of a mill worker stood before them.

"My . . . my little Bess . . . she got her hand caught in the gears of a loom."

"Tell 'em why!" a woman called out.

"Well, it was mid-afternoon, you see." The father warmed to his story. "Bess—she has only seven years—she'd been at work cleanin' around the looms since six in the mornin'. An' I s'pose she fell asleep—maybe still standin' up." He paused.

"Go on!" someone shouted.

"The overlooker on her floor—ye all know Benson?—he's one of those likes to use the lash. I never wanted my girl on that floor. He . . . he whipped at 'er and she were so startled, she stumbled an' . . . an' . . . it just happened. The gears. Mangled her hand, they did. They called the doctor. Me an' her mama was called down to the second floor, too."

"Then what happened?" a woman in the front asked in a quieter tone.

"The doctor . . . he . . . he cut off her hand!"

Hannah gasped in horror.

The father's voice ended on a suppressed sob, then he caught hold of himself. "He hadda do it. I could see that. But my poor, pretty little Bess. What kinda life's she goin' ta have now? Who'll want ta marry her when she's all growed?" His note of despair gave way to general murmurs of sympathy and outrage.

Hannah was shocked and incensed at what she had heard. She instinctively jumped to her feet. "Mr. Chairman!"

"The chair recognizes Miss Whitmore."

"First of all, I want to express my sympathy to the Osborn family." She paused as her condolences gave way to fury. "But I should like to point out that this was a senseless, wholly unnecessary accident. It need not have happened!"

Again, there were murmurs of "Hear! Hear!" but Hannah ignored them and went on.

"The root of this problem—the cause of what happened to Bess Osborn *and* the Tettle family—lies with mill owners and their stewards who care far more about their profits than they do about the people who produce the goods—and the profits! *They* are ultimately responsible for what happens to innocents like this poor child! Without their tacit approval, overlookers like Logan and Benson would never be allowed to mistreat women and maim children as they have!"

"Right she is!" a male voice said. Others offered loud agreement.

"Somebody should show 'em they can't treat people like animals an' get away with it," a younger man said vehemently. Hannah thought his name was Ian Cochran. She was not personally acquainted with him, but she knew he was fairly new to Crofton. Later, when the meeting had dissolved into an angry uproar, she observed Cochran in heated conversation with Osborn and another man whom Benjamin identified for her as Osborn's brother.

With more words of approval, several people thanked Hannah for speaking out as she had. Once she calmed down a bit, though, Hannah herself felt somewhat chagrined over her outburst. Truth it may have been, but she had been carried away by her own sense of outrage—again. She went home unable to shake the feeling that she had gone too far.

The next day, she knew she had.

Henry Franklin met her and Jane as they left school in the afternoon. Jane greeted him warmly.

"Mr. Franklin. What a nice surprise."

Hannah found herself envious of her friend's obvious happiness in the mere presence of the man. Would the vicar's daughter ever have cause to feel so about a member of the opposite sex? And why, in heaven's name, did the image of the viscount pop suddenly to mind? She shook her head, annoyed with herself.

"I have come to see you two lovely ladies home," Franklin said, guiding them to a waiting carriage. "Also, because I need to speak with you, Miss Whitmore."

"Oh. Well, I can walk home as usual." Jane looked and sounded a little crestfallen.

"Not at all," Franklin said genially. "I would not dream of your going alone."

Jane protested, "This is Crofton—not London or Manchester or—"

"Humor me, Miss Thomas," the lawyer said, nudging her gently toward the carriage.

Hannah entered after Jane and deliberately took the opposite seat. When Franklin sat next to Jane, Hannah saw a flush of pleasure cross the other woman's face.

Hannah turned her attention to Franklin to ask, "What is it?"

"I heard about last night's meeting," he began in what Hannah thought must be a non sequitur.

"Then you know about that poor child being injured so horribly—and needlessly." Hannah felt her ire rising all over again. "And only because *some* people just want to be richer and richer—and never mind the cost in human misery!"

"Hannah," Franklin admonished in the manner of one who had once climbed apple trees and tickled trout with her. "You are getting carried away again."

"Some things are worth getting carried away about," she replied, but in a more subdued tone.

"I agree," he said. "However, I have just come from the Glosson Mill and there are some things you should know."

"Such as . . . ?"

"Viscount Amesbury dismissed his steward, the steward's secretary, and the overlookers on each floor of the mill this morning."

"He *what*?" Hannah sat in wonder as Franklin repeated himself. Then she asked in a near whisper, "Why?"

"The incident with the Osborn child was the precipitating factor, but he has had those men under investigation for some time."

"Really?" Hannah was both curious and surprised.

"As a matter of fact, I think his investigation of his brother's death has been thwarted by the action he took this morning, but Theo said it was time—past time—to take action on other matters."

Hannah noted Franklin's use of the viscount's given name. When had those two become so close?

"Other matters?" she asked.

"Yes. We talked at length and I think you should know he is genuinely concerned about such things as workers' hours, the conditions in which they labor, and workers' housing."

"Well, I must say he has taken his own sweet time to come to those concerns," Hannah said.

"You always want everything to have happened yesterday," her friend accused. "Perhaps he *has* been rather slow to take action, but I know for a certainty that he only recently acquired some of the information he needed to act with justice and firmness."

"I . . . see." Hannah tried to sort out in her mind just what it was she did see. What she saw immediately was that she undoubtedly owed Lord Amesbury an apology.

Jane, who had been quietly interested in the conversation, now said softly, "It . . . it would seem we have misjudged his lordship."

Shooting Jane a look of gratitude for that generous "we," Hannah murmured, "Oh, dear." Hannah Whitmore hated having to apologize at any time, but this apology was going to be especially difficult.

Franklin said, "In view of your comments at last night's meeting—if the report I heard is true—I thought you should know what transpired today."

"Yes. Thank you," Hannah said. They were all three silent for the few moments remaining until they reached the vicarage. Hannah bade them both good-bye and entered the house, deep in thought.

Later, after supper, she sat in the parlor with the rest of her family. The vicar had mentioned with approval the actions taken by the viscount that morning. Mrs. Warren, the housekeeper, entered quietly and said to Hannah, "Young Mr. Britton is here at the kitchen door, miss. He insists he must speak with you."

"Benjamin?"

"Yes, ma'am. You want I should send him away?"

"No, no. I will see him." She rose and followed the housekeeper back to the kitchen.

She found Benjamin looking very agitated. "What is it, Benjamin?"

"Miss Whitmore! The Osborns and another feller— they're goin' to—to grab Lord Amesbury."

Apprehension clutched at her. "Wha—what do you mean, 'grab him'?"

"They're plannin' to beat him senseless, they said. Give 'im what for, they said. Pay 'im back for what happened to the girl." Benjamin reported all this in a breathless tone.

"Oh, my heavens! Oh, my heavens! We—I—must *do* something. Where? When?" She knew she was babbling in panic and fear. She took a deep breath, willing herself to think clearly.

"The Osborns an' this other feller—they didn't go to work this mornin' an' they been off drinkin' somewheres. My da heard 'em talking an' he sent me to warn Lord Amesbury—but he's not at the Hall."

"Perhaps the Osborns will not be able to find him either," Hannah said, clutching at this straw.

"Da said somethin' about them goin' out to wait on the road to Horton," Benjamin said.

"Horton?" Horton was a small village about five miles from Crofton. Hannah knew the Glosson interests spread that far and much farther. "Was his friend Mr. Moore with him? I believe he has been a guest at the Hall for several days." If there were two of them, she thought, the viscount might escape unharmed.

"No. *He* went to Manchester. I checked with a Glosson stablehand when that toplofty butler wouldn't tell me nothin'."

"I see," she said admiringly. "You are a resourceful lad, aren't you, Benjamin?"

"Yes, ma'am." He glowed momentarily at the praise. "But we got to stop 'em, miss. We got to."

Hannah was a little surprised at Benjamin's intensity, but then he had always been good-hearted. She was not surprised at the intensity of her own feelings. She was overwhelmed by guilt. Perhaps if she had not been so vehement in that meeting . . . And all the while Lord Amesbury *had* been at least considering improvements for his workers. She had laid sins at his doorstep that did not belong there—or at least not to the degree she had accused him.

Hannah made her decision quickly. "Yes. We must stop them—or at least try. But we must act discreetly. There is no point in having the unfortunate Osborns hauled before the law." *Especially for something that might not have happened at all, but for me*, she thought. "I think I can talk them out of any adverse action they plan—if you will help me."

"Anything, Miss Whitmore."

She sent Benjamin out to the stable to order three horses saddled and to explain the situation to Noel, the vicar's stablehand and general handyman, and ask him to accompany them. Thank goodness her clergyman father was not one of those poverty-stricken churchmen who could barely afford a hack for himself! She returned to the parlor door and caught her father's attention to draw him out. She quickly explained things to him.

"Hannah! You cannot go haring about the countryside at night. 'Tis far too dangerous."

"Papa. I must. It is probably my fault, you see. I am sure the Osborns will listen to reason. They are good people, deep down. And Benjamin Britton is going with me."

"He's only a boy!" her father protested.

"A very big boy, Papa. He is nearly six feet tall and he holds down a man's job. And I shall have Noel with me as well."

Her father reluctantly acquiesced, and Hannah dashed to change into a sturdy riding habit. Fear and anxiety turned her fingers into thumbs. She envisioned horrifying images of the viscount helpless and vulnerable to attack.

Once they were under way, Noel said, "The most likely place for an ambush on Horton Road is that little knoll just beyond the Newland farm. There's a little copse of willows along a creek there."

Hannah nodded and bit her lip as she urged her mount to

a faster pace. Even angry and upset as he was, she doubted that Mr. Osborn intended to kill the viscount, but accidents happened, did they not? An image of Lord Amesbury lying lifeless on the road flashed through her mind and she felt an appalling sense of loss surge through her.

"Please hurry," she called anxiously to the others.

"We daren't run the horses too hard in the dark, miss," Noel said. "We're just lucky to have so much moonlight as we do."

Clouds skittered across the moon even as he spoke, casting darkness everywhere, but only for a few moments. Then the road was quite clear—a ribbon lying before them with occasional shadows cast by wayside trees.

They rode as hard as Noel said they dared, but every minute dragged interminably for Hannah. She knew it would take a half-hour or more before they reached the spot Noel had mentioned. Horrible images of what could happen in a half-hour flashed through her mind. She was nearly sick with apprehension.

Suddenly, as they rounded a curve in the road, one of those terrifying images erupted into reality. The play of shadows on the road made it difficult to take in the scene wholly. However, a figure lay on the ground and two—no, three—others stood over him. One of those standing raised a club high in the air.

"No-o-o!" Hannah screamed and dug her stirruped heel into the flank of her horse, driving the animal directly at the man with the club.

Fourteen

The last two weeks had been extremely busy ones for Theo. He was well aware that the men involved with misappropriating funds from the mill would have to be dismissed—especially Taggert, who appeared to have engineered the whole thing. However, Theo wanted a smooth transition, which meant having people in place to take over those supervisory positions before he rid himself of the thieves. After all, they had been stealing for years—a few more days or even weeks would do little harm.

At least that was his thinking before the Osborn child was injured. Out that day checking on some overdue improvements on tenant farms, he had returned late in the afternoon to find his steward waiting for him. Theo sensed a degree of agitation that the steward tried to hide.

"What is it, Taggert?" Theo gestured to a chair in the library and bade the man sit.

Taggert sat on the edge of his chair, looking distinctly uncomfortable. "There's been a bit of a mishap and one of the younger workers was slightly injured."

Theo raised an eyebrow. "Slightly injured?"

"She apparently fell asleep and stumbled into some machinery. One of her hands was amputated."

"An amputation? You call that 'slightly injured'? Good God, Taggert." Theo stared the man down. "How old is she?"

"Seven or eight."

"A babe. And working around dangerous machinery."

"There's younger ones than that, my lord," Taggert said in a slightly patronizing tone. "Both in the mill and in the cottages."

"The fact that it *is* done does not mean that it *should* be done." Theo paused. "Fell asleep, you say?"

"Yes, my lord."

"How long had she been working?"

Taggert ran a forefinger around his neckcloth. "Uh . . . I'm not sure. Probably arrived around six—after that, workers are fined for being late."

Theo did not immediately respond to this. At six in the morning he had only just arisen from his bed—and a child of eight years was expected to report for work then!

Taggert spoke nervously. "The thing of it is, my lord, Osborn . . . he's . . . well, he's a bit of a hothead. No telling what he might take it in mind to do."

"Have you spoken with him?"

"Uh . . . no. Osborn and his wife took the girl home right after the doctor came. The doctor went with them and then he came back to report to me."

"All right. Here is what you will do," Theo said. "You are to go to Osborn's place and offer our sympathy and assure the parents that the child will be properly looked after."

Taggert's jaw dropped. "You want me to visit a mill worker in whatever hovel he occupies?"

"Precisely." Theo's tone was matter-of-fact.

"But I don't have much to do with workers," Taggert protested. "The overlookers handle those things. And how are such expenses to be handled? I don't mind telling you the doctor had to be assured of payment before he would treat a mill brat."

"A true son of Hippocrates, eh?" Theo could see his irony was lost on the steward, so he added with a significant look at Taggert, "I am sure the mill profits can handle the doctor's expenses."

Taggert refused to hold Theo's gaze. "Uh . . . yes. I suppose they can."

"I am quite confident they can. But the important thing

now is to assure the Osborns of our concern. I would go myself, but I have a pressing matter to attend to this evening. And, as you are more immediately connected with them than I, the Osborns would probably welcome your assurance more than mine at the moment. You may inform them that I will call upon them tomorrow."

"Yes, my lord." Taggert was obviously not happy with this chore, but he voiced no overt objection to an order from his employer.

When Theo returned late that night, Knowlton handed him a note from the steward. Taggert had conveyed the viscount's message to Mrs. Osborn, but her husband had gone out for the evening. Theo had also had a full account of the incident from Yardley and another worker, who were both incensed at the cavalier attitude taken by the overlooker, whom they saw as the culprit in the accident.

Theo had been deliberately vague with Taggert about the "pressing business" requiring his attendance that evening. At a respectable inn not far from Crofton, Viscount Amesbury was to meet with other owners of textile mills in Derbyshire and Lancashire. Ten or twelve men were crowded into the small, private parlor, but Theo soon recognized that only about five of them would carry the evening's debate. Besides Theo, the five included Lords Kitchener and Mayfield, a Mr. Bridewell, and a Mr. Childress, who had initiated the meeting.

Theo knew, on receiving the invitation, that he would be an outsider at such a gathering. After all, he was a newcomer to their brotherhood. Also, there was his unorthodox introduction to the area. All except Mayfield greeted him with an attitude suggesting they reserved judgment. Mayfield was not precisely hostile, but neither was he openly welcoming. Theo wondered what had been said prior to his late arrival.

"Strictly speaking," Childress said when the new arrival had been greeted, introduced all around, and offered refreshment, "this meeting is probably illegal." He was a short man of middle years with a round body, a round face, and close-set, dark eyes. "However," he went on, "we are not here to set wages or prices—are we?" He winked and then chuckled knowingly. "Besides, who would bring charges against *us*? Several of us are magistrates ourselves."

"Right," Lord Kitchener agreed. He, too, was a man of middle years. He was tall, with a shock of white hair that gave him a distinguished air.

Theo instantly disliked both men, but he had come to this meeting to listen—and listen he would.

"Well, let's get down to business," said Bridewell, who was probably ten years older than Childress and Kitchener. "We need to present a united front—especially after that Pentrich incident."

Mayfield shot Theo a telling look at this comment. Theo maintained an attitude of polite interest, but refused to jump in with immediate agreement.

"Yes." Childress seemed determined to hold onto the controlling position in the meeting. "We must not bend to the unreasonable demands of rabble-rousers."

The others in the room nodded agreement.

"What of reasonable requests from one's own workers?" Theo asked.

Lord Kitchener took the condescending tone of a schoolmaster toward an ignorant pupil. "I think you will find, Amesbury, that most of their 'requests' are arrant nonsense."

"Instigated by greedy bounders who profess to speak for the multitudes," said Bridewell, clearly unwilling to surrender his authority as the eldest member of the group.

"I have not found this to be *my* experience," Theo said calmly.

"You are too new to this business of running a mill," Kitchener said, using his schoolmaster tone again.

"True," Theo conceded. "However, I am not new to directing people to achieve an objective."

"This is not the army, Amesbury," Mayfield said derisively.

"Also true," Theo said, swallowing the retort he would like to have given the other. "However, the people with whom we work are not unlike soldiers in the field."

"Ex-soldiers!" Bridewell sneered. "They are the worst of a bad lot. I tell my steward not to hire those sorts if he can help it."

"And we don't work *with* them," Mayfield added. "They work *for* us. You need to keep that fact in mind."

Knowing he was unlikely to sway their views, Theo did not respond. He listened with growing dismay to their calls for stricter measures and for magistrates to exercise their authority to suppress even the faintest hint of revolt. Of course, the word *revolt* was open to interpretation, but a preemptive measure was by far preferable to letting things get out of hand—or so the argument went.

"Well, gentlemen—are we agreed?" Childress asked finally.

There were general murmurs of agreement.

"Amesbury?" Childress challenged.

Theo was deliberately noncommittal. "You have given me much to think about, gentlemen."

"You're either with us or against us," Mayfield said.

"What does that mean?" Theo did not bother to suppress the edge to his tone.

Childress tried to smooth over any rift before it started. "Lord Mayfield is merely suggesting that we be united in our stance regarding worker agitation. As the representative of the largest textile enterprise in our area, you, especially, will appreciate the necessity of—shall we say—keeping a lid on things."

Theo spoke quietly but firmly. "With all due respect, gentlemen, I also see a need for some changes. The nation—*the world* is changing. And it is doing so at a pace that is staggering. I believe we—people like us—should take the lead in dealing with the changes—just as we took the lead in adopting new techniques and machinery in our mills."

Kitchener snorted. "I, for one, have no intention of allowing a bunch of rabble-rousers to tell me how to run my business and dictate what their hours and wages should be. It's *my* mill. It will be run *my* way."

"Right!" Mayfield and Bridewell agreed simultaneously, and several others voiced approval or nodded vigorously.

Theo tried another tactic. "The ancient Greeks taught us that the only constant in life is change—"

Bridewell interrupted. "That's revolutionary talk!"

Theo ignored him. "In my view, the thinkers—leaders—of a people can direct the changes for good or ill. And such direction begins with men like us."

"What do you mean, 'men like us'?" Childress asked with what seemed genuine curiosity.

"I am not letting anyone dictate to *me*," Kitchener repeated stubbornly.

"Hear him out," Childress said.

Theo felt suddenly that he had come to some sort of crossroads. Somehow he had been journeying for a very long time to this precise point. It was vitally important that he bring these men with him.

"Men like us," he repeated, "men who, in effect, control the lives of the people we employ. We can use that control to make our world better—or we can let matters develop willy-nilly and live with the consequences."

"England is not ancient Greece." Mayfield barely concealed his contempt. "What—exactly—are you proposing?"

"Most workers want only what *we* want—a better life for themselves and their families," Theo replied.

"They want what we *have*, you mean," Kitchener said. "And I, for one, am not giving up anything I have to the general riffraff." He looked around smugly.

Theo looked around the room to find the majority seemed to agree with Kitchener, though some seemed to be waiting expectantly for his own reply. He drew in a breath and continued, "None of us would be giving up so very much—and it would certainly be in our own best interests to see workers better fed, better housed, better clothed—and better educated."

"Aha!" Mayfield pounded one fist into his other palm. "You are in league with that bothersome vicar's daughter, aren't you?"

"I have given consideration to Miss Whitmore's views," Theo admitted. "While I may not endorse her degree of enthusiasm, her ideas have fundamental merit."

"And she's a dashed good-looking female," someone said with a snicker.

Theo was surprised at his instant anger over a comment that was, on the surface at least, relatively innocent. He quelled the anger and went on calmly. "I have also visited a number of men all over England who own manufactories—men like Owens, Whitbread, and the Wedgewoods."

"Bunch of bleeding hearts," Bridewell said dismissively. "Just trying to make silk purses of sows' ears."

"Right," Kitchener said. "The lower classes are always with us. God ordained it that way."

"I believe that is the argument of slave owners in the Americas," Theo said dryly.

"Well, now, perhaps those fellows have the right of it," Kitchener said.

Childress intervened. "Come, gentlemen. Can we not come to some consensus here?"

"I ask you again, Amesbury," Mayfield challenged, "are you with us or against us?"

There was an expectant hush as all waited for Theo's response.

"Perhaps . . . neither," he said slowly. "I intend to make certain changes that are within my power, but I do not require that anyone else follows suit."

"Good God, man! Have you missed the point here entirely?" Kitchener asked. "We need to present a united front."

"You don't want to be a traitor to your class, now do you, son?" the aged Bridewell cajoled.

"I hardly think my loyalty is a matter of question," Theo said coldly.

"No, no—of course not." Childress again tried to smooth things over.

Pressed, Theo agreed that he would consider what the others had said, but that his final decisions would be made in the best interests of his own people. Forced to accept this ambiguous response from the man representing the most powerful textile holdings in their area, the others left the meeting rather disgruntled.

In the taproom, Theo met David Moore, who had insisted on accompanying him.

"After what happened to your brother, we cannot have you roaming about alone at night," Moore had said over Theo's protests when he returned to Glosson Hall some days before. "Why, Jeffries and Jenkins would have my guts for garters."

"Oh, is *that* why you returned to Derbyshire—to serve as my bodyguard? And here I thought it was the proximity of one Miss Bridges."

Moore had grinned sheepishly. "That, too, of course."

Now, as the two of them rode back to Glosson Hall, Moore said, "Those other fellows did not appear very happy as they came out of your meeting."

"Nor are they." Theo told Moore all that had transpired.

"Better tread softly, Theo. I don't think Mayfield likes you much." Moore paused. "Miss Bridges told me Mayfield had been to Manchester to pay his respects to Lady Olivia."

"Is that so?" Theo asked mildly.

The next morning, Theo made the promised visit to the Osborns, but like Taggert, he found the father gone from home.

"Did Mr. Taggert not tell you there would be no need for either of you to report to work for the rest of this week?" Theo asked the mother.

"Oh, yes. He told me. But my Jason—you see, he ain't been home yet." She sounded worried and frightened. "He didn't come home last night—an' that ain't like him. But he were awful tore up about Bess's hand, you see."

Theo conveyed his regrets to Mrs. Osborn and assured her that not only were both her job and her husband's safe, but that he himself would see the child properly cared for. Mrs. Osborn seemed pitifully grateful.

Prior to setting out for the Osborn residence, Theo had sent a note to Taggert requiring the steward, his secretary, and the overlooker from each floor of the mill to be available later.

When the appointed time came, Theo, along with Moore and Yardley, made his way to the steward's office. Leaving his companions in the outer office, Theo found all seven men waiting nervously in Taggert's inner office. He stepped into the room.

Waving them back to their seats, he stood, legs apart, just inside the door. "Remain seated, gentlemen. This won't take long." He paused and they waited, obviously growing increasingly apprehensive.

"May I venture to ask what this is all about, my lord?" Taggert's voice was silky.

"I think you have probably guessed," Theo said. "I am dismissing all of you for cause. You have one hour to gather your personal belongings and leave Glosson property."

"What—? What do you mean?" the man Theo recognized as Benson blustered.

"Exactly what I said," Theo replied. "You are all finished. You will steal not another farthing from my family." He looked directly at Benson. "Nor maim another child on Glosson premises."

"You're turning us all off—just like that? Just because Benson here can't hold back with the whip?" one of the other overlookers whined.

"Just like that—and without references," Theo said grimly. "Nor is it because of Benson's love of lashing helpless children. You know very well that you have all been party to ongoing thievery. I will no longer tolerate it."

"I assume you think you have proof for this ridiculous allegation," Taggert said, sounding somewhat arrogant. Theo had to admire the man's sheer brass in the face of destruction.

"I have proof enough to satisfy me of the theft—some of it in your hand or your secretary's." Theo looked at Taggert and the secretary in turn, neither of whom could hold his gaze. "And there are a number of witnesses who can confirm actual production with what was reported from each floor."

"I didn't want ta be involved with nothin' like this—they made me," said the whiner.

"Shut up, Trask," growled another. "Can't you see it's over?"

"An' you got your share," another said.

"I thought you said when that other one died, we'd be all right." The one named Trask seemed to address the room at large.

"*Shut up*, Trask!" the growler said more vehemently. Trask seemed to sink into himself.

"If you are so sure of your evidence," Taggert said, still sounding inordinately calm, "why have you not brought the law into this?"

"I may yet do so," Theo said. "Our investigations are by no means complete. When they are, you may be sure charges *will be* filed."

"If you can find us," sneered one.

"The only ones I shall look for very hard are those who may have been in any way responsible for my brother's death. Them—or him—I will hunt down like a rabid dog." A steel-like quality in Theo's tone seemed to chill them. "Now—all of you—collect your gear and get out."

"What's to keep us from chargin' at you right now?" Benson asked with more bravado than sense.

"Us, perhaps?" said a casual voice behind Theo, who stepped aside to reveal Moore and Yardley, each with a pistol in hand.

The fight went out of them and within the hour all seven were summarily escorted off Glosson property.

Theo then ordered all machinery shut down and had Yardley gather all the workers together. He found the members of the five separate crews of workers jammed tightly among the looms on the ground floor. Men and women alike were obviously nervous and frightened. They knew the overlookers had been turned off and, illogical as it might have been, they clearly wondered if they were to suffer the same fate.

Theo had mulled over many of his ideas for some weeks, but had actually planned what he would say to them only the night before—after that unsatisfactory meeting with other mill owners. Now, he laid out his proposals.

He began by telling them he was well aware of their being required to work extra hours and that their hours would no longer exceed the standards of other mills, though he expected production at the level Taggert had consistently reported on the "official" books. Then he shocked them by announcing that Glosson Mill would no longer employ any child under the age of twelve years. However, for any child under that age currently employed, the mill would continue to pay half that child's wages—*if* the child went to school. Those twelve and over could have the option of working half a day if they went to school the other half. New overlookers would be assigned soon. Theo already had certain men in mind for two of the positions, but not all of them; he invited any who might be interested to apply for those still open. He then sent them home on a paid half-holiday to think about and discuss his proposals.

Over the midday meal at the Hall, he and Moore discussed the morning's events. Miss Stimson, who was not feeling well, dined in her room.

"What are you going to do for a steward?" Moore asked. He made a sweeping gesture. "Surely you will not consider handling all this yourself. I know how you love working with ledgers!"

Theo grimaced. "I shall have to do so, though, until I can find help. Too bad you are not available. You were always good at supplies and logistics in the army."

"Hmm. I may have a solution for you." Moore grinned. "Of course, if it works out, you will owe me a large, unpayable debt."

"And if it does not?"

"You will not hold me responsible."

"I see. Heads you win. Tails I lose."

"In a word," Moore said smugly, his eyes twinkling.

Theo gave an exaggerated sigh. "All right. Let us hear this brilliant solution."

"My younger brother, Andrew."

"Young Andy? You must be joking."

Moore laughed. "He *was* 'young Andy' when you and I set off for Spain ten years ago. He is twenty-five—no, twenty-six—now. He works in London at Whitehall and hates government work. Wants to be in the country."

"And you think he could handle the job of Glosson steward?"

"I am quite sure he could—and not just because he is my younger brother."

"Then why does he not handle your own family's not inconsiderable properties?" Theo asked.

"We *have* a steward who has been with us nearly fifteen years. Neither my father nor I would think of turning him off. Nor would Andrew approve of our doing so."

"Well, if you think he would be interested in being steward here . . ."

"I shall write him tonight when we return from Manchester," Moore said.

Theo slapped the heel of his hand against his forehead. "Good Lord. I forgot we had talked of visiting in Manchester. I must go to Horton. I promised some of the cottage weavers there that I would visit today."

"Oh." Moore sounded disappointed. "Well, it was not a definite commitment. Horton it is, then. The ladies will be there tomorrow, too. At least Anne will be."

"No. No. I would not keep you from your lady love. You go ahead. And do make my apologies to Lady Olivia."

"Are you sure? Something could happen, you know."

"Do stop being such a worrier. You sound like an old woman. I shall be armed—and I will ride rather than take the coach. I shall probably be here sipping brandy long before you return."

"Well . . . if you insist . . ."

"And I do."

The trip to Horton was uneventful. Theo visited with three weavers, encouraging them to send their children to school. They promised to consider the idea. The visits had taken longer than he anticipated and the moon was fully up before he started home.

Fifteen

"No!" Hannah yelled again, urging her mount directly at the man with the club.

He threw down the cudgel and, along with the other two, immediately took flight.

"Go after them, Noel!" Hannah ordered. "Benjamin, you stay with me—I may need help with Lord Amesbury."

"Yes, ma'am."

She dismounted and hurried to the prone figure of the viscount. He was as still as death and she smothered a cry of distress. She felt at the base of his throat to find a healthy pulse, and when she put her ear next to his chest, she discovered a vigorous heartbeat.

"Thank goodness," she murmured.

"Is he . . . ?" Benjamin's tone was fearful.

Hannah, frantically trying to determine the extent of the man's injuries, did not immediately respond. Blood flowed from a gash near the hairline of his forehead. She found a neatly folded handkerchief in his jacket pocket and pressed the cloth against the cut. When she lifted it a moment later, she saw that the injury was a minor laceration, but, like all head wounds, it bled profusely. She replaced the cloth and, holding it in place with one hand, used her other hand to lift his head into her lap. She felt for other wounds to the head and found an egg-shaped lump on the base of his skull.

She breathed a sigh of relief. "I—I think he will be fine. We arrived in time."

"Good," Benjamin said. "But what do we do now?"

"His horse must have bolted. Please try to find it. I shall see if I can bring him around. It will be much easier for us if his lordship is conscious."

"Yes, ma'am." Benjamin remounted his horse and quickly departed.

Silence closed in on her momentarily. Then she became aware of the wind whispering through the willows, a cricket calling, and a frog croaking.

Hannah checked the cut on her patient's head again. The bleeding had stopped. She wiped at the smudges of blood on his face, saying a silent prayer of thanksgiving that his wounds were no worse. There was something infinitely heart-wrenching about seeing this vigorous man lying here still and helpless—he who was usually so full of energy and exuding a sense of latent power.

She gently slapped at his cheeks. "Lord Amesbury! Do try to wake up. Can you hear me, my lord?"

He moaned, twisted his head away from the last blow, and grabbed her wrist in a surprisingly strong grip. "Stop," he said. He opened his eyes and looked up into her face, clearly trying to grasp the situation. "Miss Whitmore? It is you, is it not?"

"Yes, my lord. Oh, thank goodness you've come around. I am so sorry, my lord. I never meant for anything like this to happen."

He rolled his head back and forth and attempted to rise. She pressed his shoulders back down.

"No. Please, my lord. You must lie still until help comes. Noel and Benjamin will return shortly. Please just lie still."

"I think not," he said with a touch of arrogance. He managed to rise to his knees. He put his hand to his head. "Ooh. I *am* a little dizzy." He held that position for a moment as she rose to her feet.

"Here. Lean on me," she said, helping him to a standing position.

"They startled my horse. Not an army horse, that one. He bolted and dumped me. Rather embarrassing, it is." He moaned as he touched the knot on the back of his head. "I shall have a right smart headache, I think." His voice sounded increasingly stronger. He took a step away from her, no longer needing her help to stand.

"I am so very, very sorry, my lord. This is all my fault. I should never have—"

"I am grateful that you came along when you did."

As he clearly regained his self-control, she found herself losing hers. "You don't understand!" In her anxiety, she was unable to control her rising voice or the catch in it. "It—it *was* my fault. All my fault. I am so sorry."

"*You* startled my horse?" he asked in surprise.

"No, not that. I never meant—Oh! I am so glad you will be all right. It was my fault." She sobbed, partly from guilt, partly from relief. She who had been so calm at the height of the crisis now could not control her near-hysteria.

"Miss Whitmore." He put his hands on her shoulders. "It is all right. *I* am all right."

"No!" she cried. "You don't understand. I—"

He silenced her cry by pulling her closer and settling his lips on hers. This did, indeed, silence her. She was startled into utter stillness. Then, slowly she moved closer; her arms went around his neck, and she responded fervently.

He lifted his mouth from hers even as his arms tightened to pull her closer. "It's all right," he murmured. "You must stop crying." He showered quick little kisses over her face, then sought her lips again. This time, it was a deep, searching, questioning kiss. Hannah's response was a search of her own. When they finally parted, she felt bereft—she had found no answer to the searching, the questioning.

"I . . . I . . . Oh." She felt her face flaming and was grateful for the dim moonlight. "You must think me shameless."

"I think nothing of the sort," he said softly. "I—it seemed a better idea than slapping you to shock you of your hysteria."

"Oh. I—I see."

"I suppose I owe you an apology and I do most sincerely apologize for any embarrassment or discomfort I caused you."

"No. Not at all," she said. "That is what I have tried to tell you—'tis I who owe *you* an apology."

"Whatever for?"

"Because . . . this—the attack—was all my fault." She stood before him with her hands tightly clasped in front of her. "Had I kept quiet at the meeting of the Corresponding Society, Osborn and his brother might not have acted as they did."

"So it *was* Osborn. I thought so."

"Yes, and it was my fault. I am to blame. I hope you will find yourself able to forgive Mr. Osborn. If I—"

"Please, Miss Whitmore—"

She went on, rushing past his words. "Henry told me about your turning off Mr. Taggert and the others. And—and I feel simply terrible about the whole thing." She stifled another sob.

He raised a hand in a "halt" motion. "You must stop this self-flagellation. While your enthusiasm may have encouraged those men, believe me, the decision to waylay me this night was theirs alone. *They* are responsible for their actions."

"I—you are very generous, my lord."

Whatever he might have said in reply was lost, as Noel returned just then.

"I lost 'em," he said sadly. "They took off in some heavy undergrowth an' I just lost 'em."

"Never mind," Lord Amesbury said. "They will not have gone far."

"You did your best," Hannah assured him.

A moment later, Benjamin rode up, leading the viscount's horse. "Found him grazing just as calm as you please."

The viscount helped Hannah mount her horse, then took to his own saddle. The four of them made the return journey without incident, though Hannah noticed Lord Amesbury putting a hand to his head now and then. For her part, she could not divert her mind from that shattering kiss. She blushed anew in the darkness as she remembered her own response to it: she had wanted it to go on and on. She relived every nuance of what had passed between her and Viscount Amesbury. She forced herself to attend the occasional words passing among the other three, but always her mind reverted to that kiss.

Later that night—long after sending Benjamin to accompany his lordship home, and long after seeking her own bed—she continued to replay the scene. She was embarrassed at her behavior, but thankful that Lord Amesbury had not made much ado about it. After all, what would a viscount find to interest him in a vicar's daughter?

There was also, of course, the fact that there seemed some foundation to rumors linking Viscount Amesbury and Lady Olivia Sanders. That young lady clearly had the endorsement of the Countess of Glosson—and was the marquis's lovely daughter not enjoying a prolonged visit very near Crofton?

Hannah pounded her pillow viciously and willed herself to sleep.

Theo's head had begun to throb long before he reached Glosson Hall.

"I was about to turn out the troops to look for you." David Moore sounded worried.

"I miscalculated the time," Theo said. He told Moore of the evening's events, carefully omitting that searing kiss he had shared with Miss Whitmore.

"She rescued you?" Moore asked disbelievingly.

"In a word—yes."

"Don't you know it is the *male* of the species who is supposed to go around rescuing damsels in distress—not the other way round?"

"Yes, yes. I know. But I was damned glad she arrived when she did."

"Sounds to me like it was little enough she could have done," Moore said icily.

"'Twasn't her fault," Theo said.

"Perhaps not directly, but—"

"It's over," Theo said emphatically. "Done. Finished. And right now I need to see if Burton has anything for this abominable ache in my head."

Once the cut was bandaged, a light snack and some herbal tea helped ease his pain. Theo crawled into bed, confident that he would hold the dreams at bay this night. It was a long time before he slept. He kept recalling the feel of Hannah Whitmore's body pressed to his, the feel of her breasts against his chest, her arms around his neck, her luscious lips beneath his own.

He had no business kissing her. No business at all. He cautioned himself against reading too much into her ardent response. The woman was distraught and people under the influence of strong emotion often behaved out of character. He reminded himself that there seemed to be a very strong tie between Henry Franklin and Miss Whitmore. That was a match that surely both families could approve. Moreover, the lawyer was a good man. Theo was annoyed to recognize that this admission came grudgingly.

He lay staring at the underside of the canopy over his bed. The faint light from dying coals in the fireplace picked out a pattern in the brocade that he scarcely noted.

He willed his attention to other matters. What should he do about Osborn? Tettle's trial was coming up soon. Would there be any possibility Tobias could come out of that debacle alive? And what about this George Kinney? The man had languished in gaol all this time largely on the accusation of Taggert. Why should he continue there on the word of a felon? Perhaps Theo could have a word with the assize judge before proceedings started. The judge would arrive in this circuit in July.

Theo was half asleep when the vision of Hannah Whitmore's blue-gray eyes, enhanced by moonlight, invaded his consciousness yet again.

What *was* it about that blasted female?

* * *

The school holiday for the summer had started before the date set for the trial of Tobias Tettle. Hannah, accompanied by her father, edged into the back of the crowded courtroom. As she looked around, two other members of the audience caught her attention—Lord Mayfield and Lord Amesbury, sitting on opposite sides of the room.

Prior to the court's hearing the Tettle case, George Kinney was brought before the judge.

That austere official looked down at the accused and announced, "Prisoner George Kinney has been charged with the crime of poaching. The sentence for such a crime is seven years' transportation."

A collective intake of breath was audible in the courtroom. George Kinney was well liked in Crofton and most of his neighbors considered him to be the victim of both a harsh law and a vindictive man. Hannah held her breath along with many others as the judge went on.

"The alleged crime is said to have been committed on land owned by the Earl of Glosson. Lord Glosson's son, as the earl's representative to this court, has indicated that the earl has no wish to prosecute. Therefore, the prisoner is free to go."

Smiles and murmurs of approval greeted this announcement, though other landowners seated with Lord Mayfield glanced at Lord Amesbury and scowled. It was an anticlimactic ending to months of incarceration and uncertainty for Mr. Kinney. He looked bewildered. His wife, seated behind a bar separating the spectators from the officials of the court, reached her hand toward him and wept tears of joy.

Hannah jerked her head in the direction of Mayfield and his companions and whispered to her father behind her hand, "Those gentlemen are not happy with this decision."

"They undoubtedly feel this turn of events will undermine their own authority somehow," the vicar said softly. "They dislike thinking a poacher got away with something. Crimes against property raises their hackles more than any other misdemeanor."

"If so, in this case, they backed the wrong horse. And poor Mr. Kinney has paid several-fold for a rabbit in his family's stewpot. Months in gaol!"

"But he might have been transported," her father reminded her.

There were two other minor cases that required a judgment of the assize court before the bailiff finally called the case of Tobias Tettle. A stir went through the courtroom as the prisoner was brought in wearing shackles. The prosecutor, in a quick presentation of his case, called upon the man who had found Logan's body and drew from him sensational and grisly details. He called others who testified to Tettle's making threats against Logan. He then called Lord Mayfield to the witness box. Mayfield testified as to Logan's reliability as a worker and supervisor in the spinning mill. The prosecutor made much of the fact that, in losing such a dependable, productive worker, Mayfield, too, was a victim of Tettle's heinous crime.

Tettle, as was the custom, was given no opportunity to challenge information offered by any witness against him. Nor could his lawyer do so. In fact, Tettle sat quietly throughout the proceeding, his head bowed. Hannah's heart ached for the ruined lives he represented as he sat there.

As the prosecutor finished his presentation, the judge addressed the jury. "Well, gentlemen, this case appears to be cut and dried. Would you not agree?"

The members of the jury, local people overwhelmed by the dignity of the bewigged and black-robed visiting judge, all nodded their agreement.

"There remains only the matter of passing sentence. In such a crime as this—one aggravated by the extreme brutality inflicted on the unfortunate victim—the law is not only clear but just in mandating that the perpetrator of such a deed be hanged, drawn, and quartered."

Hannah gasped. She saw Tettle visibly flinch at this announcement, but he continued to keep his head down.

The barrister appearing on Tettle's behalf now rose.

Hannah had gone to Henry to ask him to step in to provide some degree of defense to Tettle, who was sure to be convicted under any circumstances. She had been taken aback to find that Lord Amesbury had already consulted Franklin and that the two had arranged for a barrister to present Tettle's case in court. She crossed her fingers that the three men might have come up with some way of mitigating such a horrible sentence.

"May it please the court," the barrister began, "I should like to offer evidence that might moderate the court's view of the circumstances that have been laid before us today."

A buzzing of discontent came from the prosecutor and those seated near him.

The judge shared a mirthless smile with them and said, "I cannot see that one can moderate the view we have had of a vicious murder and a bloody corpse, but justice would appear to require that the defense be heard."

"Your honor, there are, in fact, extenuating circumstances to this case that have not been presented." The barrister then called several mill workers to the witness box to testify to Logan's pursuit of not only Molly Tettle, but any other comely young woman on his floor. He summed up their testimony and, after a brief consultation with Franklin, added, "I feel confident, your honor, that Lord Mayfield was completely unaware that workers supervised by the overlooker Michael Logan were, in fact, being used as Logan's personal bordello."

"Your honor!" The prosecutor jumped to his feet in protest and Mayfield shot a venomous glare at Tettle's lawyer. There was a rumble of conversation in the room.

The judge pounded his gavel. "Order! That was over the top, sir."

"I apologize to the court," the barrister said.

However, Hannah could see that the evidence and the comment had hit a sensitive nerve with the jury—and perhaps with the judge as well.

"Have you finished, then?" the judge asked the barrister.

"No, your honor. I should like to call one more witness."

"Very well."

"The defense calls Theocritus Euripides Ruskin, Viscount Amesbury."

A murmur went through the courtroom. Some of it undoubtedly centered on the new witness's unusual name, but most of it came from the unlikelihood of a peer's rising in defense of one having no higher station than that of Tobias Tettle. The judge pounded his gavel again as Lord Amesbury took the seat in the witness box.

The preliminaries over, the barrister asked, "You were acquainted with both the accused and the deceased?"

"Yes, sir, I was—with *both* the deceased persons. That is, with both Mrs. Tettle and Mr. Logan."

"Please tell the court your view of the circumstances of this case."

Lord Amesbury's voice was firm and authoritative. The room was absolutely still as he talked. "I observed things and events very much as have been described here. While I do not in any way condone the killing of Michael Logan—I have seen quite enough such carnage in my day—I can understand what motivated Logan's executioner. Logan was a man deserving of punishment."

"Then you *do* condone the killing," the prosecutor shouted, jumping to his feet again. He pointed to Tettle. "This . . . this man could not keep his wife in his own bed and his failure to do so drove him to slay the man who could."

Hannah saw Tettle wince at this and say something to Franklin. Franklin, in turn, wrote something on a note and handed it to the barrister.

"Your honor," the barrister said in a voice of exaggerated patience, "we are not here to besmirch the character of a dead woman who, by all accounts, was a good wife and mother."

Hannah had feared the exact circumstances of Molly's death would be revealed, but so far all that had come out was that she suffered a miscarriage. She was sure that few in the entire district knew the realities of the situation.

"Continue, Lord Amesbury," the judge instructed.

Lord Amesbury then described an incident in which he personally had interrupted Logan in an assault on Mrs. Tettle. "I thought that would be the end of it. But to my everlasting regret, it was not." He paused. Hannah now understood what the viscount had really meant on that awful night of Molly Tettle's death.

Amesbury continued, "Lord Mayfield has testified that, in effect, he lost a valuable property in losing Logan from his work force. But I would draw the court's attention to the fact that Logan was, in effect, stealing Mr. Tettle's property when Logan appropriated what rightfully belonged to Mr. Tettle—his wife's services. The law makes a wife the property of her husband. Any man of any worth at all has a right—a God-given right as a free-born Englishman—to redress the wrong when his property is thus stolen from him. Had Logan stolen a cow or a horse from Mr. Tettle, this very court would undoubtedly have sentenced *him* to be hanged, drawn, and quartered."

Hannah gasped in outrage at this line of argument.

She heard a chorus of soft cries of "Hear! Hear!"—including some from the jury box. It was obvious to her that Lord Amesbury had struck a sympathetic chord among the men with his argument. However, Hannah Whitmore was infuriated. How dare the man reduce any woman—especially a loving wife and mother—to the status of an animal, a mere piece of property?

"You present a very cogent argument, Lord Amesbury," the judge said solemnly. "The fact remains, though, that Prisoner Tettle did willfully kill another human being. Therefore, the court sentences him to be transported to New South Wales, where he will serve a term of not less than twenty years at hard labor."

Hannah surmised that this, too, was probably a death sentence, but there was an outside chance that Tobias Tettle would survive. She knew that former prisoners had been known to return to England—or, more often, to make for themselves satisfactory lives in that fledgling country "down under."

So, perhaps Lord Amesbury's argument had carried the day. Still, Miss Hannah Whitmore found his basic premise to be both specious and highly offensive.

As he left the courtroom, Theo was feeling decidedly pleased with himself. He had managed to have one man restored to his family and had seen that the life of another was spared. Not a bad day's work. Not bad at all.

In the hall outside the courtroom, he saw the vicar and his daughter standing with Henry Franklin. He smiled cordially and would have greeted them and stopped to chat, but Miss Whitmore gave him a cold, forbidding stare that put him off.

So—she had had second thoughts about that kiss. He watched with some regret as she took the lawyer's arm and the two of them left the building with her father.

Sixteen

Hannah always considered the summer holiday far too short. Invariably, she had twice as many projects for that season as there was time to achieve them. This year she cut her customary month-long visit to the Folkestons to two weeks. She had traveled to Folkeston Manor, grateful for even a short holiday with them. She and the baroness lingered over a late breakfast one morning.

"I *must* return early," she replied to Claudia's protests. "Lord Amesbury has encouraged his workers to send their children to our school and I am hoping that other mill owners will agree to do so, too."

"Is your *whole life* involved with that school?" Claudia's tone was gentle, but disapproving.

"It does take up much of my time—yes."

"Surely Crofton has something to offer in the way of society," Claudia wailed. "Surely there are dances and soirees of a sort. Surely there are some eligible gentlemen in the district."

"Oh, dear," Hannah said in mock surprise and dismay, "you are not singing *that* song again, are you? I had thought us quite finished with that last year."

"*I* am not finished at all. Nor should you be. You are not so long in the tooth as to be ineligible. And you *do* have a satisfactory portion in that legacy from your godmother."

"Yes, the Winslette estate near Barnsley is a handsome legacy, indeed. I suppose one day I will live there with some ancient maiden relative as companion."

"Oh, Hannah, you cannot mean that."

"But I do," Hannah said cheerfully. "Mind you, I would not be averse to marrying—if my heart were engaged. So far, however, that organ remains firmly indifferent." Well, perhaps not quite so firmly where a certain viscount was concerned, but Hannah was not about to admit this to Claudia.

"You know," Claudia said slyly, "I ran into Horatio Smythe-Jones in town last winter. He is Baron Castlemaine now."

"I heard he had succeeded to the title."

"He asked about you most particularly."

"Did he now?" Hannah asked with a quirk of one eyebrow. "Did he also make a point of mentioning that the Castlemaine property is adjacent to the Winslette estate?"

"He may have done so. But so what? Many a fine marriage has begun with just such a consideration in mind. And the man *is* sinfully handsome."

"Not to mention wholly self-centered."

"We all have our little faults," Claudia said airily.

"So he is Lord Castlemaine now," Hannah mused aloud. "At last he has equal standing with his friend Lord Mayfield. I always thought Mr. Smythe-Jones resented being a mere 'mister.'"

"Perhaps he did. 'Twould not be unusual."

Hannah deliberately changed the subject. "I suppose you also saw my sister Katherine during the season?"

"Yes, I did—occasionally. Such a sweet girl." Claudia sipped her coffee. "At least your aunt allowed *her* to dress in more flattering gowns than she ever assigned to you."

Hannah chuckled. "Katherine has a stronger will about such things than I did—*and* a greater sense of style."

"Rutledge's heir was paying her a good deal of attention."

"So I heard. Katherine was quite flattered. Poor Dorothea. Her nose would be quite out of joint if our younger sister were to catch the heir to an earldom."

"How would she feel if her older sister were to do so as well?" Claudia asked.

Hannah tried to keep her composure. "I have no idea what you are talking about."

"Oh, do you not?" Claudia teased. "There has been no announcement of Amesbury and Lady Olivia Sanders—though the whole town knows she spent all those weeks in Manchester trying to bring him up to scratch."

"I wouldn't know," Hannah said.

"In any event, he is still an eminently eligible gentleman."

"Who will marry Lady Olivia if his mother has *her* way."

"The man strikes me as being far too independent to allow that to be a deciding factor," Claudia said. "Look at how he is defying the general trend regarding mill workers."

"Perhaps you are right." Hannah found herself foolishly hoping Claudia *was* right. But that way madness lies, she cautioned herself and changed the subject again by asking her friend about the Folkeston children.

When she returned to Crofton, her first project was to talk to other mill owners to try to persuade them to follow Lord Amesbury's lead.

She met with little success.

Lord Kitchener and Mr. Reginald Childress owned mills near enough to Crofton that children of their workers might have attended the Crofton Parish Day School. Neither of these owners was eager to listen to her pleas.

Kitchener saw no need to educate people "above their station."

When Hannah asked if he might not profit from having a better educated cadre of workers, his reply was, "It does not take a literate man or woman to pull the handles and work the pedals of a loom." His tone was cold, his manner unbending.

Hannah pointed out to him that Lord Amesbury, in charge of thc most extensive holdings in the district, was encouraging his people to take advantage of what her school offered.

"Amesbury marches to his own set of pipes," Kitchener said with a hint of a sneer. "If he is wise, he will stop going it alone as he is presently doing."

She found Mr. Childress unwilling to go against the general opinion of other mill owners. "Too much schooling might make the lower classes even more demanding, and the good Lord knows they already are behaving outlandishly. Above themselves, they are. All this agitation for a greater say in Parliament—when everyone knows we take right good care of them."

Hannah forbore pointing out to this obtuse man that perhaps the point was that folks would like to speak for themselves.

Finally, she met with Lord Mayfield again. She did so most reluctantly. As he had with her visits to the other two mill owners, the vicar accompanied his daughter. Both the daughter and father were well aware that it would never do for a young, single female to make such calls on her own. They met with Lord Mayfield in the library of Mayfield Manor. Hannah looked around at the multitude of leather-bound volumes with rich, gold lettering. Impressive, she thought, but I wonder how many of these books have even had their pages cut?

Taking a seat behind the fortress of his desk, Mayfield was cool, but polite—at least at first. "I suppose you have come about your school." He sounded a bit put-upon—*and* condescending, but at least he addressed his remarks to *her*, not her father. "I understand you have already been to Kitchener and Childress."

"Yes, I have been," she replied. "They were not very cooperative. However, I thought if I could persuade you of the great benefits to be offered children, they, too, might come around, for *you* seem to have the position of leader among mill owners." Hannah and her father had agreed that a little flattery might work with Mayfield.

The baron quickly quashed that idea. "My views have not changed one iota since our last discussion on this matter."

"Lord Amesbury seems to think an educated workforce would be advantageous to the running of a mill." She saw immediately that mentioning Amesbury had been a mistake.

Mayfield's countenance took on a stony quality. "What Amesbury does, he does without any consideration of how it might affect others. He is an outsider and he is making trouble where it need not exist."

Not knowing how to respond to this, Hannah glanced at her father, then said, "I . . . uh . . . had no idea you felt that way."

"Well, I do. The man is creating problems for the rest of us. And I am certainly not going to aid and abet him in the idiotic ideas he promotes."

"About educating children, you mean?"

"Among other things," Mayfield said vaguely. "Now—for the last time, Miss Whitmore—let me make this perfectly clear to you so you will not feel compelled to waste either my time or your own again." He spoke very deliberately, as though he addressed a want-wit. "The children of workers at Mayfield Mill will *not* be attending your school. Not now. Not ever."

"I am not sure I understand, my lord." Good heavens, she was sounding like a want-wit herself.

"Allow me to make it even plainer to you." His tone bordered on being nasty. "If any Mayfield worker attempts to enroll a child in your school, he, his wife, and any other brats they have working in my mill will no longer be Mayfield workers. The same goes for those ill-conceived adult classes you have been conducting. Is that quite clear enough for you?"

Hannah was stunned by his vehemence. "I am sorry you feel as you do, Lord Mayfield. I have an idea your attitude will end by making it more difficult for you to maintain the best workers."

Mayfield smiled with a distinct lack of warmth. "Amesbury cannot possibly hire *all* the textile workers in this part of Derbyshire."

Hannah merely gave him a cool little nod. "Come, Papa. I believe my business here is finished. Thank you for your time, Lord Mayfield."

"I wish I could say it has been a pleasure," he replied as he rose. "I trust you will not waste my time with this matter again."

"On that, you may rest assured," she said. "I will not approach *you* again. But neither will I stop trying to persuade people of the merits of educating their children."

"You stay away from Mayfield workers," he said in a threatening tone.

The vicar spoke for the first time since polite greetings had been exchanged as the meeting began. "My daughter knows her own mind, sirrah. She will do what she thinks is right, though I can assure you she will respect your *property* rights."

Once they were outside, Hannah said to her father, "I did not handle that well, did I?"

"He is a hard man—accustomed to having his own way and to being in charge. You have challenged him—and he cannot like that."

For the next few weeks, Hannah talked up the merits of education to anyone who would listen. She addressed the issue formally at a meeting of the Corresponding Society, praising Lord Amesbury's encouraging his people to take advantage of the school. She could see that this was a point of some pride with the Glosson Mill workers and a cause for envy with those employed by other mills. She also pressed her case with individuals at church, at the butcher's, at the baker's, and on the streets. She knew that delegations of workers had tried to discuss the issue with Mayfield, Kitchener, and Childress—but to no avail.

A few weeks after the new school term started, she began to notice that workers' enthusiasm for sending their children to school seemed to diminish. Even some of the Glosson workers and cottagers seemed reticent to entertain the idea of sending their children to what was commonly known as "Miss Whitmore's School." Parents actually withdrew a couple of students. Hannah was mystified and no one would discuss the matter with her.

Then events accelerated and her problems seemed minuscule by contrast to what was happening to others.

Theo struggled during the weeks of late summer and early autumn to learn all he could about the earldom he would one day inherit—much of which he was already responsible for.

Andrew Moore was detained in London, so initially Theo was forced to be his own steward. He managed to find suitable replacements for the five overlookers he had turned off. Two of the five were the former sergeant, Yardley, and Tim Hessler, whom Theo hired away from Mayfield's mill. Tim happily joined Glosson workers. Another was the man Melton, who had been a spokesman at that early meeting Theo had observed between Taggert and the workers' representatives. The other two were men readily acceptable to people they would supervise.

In a short while, things seemed to be working smoothly. There were no more fourteen- and fifteen-hour workdays, so the workers were happier, though clearly some felt the financial pinch when their young children were no longer employed. Production held up—and was even better than shown on the specious books Taggert had given his employer. Theo surmised that the offer to pay for children attending school was not likely to take as big a bite out of the mill's profits as he had feared.

He happily welcomed the delayed arrival of Andrew Moore as his new steward. The young man quickly settled into his new position.

"He's as good as you said he would be," Theo told David Moore at the end of the younger Moore's first week in the position.

"I am glad to hear it," David said. "One always has some apprehension about recommending a family member to someone else."

David Moore had stayed intermittently with Theo for some months now, going to London for a few weeks at one time and, on another occasion, paying an extended visit with his family. Theo knew that David was actively courting Miss Bridges, but the young woman's father was apparently holding out for a title for his daughter. When David was absent, Jenkins or Jeffries were likely to arrive for visits. When none of them was available, Theo was aware that Hessler and Yardley seemed frequently in the vicinity of the Hall. He knew very well what they were all doing, and he was grateful for their concern. Until the death of his brother was resolved once and for all, it was far better to err on the side of caution. What if that incident with the Osborn brothers had been the work of Francis's killer?

Theo had had a long, serious set-to with the Osborns and their friend. In the end, the three had been genuinely contrite, so he had kept them on. Somewhat surprisingly, they turned out to be among his most loyal and able workers.

One evening Yardley asked to speak with Lord Amesbury. Knowlton again delivered the former sergeant to the library.

"What is on your mind, Yardley?" Theo asked cordially as the two of them sat down. "I trust there is nothing untoward with your work?"

"No, my lord. The work is fine. I've come about some strange rumors that are going around, and I thought you ought to know about them."

"Rumors? What about?"

"Two things," Yardley said. "One of them concerns Lord Mayfield. Not that I don't think he probably deserves anything bad as happens to him."

"What is it?" Theo asked, feeling an inkling of foreboding.

"I'm not real sure *what* it is—like I said, it's mostly rumors."

"But you do think there is something to them," Theo stated rather than asked.

"I think there *might* be. The fellows involved are being pretty tight-lipped about it. But there's talk of a bunch of 'em goin' to smash machines in Mayfield's mill."

"Good God! Why?"

"It sort of started with that Tettle business. Nobody liked the way Mayfield just let Logan loose on the women that way."

"Is that all?"

"No, my lord. Seems that Mayfield Mill has financial problems and Mayfield's overlookers have been driving the workers real hard—longer hours, one man doin' the work of two—that sort of thing. People don't like that. Especially when they see what's happening here." Yardley grinned and went on. "Anyways—you know someone named Cochran?"

"Ian Cochran. I know who he is."

"Well, there's some as don't trust him at all. He was real cozy with that Oliver fellow who caused that ruckus at Pentrich."

Theo rose and stood near the fireplace. "So what has he done?"

"Nothin' real partic'lar—it's all sort of vague and shadowy—but it seems he's the one been eggin' folks onto smashin' machinery—he tells 'em General Ludd should rise again."

"And Mayfield is their target?"

Yardley nodded.

"Only Mayfield?"

"So far as I can tell. Lots of innocent folks could get hurt in a thing like this."

"You are absolutely right," Theo said, "and I thank you for bringing it to my attention."

Yardley nodded again. "I s'pose you know Taggert is still around? Seems all them others got out of Crofton quick as they could. But Taggert—he's workin' for Mayfield now. Struttin' around, big as you please."

"Hmm." Theo found this news somewhat disturbing, but surely Mayfield was aware of the nature of his new man. "That was not your second set of rumors, though, was it?"

"No, my lord. That's pure fact." Yardley paused, looking a bit uncomfortable. Finally, he blurted out, "The other rumors concern Miss Whitmore."

"Miss Whitmore? What about her?" Theo felt an even stronger sense of alarm. He had seen little of the vicar's enticing daughter since the trial, though she had made a point of calling with her father to thank him for his support of her school. He had thought she would be glad of Tettle's reprieve from hanging, but she had offered nothing beyond saying it was nice that his life had been spared.

"Some are sayin' she is too forward a female and she is a bad influence on children."

"She is *what*?" Theo was instantly angry. He saw Yardley flinch at his tone.

"That's the rumor, my lord. A bad influence, they say. They're also sayin' she jilted a lover and she should not be allowed to associate with children and young people."

"Corrupting the youth, eh?" Theo said, thinking of an ancient teacher who had fought the same shadowy adversary. Socrates had at least had a full life prior to such an accusation.

"That's the idea," Yardley said, his tone solemn.

"Ridiculous!" Theo snorted. "Why, the woman cares more for her pupils than most of their parents do."

"I know, my lord. But some are sayin' her morals are weak."

"Ridiculous!" Theo said again. "*Who* is spewing out such garbage?"

"No one I've talked with seems to know where it started an' a good many folks ain't believin' it—but they's enough that do to keep the rumors flyin'."

"Oh, my God," Theo said in disgust.

"You know how some folks like to see others taken down—an' her bein' a vicar's daughter—"

"Makes her a ready target," Theo supplied.

"Yes, my lord."

"Perhaps this will blow over—after all, there is no fire at all for *this* bit of smoke." Theo projected more confidence than he felt. A jilted lover in her past? Could that be? He felt a surge of what he clearly recognized as jealousy at the very idea.

"That was my thought, too," Yardley said, "but I thought as you'd like to know about it all the same—given what you've said about the school an' all."

"Thank you," Theo said quietly.

After Yardley left, Theo sat for a long while musing over the conversation. He felt a fierce protectiveness toward the vicar's daughter, but he could see no way to express such in a public manner. Also, he felt he should warn Mayfield, but he knew the other man was still furious because Theo had not toed the line drawn by the collective mill owners. Franklin would probably have no more success than Theo himself. That "bordello" comment at Tettle's trial had made the rounds and Mayfield was intensely sensitive to anything that smacked of ridicule. Theo went to bed, still uncertain what course he should take.

Early the next afternoon, he had an unexpected visitor in the person of Miss Whitmore, accompanied by her maid. Elsie was sent off to the kitchen to visit with Glosson servants as Miss Whitmore was shown into the drawing room, where Theo sat talking with his Aunt Stimson and David Moore. Theo had told them of Yardley's visit and the unsavory rumors Yardley had reported. They discussed possible avenues of action.

Miss Whitmore arrived at the usual time for "morning" calls, though she must have come directly from her duties at the school.

After an exchange of polite, cordial greetings, Theo, still standing, said, "Miss Whitmore, if you have come to visit my aunt, David and I will make ourselves scarce."

"How very kind of you," she said. "I always enjoy Miss Stimson's company, but I actually came to discuss a . . . a problem with *you*, though Miss Stimson and Mr. Moore are ever so welcome to share it as well."

"Oh, well then . . ." Theo and David resumed their seats. "How may we help you?"

"It is not for me—not precisely. I—have you heard anything of plans some have to resume the actions of the infamous General Ludd?"

"Actually, we have." Theo gestured to his companions. "We were just discussing that very topic."

"Good. I need not recount all the rumors, then. I think there is something planned for tonight," Miss Whitmore said.

"Tonight? Oh, my!" His aunt's surprise verbalized Theo's own.

"Why do you believe it will be so soon?" Theo asked.

"Frankly, you might say I was eavesdropping. I overheard

two of my students talking. People are sometimes very careless about what they say in front of children."

"They forget that 'little pitchers have big ears'—is that it?" David asked.

Miss Whitmore smiled. "Yes. But given the proliferation of rumors lately about just such an event, I think there may be more to this matter than the usual chatter of children."

"Why?" Theo asked. "I mean why do you think this any more pertinent than other information?"

"My father heard the first rumors and went to Lord Mayfield to warn him."

"Oh. Well, Mayfield *has* been informed, then," Theo said with a nod of satisfaction that included all three of the others.

"He has, indeed," Miss Whitmore said. She continued to wear a worried frown.

"Come. Out with it," Theo prompted. "You did not come here only for this."

"Well, the truth is, Lord Mayfield did not seem at all surprised by my father's news. He assured my father that he was well aware of what was going on and that he had the matter fully under control."

"Yet *you* are concerned," Miss Stimson said.

Miss Whitmore turned toward the other female. "Call it woman's intuition, but I cannot shake the feeling that Lord Mayfield is up to something—and that it bodes ill for certain members of the Corresponding Society."

"Never underestimate the power of a woman's intuition," Miss Stimson said with a significant look at the two men in the room.

"Surely the Corresponding Society is not condoning violent behavior," Theo said.

"Those Societies are usually much more circumspect," David put in.

"And so is this one," Miss Whitmore insisted. "But . . . well . . . people can behave in an untoward manner if they are provoked enough."

"People are being deliberately provoked to go around the

countryside smashing machinery?" Theo's aunt asked. "Good heavens, why?"

Theo, who had been thinking of little else for most of two days, now felt he had an answer. "For the same reasons those poor fools were led to their 'revolution' in Pentrich."

"You think there is a government spy involved in this?" David asked.

"*Someone* is leading them down the primrose path," Theo replied.

Miss Whitmore nodded, her expression grim. "That is what I think, too."

"Can we stop it? Tonight?" David asked.

"We can try," Theo answered. "We *have* to try."

Miss Whitmore seemed to breathe a sigh of relief.

Seventeen

Hannah had debated with herself—and discussed the situation with her father—before consulting Lord Amesbury. The vicar, on returning from his meeting with Lord Mayfield, shared his concerns with his daughter, who had met him at the door and followed him into his study.

"I had the distinct impression when I spoke with him that Lord Mayfield did indeed know all about this plan long before I approached him," the vicar told Hannah.

"Is he taking steps to stop it?" she asked. "I have heard nothing of extra guards at his mill."

"Nor have I," her father said. "There has been no word of such on the street—nor in any of the meetings I have attended this week."

"Very peculiar," Hannah mused aloud.

"Not so very peculiar, if you think about it," he said. "Suppose you knew someone was planning something of a nefarious nature. Would it not make sense to allow them to proceed and nab them in the act?"

Hannah was shocked. "Deliberately allow people to be led into committing a crime that is a hanging offense? That is diabolical."

"I quite agree, my dear, but I cannot see another way to view this. And it worries me grievously."

"Father, it must be stopped. We cannot sit by and see people transported—or *hanged*."

"I know, Hannah. I have also tried talking with some of the mill workers who are members of our church, but they are generally unwilling either to listen to my concerns or share their own."

"And Lord Mayfield was adamant?" she asked.

The vicar rubbed his chin and Hannah thought he looked tired. "When I mentioned the serious consequences of letting the situation proceed, Lord Mayfield told me in no uncertain terms that it was not my affair. He insisted that the owners are tired of costly demands from workers and perhaps one good lesson will show them the error of their ways."

"I shall discuss it with Mr. Franklin in the morning," she said. "Perhaps he can reason with some of the mill workers."

"I hope he can." There was not much conviction in her father's voice.

Later, as Hannah considered the issue yet again, she could not bring herself to believe that Lord Mayfield's comments to her father included *all* the local mill owners. Lord Amesbury had made changes in his mill. He might well have an arrogant, domineering view of women, but he had ensured that mill children—children from *his* mill—could be schooled. Also, he had stopped employing very young children. He seemed to care for his people—or at least to look out for their welfare.

Of course, she reminded herself, such care of his employees was ultimately in his own best interests, was it not?

She knew from her discussions earlier with the three other local mill owners that Lord Amesbury was not exactly welcomed to their ranks with open arms. Still, he *was* one of them. Perhaps he could head off this impending disaster.

Then she overheard those two boys talking and the matter took on greater urgency.

Hannah had not been invited to take part in any of Franklin's discussions with workers. Nor had Lord Amesbury and Mr. Moore offered to make her privy to *their* plans. She fumed a good deal about the arrogance of men. She was determined to be on the scene that night—regardless of whether these superior males approved.

However, she was not so defiant of propriety—or so fearless—as to jaunt about the countryside alone at night.

"I don't know, miss," Noel said, looking worried. "Your da—he won't like this."

"I will take full responsibility, Noel. I assure you—you will not be turned off for my actions."

"Still . . ."

"Look. If you will not accompany me, I shall have to take Elsie with me and you know as well as I do that if anything *were* to happen—well, it will not, of course, but if it *were*—you would be a far better companion than she."

"Yes, but . . ."

"Or, I *could* go alone." Hannah knew she was putting poor Noel in an untenable position.

"All right, miss," he said with a reluctant sigh.

Near midnight, Hannah met Noel in the stable where he waited with two saddled horses.

"Are you real sure about this, miss?" he asked with the air of one making one more try to reason with the unreasonable.

"Yes. Let's go."

They rode to the edge of Crofton where the Mayfield Mill was located.

"We shall wait in those trees across from the mill," she said.

"How long?"

"I have no idea. Not more than an hour or two, I should think."

They dismounted and found a fallen tree on which to sit and wait. They had a clear view of the darkened mill and the road that ran in front of it. It was a chilly November night and, while it was not raining, the air was damp. They both pulled their cloaks tighter about them. As they waited, Hannah's eyes became increasingly adjusted to the darkness and she could distinguish lighter shadows from darker forms. The windows of the mill showed up clearly against the night-colored walls.

After a while she said, "Listen. Did you hear that?"

"I didn't hear nothin'," Noel said quietly. "Oh. Maybe. A kind of shuffling sound."

Soon enough, she could make out shadowy figures approaching the mill from different directions. All was relatively quiet. She was about to yell at them when there was a loud crack! as of a door being forced open. Shortly afterwards, a light appeared on the first floor and there was the sound of huge hammers against cracking wood and metal.

Suddenly, there was pandemonium and things happened so fast Hannah really only pieced the events together later.

Even as a lone rider approached, dismounted, and entered the building, there were yells of surprise and pain and triumph from within. At the same time, a small group of riders approached along the road and several figures darted from the building with others in pursuit.

One of the figures fleeing from the mill ran straight toward Hannah and Noel. She recognized Benjamin Britton. Before she could call to him, one of the approaching riders came between them.

"Here! You!" the rider yelled. Hannah recognized the voice of Lord Amesbury. Then his voice rose in surprise. "Britton? What in hell are you doing here?"

"Uh . . . I dunno . . . now." The boy sounded scared.

"Well, never mind for now." Lord Amesbury quickly dismounted. "Here. Hold my horse—and try to make it look like that is all you are here for."

"Y-yes, my lord."

The other riders, too, dismounted. "Damn! We are too late," Amesbury said. "Mayfield must have had men inside waiting for these poor lobcocks."

"Th-they was," Benjamin said.

"What do we do now, Major?"

Hannah could not identify this speaker.

"Control the damage—if we can," Amesbury said.

Deciding to make her own presence known, Hannah stepped forward and asked, "May I do anything to help, my lord?"

Amesbury whirled toward her. "Good God! Have you no sense at all, woman? You have no business here!"

She raised her chin. "Well, I *am* here all the same."

"So you are," he said grimly. "Just see you stay out of the way. Britton, watch her—along with my horse."

"Yes, my lord."

Hannah fumed at his dismissing her so summarily, but she did as he told her—until men with torches began herding others out of the mill. She recognized several of those who were clearly captives as members of the Corresponding Society, including Mr. Henshaw. Also being prodded along with the other was Henry Franklin.

"Oh, Henry! No!" she screamed and ran toward her friend.

She felt strong arms grab her and hold her in place. "I *told* you to stay back," the viscount growled in her ear. "Here, Hessler. Keep her back."

The man took her arm rather firmly in his own. "Sorry, miss."

The two groups of people were close enough now to identify each other.

"You're too late, Amesbury." Mayfield sounded intoxicated with his triumph. "We've captured the ringleaders—including that damned lawyer, Franklin. I always knew he was in this business right up to his ears."

"No!" Hannah yelled. "No! He was trying to prevent a tragedy."

"What?" Mayfield said in surprise. "The meddlesome schoolteacher, too? Oh, this *is* good!"

"Hold on, Mayfield," Lord Amesbury said. "Miss Whitmore arrived with me and I am sorry to see that we arrived too late to avert this mayhem."

"Hmphf!" Mayfield snorted contemptuously. "*Perhaps* she came with you. But in any event, you are right—you are too late. And I intend to see that these criminals hang—every last one of them!" He waved a hand at his small army, which included the sheriff. "Take them off to gaol, men."

Whooping with their victory, they did just that.

"I bid you and the . . . uh . . . lady . . . good night," Mayfield said in a superior manner as his carriage, which had been well hidden, approached. He climbed into the vehicle and was gone.

It was silent on the roadway except for the occasional snort from a horse and stamp of a hoof. Hannah stood stunned by what had happened.

"Sorry, Theo," David Moore said. "We were only moments too late."

Hannah tried to control her voice. "What will happen to them?" It was a rhetorical question, for she knew very well how events would transpire.

Amesbury merely voiced what she knew—and feared. "There will be a trial and they will probably hang."

"Even Henry—Mr. Franklin?" She controlled a sob. "He—he really was only trying to stop those men—keep them from smashing the machines."

"I am sure he was," Amesbury said. "But I am equally sure that Mayfield thinks he has caught himself a very big fish. Unfortunately, Mayfield is not without friends in high places."

"Oh, dear." Hannah felt tears sliding down her cheeks. She turned away lest they be seen even in the dim light available now that the torches were gone. She would *not* turn into a watering pot in front of these men—especially in front of Lord Amesbury.

Theo had been astonished when Miss Whitmore made her presence known. Then his temper had flared at her utter foolishness. Now he clearly heard the controlled tears in her voice. He wanted to take her in his arms and comfort her. On the other hand, he wanted to throttle her. His anger won out—largely as a way of averting her tears.

"What *were* you thinking?" he demanded. "You'd no business here. No business at all."

"I— I had to see, to know—"

"You could not just wait for someone to report back to you? And you came here *alone*? That was outside of any semblance of common sense."

Her indignation conquered the tears. "No. No, I could not sit and wait. And no, I did *not* come alone. Noel?" she called.

"Right here, miss."

Theo recognized the man who had accompanied her on the Horton road when he had been attacked. "Well, so you were not *quite* the shatter-brain I took you for," he said, some of the harshness fading from his voice.

She did not reply to this and the others stood around in embarrassed silence. He saw her lift her chin and he knew she hated having to acknowledge that he was not only right, but that he had stepped in to protect her.

"My . . . my judgment may have been faulty," she conceded. "I—I thank you for telling Lord Mayfield I arrived with you."

He gave her a mocking bow. "You are welcome, ma'am."

"But . . ." He could tell the tears were near the surface again. "Can nothing be done for Mr. Franklin—and the others?"

Theo noted with a twinge of dismay that her first concern was for the lawyer. Was she so concerned about Franklin that she would risk her reputation for the man?

"I do not know at the moment *what* can be done," he said, unwilling to raise false hopes. "I shall look into matters and see what I can do. I, too, have a few friends in high places. Franklin is a good man."

"Yes, he most assuredly is," she said.

Theo and his companions saw Miss Whitmore and the vicar's man, Noel, home. They had gathered up Franklin's horse so the boy Benjamin was mounted. As soon as they had deposited Miss Whitmore, Theo turned on Benjamin.

"All right, Britton. What were *you* doing there tonight?"

"I . . . I told my friend Jack Slater I would stand by him when it came to doing something about . . . about their working conditions."

"*Their* working conditions. But you work for me."

"Y-yes, my lord," the boy said in a small voice.

"Are you unhappy with your own work situation?" Theo asked, genuinely curious.

Benjamin raised his head. "Oh, no, my lord. I was just aimin' to help Jack and them others. They ain't got it so good, you see."

"Well, it looks to me as though they took on more than they could handle tonight," Theo said.

"Yes, my lord." Benjamin sounded glum.

"You'd best tell anyone who asks that you were with me tonight," Theo told him. "Hessler and Yardley will back you on that." His last statement was directed so as to include those two, who quickly murmured their assent. "And perhaps you should stay close to home for a few days," Theo added.

"Yes, my lord. An' . . . thank you, my lord."

Theo and David saw the boy home as Yardley and Hessler went to their own quarters. Both men were silent as they rode into the Glosson stables, where a sleepy groom saw to the horses.

"Not exactly a glorious night's work, was it?" Theo commented as they walked toward the Hall.

"We've had some that were better," David said. "*And* some that were worse. At least we tried."

"I hate failure, though—and I know you do, too."

"Perhaps an occasional failure makes us appreciate successes all the more."

"Ah, David. Don't go philosophical on me. 'Tis far too late in the night for that."

Entering the Hall, they went directly to the library. Theo stirred up the fire and offered his friend a nightcap of brandy. He poured two scant drinks.

"What now?" David asked, settling into a chair near the fire.

Theo sat across from him. "I honestly do not know. I think Mayfield will present a very strong case when the assize court meets."

"When?"

"It usually meets twice a year. Next one is scheduled for the spring."

"I see. Well, that gives you a bit of time anyway."

"But to do *what*?" Theo ran his hand through his hair. "Those workers were caught in the very act. Mayfield will see them prosecuted to the fullest extent of the law just to make examples of them."

"It does seem a matter of more than simple justice with him," David said. "Not to mention he perhaps thinks he can score against *you*."

"Poor Franklin—he was certainly in the wrong place at the wrong time."

"Do you think you can do anything for *him*? It appears he was there by happenstance. But from what you've told me, I gather Mayfield has no great love for him, either."

"No, he does not. I shall try. I promised Miss Whitmore I would try."

David gave him an oblique look, but said no more. They quietly finished their drinks and sought their beds.

The next afternoon, Theo visited Franklin in the Crofton gaol. He found that Franklin already had visitors—Miss Whitmore and Miss Thomas. Both women looked especially dejected and Theo thought Miss Thomas had recently been crying.

The women greeted Theo, then took their leave of Franklin, each extending a hand to the prisoner, who clasped them firmly and admonished the two not to worry themselves over him. Theo thought the lawyer and Miss Whitmore were showing extraordinary decorum.

"How are you faring, Harry?" Theo asked when the women had left.

Franklin's face lost some its forced cheerfulness. "Not too badly, I suppose—given the circumstances."

"Did you suspect a trap last night?"

"Yes. That is, of course, why I was there. I had hoped to convince the men *before* they went in, but I was too late."

"There was a lot of that last night," Theo said.

"Miss Whitmore told me—and of your kindness to her and young Benjamin. I thank you for that."

So—Franklin was claiming the right to thank Theo for protecting Miss Whitmore. Theo had been correct, then. This thought came with a distinct feeling of regret and even loss. He mentally shook himself for such foolishness. Still, there had been that unforgettable kiss. . . .

"I intend to see what I can do to help you," Theo said. "We have several weeks, you know."

"Yes. Perhaps you would not be averse to contacting Samuelson for me? He was the barrister we had for Tettle."

"Yes, I remember. I shall see him tomorrow."

They talked of other—mundane—matters for several minutes, carefully avoiding further mention of what was likely to happen to Franklin. How is it, Theo asked himself, that in the face of great crises people resort to talking of the weather and grain prices?

Theo left with a final word of encouragement. "Keep your spirits up, my friend. This is definitely not over yet."

"Thank you."

"And do not for a moment think I have forgot you—though I will be gone from Crofton in the next few weeks."

"Never." Franklin extended his hand through the bars of the cell door. Theo took it and held it warmly, vowing silently that *something* would be done to help this man, both for his own sake and for Miss Whitmore's. If she wanted Franklin—well, then, she should have him!

As he had indicated to Franklin, Theo was absent from Crofton for the next several weeks. He spent December and the Christmas holiday in Wiltshire with his parents, who also welcomed his sister and her husband and their growing family. Theo was glad for this "family time," but he found himself missing life in Crofton and the people there. The image of the vicar's daughter haunted him. Those blue-gray eyes seemed stormy in his vision—berating him for not acting more expeditiously to save her—her what? Her friend? Her lover? Her would-be husband?

And always he fought those infernal battlefield dreams and the recurring images of his brother's death.

Shortly after the new year, his parents returned to London and Theo went with them. Members of the *ton* were gradually returning to town for the impending opening of Parliament and the new social season.

Theo, who was also in continual communication with the barrister, Samuelson, was in town primarily to see what he could do behind the scenes regarding the upcoming court case in Crofton. He visited several men prominent in law circles, made his positions clear to them, and listened intently to their sometimes conflicting advice.

One afternoon as he returned, Morton met him at the door to say, "The earl has a guest in the library and asked to have you join them as soon as you returned."

As he shrugged out of his greatcoat and handed it and his hat and gloves to the butler, Theo was amused at Morton's intonation on the word *guest*. He wondered briefly who might have incurred such disapproval.

It was a Bow Street Runner.

"Hansen here has just returned from Ireland," the earl announced.

"And did you find our man?" Theo asked.

"Not exactly, my lord. Seems he left for North America soon after his return to Ireland. Told one of his mates he had to get as far away as possible because he'd killed an English lord."

"So he is in the United States? Or Canada?" Theo asked.

"Neither, my lord. He's dead. Killed in some Indian battle out West, they say."

Theo was skeptical. "We know this for sure?"

"Well, my lord, as sure as we can be." Hansen sounded a bit defensive. "His mother showed me a piece from an American newspaper naming her son as one of the casualties in a battle at some fort on the Missouri River."

Theo looked at his father, who seemed to share his own despair. "Another dead end, eh?"

"It would appear so," the older man agreed.

When the runner had gone, Theo asked, "What now?"

"Unless something turns up in Derbyshire, I suppose we simply have to accept that we will never really know for sure why Francis died." The sadness in his father's tone touched Theo's heart.

"I think, Father, that we do know *why*. We just do not know for an absolute certainty *who*. I am convinced Francis died because he, too, found out about Taggert and those others driving the workers to produce more and more—and he knew about their stealing. That was, I am sure, the *why*. Apparently this dead Irishman was the actual instrument of my brother's death, though others were and are equally guilty in my mind."

"But we shall probably *never* be able to prove that," the earl said bitterly.

Theo's own tone was just as bleak. "Probably not. I think sometimes life simply refuses to give us neat, tidy solutions to even the gravest of problems."

His father smiled faintly. "It is old men like me who are supposed to come up with such explanations for the inexplicable, my son."

Theo smiled back at him. "A lucky guess?"

The Countess of Glosson continued her quest to see her son married. Now that he had returned to town—for whatever reason—she was determined at least to put him in the path of possible matrimony.

Theo was not totally averse to her machinations. He was quite ready to give up the single life. Obviously, the great love with which his parents had been blessed was not to be his lot in life. Whenever this thought assailed him, he found himself face-to-face with an image of Hannah Whitmore. He wondered how events might have transpired between them were the lawyer Franklin not in the picture. You cannot spend your life dwelling on what might have been, he told himself sternly. That argument rarely worked with his dreams of dead men on the battlefield—why should it work in this area of his life?

To his mother's delight, Viscount Amesbury set himself to the serious business of finding a bride. He was frequently seen at social affairs with the beautiful Lady Olivia. The betting books at both Brooks' and White's gentlemen's clubs favored Lady Olivia, though it was duly noted that he was also seen from time to time in the company of other very eligible young women.

"Do you think you are being quite fair to Olivia?" his mother asked him one morning after yet another elegant ball. At her request, Theo had presented himself in her sitting room for what he knew full well would be one of her mother-son inquisitions.

"What do you mean?" he asked.

"She has been out for—what?—four, perhaps five years now. She cannot wait forever for you to declare yourself."

"She has any number of suitors from whom she might choose," Theo said defensively.

"Possibly—as second choices," his mother replied.

Theo laughed. "You flatter me, Mother."

"No, I do not." Her tone was very calm, very deliberate. "You are assuredly one of the most eligible—and most elusive—gentlemen in society. And you have been for quite long enough, I should think."

"I thought your enthusiasm for Lady Olivia had waned after the visit to Derbyshire," Theo countered.

The countess looked uncomfortable. "Well, perhaps it did," she admitted, "but you seem attracted to her—and, after all, 'tis not *I* who will live with whomever you choose."

"Right," Theo said vaguely.

"You *are* attracted to her?"

"Yes. Of course. She is quite a lovely woman. Good heavens! She never fails to be surrounded by a whole cohort of would-be suitors."

"And she has all the right connections and proper manners," his mother added. "She will be a fine countess. Is she not an enjoyable companion?"

He shrugged. "I suppose so." He tried to ignore the little voice that silently added if one confines one's conversation to subjects of fashion and the latest *on dits* of gossip. Well, whoever said a wife had to have an interesting intellect? Was that not what male friends were for? And it would be easy enough to keep the nightmares from her—separate bedrooms would achieve that end nicely.

"So what is holding you back?" his mother asked bluntly.

"I do not know," he said honestly, but with a touch of exasperation. "I do not know," he said in a quieter voice.

"Someone else?" she asked gently.

"No," he said slowly. But that was a lie—was it not?

"Theo?"

He shook his head. "I promise you, Mother, that before this year is over, I shall choose your successor, and you may lavish as much time and attention on her as you will."

In the event, however, the choice was taken out of his control.

Eighteen

For Hannah the winter weeks dragged. When Katherine left for her second season in London, Hannah briefly considered going with her. The widowed Mrs. Pilkington, who often helped at the school, would have happily served as a substitute teacher. In the end, though, Hannah could not bring herself to rob Jane of the support that the young woman needed in this trying time.

The two of them sat at either end of a long table in the office of the school one day in mid-January. Both of them found the interminable paperwork of teaching more palatable if it was a shared task. Hannah looked up to see Jane staring off into space, tears trickling down her cheeks.

"Oh, Jane." Hannah rose and put her arms around the other woman's shoulders. "You must not allow yourself to sink into despair. It will work out. I know it will."

Hannah *knew* nothing of the kind, but she, too, had to hang onto that shred of hope Henry had offered when he told them of Lord Amesbury's promise. Amesbury had been gone for weeks now, though, and there had been no word in Crofton of his efforts on Henry's behalf. There had, however, been plenty of information in the gossip columns of newspapers from London linking the names of a certain Lord A with Lady O at this or that *ton* gala. Hannah wondered spitefully when he could possibly have *time* to deal with any matter to do with Crofton.

Jane sniffed and wiped her eyes. "I *am* sorry, Hannah. It is just so very hard—this waiting, not knowing. Sometimes at night I wake up all cold and so terribly frightened. I love him so much. How will I go on without him?"

Hannah gave her a gentle shake. "Hush, now. We do not know that you will be required to do so. *Henry* is hopeful—so you should be, too."

"He—he puts on a show of cheerfulness when you or I visit him, but I can tell he thinks it will go badly at the trial."

Hannah knew this to be true, for when she had visited Henry alone, he had been more forthright with her than he had with Jane, whom he sought to protect.

"Take care of her, Hannah. Please. Don't let her mourn forever," he had said once.

"Don't talk that way, Henry."

"I have to face possibilities," he said. "I have had a great deal of time to think while I have been here."

"Shall I bring you a Gothic novel to distract you?" she asked lightly.

Henry was not to be deterred so easily from his contemplative mood. "You know, I should have just taken my chances and declared myself to Jane long ago. I have loved her since—well, since we were all children together, I suppose."

"Tell her, Henry! She needs that to sustain her through the next few weeks."

"You—you think I have a chance?" he asked uncertainly.

"Oh, Henry." Hannah chuckled. "'Tis ever so true. Love *is* blind."

He looked delighted—and embarrassed. "Ah, well . . ."

When Jane returned from her next visit to the gaol, she seemed to Hannah to be virtually floating.

"He loves me, Hannah. He really does love me!"

"Well, of course he does. He always has."

Now, on a bleak January day, Hannah hugged Jane tighter and said, "You cannot give up hope. Henry needs your support—and that infuriating optimism of yours."

Jane smiled through her tears. "Thank you, my 'pessimistic' friend."

"Practical," Hannah said lightly. "I prefer to think of myself as very, very practical." Would a truly practical person pin her hopes on a man who was obviously off in town enjoying himself?

In the following month, there were other such sessions with Jane. Newspapers carried continuous articles about the men awaiting trial. To keep the stories alive, journalists reached ever harder for salacious details. The accused men were labeled "the Crofton seven" and depicted as depraved, irredeemable miscreants who hardly deserved a trial. There were hideous cartoons, especially of the so-called leaders, the middle-aged Henshaw and the youthful Slater. One, in particular, showed these two as dupes being egged on by a black-frocked man with a law book in his hand.

Editorials called for the most severe punishments in the interest of preserving "law and order." The only paper that toned down the diatribe was the *Crofton Chronicle,* of which Jane's father was editor and publisher. In one edition Nathan Thomas suggested that the public might be best advised to wait for the evidence to be presented before condemning accused persons. This, as Jane reported to Hannah, brought Mr. Thomas a visit from an irate Lord Mayfield.

"He accused Papa of being in league with revolutionaries!" Jane said. "He wanted a retraction printed immediately. Apparently he thought—he really thought—my father would be intimidated by his rank and prestige!"

Hannah smiled. "Lord Mayfield cannot have been reading the *Chronicle* all these years, then."

In an attempt to keep herself from dwelling unduly on the fate of the seven accused men, Hannah redoubled her efforts to recruit students for her school from among families of mill workers. Almost daily she knocked on doors and accosted weary weavers returning from work. The rumors having died down, she managed to enroll five new students from among the workers in the Kitchener and Childress mills. Although those owners saw no reason to be educating the "lower orders," they had not been as adamant about punishing workers for sending their children to school as Lord Mayfield had been.

Hannah knew that Mayfield was hearing appeals from some of his people and there was a good deal of grumbling in his mill. The baron had even sought a meeting with Hannah's father to try to enlist the clergyman's aid in controlling the vicar's daughter.

"Perhaps you should restrain yourself somewhat, my dear," her father told her on sharing news of the visit he had had from the angry Mayfield.

"But I am doing nothing wrong, Papa. I have not set foot on his property. It is just that *his* workers hear from other workers and, well . . ."

"The man seems under a good deal of strain."

"As well he should be," Hannah said grimly. "*He* is the one who keeps those awful newspaper stories going, you know."

"Still—people under pressure are unpredictable. I would not have you hurt in any way."

Hannah hugged her father. "I shall be careful," she whispered and kissed his cheek.

The long-awaited trial was a short-lived affair. The prosecution presented its case very efficiently. There was obviously ample evidence for conviction, in addition to numerous eyewitnesses. The jury was out for an hour. The seven men were declared guilty of a variety of offenses, each of which might be punishable by death.

Hannah sat next to Jane throughout. The two women were flanked by their fathers, who occasionally offered quiet encouragement. Most of the time, Hannah and Jane sat mutely, holding each other's hands tightly. As an especially damaging piece of evidence was revealed, they occasionally flinched. Despair crept over Hannah like fog settling over a city. It permeated her being.

When the verdict was returned rather late in the day, Hannah and Jane, along with other women in the courtroom, openly wept. Many of the men wore grim expressions. They waited apprehensively for what seemed an inevitable sentence, but then something unusual happened.

Instead of immediately pronouncing sentence as was customary, the judge announced that he was taking the verdict under advisement and that he would sentence the guilty parties on the following day.

"Your honor—" the prosecutor protested.

The judge pounded his gavel and said, "Court is dismissed until ten tomorrow morning." He rose and left the courtroom.

The spectators sat in stunned silence for a few moments, then a growing murmur arose—of frustration from the prosecution's part of the room, and anxiety from that of the defense. The sheriff and his deputies quickly ushered the prisoners away. As he left, Franklin lifted a hand in the direction of Jane and Hannah and flashed an uncertain smile.

Jane laid her head on Hannah's shoulder and said in a shuddering whisper, "I don't think I can bear this."

"A delay in the sentencing can only be seen as an encouraging sign, daughter," said Nathan Thomas.

"I agree," the vicar said.

"See?" Hannah said brightly. "There's still hope."

All day Hannah had been acutely aware of the presence of Lord Amesbury. He sat quietly just behind the defense and during short recesses in the proceedings, she had seen him confer with the barrister, Samuelson. Now she observed him talking with Samuelson, who listened intently. Then Samuelson approached the prosecutor. There was a short colloquy that included Lord Mayfield. She could hear none of what was said, but she thought Mayfield was objecting strenuously to something the defense barrister said. Mayfield glared across the room at Amesbury as the prosecutor laid a restraining hand on Mayfield's arm. Finally, Mayfield gave an abrupt nod and left the courtroom, obviously angry.

As Hannah and her companions left the courtroom, Lord Amesbury caught up with them. He greeted the two women and the vicar and graciously acknowledged an introduction to the editor of the *Chronicle*. He held Hannah's gaze as he continued to speak.

"It is not over yet, but I think this will not turn out as badly as we once feared."

"That is reassuring news, my lord," the vicar said, for Hannah seemed to find herself tongue-tied.

"Oh, yes," Jane said breathily.

"I must go now," Amesbury said, still speaking directly to Hannah, "but if I may, I will call upon you later this evening."

"Of course," she said quietly.

It was, indeed, very late when Lord Amesbury called at the vicarage that night. Mrs. Whitmore had already retired and Hannah and her father waited in the study, a room both found more comfortable than the drawing room. They talked in a rather desultory manner about parish and school business, for they had long since exhausted the topic uppermost in both their minds. Finally, they heard the knocker resound in the quiet night. A few moments later the housekeeper showed Lord Amesbury into the study.

"You *do* have good news?" Hannah asked immediately.

"Partially," he replied as the vicar gestured him toward a chair.

"We were just having a bit of sherry, my lord," the vicar said. "May I offer you some? Or I have brandy, if you prefer."

"Sherry will be fine," Amesbury replied.

Hannah thought he looked tired. She resisted an inexplicable urge to rise and massage his temples to smooth away the worry lines on his face. Good heavens! You silly goose, she admonished herself. When her father had placed a glass in their guest's hand, she gently prodded, "Your news?"

"I have been meeting—for hours, it seems—with Judge Atkins, along with Samuelson and the prosecutor—*and* with Mayfield, Kitchener, and Childress. Mayfield and Kitchener—as they have all along—want everyone to hang. Positively bloodthirsty, they are."

"And will they prevail?" The vicar asked the question Hannah was afraid to ask.

"No. Only Henshaw and Slater will face the noose."

"Oh, no," Hannah moaned softly.

The viscount nodded solemnly. "I know. They are no more guilty than the others—and the real culprit goes scot-free, for it is quite clear that the instigator of that disaster was one Ian Cochran, who was sent here by Whitehall."

"And the others?" She held her breath.

"All but Franklin are to be transported to New South Wales."

She brightened. "Oh! Henry is to be freed, then. How wonderful."

"Not exactly," Lord Amesbury said.

"What do you mean? He will be neither hanged nor transported. Gaol? He will serve a prison term here in England?"

"No. Even though the evidence against him was weak, he was on the scene—and that went against him. He will be allowed to leave the country voluntarily. Mayfield and his lot were very adamant about that."

Hannah was appalled. "Leave England? Forever?"

"I am not sure about 'forever,' but I think it will certainly be for several years."

"Oh, my heavens. Poor Henry. He does love Crofton so. Why, he chose to set up his office here when he might have been quite comfortable in London, you know."

"I do know. He told me," the viscount said.

The vicar patted his daughter's hand. "At least he will be alive, my dear."

"Yes." She brightened momentarily. Then another thought hit her. "But—but where will he go? He will be free, will he not?"

"He will be free," Amesbury said. "I have made arrangements for him and a . . . a companion to sail from Liverpool to the United States."

"The colonies?" Her tone suggested even to her own ears that the proposed destination might as well have been the north pole or deepest Africa.

Amesbury's mouth twitched in a brief smile. "The former colonies. He will be able to practice law there—I have a contact in Philadelphia who will be glad to help him."

"Wh-when?" she asked, overwhelmed now by the sudden swirl of events.

"The ship sails in three days."

"Three days!"

"Yes."

"Oh, my heavens," she said again. "So much to do."

"Tell me, my lord," the vicar interjected, "how was it that you managed all these arrangements this evening?"

"The truth is, I did not," Amesbury replied.

"Then how—" Hannah started.

Lord Amesbury cut her off with a gesture. "I discussed the *possible* outcomes of the trial with men in government and law while I was in London. When it became apparent that this fiasco—like the one in Pentrich earlier—was at least partly the work of a government spy, a good number of men in high places had second thoughts about this case. To be frank, they have not recovered from the earlier debacle and they want this one to go away as quietly as possible."

"Henry thought Lord Mayfield had his own spy in the group," Hannah said.

Amesbury nodded. "He did. He admitted as much when the events of that night were discussed in London."

"Lord Mayfield was privy to the London talks?" the vicar asked.

"He was," Amesbury affirmed. "However, even Lord Sidmouth found him immovable on the possible sentences. And the law was on his side, of course."

"But he *was* finally persuaded?" Hannah asked.

Lord Amesbury's smile was full and genuine this time. "He was sort of bullied into it. Have you ever heard of the 'Fearsome Five'?"

"No-o," she said slowly.

"I have," her father said. "Five very important men in the inner circles of Parliament," he explained to his daughter, then addressed their guest. "I believe your father is one of the five."

"He is. And once that lot gets their teeth into something, they refuse to let go."

"They were very persuasive, I take it," the Reverend Mr. Whitmore said.

"Let us merely say they knew where and on whom to put pressure—and they brought some heavy weapons to the bargaining table," Amesbury replied.

Hannah had been quiet for a few moments, mulling over what had been said. "I . . . somehow this seems almost a circumvention of the law. I wonder that the judge condoned it."

"That was, of course, a concern to everyone involved," Lord Amesbury said, sounding weary. "But the law is rather unbending and the alternative of hanging seven men who were virtually trapped into doing what they did was an embarrassment the government was unwilling to tolerate."

"But the judge—?" Hannah persisted.

"He is a practical man—*and* he is ambitious. He eventually wants an appellate court seat."

"So two men must die purely for political reasons," she said. She was immediately sorry as she saw a flash of genuine pain in the depths of Lord Amesbury's eyes.

He passed a hand over his face and said, "You might see it that way. But it is two—not seven—and both are clearly guilty of the singular crime for which they were charged."

"I know," she replied, "and I am sorry. I must seem terribly ungrateful and I do most sincerely appreciate all you have done."

He nodded. "It is late. I must go."

"I shall see you to the door, my lord," she said.

All three of them rose and the men shook hands. In the hallway, Hannah, never one at a loss for words, fumbled for the right ones to thank him.

"I—I cannot tell you—"

"There is no need," he said.

He stood very close to her; she could smell his shaving

lotion—or something that smelled of spice and . . . and something else, something earthy—and captivating. In the dim light of a single shielded candle in the hall, she tried to read his expression. The weariness she had seen earlier was still there, but there was also a kind of sadness and . . . perhaps . . . regret? He reached out to put his hands on either side of her face and gently kissed her forehead, his lips barely brushing her skin.

"Try to be happy, Hannah Whitmore," he whispered. "It will all have been worth it if you are happy."

"Oh, I am," she assured him, though she was puzzled by the intensity of his words and demeanor.

He gathered up his hat and gloves and bade her good night.

Having arranged the day before for substitute teachers for Jane and herself, Hannah went early to the Thomas home to tell Jane and her parents the news. They were having an early breakfast and invited Hannah to join them. She readily accepted a cup of tea. The Thomases were, of course, relieved that Franklin's life would be spared.

"But—leave the country? Leave England?" Jane was as astonished as Hannah had been. "I shall never see him again." Tears welled in her eyes.

"Lord Amesbury has arranged for you to go with Henry."

"Me? His lordship knows about Henry and me? I—I only recently shared the news with Mama and Papa."

"Which of course came as an astonishing surprise to her mother and me," Mr. Thomas said with an indulgent smile at his daughter.

"Perhaps Henry told him," Hannah said. "In any event, passage is booked for Mr. Franklin and a 'companion.' I assumed you would be that companion."

"But . . . leave Crofton? Leave my family? My friends? The school? How could I possibly do that?"

Jane's mother, too, was crying now. "Oh, Nathan, no. I cannot have my darling girl go off to the wilds of the colonies."

"Philadelphia is not exactly the wilderness, my dear," her husband replied. "And I seem to recall a certain Highland lass who left Scotland to marry a lowly newspaperman."

"That was different," Mrs. Thomas said. "Scotland is only a few days' journey away."

"And Philadelphia is only a few weeks' journey away," Nathan Thomas said to his wife. He turned to his daughter. "Follow your heart, Jane. You have loved that boy since you first put your hair up."

"L-longer," Jane sobbed. "But, Papa, this is so *hard*."

"I know," he said and Hannah could hear suppressed tears in his voice, too.

Mrs. Thomas sniffed and sat up straighter. "Your father is right, Jane. You would never be happy here with Mr. Franklin half a world away. I know that—but, oh, my! How we shall miss you!"

Her husband concurred. "That we will. But when your brother finishes school next year, we shall all come to visit you and—who knows?—perhaps the former colonies could use another newspaperman as well as another lawyer."

"Oh, Papa." Jane tried to smile through her tears. She rose and hugged both her parents; then she and Hannah, along with Jane's father, departed for the courtroom and the sentencing.

The scene in the courtroom was solemn as befitting life-and-death matters in human affairs. The judge gravely passed sentences precisely as Viscount Amesbury had explained them the night before. Cries of anguish from the families of Henshaw and Slater dampened the rejoicing of other families.

Hannah was torn between jubilation at her friend Henry's reprieve and impotent fury that two men would hang and others would suffer untold hardships—and all for what? For the arrogant pride of a few and ignorant fears of many.

Nineteen

Theo visited Franklin in gaol immediately after the sentencing and the two of them sorted out the details of the lawyer's upcoming journey. Franklin was to be incarcerated until the last moment.

"Mayfield's last stab at me," the lawyer said.

"He does not take defeat well," Theo replied, "but then I suppose none of us does."

"My clerk, Larkin, has offered to sort through my books and files and pack up what I will need. Miss Whitmore and Miss Thomas will take care of my personal effects."

Theo did not welcome the vision of Hannah Whitmore lovingly sorting through another man's "personal effects," so he changed the subject.

"About your man Larkin. Would you give him a good recommendation?"

"Of course. He is a first-rate clerk and has a fine hand. Why do you ask?"

"My new steward is in need of a clerk or secretary. I knew he would be, of course, but the need seems more urgent than I had anticipated," Theo explained.

"You could do much worse than Brandon Larkin," Franklin said.

"I shall speak to him soon, then. So—you will be ready early Thursday morning?"

"We will be ready. I really wish it could be a day earlier, though."

"I agree," Theo said. He knew all the prisoners were being

forced to witness the hangings scheduled for Wednesday. Theo, too, would be a witness to them—not because he was forced to do so, but because he felt an obligation, a duty to lend the two his support, especially Henshaw, who had befriended a young mill worker named "Leo Reston."

Before leaving the gaol, he spoke with Henshaw and Slater as well, for the seven convicted men were still all being held together. Henshaw had been stoic about his fate and seemed to have a calming effect on the younger Slater, whose fears were readily apparent.

"Will ye be there to see me off?" Henshaw asked Theo. He might have been speaking of a journey to Scotland or Wales.

"I shall be there," Theo promised.

After leaving the gaol, Theo rode to Manchester to seek an audience with Sir Dennison Stewart, Lord Lieutenant of the district. As the king's representative in county matters, Stewart's authority superseded that of local authorities.

"I *am* sorry, Amesbury. I cannot step in and commute those sentences," he replied to Theo's request. "Technically, I *might* have the authority to do so, but in this day, with outbreaks of violence—or threats of such—every week . . . well, it just would not be wise for London to usurp power from locals."

Theo's shoulders slumped in defeat. The Lord Lieutenant had been his last hope for the two men condemned to die. He could see that Stewart was not to be moved by further argument. He was, Theo thought, the sort of man who enjoyed the prestige of a high position, but shrank from the responsibility of making decisions.

That night new faces joined Theo's gallery of ghostly accusers. Once again, his own cries of anguish jerked him awake. Since there were currently no guests in the Hall and his aunt was not only a very sound sleeper but also slightly hard of hearing, Theo had thought it safe to allow Burton to return to a more comfortable bed in the servants' quarters. Now, consciousness found the former army officer sitting on the edge of the bed in a cold sweat.

He tried to analyze yet again why these damnable dreams

returned—and always without warning. He had been free of them all winter—except for three or four nights. He could understand fully why those poor devils on the battlefield plagued him. God knew, *they* had a right to. As their commander he *might* have done something. He *should* have done something—anything. Guilt was logical in that instance. But his brother? Molly Tettle? Even Logan? And now Henshaw and Slater? How could anyone logically hold Theo Ruskin, Viscount Amesbury, to blame for those deaths? It did not make sense. He shook his head and lay back down.

Sleep did not return, though.

The next morning, Theo busied himself with estate business. Andrew Moore was proving to be a fine steward, but there were a number of matters that had been put aside awaiting Theo's return. The young man was properly grateful when Theo informed him that the clerk, Larkin, would be helping out in a week or so.

Theo dreaded the afternoon and that double hanging. He had witnessed executions before, but never with any sense of satisfaction. Battlefield deaths were one thing. Accidental deaths were another. One mourned tragic losses. But institutionalized killing? No matter how it was dressed up and justified in courts, it boiled down to certain people assuming the right to say who should live and who should die. Unfortunately, he thought, we poor human beings are not infallible.

In the event, both Henshaw and Slater died with as much dignity as a public hanging could possibly offer. Theo suspected that young Slater, especially, had had the aid of some liquid courage. If their families could manage it, condemned men often arrived on the gallows intoxicated.

The crowd at such a spectacle usually took on a carnival-like atmosphere with much merriment and catcalls and pickpockets plying their trade among the spectators. The crowd in Crofton on this day was somber and sullen. Mill owners such as Mayfield, Kitchener, and Childress had encouraged workers to attend the hanging—"so as to teach us a lesson," one of the men standing near Theo grumbled. Theo thought the "lesson" had probably gone terribly awry, for, far from instilling fear and obedience, hanging these two seemed to intensify resentment and determination.

"I think this day's business will come back to haunt us," Theo said quietly to himself as he left the dismal scene.

The next morning he arose early for the journey to Liverpool with Franklin and Miss Whitmore. He was not looking forward to the trip, but he had offered the lawyer his services and support and he could hardly withdraw them now. They had arranged to meet at Franklin's quarters at an early hour. Theo assumed the coachman and footman would load up Franklin's luggage and then they would pick up Miss Whitmore at the vicarage.

When he arrived at Franklin's place, he found not only Henry Franklin standing outside, along with a pile of luggage, but also Miss Whitmore, another woman, and an older couple. Soon he recognized Miss Thomas and her father. The other woman appeared to be Miss Thomas's mother. Theo was rather surprised that Miss Whitmore's family had not come to see her off.

Alighting from the carriage, Theo said cheerily, "It looks as though you are all set."

"That we are," Franklin replied. "As soon as the luggage is stowed, we can be off."

The coachman and footman set about that task as Franklin said his good-byes to Mr. and Mrs. Thomas.

Theo stood holding the coach door. "Miss Whitmore?"

"Yes, my lord?"

"Would you like to get settled for the journey?"

She looked surprised. "I beg your pardon?"

"You may get into the carriage, if you wish. The sooner we are all settled in, the sooner we may leave."

Now the others were looking on with rather confused expressions. After a moment, Miss Whitmore started to giggle. A look of understanding passed between her and Franklin. Franklin grinned, then burst into laughter.

"What is it? I do not understand," Miss Thomas said.

There was a gurgle of laughter in Miss Whitmore's voice. "I—I think Lord Amesbury is under the impression that *I* am to be Henry's 'companion' on this voyage."

Henry stepped closer to Miss Thomas and put an arm around her waist. "I fear my wife might object to that."

"Your wife?" Theo asked in amazement as all the others stood grinning at him.

"Henry and Jane were married only about two hours ago," Miss Whitmore replied.

"The moment I managed to return with their special license," Mr. Thomas said. "The vicar kindly got out of bed early this morning."

"I—I see." Theo tried to digest this turn of events. He smiled broadly and offered Henry his hand. "Well, then, my congratulations." He bowed to the new Mrs. Franklin. "And my best wishes to your bride."

The bride blushed becomingly. Then there was a flurry of good-byes. Theo tried not to be too obvious in observing as Miss Whitmore embraced first Franklin, then his wife in saying her farewells to them. All three women were weeping.

Finally, the three travelers were settled in the carriage and they were off with waves and promises to write. Theo surmised that the new Mrs. Franklin was physically and emotionally exhausted. He was not surprised to see her fall asleep before the coach had traveled only a few miles. He and Henry talked softly of mundane matters for a while, then each retreated into his own thoughts.

Now that he had sufficient opportunity to examine his own reactions to the news of the Franklins' marriage, Theo found himself positively elated. His elation, however, was tempered by uncertainty. He had himself been willing to ensure Miss Whitmore's—Hannah's—happiness despite his own feelings. Was Hannah doing the same thing for Franklin? And why had Miss Whitmore suddenly become *Hannah* to him?

He leaned his head back against the squabs of the seat and thanked a kind providence that he would not be spending the day in a closed carriage with the woman he loved and her would-be lover.

He sat bolt upright.

The woman he loved? Where had *that* idea come from? It would certainly bear some examination. Luckily, it would be a very long journey to Liverpool and back.

After a stop for lunch and a change of horses, the Franklins showed fewer signs of exhaustion and they had replaced some of the sadness of farewells with speculation about their future. Apprehension gave place to acceptance and a degree of eager anticipation.

"I believe you two will do just fine," Theo said after a while.

"At least they speak English in the former colonies," Mrs. Franklin said.

Theo chuckled. "After a fashion. There were impressed American sailors on some of our troop ships when I served in the Peninsula." He proceeded to entertain them with imitations of American accents from New England and from the Carolinas.

"I had no idea there was such variety in language over there," she said.

"The English language is nothing if not versatile, Mrs. Franklin," Theo said.

"Oh, please, my lord. I do love my new name." She smiled shyly at her husband. "But you have been such a friend to Henry, I would have you call me Jane."

Theo nodded. "As you wish, Jane. Ours has been a short acquaintance, but I suppose intensity counts for something. First names certainly seem quite appropriate."

"Yes," she replied.

For a moment, Theo knew all three of them were marveling at the vicissitudes of their relationship. Then he shifted the subject. "I gather that your friendship with Miss Whitmore is a long-standing one."

"The three of us grew up in Crofton," Jane said, "and we were just always together, it seems."

"Except when we all went away to different schools," her husband interjected.

"We all thought we would be so different as grown-up adults when we finished school," Jane said, "but we were not."

Her husband chuckled. "No. You and I were still trying to tone down Hannah's enthusiasms just as we had always done."

There followed an exchange of anecdotes, each of which began, "Remember when—" and included youthful capers and serious pursuits of the three friends. Theo listened avidly to gain further insight into the make-up of one Hannah Whitmore.

"Oh, dear." Jane laughed softly. "I wonder who will keep her in hand now? Hannah has always run right over her mother and sisters, and her father simply indulges her every wish."

"I have no idea," Franklin said.

"Perhaps *you*, my lor—er, Theo," Jane said with a teasing twinkle in her eyes. Theo wondered why she had always seemed to him such a mousy little thing.

He threw up his hands in a gesture of mock defeat. "Me? The woman seems a proper virago from what you have said."

"Hannah *is* a strong woman," Franklin observed, "but there is a certain vulnerability about her, too."

"I have an idea," Jane said in an utterly serious tone, "that our Lord Amesbury would be equal to the task."

Franklin was lost in thought for a moment. He squeezed his wife's hand. "You may be on to something, my dear."

Jane blushed at the mild endearment in front of a third party and Theo noted with amusement that Franklin did not release her hand.

They arrived in Liverpool late in the afternoon and the Franklins were ushered on board the ship immediately. The captain explained that winds and tide would allow them to set sail before midnight. Theo said his good-byes to the young couple and wished them well. They thanked him profusely and once again there were tears swimming in Jane's eyes.

Her last words to him were, "Farewell, dear friend. And do take care of our Hannah for us."

"I will," he promised and suddenly knew he *would* do so—that is, if he could persuade that prickly, independent female to allow him to.

Theo spent the night in an inn on the outskirts of Liverpool and returned to Crofton late in the afternoon of the following day. He went directly home and arrived at the Hall in time to change from his travel clothes and enjoy supper with his aunt.

"Did you stop in the village?" she asked him. Mathilda Stimson always spoke of Crofton as "the village," though it had long since outgrown that designation.

"No. I came straight home."

"You have not yet heard the news, then." She waited expectantly.

He indulged her. "What news?"

"Of the fire. There was a fire last night at the Crofton school."

Theo was instantly alert. "Miss Whitmore's school?"

"The very one."

"Was anyone hurt?"

"No. It happened past midnight. Seems to have been deliberately set."

"Set? But who—? How much damage was there?" Theo asked. Hannah would be beside herself, he thought.

"No one knows who did it, but it *is* certain that it was no accident. The damage was quite extensive. Hannah said they will have to move their classes."

"You spoke with Miss Whitmore?"

"She was here this afternoon to give me a full accounting," his aunt said proudly.

"And how did she take this unfortunate incident?"

"She is devastated, of course. All of Crofton is, I think. She has had ever so many offers of sympathy, and people are already organizing repairs. Can you believe it?"

"But *she* is all right?" Theo persisted and his aunt gave him a speculative look.

"She is fine. Mad as hops, of course. She is determined to carry on, though. Next week classes will be held in her father's church—and the Methodists offered their church, too. Mrs. Pilkington—she took Miss Thomas's place, you know—she is a Methodist. So whoever did this has not shut down Hannah's school." She ended on a note of pride again.

The next day, Theo found her assessment of the situation to be true. He rode by the site of the school and found one end of the building virtually destroyed. Blackened beams shone through the roof. A number of people were engaged in salvaging what could be salvaged from the disaster. When he asked, he learned that Miss Whitmore had been there earlier, but had gone home now. He then called at the vicarage to offer his support and to report on his journey with the Franklins. He found Miss Whitmore saddened by the fire, but undaunted. He, on the other hand, voiced caution and concern.

He invited her to walk in the garden with him. A profusion of yellow daffodils, blue flags, and colorful primroses were a treat to the eyes, but Theo hardly noticed them in his need to impress upon this irrepressible female that she should be more careful.

"The fire may have been intended as a warning." He began tentatively as they walked along the path.

"Oh, I am sure it was—but I will not be intimidated by some coward who strikes in the night."

He stopped her by putting his hand on her elbow. "Miss Whitmore. You seem to insist on underestimating the danger you may be attracting."

"What are you suggesting?"

She gazed up at him. He was momentarily lost in the depths of her eyes. An image of the sky during a summer shower flashed through his mind. "I . . . it . . . you must take care. This time, whoever it was struck at property. Next time he—or they—may strike at your person." He reluctantly released his hold on her.

"I cannot believe I am in any *personal* danger," she said. "Who would care so much about a mere school?"

"You have crossed swords with some powerful people," he reminded her.

"If you mean Lord Mayfield in particular, I am aware that he is angry with me. He called yesterday to speak with my father—again."

"What did he say?"

She shrugged. "Besides his usual complaint that my school stirs up discontent in the district, he wanted it known that of course he had nothing to do with that unfortunate fire. But he did hope it would serve as a lesson to me."

"How did you reply to that?" Theo asked.

"I was not here at the time. *I* would have sent him away with a flea in his ear!"

"Good for you! Though you would probably have angered him even more."

"Perhaps. But that man needs to understand that the whole county is not obligated to do his bidding. He tried to prevail upon my father to *order* me to limit my school to townspeople and farmers—and to leave mill people alone."

"How did the Reverend Mr. Whitmore respond to that?"

"Well, Papa did not exactly send him away with a flea in his ear." She chuckled softly. "However, he did point out that I am of age and enjoy a degree of independence."

Theo grinned at this obvious understatement. She went on.

"And—Papa also reminded Lord Mayfield that this church living is granted under the auspices of the Earls of Glosson—none of whom has *ever*, Papa said, deigned to issue commands to the vicar."

"You may assure the vicar that neither the present earl nor his successor would ever entertain the idea of doing so."

Her smile was broad, genuinely amused—and captivating.

"Oh, thank you, my lord. I am sure Papa will find that news most welcome."

Theo grunted. "I am beginning to see exactly where the vicar's daughter comes by her independence."

They walked in silence for a few moments, then she said, "I assume Henry and Jane are off to the United States safely."

"They sailed on the evening tide the day we left here."

"I shall miss them both most dreadfully."

Once again, Theo wondered if she would miss the lawyer more than the teacher, but it was not a question he had a right to ask.

"They will adjust to their new life well enough," he assured her. "Once we were away from Crofton and the good-byes, their spirits brightened considerably."

"Oh, good. But of course I knew they would—both are incurable optimists, you know."

"I think they were somewhat concerned about *you*," he said.

"About me? Whatever for?"

He was slightly uncomfortable. He still wanted to impress upon her a need for caution, though he did not want to alarm her unduly. "Well . . . they . . . uh . . . seemed to think you have a tendency to be . . . well, impetuous."

"Oh, honestly!" she protested. "Henry is always accusing me of being overly enthusiastic." She paused, then added more soberly, "At least he used to do so."

"You might bear his worries in mind," Theo suggested.

"You truly *are* concerned," she said disbelievingly.

Again he stopped. He took both her hands in his and waited for her to meet his gaze. "Yes, I am. Concerned, but not overly alarmed. However, I do wish we knew more about the fire."

"So do I," she said fiercely. "But if anyone—*anyone*—thinks that will be the end of our school, he is very badly mistaken."

"Could you not hold off on reopening for a couple of weeks? Or even a month? Allow things to die down, as it were?"

She withdrew her hands from his. "Absolutely not! Why, then they would think they had me beaten!"

"Does what anyone *thinks* matter so much? I thought you were made of sterner stuff."

"Are you suggesting I am a coward?" she asked, apparently on the edge of anger.

"Good Lord, no! However, I think a bit of prudence might be in order."

"School is reopening on Monday," she said flatly. "And that, my lord, is that."

"Are you always so headstrong?" he asked impatiently.

"I prefer to think of it as being positive and able to stick to a given task."

He could tell she had her back up and he knew he should ease off, but he did not do so. "Did that fire teach you nothing then?" he demanded.

"Now you sound exactly like that odious Mayfield." Her voice was cold.

"Look," he said with the patient air of one trying to reason with someone of limited understanding, "I am merely suggesting caution. We do not know if that fire was really directed at the school—or at you, personally. Next time—God forbid—you could get hurt. And it might not be you alone."

"Well, *of course* it was the school," she said, dismissing any other consideration.

"You cannot know that."

"I have lived in Crofton all my life. Never—*never*!—has anyone in any way seriously threatened me."

"There is always a first time," he said. "I am going to assign someone to keep watch over you."

Her voice rose in indignation and she clipped off each word distinctly. "You will most decidedly *not* do any such thing! I have given you no right to do so—nor will I."

"Miss Whitmore—Hannah! Be reasonable. I shall do this for your own good."

"No! You presume too much, my lord," she said angrily.

"And furthermore, I never gave you permission to use my given name."

His own temper had sprung to action. His voice now was laced with sarcasm as he gave her an ironic and exaggerated bow. "My most abject apologies, *Miss* Whitmore. It will not happen again."

"I . . . I think this discussion is over," she said, somewhat calmer.

"It would appear so," he said tightly. "I shall take my leave."

They were silent as they retraced their steps and their good-byes were cryptic.

Nevertheless, my foolish, foolish friend, he vowed silently, *I* will *set someone to keeping watch over you.*

And, in the end, he was glad he had done so.

Twenty

Some two hours later, Hannah had finally calmed down enough to think rationally as she paced about her room like a caged lioness. The interview with Lord Amesbury had started out so well. How on earth had it become so . . . so ugly? She tried to recapture every word, every subtlety of tone. She thought his concern for her was genuine, but did he have to be quite so autocratic in expressing it? And what was it that always seemed to turn her insides to jelly when he touched her in even the most superficial way?

She knew she had overreacted and she was embarrassed for having done so. She had just lashed out at him. And that business about her name. Why on earth had she carried on so about her *name*? In fact, she had *loved* hearing her name on his lips. She stood next to her bed and pounded her fist against the bedpost. Would she *never* learn? Henry was right. He had once told her she "needed a keeper."

Still—her overreacting did not mean that his lordship was right. There was absolutely no reason not to resume classes as planned on Monday. And so she would. The next time she saw Lord Amesbury she would merely pretend today had never happened. Should he prove to be so ungentlemanly as to bring up the topic, she could simply say, *We were both wrong*. Which was, after all, the truth.

As she was sorting this out, there was a knock on her door.

"Are ye in there, miss?" the housekeeper called.

Hannah opened the door. "What is it, Mrs. Warren?"

"You have a guest, miss. I put him in your father's study as your mother is entertaining parish ladies in the drawing room and the vicar is out."

"Thank you, Mrs. Warren. I shall be right down."

So—Lord Amesbury, too, had cooled off and they might continue their discussion rationally and he would surely see the error in his position. She quickly pinned up some stray strands of hair that had loosened during her furious pacing.

It was not Lord Amesbury who rose from a chair in her father's study.

"Mr. Smythe-Jones! Oh. I mean, Lord Castlemaine. I had not expected to see you."

"No, I don't suppose you had," he said. "I did not send a note so you had no chance to refuse to see me." He smiled as if to indicate how ridiculous *that* notion was.

He was rather solicitous in guiding her to a chair. She sat and folded her hands in her lap and waited for him to speak. He did not immediately do so. Instead, he draped himself in a rather decorative manner along the fireplace mantel. Lord Byron came to mind and Hannah smiled inwardly at the thought that Castlemaine's pose was *intended* to be "Byronic." Well, Claudia was right—Castlemaine *was* a handsome creature, with thick, blond hair, dark brows, even features, and a most attractive physique.

"You . . . wanted to see me?" she finally prompted him.

"Yes. I wanted to tell you how sorry I am about what happened to your school."

"Goodness. News *does* travel fast if you have heard about it in Barnsley already!"

He laughed. "Ah, no. Not that fast. I arrived just yesterday for a visit with Mayfield. Old school chums, you know."

"Yes, I remember," she said. Then she added politely, "I appreciate your interest in my school."

He gave her an intimate little smile. "Actually, my interest lies more with the *teacher* than the school."

She started to rise. "Lord Castlemaine—"

"No. No. Hear me out." He waved her back into her seat. She sank back reluctantly.

"Perhaps the fire was rather fortuitous for you," he said.

She was appalled. "Fortuitous! How could you possibly think it a lucky circumstance to have the building damaged, books destroyed, lives upset?"

"It *was* unfortunate in that respect," he admitted. "However, it occurred to me that it provided you an opportunity to reexamine your . . . your goals and decisions."

"Well, yes, I suppose any sudden calamity in one's life has that effect." She admitted this much, but wondered where this was going.

"I thought perhaps that you might view this particular . . . incident . . . as I do—as a sign from heaven."

"A sign from heaven?" she repeated without expression.

"Yes." He warmed to his topic. "A sign that you should be a wife and mother—that you should fulfill the only role for which God intended all women."

"I see. . . . And do you believe He intended men to be only husbands and fathers?"

"Well—no. But men are different."

"Yes, they are." She controlled the urge to laugh.

Suddenly, he was on bended knee before her. He grasped her hand. "Miss Whitmore—Hannah. I have the greatest regard for you. Please say you will do me the honor of being my wife."

"My lord, I—"

"No. Do not refuse me out of hand as you did before. That was—what?—two years ago? Surely, you have had time to reflect on what an advantageous match it would be for both of us." He reluctantly allowed her to withdraw her hand from his.

"Lord Castlemaine, I . . . I do not know how to say this any plainer than I have in the past. I . . . I simply do not believe we would suit."

"Oh, but we would. Dear Hannah, we complement each other in every way. I daresay that as a married couple we should command quite a position in the *ton*."

"But—"

"And our two properties together would make us the most important landowners in the whole area of Barnsley."

She stood and moved apart from him. He stood as well.

"I am sorry, Lord Castlemaine. It . . . would not work."

"But of *course* it would," he insisted. "I understand a woman's need to seem reluctant, but really, my dear, we have already wasted two years. Also, I should point out that I have more to offer you now that I have finally come into the title. You will go from being a vicar's daughter to a *lady*."

Embarrassed, Hannah was at a loss for words. "I . . . hardly know what to say," she mumbled.

"Never mind, my dear. I know this is all a bit overwhelming for a delicate female such as yourself."

Delicate female? He certainly could not know her very well, Hannah thought. She cleared her throat and spoke hesitatingly, groping for words that would not hurt. "Lord Castlemaine, I . . . I am of course mindful of the great honor you do me, but . . . well . . . I cannot—indeed, I will not—marry you. Not now, not ever."

His expression darkened and Hannah could see that he controlled his rage only with difficulty. "How *can* you so blithely turn me down?" he asked. "I cannot believe you are likely to get a better offer."

"Nor can I," she said gently. "But, really, my lord, we would not suit. We would make each other miserable."

"Perhaps you will change your mind," he said. "I shall be Mayfield's guest for the next month or so."

"Please do not presume that I will do so," she said as she moved toward the door.

He took the hint and left, giving her a perfunctory bow and saying, "I am not giving up so easily."

When he had left, Hannah sank back into her chair. So. Claudia had been right. That may have been my last chance to be a wife and mother, Hannah thought. But somehow she could not be sorry she had turned down Castlemaine's offer—again.

In the next several days, her life settled into a new routine. Classes held in the church were not as comfortable for either teacher or students as those in the classroom had been. But the classes did meet and students were making progress. After classes each day, Hannah made a point of checking on the progress of repairs to the fire-damaged school.

She had noticed Benjamin Britton hanging around the church occasionally as she conducted classes. Once she asked him if he would not like to rejoin the lessons he had given up a year ago.

"Oh, no, ma'am. I am working as a stable hand for Lord Amesbury now," he said proudly.

"Not as a weaver?" she asked in some surprise.

"No, ma'am. I love horses, you know. Lord Amesbury, he let me work with his stable hands. They all say I have the makings of a first-rate hand, too."

"How nice, Benjamin."

"The hours ain't so regular as at the mill, but the horses . . ." his voice swelled with pride and wonder.

"I am glad you enjoy your work, Benjamin," she said. She dismissed the conversation, and later took little notice of Benjamin's hanging around from time to time.

Hannah worked late many days, and in May when the days were starting to lengthen, she continued this practice. Late one afternoon as she left the church, a man accosted her.

"Miss Whitmore?"

"Yes?"

"This way, ma'am."

She innocently stepped in the direction indicated. Only later did she even think of the fact that the man, dressed very much as any mill worker, was unknown to her. She followed him for two steps, then felt a hand come over her face. She struggled, then everything went black.

She had no idea how long she had been unconscious. She knew she was in a carriage that was traveling at a very fast pace. She pretended to be still unconscious.

"Shouldn't she be comin' around?" a male voice asked.

"Soon," another answered.

"I ain't likin' this one bit," the first one said.

"Never mind. We're gettin' paid good. We jus' take her to the lodge and we'll be off in the mornin'."

"I don't know . . ."

"Don't go coward on me, now."

"Who you callin' a coward?"

Hannah recognized neither voice; nor had she any idea where they were. The "lodge"? That word stuck in her mind. Finally, she dredged up a connection. A very out-of-the-way building, located deep in a wooded area. It was used mostly by hunters during a certain season of the year.

This was not the season.

She lay very still, trying to think of a plan of action.

"Shouldn't she be comin' around now?" the worried voice asked again.

"Soon, I said." The confidence in this voice had a false ring to it.

Finally, the carriage rumbled to a stop. The sun had gone down and night was upon them.

"Here we go," the second man said cheerily. He put his hands under her armpits and tried to maneuver her to the door.

Hannah moaned and pretended to be only just becoming conscious. "Wh-where am I? Wh-what is going on?"

"Never mind, ma'am," the first voice said. "Just watch your step," he said as the other one guided her from behind.

She was ushered into a large room of what was certainly the lodge and then quickly propelled upstairs. She tried to protest, but the men who had brought her were efficiently guiding her and there was no one in the room they passed through.

"Here," a disembodied voice said.

She was shoved into a room and behind her she heard the thick clunk of a bar settling into place on the heavy, cross-timbered door. *No! Do not panic,* she admonished herself.

There was a lamp lit on a table. She could see a neatly made bed. A window showed dim light from a half-moon and stars. Checking the window as a possible means of escape, she found there were bars on it. She thought that a decidedly strange feature of the room. In any event, it was apparent she was a prisoner, but of whom? And why? She panicked for a moment and pounded on the door.

"Let me go!" she screamed.

"Just you settle down now, ma'am," called a male voice she did not recognize.

She pounded on the door again and tried it repeatedly and yelled out again and again. The door did not budge and there was no answer to her calls. None whatsoever. She retreated to the bed, sat on it, and examined her surroundings more closely. There was a tray on the table, along with the lamp. Investigation revealed that it held a bottle of wine, a jug of water, some bread, some cheese, and three apples. So—her captors did not intend to starve her.

She wracked her brain for some explanation of this bizarre situation. Kidnappers pursuing young women usually did not go for staid schoolteachers. Despite being in a near panic, she was determined to keep her wits about her. All would become clear in time, she told herself.

She sipped at the wine and nibbled at the bread and cheese. Eventually, sheer boredom overrode her fear and pressed her back against the pillows. She dozed until she heard the bar scraping on the door.

Theo, waiting in the library for his aunt, had just come down for supper when he heard a commotion in the entranceway.

There was a youthful shout of, "You jus' better let me see 'im, old man!"

Theo stepped into the foyer.

A flustered Knowlton said, "My lord, I am sorry, but this . . . this person—"

"It's all right, Knowlton. Let him in."

Knowlton sniffed, but opened the door to admit Benjamin Britton.

"Britton! What are you doing here?" Theo dreaded what the boy's answer would be.

"You said as how I was to keep an eye on her—Miss Whitmore, I mean."

"Yes. What has happened?"

"Two men. They grabbed her and took her off in a closed carriage."

"When?"

"An hour—maybe two hours ago."

"What?" Theo wanted to strangle the lad. "And you waited until *now* to tell me about it?"

"I was exercisin' that little black mare, my lord—you know, sort of killin' two birds with one stone."

"Get to the point," Theo snapped.

"I followed 'em."

"You followed them?"

"I hadda see where they was goin'."

"And did you?"

The boy nodded, obviously pleased with himself. "I did. They went south 'til the road forks at the Hays cottage, then they went left—an' the only thing down that road is an old huntin' lodge—but it ain't used except during grouse season."

"How far?" Theo asked, his mind furiously absorbing details.

"Hmm. 'Bout two miles from that fork in the road. An' it's maybe four or five miles to the fork."

"Two men?" Theo asked.

"An' a driver," Benjamin said.

"At least three, then—plus whoever is in the lodge."

"The lodge is usually deserted except for one month in autumn," Benjamin repeated.

"Thank you, Britton. You have been a great help."

The boy did not waste time basking in Theo's praise. "Can I go with ye to find her?"

Theo wished fervently there *were* someone to go with him. He did not like the odds he would find at that lodge. But a young, untried boy? He wished David Moore were here, but he was still in London pursuing his courtship of Miss Bridges.

"No, Britton. Not right away, at least. I would like you to run a couple of errands for me, though."

"Yes, my lord." Benjamin was disappointed, but Theo knew he would carry out the tasks.

"First, go over to the vicarage and inform the Reverend Mr. Whitmore of what has happened. *Only* the vicar, now, you hear? Let him decide whether to tell his wife."

"Yes, my lord."

"Tell the vicar not to worry. I *will* bring his daughter back to him."

Benjamin nodded.

"Then go and find Tim Hessler and Dick Yardley and bring them out to that inn as fast as you can."

"Yes, my lord." Benjamin's enthusiasm picked up at the idea of his being truly included after all.

"And Britton—"

"Yes, my lord?"

"Not a word to anyone else, you hear? We must try to protect Miss Whitmore's good name."

"Yes, my lord."

Theo did not pause to change his clothes. He did take the precaution of arming himself with a pistol and a knife. Following Benjamin's directions, he rode as fast as the limited light from the moon and stars would allow—when those sources of lumination managed to make themselves known through a cloudy sky. Rain was in the offing and he just hoped it held off until this business was over. He had difficulty finding the lodge and, at one point, he thought he might have taken a wrong turn. Then suddenly, there it was, a large, darker shadow against the dark shadows of trees that surrounded it. A faint light shone from an upstairs window and a brighter light issued from one below.

He left his horse some distance away and edged quietly toward the building, praying all the while that no harm would have come to Hannah. He circled the lodge and managed to peep into the downstairs windows. Two men were playing cards in one of the rooms. Another man seemed to be dozing in a chair in what must have been the main room on the ground floor. A stairway along one wall led above to the first floor where, Theo conjectured, Hannah was being held.

Deciding that straightforward surprise might be his best strategy, he quietly ascended the outer steps and burst through the entry door, pistol in hand.

"Where is she?" he demanded.

The dozing man came to attention abruptly and waved away the gun in something of a panic. "Hey! They ain't no need of that. She's above—as planned. Hey! Cyrus—the nob's here—just like you said."

A burly, dark-haired man looked out from the side room. He held playing cards in one hand. "Well, take 'im upstairs like you was told."

Puzzled, but alert, Theo kept a grip on his pistol, but he did lower it. He wondered at the reference to a "nob," but he decided to play along for the moment. As he and the dozer started up the stairs, Theo replaced the pistol in his belt.

The burly one called up behind them, "Remember what you're supposed to do."

"Right." The dozer sounded annoyed at being reminded.

As they reached the top of the stairs, Theo noted four rooms, each with a heavy door, one of which had a thick bar in place. The dozer removed the bar and opened the door.

Theo stepped into the room, but did not immediately see Hannah. He stepped farther across the threshold and just as he turned to look around the room, something large hit his head with a decided "thunk." He was thrown off balance for a moment; then he heard the door close behind him and the heavy bar fall into place.

Twenty-one

Hannah, startled into wakefulness, experienced a moment of sheer terror as she heard movement at the door. She jumped from the bed, looking around for a weapon—any weapon. She spied a chamber pot on the lower shelf of the bedside stand. "Too bad it is empty," she muttered to herself even as she grabbed it and scuttled behind the door.

As it opened, she was treated to the view of a set of broad, well-clad shoulders. Knowing she would have only one chance, she gripped the handle of the pot and swung her weapon mightily at the dark head sitting on those shoulders. Unfortunately, her aim was off and the pot did not hit her target directly.

Her dazed victim turned and she recognized Lord Amesbury. Her relief and delight were tempered by horror at what she had done. She heard the door swing shut and the bar fell into place.

"L-lord Amesbury! Oh! I am so sorry."

He shook his head as though to clear it and rubbed a hand over the spot she had hit. "Good God, woman, is this any way to greet someone come to help you?"

She dropped the pot onto the carpet and stepped toward him. She raised a hand to try to examine his wound in the dim light. "I said I am sorry. . . . And, besides, how was I to know you were a rescuer?"

He did not immediately answer her question. Instead, he caught her exploring hand, pulled her close, and just held her for a time. It seemed the most natural thing in the world—as though *this* was where she had always belonged.

"Damn!" he muttered against her hair.

"Wh-what is it?" she asked, stepping back a little but not willing to lose the comfort of his arms. "Are you all right? Did I hurt you terribly? Th-the skin is unbroken."

"No. I mean—yes, I am all right—though you *did* manage a telling blow!" He looked into her eyes and said ruefully, "I came here fully intending to rescue you—and it looks as though all I have managed to do is have myself entrapped along with you."

"Oh!" Fear and concern shadowed her eyes.

"Are *you* all right?" he asked. "Did they harm you?"

"No. They *frightened* me out my wits, but nothing else—at least, not yet."

"You will be safe now," he assured her, not at all certain it was wholly true. "Have you any idea what this is about?"

"None whatsoever," she replied, reluctantly giving up the comfort of his embrace. "They said nothing that made any sense to me. And then they put me in here. That was perhaps two or three hours ago."

"One of them said something about a 'nob' when I arrived."

"A gentleman? I have seen none," she said. "You don't suppose Lord Mayfield . . . ?"

"That is exactly what I suppose," he said grimly. "At least, that was my first thought. But then they seemed to think *I* was the 'nob' they expected. It makes little sense."

She sat on the edge of the bed. "I am sorry you have to be involved, though I am ever so grateful you are here. You were right, of course."

"About what?"

"About my being in some sort of personal danger. I just could not accept that idea. But you were right."

"If it is any consolation to you, I take no satisfaction in that fact, Miss Whitmore." When she said nothing in reply, he went on in a heartier tone. "So. I assume you have examined our prison cell. Is there a way out?"

"The chimney—if we were starving children with fewer than six years. There are bars on the window and that door is extremely thick and heavy—not to mention that there is a substantial bar across it on the outside."

"So I noticed," he said, pacing the room, examining every aspect of it closely. It was a small room, so this did not take long. He finally seated himself on the only chair, a straight-backed, wooden chair such as might be found in a country kitchen. He glanced at the bread and cheese. "At least they do not mean for us to starve."

"How long do you think they intend to keep us?" she asked.

"I suppose that depends entirely on *why* we are here. I doubt it will be overly long, though, for I have people following."

"How did you know?" she asked, rejecting a momentary suspicion that he might be trying to teach her a lesson. No. Surely no one would go to such lengths just to say, I told you so."

"Benjamin Britton."

"Benjamin?"

"He has been keeping an eye on you for me."

Her temper flared. "You had that boy spying on me? How dare you!"

"Looking out for you. And a good job he did so. I might have been too late."

She lifted her chin belligerently. "Well, I don't like it."

He rose and pulled her to her feet. He put a finger under her chin to force her to meet his gaze. "What don't you like?" he asked softly. "That I am here?" His lips brushed hers and she trembled, her lips automatically responding. He lifted his head momentarily. "No, that's not it, is it?"

Her arms crept up and around his neck. She leaned into him, responding to the next kiss with characteristic enthusiasm.

He emitted a triumphant little laugh. "No, not that at all."

She felt herself blushing furiously and she would have moved away, but he held her even tighter—and she found she did not mind in the least.

He laced his fingers together behind her and leaned his shoulders back to gaze into her eyes. "So, my prickly Miss Whitmore, what is it that you don't like?"

She felt foolish at being so easily disconcerted. "Y-your ignoring my wishes," But she was honest enough to admit—if only to herself—that she was glad he had done so. "Oh, fap!" she muttered in defeat.

"Fap?" He chuckled. "What kind of a word is that?"

She lifted her chin, but smiled. "A perfectly good one for the occasion—and it is certainly an improvement over your swearing!"

"Miss Whitmore, dare you chastise me as yet another schoolboy?"

Pulling her close, he kissed her again, exploring her mouth with his, tentatively at first, then with far more urgency. She lacked experience in the art of kissing, but she did not lack enthusiasm. She felt herself discovering a whole world whose existence had heretofore been virtually unknown to her.

He drew back and said a bit shakily, "Miss Whitmore, I-I think we should perhaps . . . uh—"

"Hannah," she whispered.

"Wh-what?"

"Call me *Hannah*. I want to hear you saying my name."

He smiled in gentle mockery. "So—Miss Whitmore is granting me permission to use her very name?"

She gave him a shake—of sorts. The man was rather like an immovable boulder. "I might have expected you to throw that back in my face," she said. "However, under the circumstances . . ."

"And what circumstances might those be, my dear Hannah?" he murmured just before his lips claimed hers again.

And again, she responded mindlessly, though they finally paused long enough for her to say, rather dazedly, "These?"

"Yes, first names are definitely in order under these circumstances." He kissed her again. "Hannah."

"Theo," she murmured experimentally, rolling the two syllables aloud over her tongue.

"Good." His tone was almost normal as he stepped back and, holding her hand, propelled her toward the bed, where they both sat on the edge. "Much as I should like to continue exploring our . . . uh . . . circumstances," he said, his tone both wry and suggestive, "I think we'd best postpone them."

She felt herself blushing, but she had to agree with him. "H-how long do you think we will be held captive?"

"I have no idea. It would help if we knew why these rascals grabbed you. And what 'nob' they were obviously expecting."

"I thought we agreed that Lord Mayfield—"

He cut her off. "I think Mayfield is involved somehow, but there is more to this than merely trying to discourage an inordinately stubborn schoolteacher."

"What else *could* it be?" she asked and a sudden stillness came over her. "No. No, it could not be."

"What?" When she did not respond, he gave her a shake and repeated, "What?"

"Lord Castlemaine is visiting Lord Mayfield."

"I heard as much, but what has that to do—"

She found herself unable to meet his gaze. "I—he came to visit me."

"To visit you?" he prompted patiently.

"He—he asked me to marry him. Again."

"Castlemaine is in love with you?" he asked, clearly surprised.

She took umbrage at his tone. "What would be so amazing about that?" she challenged.

He chuckled and put an arm around her shoulders. "Not a thing, my sweet. Not a thing. It is just that the man has always struck me as being far too enamored of himself to admit another to his circle of admiration." He kissed her temple.

"Oh. Well, I suppose you are right. And, to be quite truthful, his real interest in me is a piece of property I am one day to inherit from my godmother. It lies next to Castlemaine's primary holding."

"I doubt that is his *only* consideration," Theo said.

"You needn't play the gallant with me," she said.

"Nor am I. However, if this *was* some bizarre plan of Castlemaine's, I think we have effectively foiled him." He gave her a peck on the cheek. "Climb up there on the bed and pull the blanket over your legs. It is getting cold in here."

He rose and brought the lamp to set it on the bedside stand. Then he brought the tray with the bread, cheese, and wine. He gave her the tray to hold as he settled himself beside her. He took the tray, retrieved his knife, and began to slice cheese, then pare an apple.

"We may have quite a wait," he said in response to her look of astonishment. "Soldiers learn to eat and rest when they have opportunity to do so."

"How long?" she asked again, pouring wine into the only available drinking vessel, a pottery cup.

He appeared to be doing some mental calculations before he answered. "Well, it probably took Benjamin at least an hour to see your father and then locate Hessler and Yardley. They will not make as good time as I did because—in case you've not noticed—it has started to rain. Nor is there any longer moonlight to go by."

"Raining? Oh, so it is." She now heard the rain on the roof that she had been too distracted to hear before. "It must be nearly midnight by now," she said dolefully.

"It is. So eat up. Get some rest."

There was something wonderfully intimate about their sitting together on the bed—though the blanket clearly separated them—sharing food and drinking from the same cup. Her senses were heightened, but she succumbed nevertheless to emotional exhaustion as the wine mellowed her anxiety. Eventually, she became drowsy.

Theo was glad to see her begin to relax. They even managed to chat about mundane matters—the rain would be good for gardens; an improved canal system was helping transport of goods to markets; Henry Franklin and his bride would be docking in America soon.

Theo had feared the last topic might be a sensitive one for her, but she seemed perfectly at ease with it. Besides, those kisses she had readily shared with him certainly did not bespeak an enduring *tendre* for another man.

Which was just as well, Theo thought, for, though he was quite sure the enchanting vicar's daughter had not yet realized it, she would have to marry *him*. He wondered if he should broach the subject now, but thought better of it. He set the tray on the floor, slipped an arm around her, and settled her head on his shoulder. Eventually, he, too, dozed.

He had no idea how long they had slept when he heard a commotion from below. He stroked a hand gently along her jaw.

"Wake up, Hannah. Something is going on downstairs."

"What? What is it?"

"I don't know. Listen."

They listened intently. Muffled shouts swirled up from below, but the voices were indistinguishable. Soon, they heard pairs of feet ascending the stairs. Theo jumped off the bed and took a position where Hannah had stood earlier. He waited, pistol in hand. The door rattled as the bar was raised. He could hear a male voice, very distinct and very angry.

"You blithering idiots have certainly made a mull of a simple enough task."

Theo looked at Hannah, who mouthed the name *Castlemaine*. He nodded.

The voice of one of their hosts whined, "How was we to know? That sly by-blow what hired us said a gentleman would come for her. Well, a gentleman did show up. Dressed to the nines, he were."

"I am sure Mr. Taggert must have given you far more explicit instructions than that," Castlemaine said. "You were just too stupid to listen. Now get this door opened!"

Taggert! The name startled Theo until he remembered that Taggert now worked for Mayfield. So, there really was a connection here.

The door swung inward and Castlemaine rushed in, two others behind him.

"Oh, my dear Hannah, my darling girl. Are you all right?"

His voice dripped solicitude. "Have these ruffians harmed you at all? I shall have their hides. I would have been here much sooner, but the road is so wretched and my carriage kept sliding and knocking me about so."

Hannah threw the blanket off her legs and stood even as one of their captors said, "Where's the other one—that first nob?"

"Right here," Theo announced and all three men turned to look at him, their eyes riveted on the pistol in his hand.

"Oh, God! I forgot he had a barker," said the man who had been the first to encounter Theo earlier.

Castlemaine hurried to Hannah's side and pulled her to him. "It is all right, my darling. You are safe now. I have rescued you. Everything will be fine. You shall see. We will be married and there will be no talk of this night."

Before Theo could growl out his vehement protest to this notion, Hannah gave Castlemaine a hard shove that put him off balance for a moment. "You . . . you arrogant ass!" she spat out at him. "You! You engineered all this for the sake of a few acres of property? What kind of vermin are you, anyway?"

"I know you are upset, my dear—"

Before he could finish what he was saying, there was more commotion from downstairs.

"Castlemaine!" a voice called. "Are you here?" It was Mayfield. "I have Mrs. Grimes with me." Mayfield's tone was hearty as he climbed the stairs. "She has volunteered to lend Miss Whitmore some semblance of propriety."

Mrs. Grimes? This was not a name Theo immediately recognized. Then he recalled his aunt's labeling the woman the worst gossip in three counties. With that, the last piece of the puzzle slipped into place, though the picture had already been quite, quite clear.

Lord Mayfield crowded into the room, ushering Mrs. Grimes ahead of him. She was a portly, gray-haired woman of middle years with sharp, pale-blue eyes that darted about, missing nothing. Theo groaned inwardly.

Mayfield looked rather self-satisfied until his gaze fell on Theo, whose pistol had not wavered. "You! Amesbury, what are *you* doing here?" he blustered.

"One might ask the same of you, *my lord*," Theo said calmly. "Just how is it that a gentleman comes to lend his credence to the sordid business of trying to compromise a young woman?"

"Oh, come now. Castlemaine and I only happened to hear of this and came to rescue her. I have even brought Mrs. Grimes—"

"To be sure the story is well and truly aired," Theo finished for him.

"I assure you I had nothing to do—"

Again Theo interrupted. "Cut line, Mayfield. We all know this fiasco was arranged by Taggert—*and* we know that Taggert now works for you. Taggert himself would have little interest in Miss Whitmore's affairs, but you—and Castlemaine—certainly would."

Mayfield drew himself up in a pompous show of umbrage. "You cannot seriously think *I* would be a party to what you are suggesting. Why, that is preposterous!"

"Oh, is it?" Theo asked.

Just then there was another loud commotion coming from the entrance below. Theo stepped nearer to Hannah, who had been inching closer to him all the while. He now moved in front of her and, gesturing with the pistol, said, "Everybody, downstairs."

It took some maneuvering to get the small mob down the narrow stairway, with Theo and Hannah bringing up the rear.

"Don't worry," he said softly to her alone, "it *will* be all right."

She merely looked at him, her eyes revealing a stricken bleakness. It crossed his mind fleetingly that she now grasped the whole situation.

When the entire group had reassembled in the larger room downstairs, they found that Yardley, Britton, Hessler, and the vicar had arrived moments before.

"Papa!" Hannah flung herself into her father's arms.

Theo could not make out the soft words of comfort the clergyman offered his daughter.

"Well, Major," Yardley said with a show of disgust, "don't appear to me like you needed us at all."

"Not until now," Theo said, "but I am glad you have come, all the same."

Light was beginning to show in a leaden sky by the time things had been sorted out and everyone could leave. Theo sent the vicar and Hannah home in the carriage that had brought her to the lodge, with Benjamin Britton as driver now. Mayfield and Castlemaine, still blustering about their respective innocence—they had only happened on the scheme accidentally—were allowed to leave in Mayfield's carriage. They took Mrs. Grimes with them.

This left the final three, who had apparently been duped—and bribed—into their part in the incident. Theo was in a quandary concerning them. What he *wanted*—and surely what they deserved—was that they be tried for kidnapping Miss Whitmore and then be sentenced to a very long term at very hard labor. Theo sat silently for a while, trying to sort out his options.

Finally, Tim Hessler voiced the question on all their minds, including Theo's. "What're you goin' to do about *them*?"

"Be easy enough ta just kill 'em. Hide their bodies in the woods. They just disappear like," Yardley said with a casual shrug that *seemed* real enough.

"I suppose." Theo pretended to give the idea serious consideration.

"No! You can't do that," cried the burly one who had been playing cards much earlier.

"The lady wasn't hurt none," said another in a supplicating tone.

"Hmm. There is that," Theo agreed.

"Ah, just haul 'em off to gaol," Hessler said. "A few years of hard labor would serve them well."

"I say just kill 'em," Yardley said again. "Nobody would know nothin.' I woudn't even think twice about it."

"Yeh," Hessler agreed. "*They* sure didn't think twice when they done what they did to Miss Whitmore."

"We was told she would *like* the idea," the burly one protested. "The way we got it was that their nob was goin' ta marry her—an' this was just a bit of play-acting."

"Play-acting!" Theo exclaimed, his anger only partly feigned. "You would ruin a woman's life for a bit of 'play-acting'?"

"We needed the money," said the third one, who had been silent until now.

"And did you get your thirty pieces of silver?" Theo asked bitterly.

"Our *what*?" The burly one's face wrinkled in consternation.

Theo made a dismissive gesture. "Never mind."

There was more silence.

"Well?" Yardley prodded after a while.

"Search them for weapons," Theo said. He watched, holding his pistol at the ready, as Yardley and Hessler patted them down, but they found only a small pocket knife. "Shut them up in the room they had Miss Whitmore and me locked into. I shall return to Crofton and send you some assistance. I think the Osborns would be willing to help."

"Then what?" Hessler asked.

"You will take them to Liverpool and find a press gang looking for some extra ship hands."

"Impressment?" one of the three asked in horror.

"There *is* the alternative of the woods," Theo said coldly.

Yardley gave an exaggerated snort. "Civilian life has gone and made you soft, Major. You're too easy on 'em."

"Perhaps."

Hessler and Yardley took the three upstairs. Theo heard the heavy bar on the door thud into place; then they returned.

"You will be all right?" Theo asked.

"Sure. There's food in the larder—enough for today, anyway," Hessler said.

"The others should be here by noon," Theo said. "With luck, you can all be back in Crofton by late tomorrow."

"I hope that damned Taggert gets what's comin' to him

for his role in this little bit of 'play-acting'!" Yardley said vehemently.

"I would surmise that Lord Mayfield has already seen to Taggert's disappearance," Theo said with more than a little regret. He would have taken great satisfaction in seeing to that task himself.

Which was, in fact, exactly what he did, however inadvertently.

Twenty-two

Late in the afternoon, there was a knock at Hannah's door.

"Hannah, dear," her mother called. "Please, daughter. You cannot hide in your room this way."

Hannah opened the door. She knew she looked a fright, and she saw by her mother's reaction that her appearance was even worse than she had supposed.

"Just today, Mama. I cannot face any visitors yet."

"Lord Amesbury was here asking to see you," her mother said. "I told him you were not up to receiving visitors."

"Good."

"But that you would be receiving tomorrow."

That gives me twenty-four hours to contract the plague, Hannah thought.

"He spoke at great length with your father," her mother went on.

Wonderful, Hannah thought. That was *not* news she really wanted to hear. Not that it was even news; she had expected exactly that.

The carriage ride back from the lodge had allowed her to sort out some things, with her father acting as a sounding board. Hannah had managed to hold her tears until the carriage was under way.

"Oh, Papa, this is so awful." She tried unsuccessfully to stifle the sobs. "Everything I have worked for—for years, and now it is gone. Just gone—in a blink!"

"We cannot know that, my dear."

"Mrs. Grimes will not waste a minute spreading this

around. It will add fuel to those other rumors and innuendoes."

"It will die down." However, there was little conviction in the vicar's voice.

"If the school is to survive, I can no longer be intimately associated with it."

"You could be right about that," her father conceded sadly. "I know how much your teaching has meant to you. Yours is a calling—not unlike my own."

"Do you suppose Mrs. Lewis could be persuaded to take over my classes?" Mrs. Lewis was one of the vicar's widowed parishioners who often assisted in Sunday school lessons.

"I am sure she would be glad to do so—at least for the few weeks left in this school term. And—who knows?—this may prove to be a nine days' wonder." But, again, he did not sound convinced.

They were both lost in thought for a while; then the vicar spoke again.

"Would you like to go away for a while? You could visit Lady Folkeston, perhaps—or Dorothea."

"No!" Hannah said vehemently. "I will give up my teaching for the sake of the school, but I will *not* sneak out of town like a guilty criminal. Papa, *I have done nothing wrong*!" She pounded her clenched fists on her knees.

"I know you have not," he soothed. "Your mother and I will stand by you, whatever the outcome of all this."

Her father's verbalizing her parents' support was at once comforting and more distressing as Hannah considered what her family would endure once the scandal broke. The vicar's daughter alone in a bedroom with a man for God knew how long—that bit of gossip would be far too juicy to keep.

Once they arrived home, she busied herself making detailed notes for Mrs. Lewis, who had readily agreed to fill in for the remainder of the school year. For Hannah, this mundane task was a helpful diversion. Still, she succumbed to occasional but short-lived bouts of tears. She took both luncheon and supper on a tray in her room. Knowing her parents were worried about her, she tried to reassure them.

"Just let me have today. I will be all right tomorrow."

She slept fitfully that night, but forced herself to resume as normal a schedule as possible the following morning. She went down to breakfast and then offered to help her father with some copying and filing. She was engaged in this task when Mrs. Warren announced the arrival of Lord Amesbury.

He greeted her and her father politely, then invited Hannah to walk in the garden with him. Feeling a bit panicky, she looked toward her father, who gave her a reassuring smile.

"A lovely day, is it not?" Her voice was high and stilted.

He agreed politely and steered her toward the bench under the large elm tree that provided a haven of green. When they were both seated, he said, "I think you know why I am here, Hannah."

She nodded, unable to meet his gaze.

"Hannah?" He put a finger under her chin to turn her face toward him. She reluctantly raised her eyes. His voice was gentle. "We must marry, you know. I spoke with your father yesterday. He and I agree that this is the best course of action."

"No," she said quietly.

"No?"

"No. I will *not* be forced into marriage—nor will I welcome a husband who feels *obligated* to offer for me."

"Perhaps I was a bit clumsy in the asking. But Hannah, be reasonable. We must do this. And after the other night, I cannot believe you harbor some aversion to me personally."

She felt herself blushing. "That was . . . well, the circumstances . . ." She paused and blushed even harder at her choice of words. "What I mean is, we were in a strange situation and . . . well . . . things happened that should not have."

"Are you sorry? Do you regret my kissing you? Your kissing me? Did you find the experience repulsive?"

"No, of course not," she admitted, slightly exasperated. "However, that should not be a primary consideration for marriage."

"I disagree—it is a *very* important element."

Refusing to allow tears, she ended by sounding stiff and formal. "I am sorry, Lord Amesbury. I simply do not think we would suit."

"It was *Theo* at the lodge," he reminded her. "And you have offered no reason for that vague 'we would not suit.'"

"I should think that would be explanation enough for a gentleman," she said, now a bit haughty as well.

"Perhaps there is still more soldier than gentleman in me," he said. "And know this, Hannah Whitmore—I do not retreat easily. I shall return tomorrow to resume this particular battle."

"Please, my lor—Theo. Do not do this to me."

He caressed her cheek with the knuckles of two fingers. "I fear I must, my sweet. In the meantime, you should discuss my offer with your parents. I think they will agree this is the right thing to do."

After supper that evening, she did, indeed, bring up the subject of Lord Amesbury's offer. She fully expected her parents to support her decision. Had they not done so—however reluctantly on her mother's part at times—with every other important turning point in her life?

"Are you serious?" her mother expostulated. "You turned down an offer of marriage from a decent man who will one day be an earl?"

"I am not hanging out for a title," Hannah said defensively.

"Obviously." The vicar's wife gave a ladylike snort. "And just as obviously, you have given no consideration to your family in your hasty decision."

"You—you accuse me of being selfish? Mama, how could you?"

"Because that is precisely what it is. Selfish pride. Lord Amesbury is doing the honorable thing. And you just refuse him—willy-nilly?"

Hannah controlled the urge to weep. She had done enough of that lately. "I do not want him *obliged* to marry me!"

"Hannah," her mother said with a great show of patience.

"You cannot afford girlish nonsense. You were alone with the man for several hours. Everyone knows that. You have been quite thoroughly compromised."

"But nothing happened. I . . . I mean . . . nothing that would require marriage as a remedy."

Her mother did not notice Hannah's hesitation and said, "That is entirely beside the point. You know very well it is *appearances* that matter in cases like this. Good heavens! You do remember your Cousin Emily."

"Cousin Emily *wanted* to marry Harkington. She deliberately arranged for him to be caught in her bedroom at a house party."

"I know you are innocent in this, Hannah." Her mother's voice was more gentle now. "But you must think of your sisters—especially Katherine. A scandal like this could well ruin her chances at making a good match. Tell her, Charles. Please. You are the only one she ever listens to."

"Mama!" Hannah protested.

"I am afraid your mother is right," her father said, sounding reluctant and infinitely sad. "Lord Amesbury has made you an honorable offer. And I think the two of you have no real aversion to each other—have you?"

"Well . . . no," she conceded. "But I hardly think 'no aversion' much of a foundation for marriage!"

"Many a marriage has succeeded on less," her mother said.

"Papa? You . . . you really think I must do this?"

Her father gazed at her in sympathy and pain. "I think it the best course for *you*, Hannah. The family would survive the scandal eventually, but it would follow *you* all your life. I would not urge you to do this if it were Castlemaine—but Amesbury is a good man. He will honor you."

Hannah felt tears streaming down her cheeks. She wiped at them in a gesture of futility. "All right. I agree. I shall accept his offer."

Her mother breathed a loud sigh of relief.

With a special license, Lord Amesbury claimed his reluctant bride ten days later. It was mid-June and the wedding day turned out to be one of those days that seemed designed especially for such events. Hannah tried to put a good face on the situation. Under different circumstances—if he loved her—she would have been ecstatic at the idea of marrying Theo. She readily admitted to herself that she was in love with him.

She knew—from those kisses in the lodge and a few since that had been more chaste in nature—that they would undoubtedly enjoy the marriage bed. Moreover, they would probably rub along well enough together outside the bedroom, too. As the appointed wedding day approached, she grew more and more accepting of her fate. However, she still deplored the idea of having a man coerced into marrying her.

She even took a strong interest in the gown she would wear, a rich, cream-colored silk. Owing to the limited time the seamstress could be given, the style was very simple. Hannah thought it suited her very well. Theo had presented her a diamond-and-pearl necklace the day before, which complemented the betrothal ring he had given her when he returned that day to renew his suit.

The wedding ceremony took place before a relatively small audience of immediate family members. Theo's parents and sister had arrived three days before the event—as did Hannah's sisters, along with Dorothea's husband. David Moore and Katherine served as their official witnesses. The Reverend Mr. Whitmore officiated as his daughter became Lady Amesbury. A wedding breakfast at Glosson Hall was followed in the afternoon by a grand outdoor party for tenants, cottage weavers, and mill workers attached to the Glosson earldom.

Hannah had steeled herself for the occasion, determined to keep a smile pasted on her face the whole while. However, she found herself genuinely enjoying the day. She was gratified that her new in-laws readily accepted her.

"I don't know why I did not think of it myself," the Countess of Glosson said. "You are perfect for my son."

"Just be happy, daughter," her father whispered to her as the two of them shared a moment before the breakfast.

The mill workers were grateful for a holiday and a feast hosted by the earl himself, but Hannah could tell that beyond their paying dutiful tribute to the earl, the Glosson people truly liked and admired the man currently in charge of Glosson concerns. Their affection for Theo readily extended to his new bride, whom they had always esteemed in her own right. Now that any hint of scandal had been averted, they showed no reluctance in their acceptance of her new position in their midst. After overhearing several flattering comments about her person, she found her anxiety fading.

The wedding day dragged on and despite her nervousness, Hannah was glad when Theo insisted in the early evening that they make their good-byes and leave the party, which would continue without them. There were good wishes, teasing comments, and knowing glances as they left.

Hannah's personal belongings had been transferred to Glosson Hall. The countess and the housekeeper had given her a tour of her new home three days before.

"Of course, you and Theo will occupy the master suite," the countess had informed her. "Edward and I prefer the London and Wiltshire properties and we are perfectly happy in a guest suite here at Glosson Hall."

"That is wonderfully generous of you, my lady," Hannah replied.

The countess laughed. "Nonsense. Edward and I are shirking our responsibilities shamefully and laying them on you and Theo."

"I think there are probably enough responsibilities to go around," Hannah said hesitantly. "Lord Amesbury—Theo—does not seem to feel put-upon."

"Not now. But he did at first," the countess said frankly. "I am glad he will have *you* to share his duties."

Hannah had not yet really thought of this aspect of her new status. But, yes, sharing the duties of managing the Derbyshire holdings of the Earl of Glosson would, indeed, help make up for the loss of her teaching position. She began to feel better about this forced alliance. Even if her husband were not in love with her, he would be kind and affectionate. Her life here could be every bit as fulfilling as the one she had envisioned for herself prior to that night in the lodge.

"Ah, here we are," the countess said, swinging open the door of the master bedroom. Hannah felt as though she were somehow invading Theo's privacy. There were two dressing rooms connecting with another bedroom as richly decorated as the master chamber, but in a far more feminine mode. Both rooms reflected a style popular in the previous century.

"Faded elegance," the countess pronounced. "Of course, you will want to have them redone. You know, if you and Theo shared the master chamber, this room would make a marvelous private sitting room. It catches the morning sun."

Blushing furiously, Hannah mumbled, "Yes, it would seem so."

"Oh, my. I have embarrassed you, haven't I? Do forgive me, my dear. My family are always saying I am far too blunt."

"Not at all, my lady."

"Hmm. That 'my lady' is far too formal. I cannot be your mama, for you already have one. Perhaps you will call me *Mother* as Theo does. Would you be comfortable with that?"

"Yes, my lady—after the wedding, I would." Hannah had been glad to have the subject shifted away from sleeping arrangements.

Now, as Theo steered her upstairs, she nervously considered that very subject. He opened the door of his own chamber and invited her in with a sweeping bow. A small fire burned in the fireplace and a single lamp cast a gentle glow about the room, making the elegance seem less faded. A cold supper was laid out on the table; a bottle of champagne cooled in a container.

"I see my mother's hand in this," Theo said, breaking the silence as he closed the door firmly.

"Very nice," Hannah said.

He stopped in the middle of the room and put his hands on either side of her face. "I've wanted to do this all day." His kiss—slow, gentle, and infinitely sweet—ignited a smoldering longing in her.

"I want you to share this room with me—always," he said softly. "However, if you prefer your own chamber, I will respect your wishes."

"I have not shared a bed with anyone since my sister Dorothea married," she replied. "But I . . . I like the idea of sharing with you."

"Ah, Hannah." He pulled her closer and kissed her far more deeply this time. As usual, she felt that wonderful tingling, quivering sensation that left her breathless with desire for more and yet more.

He began to unpin her hair, trailing his fingers gently through the freed tresses. "I have dreamed of this," he said, his voice husky.

"I have, too," she admitted, "but I fear you have the advantage of me."

He paused. "What do you mean?"

"I . . . I think you probably know precisely where we go from here—but I am woefully ignorant."

He laughed. "A 'problem' that is easily remedied, my love."

His hands worked busily at tiny buttons down the back of her gown. He showered sensual kisses down her face and neck as he pushed the dress off her shoulders. Her own hands were not idle. She loosened his neckcloth, unbuttoned his waistcoat, and pulled his shirt from his trousers. She slipped her hand under the shirt and thrilled at touching the bare skin of his chest.

"Just a moment," he said. He kicked off his shoes and shrugged out of his upper garments. Hannah followed his lead by stepping out of her gown and removing her slippers. She stood before him trembling, but with anticipation, not cold.

He pulled her close again, and through the thin lawn of her chemise she felt his firm chest against her breasts. He kissed her again, his hand cupping one breast. She leaned into his touch and felt her nipples eagerly hardening. Against her belly, she felt an answering hardening of his body.

"Hannah," he moaned and gently pushed her toward the bed. He lifted the hem of her chemise and drew it over her head. Modesty had her drawing her arms across her chest.

"No. I want to see you—all of you," he said softly, seductively. And—wanton that she was—she wanted to show him. She held his gaze as she loosened her arms and slowly wriggled out of her pantalets and began to roll her stockings down from her thighs.

"My God!" he whispered in wonder. He pushed her down onto the bed and began caressing every inch of her body, kissing, nibbling, and licking as he explored. His mouth closed over first one nipple, then the other, and she thought she must surely go mad with wanting.

Then his hand moved up the inside of her thigh and she held her breath in eager anticipation. His fingers probed into that most secret part of her body and began to stroke gently, but firmly. Now she knew she had gone mad as her body thrust against those beautiful, wonderful strokes. She heard a whimpering sound and knew it came from her own throat.

He swung away from her for a moment.

"No," she wailed.

He laughed down at her as he removed his trousers and socks. Now he, too, was as naked as she. She gazed in wonder at his stiffened member and momentarily doubted if it would fit her body.

He lay back down beside her and pulled her close. She gloried in the feel of skin against skin the full length of their two bodies. He began those magnificent caresses again and she savored each one of them. His fingers again moved inside her. Then he was *kissing* her there, his tongue stroking where his fingers had before.

"Oh! Theo! Please. Please."

He raised his head and kissed his way up her body.

"Please what?" he teased.

She tossed her head from side to side. "I—I don't know!" she said. "I just want . . . want—"

"And you shall have it, my darling," he whispered. He held her head still and gazed into her eyes. "Hannah? This will hurt the first time—are you sure you are ready?"

She nodded and strained her head up to kiss his mouth as she whispered, "Yes. Oh, yes!"

He positioned himself above her and she felt the smooth, firm warmth of him slide into her. He pushed against her and there was, indeed, a sharp pain.

"O-oh!" she gasped and froze.

He stilled his movements. "Hannah? Are you all right?"

She hesitated, trying to decide whether she *was* "all right."

"Hannah?" His voice was concerned.

"Yes. I am fine," she said, now relishing the magic of the total oneness of their two bodies. Her arms around his neck stroked his shoulders.

He kissed her again, deeply, and she opened completely to him. As his body stroked into hers, she instinctively lifted her hips in eager welcome.

"Oh!" she gasped again as a shattering warmth spread through her. She gripped his shoulders even tighter.

Within moments, his final thrusts came and he collapsed on top of her. He lay there for a moment, then rolled to her side, hugging her to him.

"Theo?"

"Hmm?" He sounded sleepy.

"Is it always like this?" she asked.

"What?" He was clearly alert now.

"Is it always like this?" she asked, impatient now.

"It will get better," he assured her.

"Oh. . . . Oh!" she said in wonder, then added shyly, "I . . . I thought this was . . . well . . . quite wonderful."

He chuckled and drew her even closer. "So did I, sweetheart. So did I."

She had worried needlessly about this aspect of their marriage. She might have a husband who had been forced into a marriage he did not want, but he was a gentle, considerate lover. She could have done much, much worse.

Twenty-three

He was breathing with difficulty. The horse constricted any movement of his legs. The dead accused . . . and accused . . . and accused . . .

"No," he groaned. "No. Not now."

He jerked awake to find Hannah raised on one elbow staring at him, fear and sympathy reflected in her eyes along with the lamplight.

"Theo? What is it?"

He blinked. The horror receded. "Nothing. Just a dream. Go back to sleep."

"No. You cannot put me off so easily. Tell me."

"It's a dream. It's not real. Well, perhaps some of it is."

"Tell me," she insisted. She pushed her pillow up and reclined against it. With no hint of shyness, she drew his head to her bare chest and whispered against his hair, "Tell me."

And so he did. Later, he was not sure why he chose that moment to unburden himself, but he recounted the entire dream to her—and the incidents that were behind it.

"You have been living with this horror for two years?"

"Longer."

"You blame yourself for those deaths." It was not a question and there was no hint of skepticism in her voice.

"I suppose so—yes."

"Even Molly Tettle and your brother—and that beastly Logan—as well as Henshaw and Slater?"

"I know it does not make sense—"

"Such things rarely do," she said.

"But it is so *real.*" He tried to control the shudder that wracked his body. "I should have . . ."

"Should have what?" she asked. "Died with them? But you didn't. And thank God you did not!"

"I don't know," he mumbled.

She raised his head to force him to meet her gaze. "Theo, think! What would have happened if you had countermanded an order from a higher officer? Might it not have had some repercussion elsewhere on the battlefield? Can you really know what the outcome would have been?"

He stared at her in wonder. It was such a simple question. But—no—he had never really considered the issue in that light.

"And as for Molly and the others," she continued, giving him an admonishing shake, "those are not your fault, either. Molly knew what Logan was. She felt she had to do what she did. We all make the choices we *have* to make at any given time. It does no good to relive them over and over—even if they *were* mistakes."

"You don't understand—"

She ignored his interruption. "And yours were *not* all mistakes. You saved the lives of five men a few weeks ago. You gave Henry and Jane a real chance at life."

He took a deep breath and sat up straight. He pulled her into his arms and just held her tight for several moments, thinking of what she had said.

"Theo?"

"Hmm?"

"Are you all right?"

"Yes, I think I am—now." He pressed his lips to her hair, drinking in the faint scent of lilac. "I had no idea I was marrying such a fount of wisdom."

She hugged him and turned her head up for a lingering kiss. Then she giggled. "A fount of hunger at the moment."

"We missed our supper!" He threw back the bedcovers, went to the table, and filled two plates with delectables. "Here." He handed her the plates and returned for two glasses of champagne, then rejoined her in the bed.

"I love picnics," she said.

"Wait 'til we get to dessert," he said suggestively and took great delight in her blush.

Dessert proved to be very worth the wait.

It was nearly noon the next day when Theo and his blushing bride emerged from their sojourn in Paradise. They had broken their fast in their room and enjoyed another satisfying "dessert" before making their way downstairs. She truly *was* blushing and he knew he wore a self-satisfied grin. They found the countess and her daughter in the drawing room playing with Cassie's two small children.

"Good morning." His mother greeted them just as though this were a normal hour and a normal day. Theo shot her a look of gratitude and she winked at him.

Cassie smiled knowingly and echoed her mother's greeting.

"The men have gone out—they *said* they were going to shoot rabbits, but I think they were tired of 'girl talk,'" his mother announced with a laugh.

"We shall be leaving tomorrow," Cassie said. "Dwight does not like to be away for too long."

"So shall we," his mother said. "Glosson has business with the infamous five."

Later, his mother cornered Theo for one of her little mother-son *tête à têtes*. She tracked him down in the library.

"Your Aunt Stimson is showing off some new exotic plants to Cassie and Hannah. I only just managed to escape," she said with a smile.

"Lucky you." He seated himself beside her on a settee.

"You mean *clever* me, for now I have a moment alone with you." Her voice turned serious and she patted his knee. "You *will* be happy, won't you, Theo? I could not bear it if you were unhappy."

"You needn't worry, Mother."

"I *do* worry. That is what mothers do, you know. I mean,

this all happened so suddenly and the circumstances . . . well . . . it will be only a nine days' wonder, now, but—"

"It is *all right*, Mother. Hannah and I will rub along quite well together." He lifted her hand and kissed it. "Perhaps even better than either of us might have expected."

The countess gave her son an assessing look. "Good heavens! You are in love with her—truly in love with her!"

Theo grinned and said wryly, "I suppose I am. I mean, yes. I am. But I don't think Hannah is quite ready to have that thrust upon her."

"Do not underestimate that young woman, my son. She is stronger than you think."

"Perhaps . . ." he said vaguely.

"Tell her. Soon."

They were interrupted as the earl and Cassie's Dwight returned from their hunt. When they admitted to returning empty-handed, the countess gave Theo an I-told-you-so look and smiled.

In the next several weeks, life within the walls of the master chamber of Glosson Hall was nearly idyllic. However, Hannah and Theo were not oblivious to events swirling around them.

Theo had been considering plans to build better housing for his workers. He would start with two buildings of flats that would accommodate families of six or more.

"That is a very generous idea," Hannah said when he broached the subject to her one night as they prepared for bed.

"No, it is not—not at all. It is actually a very self-serving plan."

"How so?"

"People who have a decent place to live and are able to feed their children properly will, in the long run, be far more productive in the mill."

"And of course that is your only consideration."

"Of course," he said and effectively cut off the conversation by nibbling at her earlobe and neck.

Hannah found her new status as Lady Amesbury carried far more weight than she had anticipated. The town committee for rebuilding the school insisted she should head the group. There was no mention of the circumstances of her marriage. Invitations poured in for the newlyweds, and Hannah took advantage of every opportunity to advance her ideas of educating underprivileged children. It was a particular triumph when she managed to enlist the aid of Lady Kitchener and Mrs. Childress. These two apparently thought there would be some social advantage to being associated with a woman destined to be a countess one day.

David Moore returned for a visit. Hannah suspected the former soldier had reasons beyond mere friendship for his frequent visits to the Hall. She liked him immensely and found him an easy comrade. He put her in mind of Henry Franklin.

The evening meal often saw only the four of them—Theo, Hannah, Aunt Stimson, and David—at one end of the long dining table.

"Have you heard a rumor of trouble at the Mayfield Mill?" Miss Stimson asked one evening. "The Gilmore sisters were here this afternoon and they were going on about such."

"Mayfield has been having his ups and downs on many fronts," David said.

"Such as?" Hannah prodded.

David grinned. "Well, he thought he had that pesky teacher out of his hair—but darned if she didn't bounce back stronger than ever."

Hannah smiled and Theo gripped her hand briefly, a gesture that was not lost on their companions.

David went on. "And now that husband of hers backs her more than ever." He glanced at Theo. "You know, of course, that Mayfield is openly courting Lady Olivia?"

Hannah went very still, waiting for Theo's response.

"Yes. I had heard. Jenkins mentioned it in his last letter," Theo said casually. Too casually? "I am far more interested in the progress of another courtship, though," Theo said pointedly. "When are we to wish *you* happy, my friend?"

Moore reddened and said, "Soon, I hope. Anne is beginning to wear her father down."

"Very good," Theo said.

"Back to Mayfield, though." David hunched forward in his chair. "He blames his troubles on you, Theo. I'd watch my back if I were you."

"Why on earth would he blame my nephew?" Miss Stimson asked.

"His troubles?" Hannah asked. "You mean that fire in his storage barn?"

"Right. It destroyed a good deal of raw cotton for his mill."

"He could hardly blame Theo for *that*," Hannah insisted.

"I am sure he knows full well I had nothing to do with the fire," Theo said reassuringly.

"Of course he does," David replied. "But he also knows that his own workers are unhappy and that yours are intensely loyal. And believe me, the whole county knows who was really behind that kidnapping—despite his having turned off that Taggert fellow."

"Your little brother talks a great deal," Theo said, sounding slightly annoyed.

"Well, Andrew listens," David said. "He is concerned, too. Doesn't want to see anything happen to you and Lady Amesbury. He likes his job—and you—and your wife."

Miss Stimson changed the subject by asking Mr. Moore about a recent trip he had made to Brighton. He entertained them with descriptions of a grand ball at the Prince's pavilion there.

Later, Hannah asked Theo, "Do you think Lord Mayfield would really do anything . . . well, truly hurtful?"

"Aside from aiding and abetting a kidnapping, you mean?" Theo responded bitterly.

"H-he thought he was helping a friend in that event," she said.

"But it *could* have been disastrous," Theo said. "Come. Forget about Mayfield. I want to take my wife to bed."

Putting all thought of Mayfield out of her mind, his wife readily agreed to that plan.

Theo wanted to strangle David for discussing Mayfield's affairs so openly and causing concern to Hannah. Undoubtedly, she knew most of what touched on anyone in Crofton. Still, she need not have things spelled out quite so explicitly. Theo, too, made it a point to try to keep his finger on the community's pulse. He was fully aware of the unrest among workers at other mills. He also knew that many owners resented the changes he had instituted in the Glosson enterprise.

He no longer tried to persuade others to his point of view, but he knew word had got out that, despite shorter work hours for adults and eliminating very young children as workers, the Glosson Mill was still turning a healthy profit. That had to annoy those waiting for him to fall on his face. He tried to confine himself to his own concerns and let others go their own ways.

Then came word of two more mishaps aimed at Mayfield. A barge transporting Mayfield's knitted goods to market sank under mysterious circumstances. Mayfield hired several investigators, but they turned up nothing. A few days later, Mayfield's mother, the baroness, was held up by highwaymen as she traveled to London in her son's elegant coach. While the scoundrels did steal her jewelry, their real aim seemed to be to terrorize the old woman.

"Theo," Hannah said on hearing of this last incident, "this must stop. Frightening an old woman half out of her wits is beyond enough!"

"You are right, my dear. I shall see what I can do." In truth,

Theo thought Mayfield deserved his ill fortune, but Hannah was right—it had gone far enough.

He called a meeting of Glosson overlookers and a few other leaders among his mill workers and cottage weavers. They crowded into his steward's office along with Larkin and David Moore.

"I am quite certain," Theo began, "that none of our people are involved in these incidents directed at Lord Mayfield. However, these things can take on a life of their own and escalate out of hand."

Yardley and others nodded, though Theo could see little enthusiasm in their agreement. They, too, probably thought Mayfield had earned his misfortune.

"What do you want us to do?" the man named Cranston asked with a shrug.

"Not encourage it, for one thing," Theo answered. "I want the word to go out that I will personally take an interest in any further such event. And I will see those responsible—*whoever* they may be—punished to the fullest extent of the law."

Yardley reported later that there was some grumbling about how "owners always manage to stick together," but attacks on Mayfield came to an end.

School, of course, was in summer recess, so Hannah's educational concerns centered on the reconstruction of the fire-damaged building. She had also maintained her interest in the Corresponding Society, though she had been hesitant to be too pushy in her interest there. She feared members would reject her participation. After all, she was married to one of the owners, and, while Theo was looked upon with much more favor than other owners of mills, he was nevertheless one of "them."

To her surprise and delight, members of the Society continued to welcome her. While the group was largely made up of mill workers—with only a smattering of merchants and professional people—the meetings generally focused on political issues rather than working conditions.

In fact, throughout the spring and early summer, leaders of the Society stressed over and over that the group—along with other similar clubs and societies—was interested only in promoting *political* reform. They were well aware that advocating radical ideas of trade unionism and revolution was strictly illegal. The goal was to stay within the letter, if not the spirit, of the law.

Their desire for reform thus focused primarily on two issues. The first was that the House of Commons should be reorganized so as to be more representative of the population at large. Furthermore, certain seats in Commons would no longer be under direct control of this or that member of the House of Lords. The second major issue was a demand for universal suffrage. Other concerns were the government's continued suppression of freedom of the press and the attempts to prevent large public meetings by labeling them "seditious" and "revolutionary."

"These are not unreasonable demands," Hannah insisted when she discussed them with Theo one afternoon as the two of them enjoyed a stroll in the Hall's extensive gardens.

"I suppose that depends on one's point of view," he replied mildly. "Members of Lords who control seats in Commons are unlikely to agree with you."

"But, Theo, that is precisely the point."

"And universal suffrage? No property qualifications? Just anyone is allowed to vote?"

"No," she said in disgust. "Only men. I did point out that it could hardly be termed 'universal' if half the adult population of the country is deemed unqualified!"

Theo gave a hoot of laughter. "Were you serious?"

"Well . . . yes. But even in our own Society meetings we women are not allowed to vote. Mind you, we can *talk*, but not vote. Now—is that not ridiculous?"

He chuckled and gave her a hug. "Ah, Hannah. You are a woman before your time! I shall have to keep you away from my mother. The two of you might prove dangerous to the natural superiority of males."

"Be serious," she said.

"All right, I shall. What do you know of this massive meeting planned at St. Peter's Fields?"

"It has been in all the newspapers. Oh, Theo! It is going to be so wonderful! Hundreds—perhaps thousands—of people will be there to hear Orator Hunt speak on these very things."

"Sounds like a recipe for chaos to me," her husband said.

"Chaos? Oh, no. People are being advised by all the organizers—especially Mr. Hunt himself—to proceed in a very orderly manner."

"I hear they are being trained to march with military discipline," he said.

"There has to be *some* organization if it is to involve so many people."

"Are you determined to participate in this affair?"

"Yes. Why should I not?"

"Hannah, you know as well as I do that Hunt's orations tend to be overly zealous. The organizers of this thing skate on the very edge of revolution and sedition."

"I think Mr. Hunt is rather scrupulous in avoiding such issues," she said.

"Not everyone agrees with you. Hunt is not universally trusted. The man is likely to be arrested before he even opens his mouth. Trade unions and radical reform are not popular ideas in government circles."

"No one plans to push such ideas at this meeting!" she said heatedly. "Why can people like you not accept the idea that reforms are necessary?"

His voice became dangerously quiet. "What does that mean—'people like me'?"

She plunged ahead, heedless of the change in the tone of the conversation, intent only on having her say. "The ruling classes. The landowners of this county are so fearful of losing their hold on wealth and power that they attempt to stifle every attempt to make life better for the majority of the people."

"Is that right?" he asked sarcastically.

"Yes, it certainly is! And it is beyond time they learned to share."

"Are you not ignoring the fact that some of your so-called reformers are interested in little more than gaining some ill-placed glory for themselves? They like seeing their names in headlines and banners. For some the real goal is grabbing a little of that power strictly for themselves—those are the sorts that are hardly interested in promoting the welfare of some anomalous being known as 'the people.'"

"What a horrible thing to say."

"But true. They are not universally honorable and noble individuals."

"You attempt to demean the ideas by attacking the character of those proposing them?"

"No. You seem intent on twisting my words—but that is beside the point. This meeting is likely to be disastrous and you would do well to avoid it."

"Are you forbidding me to be part of this gathering? After all, the wedding vows required me to promise to 'obey'—you have the power there, too."

He scowled. "No, I am not 'forbidding' you anything. When have I done so? I am merely suggesting you exercise some common sense. However, if you insist on this venture, I will do my duty in escorting you."

"You need not trouble yourself, my lord. I plan to accompany the speaker and the others who will be on the platform. That is, unless you forbid it."

"Do as you wish," he said coldly and walked away.

Hannah wanted to cry but refused to allow herself that luxury. How on earth had this discussion taken such a disastrous turn?

Twenty-four

The argument left Theo angry, irritated, and saddened. He had thought Hannah was truly coming to care for him. Had it only been an illusion, then? Poor, deluded Theo needed her so much that he would imagine affection where it did not exist? Her passion and desire in the marriage bed belied this view. Yet her words and tone in the argument clearly labeled him one of the "others" in an ongoing war of some sort. Just as clearly, Hannah saw herself as a defender, and him an oppressor, of less fortunate beings.

Were they—in his wife's view—on opposite sides? More important, was this a social and intellectual gulf of such monumental proportions that it could not be bridged? Would they end by smoothing over the surface argument and never deal with the profound issues at its root? Would they muddle along, being meticulously polite to each other, never allowing a spark of opposition for fear of what it might bring? He knew he would find such a sterile existence intolerable. The question was—how to resolve this conflict before it dissolved into polite indifference.

He taxed himself mightily with this dilemma as he worked through some of his frustration on the back of his favorite mount. He rode furiously for a time, then slowed the horse to a walk. Finally he returned to the Hall, still dispirited. He had resolved nothing.

He entered the library to find David Moore lounging on a couch, reading a newspaper. David gave him a questioning look and asked, "Troubles in paradise?"

Theo responded evasively. "Why do you ask?"

David sat up and shrugged. "No reason. It's just that I saw Hannah a while ago and she was wearing the same bereft expression you are sporting."

"Is that so?" His tone did not invite further discussion on *that* topic. "Is there anything in that paper worth reading?"

David took the cue. "Interesting, if not worthwhile. Says here that rally in St. Peter's Fields in Manchester is being postponed a week."

"Postponed? Why?"

"Apparently to ensure that the demonstration goes off in as orderly a manner as possible."

"Hah!" Theo said. "What it really does is allow the magistrates to organize their opposition."

"They cannot stop it, can they? The gathering is perfectly legal, as I understand such things."

Theo ran a hand through his hair. "If they want to stop it, they should do so now—before it gets started. But you are right—it *is* legal, so the town fathers will sit around, wringing their hands until they confront a real crisis." His tone was bitter.

Before David could respond, Knowlton came in to deliver a note. Theo read it quickly, then handed it over to David. "From Yardley. Strange."

David read it and handed it back. "What is so strange? He says he has something to tell you. He has conveyed information to you before, has he not?"

"Yes. But this asks me to meet him at The Wild Boar. He usually just comes here—or we have met at The Silver Shield."

"'The Wild Boar'? Sounds unsavory."

"It is," Theo said. "Still, perhaps Yardley has some reason for choosing this place."

"Could be a ruse of some sort," David warned.

"Not from Yardley. I'll have to go. If I have not returned by suppertime, make my excuses to Hannah, won't you?"

David nodded, but wore a worried frown.

As he rode out to The Wild Boar, Theo was reminded of his

last visit to this establishment and the discovery of Logan's body. Entering the tavern, he did not see Yardley. The publican took one look at the newcomer and nodded in the direction of a hallway leading to a private room. "The gent's awaitin' fer ye."

Theo's senses were instantly alert, and he was glad he had thought to put a pistol in his belt, uncomfortable as it was. He opened the door decisively. The room had only one heavily draped window, so the light was dim. Theo did not immediately recognize the man seated at the table with his back to the window, his features shadowed. The hair on the back of his neck rose as he sensed, but did not see, another person in the room.

The man did not rise as he gestured to a chair. "Welcome, Lord Amesbury." The tone was sarcastic and triumphant.

"Taggert! What do you want? What have you done with Yardley?"

Taggert's laugh was an ugly sound. "Why, I've not seen your pet boy in some weeks now."

"The note is a forgery."

"Quite good, don't you think?" Taggert asked. "'Tis a talent that comes in handy occasionally."

Theo, still standing, demanded again, "What the hell do you want?"

Taggert's voice lost any semblance of geniality. "I intend to get my own back at you, *my lord*. You queered a very nice life for me. But that wasn't enough, was it? You even interfered with my little enterprise with Mayfield. It's your fault he turned me off. You'll not get away with it—not any more than your nosy brother did."

Taggert gestured and two rough-looking men stepped out of the shadows and grasped Theo's arms. One of them relieved him of the pistol.

"Now," Taggert said smugly, "we are going for a little ride in the woods. Unfortunately, one of us will not return." The former steward now had a gun in his hand.

"You won't get away with this." Theo tried to stay calm. He would wait for a chance to use the knife still in his boot.

"Everyone will simply assume Lord Amesbury ran afoul of some poacher," Taggert said. "And *we* shall be long gone by then."

"You would have been wise to have been long gone before now," Theo said. "I shall see you hang for killing my brother."

Taggert ignored this and barked out orders. "Sam, tie his hands. Carl, check the taproom and the hallway—we don't want any unexpected visitors."

Carl returned shortly to report all was clear and Theo, his hands bound, was propelled down the hallway to a back door, then out to the stable yard.

They stopped in the shadows at the side of the stable. "Get the horses," Taggert ordered Sam, who, a few minutes later, returned with Theo's still-saddled mount and other similarly equipped animals.

"I do hope you will enjoy your last ride," Taggert said in a nasty caricature of polite courtesy as the man named Carl helped the bound Theo mount.

"I would not count on this being his last ride," said a voice from behind them.

Taggert and the others swung around quickly. Sam squeezed off a hasty shot in the direction of the voice. Theo, unbalanced as he was, dug his heels into his horse's side and, using his knees to guide the well-trained animal, managed to knock Carl to the ground.

"No! You will not get away," Taggert screamed and aimed his pistol directly at Theo.

The shot went wild and Taggert himself was dead before his bullet found a target.

David Moore and Dick Yardley rushed to the other two and quickly subdued them and released Theo's bonds. The shots had brought patrons out of the tavern.

"Not again!" the publican moaned. "Things like this can give a respectable tavern a bad name."

When the sheriff had been sent for and the excitement had died down, Theo tried to thank Moore and Yardley.

"I'm just glad we got here in time," Yardley said, "though I must say, this is gettin' to be kind of a habit, ain't it, Major?"

Theo clapped him on the shoulder. "I sincerely hope not." He turned to Moore. "What made you follow me?"

"I don't honestly know. Battlefield hunch, I suppose. I just went out to find Yardley here and knew we had troubles when I found him."

"Well . . . thank you." Theo gripped his friend's hand tightly.

They were late—very late—for supper and found Hannah nervously waiting for them. She explained that Aunt Stimson had taken a tray in her room. Although their first inclination had been to conceal the whole business from Hannah, Theo and David had agreed on an abbreviated version of the evening's activities for her. Gossip would eventually reach everyone in Crofton.

Still later, Theo discovered that his wife was not as mollified by their story as she had pretended to be in front of their guest.

He sat in his dressing gown in a comfortable chair near the fireplace in their bedroom, waiting for her to finish her evening ablutions. He pretended to read as he wondered if this would be the night Hannah chose to avail herself of the bed in the room next door. What would he do if she did?

"You might have been killed," she challenged as she emerged from her dressing room in her nightrail.

He tried to shrug off her concern, not wanting another confrontation when he, at least, had not yet recovered from the one earlier. "I might also break my neck falling down the stairs."

She ignored this sally. "You could at least have *told* me before you went jaunting about the countryside chasing God-knows-what phantom."

"There wasn't time. The note sounded urgent."

"Still . . . all I had was a cryptic message from Knowlton,

who told me Mr. Moore had said the two of you might be late. I thought . . . well . . ."

"Well, *what*?" he asked, rising to stand in front of her.

"I thought perhaps you were still angry with me . . . and you had—oh! I don't know!" She threw up her hands in a gesture of helpless frustration.

He caught her hands in his and chuckled softly. "You thought I had gone off to sulk?"

She laughed nervously. "Well . . . yes."

"I did," he admitted sheepishly. "But I did so earlier with a long, rather vigorous ride."

"Oh." She sounded equally sheepish as she said, "I spent that time at the pianoforte, abusing poor Handel."

He chuckled again and drew her close. He began to trail teasing kisses from her shoulder to her ear.

She stood very still, unresponding, but not rejecting his caresses. "Theo. You needn't think I will be so easily distracted. You might have been killed!"

"But I wasn't, was I? Now—please—let us get back to distraction."

He knew he had won when she put her arms around his neck and drew his head down to hers for a long, searing—healing—kiss.

But he also knew that the earlier wound was merely crusted over. Eventually, they would have to deal with it. Only not tonight. Not now.

Their lovemaking had lost none of its vigor, but Hannah sensed each of them somehow holding back, almost fearful of exposing too much of the inner self. Something had been lost in that quarrel earlier in the day and she wondered if they would ever regain it. Perhaps they could—tomorrow. Not now, though. For now she would simply revel in his being safe and in their being together.

Thus did life continue for the next few days. Each of them went about various duties during the day. At night they continued their mutual delight in new ways to titillate, arouse—and satisfy. Neither brought up the topic of the coming meeting at St. Peter's Fields. On the appointed day, there came a knock on the door to the dressing room.

"Yes?" Hannah called, sitting up in bed.

"You asked to be awakened early," the maid called through the door.

"Oh. Yes. Thank you." She looked down at Theo, who was wide awake.

"So. You are still planning to go to the meeting." It was a flat statement, devoid of approval or disapproval.

She lifted her chin. "Yes. I gave my word. I am going with the Meltons and the Sturgeses." She did not say, but she knew he would understand that the presence of other women lent propriety to her accompanying the men. Mr. Sturges, president of the Crofton Correspoding Society, would, along with Hannah, be among the committee to welcome the honored guest and join him on the hustings.

"I shall probably see you there, then." His voice was casual.

"You are going?" she asked in surprise.

"Wouldn't miss it." His note of joviality did not ring entirely true to her ears. "This promises to be a history-making event."

She did not respond and quickly set about preparing for the big day. She wore a red-and-white-striped gown of finely woven cotton, for it was likely to be a warm day in mid-August. She also wore a new straw bonnet with a wide brim and a profusion of red silk flowers.

God had decided to smile on this day, even if one Theo Ruskin, Vicount Amesbury, had not, she thought. It was a gorgeous day with blue sky and warm sun. And all roads seemed to lead in the same direction—to St. Peter's Fields, so called because of the huge open-air space connected to St. Peter's Church.

Hannah and her companions rode in an open carriage hired especially for Crofton's dignitaries. The carriage bore a banner announcing *Crofton Corresponding Society*. They passed by many groups of people, some few in carriages, but mostly walking. The people laughed and sang as they made their way. Men, women, and children—all dressed in their Sunday best—were out for a holiday. That there was a serious undertone to the planned meeting did nothing to dampen the spirit of the crowd.

The closer they came to Manchester, the denser the crowds became, yet there was an astonishing sense of order. All that training on fields and moors was paying off, Hannah thought. She was struck not only by the order, but by the profusion of color and high spirits. Women wore perky bonnets—many purchased for this occasion, Hannah conjectured—and the men, too, had added holiday touches to their attire, with a flower in a lapel or a ribbon on a hat. In fact, she noted that some groups sought to distinguish themselves with certain colors of ribbons. She also noted that many of the men wore the scarlet velvet headgear known as "Liberty Caps." Children scampered playfully, or hung shyly on their mothers' skirts.

Overall, there was a sense of eager anticipation. Hannah was at once proud of her neighbors and eager herself to listen to one of England's finest orators. She did wish that Theo were with her, but would not allow his absence—or his attitude—to dampen her spirits.

Arriving at the edge of the field, the driver halted their carriage. Some Crofton people came to retrieve the banner and carry off the Meltons.

"We have seats for you and your wife and Lady Amesbury on the hustings," a man said to Mr. Sturges. "What we'll do is, we precede the carriage with Mr. Hunt and then we all just go right up on the platform with him."

"A carriage and horses in this crowd?" Hannah asked.

"A carriage, no horses," the man replied proudly. "Men have been fairly fighting over the privilege of drawing Mr. Hunt's carriage."

Suddenly the pace of activity escalated. Hannah was hastily introduced to the great man, who nodded respectfully.

Henry Hunt was a man of unprepossessing stature. He wore buff-colored pantaloons, a modest neckcloth, and a dark waistcoat with a matching formal topcoat whose tails reached to the back of his knees. He wore polished boots and carried a white top hat that had become his particular symbol. He placed it on his head at a cocky angle as he climbed into the man-drawn carriage.

"Oh, my!" Mrs. Sturges whispered to Hannah. "I expected him to be much more flamboyant, somehow."

"They say he saves his flair for his speeches," Hannah said.

"Let us hope so," the other replied as the two women were hustled along with the other designated dignitaries onto the raised platform.

Hannah saw that the crowd was divided as two broad lanes opened away from the platform from which Hunt would speak. One lane led beyond the crowd to a multi-storied building in the background. People hung over the edges of windows on the upper floors of that and neighboring buildings. The key building, Hannah learned, housed the magistrate's office. She observed several well-dressed men take their places on the balcony of this building. She was not overly surprised to see her husband as one of the group. She noted that this lane was lined by a number of uniformed constables determined to keep the crowd from flowing into the lane.

The other lane down which she and the others led the men drawing Hunt's carriage was kept open only so long as it was needed for passage. She felt and heard the crowd coming together behind the procession. Sounds of happy anticipation passed back and forth among the people. Hannah felt a wonderful sense of belonging to something big and important, something that might make a real difference in people's lives.

Once she was on the platform, she looked out on a veritable sea of faces. At once she felt overwhelmed by the magnitude of this event. Theo was right. It *was* historic, even epic, in its proportions. Several banners dotted the field, identifying different groups, who stood in an orderly manner despite their enthusiastic welcome of the speaker. There were also banners reading

Unity and Strength, *Liberty and Fraternity*, *Parliaments Annual*, and *Suffrage Universal*. The crowd cheered wildly as Hunt ascended the platform steps, his white hat acting as a beacon in the sunlight. The people cheered and cheered and cheered.

It was only after several false starts that the man was finally able to begin his talk. He had spoken for only a few moments when pandemonium broke out.

Orderly as they were, the crowd pressed inexorably forward to hear the speaker better. The constables who lined the open lane from the speaker's hustings to the magistrate's balcony, and those who surrounded the platform itself, were having difficulty holding people back. Hannah heard a constable standing just below her shout, "There's the signal. Arrest the bastard." It seemed only seconds later that she saw a body of uniformed men on horseback coming to the aid of the constables. They were the Manchester Yeomanry.

"Oh, no. No," she moaned softly.

Theo had feared just such a turn of events, though on first arriving at St. Peter's Fields, he had been favorably impressed by the order and discipline being exercised by the crowd. Still, he was glad he had run into the commander of the 15th Hussars some days ago. Colonel Guy L'Estrange assured Theo that the Hussars, based as they were near Manchester, were ready to fulfill such police duties as they might be called upon to perform. However, both the colonel and the ex-Major Ruskin knew this highly trained element of the King's Army would be used only on orders from a civilian authority.

The colonel snorted. "Typical British distrust of the military—but guess who always gets the call in emergencies!"

As one of the highest-ranking peers on the scene, Theo was immediately invited to join the magistrates and other county officials on the balcony overlooking the massive gathering. Nearly twenty well-dressed men crowded onto the limited space there. Besides governing officials, there were several other mill owners, who were sometimes also magistrates in their districts. Theo nodded to Kitchener and Childress and noted that Mayfield was also present.

"My God! They just keep coming," someone said early on.

They watched in awed silence, then another asked of no one in particular, "How many would you estimate there are?"

"Forty thousand," a voice responded.

"Closer to fifty or sixty thousand, I'd say," another offered.

"Who would have thought such riffraff could be so organized?" asked an awestruck country squire.

Theo could see the man's awe transform itself into apprehension and then fear in the expressions of those around him.

"Good God! If they are capable of this sort of organization for a peaceful gathering, what will they not be capable of if they obtain weapons and start a revolution? They will make the Paris mob look like a herd of placid sheep." The speaker was Lord Kitchener.

"You're right. Absolutely right!" Childress chimed in.

Mayfield addressed the chief magistrate in an authoritative voice. "Hulton, you must put a stop to this business at once!"

"The gathering is legal!" Hulton protested. "The constables are ready to arrest the man the moment things get out of hand."

"With this sort of multitude, things are already out of hand," Mayfield said with a strong sense of urgency. "Just look down there—they are deliberately crowding in on the constables! Those poor devils need help! And they need it now!"

Theo hated agreeing with Mayfield, but the constables *were* having difficulty. The trouble was, sending in the Yeomanry would only exacerbate the situation.

"All right," Hulton said, annoyed. He gave the signal for the constables to arrest Hunt and at the same time he signaled the release of the Yeomanry, who were to provide aid in controlling a crowd sure to object to the arrest.

The Manchester Yeomanry consisted largely of shopkeepers, butchers, bakers, clerks, ironmongers, and a few manufacturers who enjoyed parading around in uniforms and participating in quasi-military "drills." Theo knew they were seen as something of a joke in the district. Still, in the absence of a police force, perhaps they would be effective.

They were not.

He watched in horror as the ill-trained Yeomanry rushed their equally ill-trained horses into the crowd. He could hear their cries at people to disperse. However, the people were packed in so tightly, there was no room for them to do so. When their orders were not immediately effective, the Yeomanry urged their mounts harder—but to little avail, for the horsemen were trapped by the press of human bodies.

Then the crowd began ridiculing and heckling the trapped horsemen, who retaliated by swinging their sabers indiscriminately. People fell from saber wounds and were trampled under horses' hooves and the booted feet of the stampeding crowd.

"Oh, my God!" Theo said. "It's a massacre."

Others, too, were horrified as women and children fell amid screams of pain, surprise, and outrage.

"This is a disaster," some wit on the balcony observed.

"I was at Waterloo," another said. "*It* was like this."

Theo turned to a gentleman who had so far said very little. He was Sir Dennison Stewart, the Lord Lieutenant of the entire district, the King's official representative, whose authority outweighed that of the local magistrates.

"My lord," Theo implored. "You must release the Hussars!"

"Yes. I do believe you are right, Amesbury." The man's tone was almost casual.

Waiting only long enough to see that he did, indeed, give the necessary order, Theo left the balcony, determined now to make his way to Hannah. When last he glanced her way, she had stood transfixed by the horror at her feet. However, Theo knew very well she would be in the thick of the melee long before he could get to her.

Chaos reigned on the field. The constables had managed to arrest Hunt—and smash his white topper in the process. Theo lost sight of Hannah, for she had left the hustings. Where *was* she? He felt a moment of panic. Then he caught sight of a perky straw bonnet with red flowers. As he made his way toward it, he hoped to hell it was hers!

Pushing his way through the crowd was extremely difficult. He could see that the Hussars, too, were having difficulty. Gradually, though, the well-trained units of man and horse were managing to restore order. Using the flat of their swords rather than slashing away indiscriminately, they pushed the bulk of the crowd off the field. A cloud of dust, stirred up by churning horses' hooves, hung over everything.

Those left on the field were dead, injured, or tending to the injured. Theo found Hannah cradling a wounded woman's head in her lap. She smoothed the woman's hair and appeared to reassure her with soothing words.

"Hannah!" Theo shouted from some distance away.

Hannah glanced up at his shout, her eyes shining with welcome and gladness.

"Thank goodness you are here," she said. She reached for a bag lying nearby and placed it under the woman's head. "I'll get help for you—and we will find your little girl," she assured the injured woman. "Her leg is broken," Hannah told Theo as he gathered her close and just held her for a moment.

She clung to him as he murmured, "My God! If I'd lost you—"

"Sh-h," she said. "I am all right. We must help these poor people."

They worked together through the afternoon and early evening, treating the wounded, helping to restore lost children to their parents, comforting the bereaved. When it was over, they surveyed the field where a happy holiday crowd had gathered only hours earlier. Now stray dogs picked among the remains of picnic lunches; here and there a torn banner lay in the dust; but most poignant were the odd articles of clothing—bonnets, caps, shawls, and shoes— strewn haphazardly, some of them stained with blood as well as dust.

Hannah picked up a child's doll, and Theo saw tears stream

down her cheeks as she clutched it to her chest. Up to now, she had bravely held the tears at bay.

He enfolded her in his arms. "Let's go home, love."

She nodded.

He had not known what prompted him to bring his traveling coach to Manchester, but now he was glad he had as he bundled his exhausted wife into the vehicle and signaled his driver. In the coach he and Hannah clung to each other and kissed with a fervency born of the emotions of the day. Eventually, he just held her and he felt her relax and finally sleep.

Twenty-five

Hannah awoke with a start as the carriage jolted to a stop in front of Glosson Hall. After a moment with the driver, Theo handed her out of the carriage and supported her up the steps, where Knowlton had already opened the door to welcome them.

"My lord! My lady! We were beginning to worry about you after the rumors of what happened in Manchester."

"We are fine," Theo said. "Just exhausted. A bath and some supper would be very much in order."

"Right away, my lord."

And indeed it was right away. Hannah said a silent thank you to Theo's grandfather, who had installed a huge cooker in the kitchen that had a reservoir for keeping water continuously hot.

He and Hannah took turns bathing each other and she felt the tiredness drain away from her along with the grime of the day. Her body was also leaping to life under her husband's practiced caresses. He dribbled water over her chest and then placed his hand under her breast to catch it. He caressed her nipples and smiled as they instantly hardened. He ran his hand further down her body, probing between her legs.

His voice was husky. "Shall we have supper first? Or shall we start with dessert?"

"Dessert," she said without hesitation.

They slowly toweled each other off, doing so in long sensuous, teasing strokes. They made their way to the bed, where they managed to erase much of the horror of the day in the sheer beauty and ecstasy of two people coming together—the act of creation expunging the residue of destruction.

When it was over, Hannah wanted nothing more than to have Theo hold her forever, but she felt a compelling need to talk, too.

"Theo?"

"Hmm?" His hand lazily stroked her body.

"I'm sorry."

"About what? I thought this was quite good."

"It was, you conceited man! I am sorry about that quarrel. I should never have accused you of being insensitive to people's needs."

"Well, I do try to be sensitive to *your* needs." He allowed his fingers to stroke a particularly sensitive spot.

She sat up and pushed him away. "I am trying to have a serious discussion with you, you boorish man, and all you can think of is . . . is . . ."

"Making the beast with two backs?" he offered.

"Leave Shakespeare out of this."

"All right." He pushed himself up to sit against the head of the bed and turned to face her. He reached to toy with a strand of her hair. "You needn't apologize, Hannah. We all say things in anger we don't really mean. And I *was* trying to keep you from doing something you felt was important."

"But I failed even to consider all that you have done—the changes you have brought to the Glosson Mill, and the weavers, and the tenant farmers. Nor did I even think about what those things have meant to the entire parish."

"I admit to being something of a slow top at times," he said. "I should have done more sooner, I know."

"The point is you *did* do them—and after today, I think perhaps slow but sure is not all bad."

"Hannah, eleven people died today and hundreds were injured in what surely will be seen as a power clash of some sort."

"Perhaps both sides were carried away," she said.

"Perhaps. But I would not want *your* enthusiasm to diminish for things important to you."

"Truly?"

"Truly," he answered, his finger trailing over an exposed breast.

She caught his exploring hand. "I love you for not saying 'I told you so.'"

"Only for not stating the obvious?" he teased.

She went very still. Well, why not? "No," she said. "I love you for everything you've done for me, for the mill people—for everything you *are*." As he stared at her in wonder, she repeated herself nervously. "I love you, Theo—that is the end all, be all of it."

"The alpha and omega," he said quietly, drawing her close. "I love you, too, Hannah, more than I can ever say."

"Then don't tell me. Show me," she whispered.

And he did.

HISTORICAL NOTE

The debacle at St. Peter's Fields was almost immediately labeled the Peterloo Massacre as an ironic reference to the great victory at Waterloo. Peterloo was a triumph of the sheer power of government over the people. However, it had repercussions that resonated for years afterwards. This was not the way an English government should treat English people assembled to discuss issues in a peaceful manner.

The London government immediately took the side of the magistrates and pronounced support of actions they had taken that day in August. Even more repressive acts were rushed into law that autumn of 1819. The new laws increased the powers of the magistrates. They could now search private homes at will (ostensibly for weapons) and they had virtual veto power over any public gathering. The new legislation also placed even greater restrictions on freedom of the press and freedom of speech.

This unprecedented government attack on traditional English liberties aroused the opposition—Whigs, especially—who demanded an inquiry. They were defeated, but they took defeat quietly, for they, too, feared revolution of the sort that had plunged France and all Europe into chaos only thirty years earlier.

Eventually—over a decade later—sanity prevailed over fear. The first reform act was passed in 1832. The government and the people continued to struggle mightily with the cultural changes that came with the industrial revolution—social and economic changes that must have been as mind-boggling then as those we face today with the technological revolution.